HALLAN

Farenhyne

Venhyne

An 'Korathall

Narrahyne   Wederhyne

SEA OF SILENCE

Kalleron

LARIA

Gulda

Laria

Mt. Etherus

ARKALLON

Arkalla

Tormelor

KALLERON

BRUHADA

(Bruhale)

Drohendrir

Hammer & Glass

KALLERON Book IV

James D. McEwan

Hammer & Glass: Kalleron Book IV by James D. McEwan

Published by James D. McEwan

Website: jamesdmcewan.com

ISBN: 978-1-7391270-1-5

This is an original work of fiction. Names, characters, places, and incidents either are the products of the author's imagination or are used fictitiously. Any resemblance to actual persons, living or dead, fictional entities, or places, is entirely coincidental.

Cover concept and titles by James D. McEwan. World map designed with Wonderdraft.

Front cover text designed using Canva.

Cover artwork by Grandfailure.

In loving memory of my father.

And to Julie, my beloved wife. How many hours have you endured my constant prattle and dithering? I apologise, I hope this story is worth your duress.

Prologue

The Bruhsa

W hat truths we know, we pass to our own, and in the blood of the mothers, the echoes of history defy the silence of death. This is the way of the Bruhsa; we are the voice across time.

Peace does not come easily to mortal minds. It is a fragile state languishing between contentedness and ambition. Yet we in the Northern Lands have known peace for a century. A lasting harmony wrested from the death of Kalle, the last *immortal* King of Kalleron. His defeat at the hands of mighty Baza'rad sent the old world into disarray. The forces of Kalleron sent back across the sea to salvage what they could of a shattered legacy. Our mothers watched that day as a new dawn broke under a blood-red sky, and how they cheered the coming of the new Queen of Stone. Under her ward, the white city of An'Korathall flourished; it became a hub of trade and culture, of peace and prosperity. And though we knew jealous eyes were upon us, there were none foolish enough to stand against those legends who had vowed to protect us.

Yet, we were naïve to think such treasured times could last forever. We had neglected to consider that our once mortal Queen of Stone had kept her human heart. All those years slipping past; all her friends fading into the night. One by one they died. And soon the Queen disappeared, her grief an insurmountable foe she could never defeat. So too, Baza'rad faded from our mortal gaze; it was always a contradiction—how could a man so large become so invisible? Some say he died. But fools will be fools.

The Bruhsa feared that war would come again but something else walked the steps to An'Korathall. Kor'A, the Lord of the Earth, took to her marble citadel, locking herself away behind the fortress walls. For three decades she remained. Unseen but forever felt, her presence was an oppressive force upon us all. An unnatural peace remained for all that time; for what could be more powerful than our Queen of Stone, other than the Elemental master who created her?

Yet now, I fear our sanctuary is lost. Kor'A has gone; her aura no longer suffocates the streets. And the demeanour of An'Korathall is changing. The eyes of strangers watch the white tower and the flash of steel shows beneath their gaudy capes. Men of violence have come. All the while, the old cult whispers of new threats looming on the horizon. The sky has darkened in the fading of majesty. This is the fear that calls forth my pledge. Let my duty be recorded in the blood of the Bruhsa; I must find my King.

Chapter I

'Keep them shut, Chara, you mustn't watch.'

Eyes tight shut; that was the command, a powerful rumble next to her ear. She nodded, knew she had to obey. His hand pulled away from her face but she did not move. Freed from restraint she was captive to his words. Not a chink of light, nor a curious peek; she would not watch, did not want to see what was to come. All too soon she had learned there was no other like him, this man and his unearthly hammer. Listening in silence to his gruff breath, Chara heard an endless sigh of discontent. The shadow pulling away, a mountain rising to its feet. She understood—he was going to do what must be done. His promise to keep her safe, a promise that carried a grim reckoning. Without sight she focused on the familiar sounds: the click of a stud, a hand grasping metal. It was a terrible herald, and Chara trembled as the ground shook; a mighty weight pummelled into earth.

Voices in the air. Not his. These tongues babbled with malcontent and she understood their fervour. They wanted *her*. He had warned this would happen, foretold her precious black skin would bring unwanted attention. But he had sworn to protect her in the days after her mother had vanished; gone without a word. An'Korathall had been her fortress home but its doors had been left wide open. Those first tentative steps in the new world and human eyes had fallen upon her; mesmerised by her body of onyx. It was a puzzle to solve; why did they covet that which lay beneath their feet? The question would wait; with mother gone there was no ward against their greed. Leaving the citadel, she had travelled to the hills, following the echo of mother's words. *All men are dangerous, Chara*, she had said, *but the man who lives among stone is a man apart from flesh.* And Chara had known then, nothing could protect her, nothing except him—and that frightening weapon.

A clamour of voices raised against the silence of her guardian. Incessant, impatient. His reply was an angry huff snorted through nostrils she imagined would be flaring. A crunch of stone permeated the air. Gravel tortured under the grinding metal block of the massive hammer. She could sense his tension, an avalanche of power ready to destroy. Bringing her knees tight to her chest, Chara tried to become smaller, trying to hide from it all. She understood the power of what was to come. A force of which she was afraid. She despaired of what would follow and it came as angry thunder.

In her mind she pictured the doom. Goddard, a man as big as a mountain boulder, facing twelve other men. It wasn't fair. They should have brought more. If they knew what she knew, seen what she had seen; they would let her be, they would never have troubled the man and child. A sudden rush as the air howled, sliced by a slab of unnatural metal. A terrible and bone-crunching sound as the hammer found its mark. Chara burying deeper into her knees. It was not what she wanted, a reminder of what she was; as these men, she too was breakable. So different from mother.

The voices roared in anger but the noise was pitiful compared to the hammer. Tighter and tighter she hugged, wishing for it to stop. In darkness she imagined the mountains above An'Korathall, imagined the earth shaking and the proud peaks shedding their granite skins. Avalanche upon avalanche bringing thunder to the earth. This was the noise of Goddard's wrath. After countless echoes of that awful percussion, the calm returned.

In her world of darkness, she felt reassuring hands squeeze against her arms.

'It's over. But keep them closed, Chara. Don't look back.'

In one effortless movement she was lifted to her feet. She felt his hand fall upon her shoulders. A huge man, she was so small beside him. Safe beside him as she was with mother. Chara shuffled along the trail, allowing his hand to steer her path.

'Careful, mustn't step on...' he said.

The pause, words not spoken; he had meant *bodies*. She imagined trunks of gnarled trees, large and crawling as those she had observed from the citadel. Not once did she try to look down. Staring ahead into darkness, she allowed him to guide her away. The sound of the track beneath their feet was the conversion; dry earth and shattered stone. A long talk about nothing at all.

'Can I open them?' she asked.

A grumble of laughter. 'Sorry, yes.'

The light flooded in and she turned, craning her neck to look up to her protector. Chara wobbled as she righted her balance, her guardian almost twice as tall as she. He was safe, Goddard was well. Under his cloak, his old armour still shining—not even a dent. His dark skin clean. Not a hair out of place in his greying, braided beard.

'You're unharmed?' she asked.

He smiled with a wide grin. A huff of sorts. But he did not answer.

'Thank you,' she said.

A grunt.

'Is it far?'

Goddard stopped. 'Far?'

'The safe place?' He had said a safe place. Wasn't that why they had left the city? His smile faltered; a frown creasing his old brow.

He said, 'Chara. I am the safe place.'

Chara slept as though a child. *A child.* She was in her third decade, that much she had said. It marked time, not age, not something to equate with stone. Goddard couldn't understand her purpose. He had suspicions, questions. If what she said was true, the girl had been left alone. Defenceless. Small and timid as a mouse. A riddle too ugly to solve: why had her mother, the immortal Earth, created a weak and fragile child? Why send her to his door? Of that, he had an inkling; though, she had told him too little. No matter the reason, the decision to leave Anka had been easy; the flight from the city, less so. Too many bodies, the girl flinching with every encounter. He had noted her unease, she was averse to the necessary violence. Goddard shuffled on his seat; an angular rock covered in moss. His armour clinked and immediately the girl awoke. In the darkness, her shape was difficult to define, the onyx lost in the night; Chara made visible by the flickering of the fire reflecting against her sculpted surface. He wanted to call it skin, but skin didn't shatter. Eyes of impossible black blinked.

He knew to calm her before she spoke. 'We're safe. Sorry I woke you.'

'I thought I heard swords?'

'Armour.' He patted his breastplate. 'My armour.'

Chara looked around. The amber glow danced across her naked form; her body animating with inhuman elegance. Goddard thought she moved as though a bird; twitching and alert. An irony that something removed from nature could appear so natural. In the dark of the forest, she appeared as an orphaned flame.

'Why did she leave?' she asked.

Her mother. He could only guess. He knew of her; Kor'A, the emancipated Queen of Kalleron—a lifetime ago, he had crossed paths with the Lord of the Earth, had never wished to do so again. He shook his head. Kor'A had always been an enigma, a creature of flawed perfection. She was a demi-god of dangerous curiosity. Such ferocious power bound to that sublime shape. A sexless visage of femininity; a living marble statue encased in gems. But despite her chosen form, she was no woman; nothing so close as being remotely human. A vision came to him from a century past. His Captain, Petra, dying in the white city, a consequence of her own foolishness and rage. Kor'A had come to them offering salvation. Instead, she had delivered an eternal curse; all sealed by her inhuman, Elemental touch. Those cruel moments were seared into his memory. He had witnessed the first corruption of flesh—Petra becoming a victim of the immortal's curious mind. Resurrected and becoming the Queen of An'Korathall, *The Queen of Stone.* All those years lost in time and now Chara had come to his door. Kor'A's bastard mortal. Again, the damned riddle. Why create a child so weak it could die? Why had her mother left?

'I don't know, Chara,' he replied, 'Kor'A... your mother's mind is not for men to fathom.'

'Was it something I did?'

Perhaps something she was. After Petra's resurrection, Kor'A had vanished for decades. At the time, he and the old crew had spoken of it; considered the possibility it was guilt for her sins. Was this the same? When the immortal created life, did she flee from the consequence? It was a possibility the child was a factor in her mother's

5

disappearance. Though, he thought better of telling her such sadness. He said, 'No, of course not.'

She persisted. 'But I'm so weak. She's disappointed?'

'No.' It was a thought to anger him. Chara was another toy. Seemingly one of which Kor'A had appeared to grow bored. Perhaps of which she had become afraid. 'She made you. She could've made you invincible—like Petra. Your mother made you... weaker. That's not your fault. It's her design.'

'Did your mother make you strong?'

Mother? It was so long ago. Lifetimes lost in the mist. A haze coming with age. 'I was born as a child, just the same as all human children, weak and vulnerable.'

'But you became strong?'

'I had to. It was my fate.'

'My fate is to be weak?'

He wanted to say no but by her own words, Chara hadn't changed since her creation. A shade over four-feet tall. A prepubescent and sexless body. Though, it was difficult to compare to a human; her skin of black glass an impossible thing of beauty. Decades old, remaining as a child. Perhaps her growth was too slow to observe? She was, after all, the *daughter* of an immortal. Her intelligence was evident; not that of ignorant youth. Goddard had noted his own awkwardness speaking to her as such. Girl or woman, Chara was an unfathomable, Elemental child. Something that shouldn't be.

'Weakness isn't a lack of strength.' Patting his chest, he said, 'This is physical. But it has no meaning without purpose; strength requires a focus.'

The fire flickered across Chara's skin. He heard a clink of glass, imagined a mimic of his movements. She said, 'If I find purpose, I will grow like you?'

'Perhaps.' A gentle lie. 'But for now, rest. Go to sleep, Chara.'

Reflections of amber settled down and the forest became still. Nothing stirred beyond the soft popping of the dying pit, and Goddard's mind returned to the riddle. Chara was a facsimile of human life. But it was all false. She slept, though she never remembered her dreams; she spoke of hunger, though she never ate; and she rubbed her sore muscles when her body had none at all. On the brightest days, he had seen the rays of the sun cast through her black skin. Dark but unmistakable—she had no innards except for the stone. Chara was solid onyx with a heart he could only imagine was diamond. But her mortal behaviour was real. A cruel fate imposed by Kor'A. An Elemental child to experience a life of flesh. Why?

Goddard's thoughts drifted to the past. Better days before the wars. Memories, setting with old age. Some more fuzzy than others. How much time was lost in the fog? He saw good friends greeting him. Shadow teasing the girls; Kallisa teasing Shadow. A century ago. Gone, if not lost. Those days were the warmest, those friends were the closest. Yes, those were the better days; before Fire had burned Laria and Kalleron had fallen to Fury and chaos. And now, if Chara's story was true, Earth had vacated An'Korathall leaving it open to all hell. It seemed the Elementals were marshalling to some unseen plan. He had taken the child from the city not knowing what to do. Yet there was one woman who would. An eternal face from those cherished times. Petra, the Queen of

An'Korathall, Captain of *The Melody of the Sea*. Once his Captain, forever his friend. He had to find her. She was the last power that could protect the child. Death was coming. He could feel it in his old bones. Two centuries was a good span for any man, and Goddard had lived the lives of more than one. The old King Baza'rad had had his days, exiled in Bruhada's fall and becoming Argan. Sailing the far oceans with Petra and the crew. Standing against Kalle on the plains of Stranghame, shoulder to shoulder with the great General Aracyse, braving the onslaught of Fury and King. A solemn victory to seal one-hundred years of peace. Now Baza'rad wore his final mask, Goddard. Hiding in the shadows, an old man waiting for the end. But before he could let go, he had to take the child to Petra. One last journey before he and Bruch'ail could settle. One final adventure to herald a new dawn.

The damp of a dead fire; that was the smell. A stench of floral decay. The forest. Goddard opened his eyes. A surge of panic crashing upon him, instinct thrusting his hand to the haft of Bruch'ail. Chara? The child? He leapt to his feet, the shackles of sleep dragging him down. The hammer was in the air, a wild swing on unsteady legs.

'CHARA?'

Her squeal was close. His heart pounding, Goddard rallied his concentration. She was there, crawling away from the blackened fire, scrabbling away—*from him*. Damn fool. One hand released from Bruch'ail, he held it to her, speaking softly. 'I fell asleep... I'm sorry, Chara. I should've stayed awake.'

He saw the fear flicker in her eyes but her voice was calm. 'It's all right. I'm safe. You're safe.'

He was safe? Goddard frowned, placed Bruch'ail on the earth, haft standing upright.

Chara nodded. Seated on her backside, one tiny hand held high as though warding him away, she said, 'I watched you. I watched over you while you slept.'

She protected him? His face softened, his brow relaxing. A smile eased his tension and with a glance to the surrounds, he sat. 'You watched over me?'

Chara nodded with vigour, her guard dropping to her side.

A hand on his heart, he said, 'That is strength.'

'I need to try. Be more like you.'

Looking to the firepit, he asked, 'How long did I sleep?'

'When the fire died. Your eyes shut.'

Curious, he hovered his hand above the pit. A drizzle, seeping through the canopy, had stifled the remnants. There was little heat left. Perhaps an hour or so had passed, he hadn't slept long. A thought crossed his mind; he had slept seated upright, a talent born of his sheer bulk. Most people confused it for a waking state but not the girl.

He asked, 'How'd you know I shut my eyes?'

'I saw you close them.'

'But you were sleeping?'

'Yes.'

How did she see? Midge flies biting at his skin, or confusion; either way, he clawed at his beard. He tugged on the long braid. Pointing to his eyes, he said, 'I sleep, my eyes shut. You?'

Chara shook her head. 'Open.'

'You sleep with your eyes open?'

A diligent nod. 'Mostly,' she said.

'And... you see?'

'Uh-huh.'

He wanted to tell her that wasn't sleep. But he wasn't made of black glass. He wasn't the creation of an Elemental's reckless adventure. In the night she had awoken; he had seen her blink. Had she been awake the whole time? Goddard paused. Who was he to tell her what sleep was? He could not judge that which was not human.

Curious, he asked, 'What makes you sleepy, Chara?'

She looked to the sky. Turning her head this way and that, she leapt to her feet. Through the wall of wood, she pointed. He squinted, saw it. Sunrise shuttered behind vertical columns.

Chara said, 'It tells me when to sleep and when to wake.'

He needed to be careful; didn't want to sully the illusion for the girl but it was clear. He had witnessed it on so many nights. Uncanny timing. Sun down, bed down. Kor'A had fabricated a stimulus for the child. It wasn't weariness that drove Chara to slumber. It was a convenient lie. A contrived event to match a human behaviour.

Cautious, he said, 'When I was a boy, my mother would put me to bed. But sometimes, I would sneak out to see the stars or watch the men fight in the square. Did you ever do that?'

She blinked and stared. Those eyes so innocent. Chara shook her head.

Holding out his hand, palm down, he lowered it. 'You bed down for the night?'

'Yes.'

'Do you move?' He considered his own bodily functions. A reason to wake in the night; realised they wouldn't apply. 'Do you become restless; do you need to walk about?'

Chara giggled. It was music. A child's laughter; there was nothing as sweet. She said, 'Don't be silly, I'm asleep.'

Pointing at her eyes, then his. 'And you see everything?'

A nod. That beguiling smile.

The bloody riddle. Those damn midges. He clawed again.

'Is it itchy?' she asked.

He stared at her. A sigh escaping his lungs. He nodded.

'I don't itch,' she said.

Glass doesn't, he thought. Holding his beard, he said, 'Wait till you grow one of these.'

Impossible movements animated her face. 'Can I?'

'Grow a beard?'

She nodded.

What could he say? What words wouldn't hurt her feelings?

'We'll find a special lady who can tell you.'

Chara clapped her hands with obvious glee, a percussion of crystal chiming through the forest. He gazed at her, noticed a new curiosity; her eyes were glowing with the faintest aura. Mesmerising. He hadn't seen *that* before.

'Who will we see?' she asked. The mystery in her voice was unmistakable. A child's wonder.

The memories returned. They brought a smile to his face. Once his Captain, forever his friend. 'Petra,' he said, 'we're going to find the Queen of An'Korathall.'

Chapter II

Jerune had seen death before but this was impressive. A dozen bandits, crows picking at what was left of the flesh. The carrion and beasts of the forest had claimed the feast. Jerune sighed, rising from one of the corpses. The recent damage was consistent with tooth and claw; the spread of bodies random. Chaotic signs that would confuse other trackers were easy to follow with his keen eyes. All killed on the trail, left there on the gravel. Their boots sullied by the sodden track; flecks of stone, not grass, under heel. Then dragged to the forest; not by hand. Scavengers taking them from the path of men. A wolf pack, no doubts. The weapons were gone, bounty for whoever came along after the immediate carnage. Walking to another bloody mess, Jerune knelt close. He surveyed the body, two legs, one arm, and the mess attached to the neck. The executioner's mark was clear, not lost to the canine feasting. Leaning in, he peered closer. Nothing but a squashed gourd. Unrecognisable as a skull.

'Hammer?' Jerune questioned. A huge hammer. He rose, moved to another corpse. A crow, brave and sleek, perched upon upturned boots. It fluttered a protest but bravely remained, its beady eyes observing Jerune as he stared at the tangle of flesh and fabric. There were few creatures that could inflict such measured damage. Fewer that would leave the meat. An avalanche would wreak similar havoc with soft human bodies. But this was too far from the slopes. Just one creature then.

'Is it him?' Sarellia called. Her voice too loud in the forest.

The crow hopped from left boot to right. Jerune replied, 'The body?'

'The same as before? The other bandits.'

He nodded to the corpse, the gourd. 'A blunt weapon. No doubts. What's not been eaten is evidence of that.'

Twigs snapping, she was coming closer. 'Bruch'ail?'

Jerune stood and turned. Sarellia's face was expectant. She was impatient for a revelation; her pointless quest for a lost myth. He would play along. 'All hammers crush. There's no way of telling if it's the one you seek.'

Her eyes scanned the death. 'But ten bandits?'

'There's twelve actually; two are just bones. Wolves ate well.'

'Twelve?' she clenched her fists. Jerune thought they looked fragile. 'How many?'

Her questions were irritating. Unnecessary clutter in his ordered thoughts. 'How many what? I said twelve.'

Sarellia shook her head. Jet black hair fell across her dark face. 'Victors. Whoever did this. One man or many?'

The bodies were a few days old. The trail more recently trampled by fresh boots. A scuff of combat was confused by routine wear. The missing weapons meant more disturbance. He had found two significant tracks; one giant footprint and the other, smaller, too uniform to be a foot, too rounded to be a boot. A child's print, perhaps a sandal.

'Come and see this,' he said.

His ghostly steps were followed by Sarellia. Her clumsy movements loud and grating. Reaching the path, he waited as she emerged from the bushes. Somehow, she managed to make it appear as though it was a chore; plucking thorns and twigs from her pastel blue jerkin. *Blue*. She stuck out as a sore thumb; a city-dweller playing rogue. True, she paid well; she was pretty, but by the Elementals, it was barely worth the pain.

Pointing at the massive boot print, he said, 'That there's a huge man. Heavy and tall.'

'Were there others?'

He didn't think so. Same as before. But the small print toyed with his mind. This was his realm but he couldn't decipher the silent puzzle. He knelt and put his finger on the earth. Tracing the outline, a sparkle caught his eye. It was out of place among the grey gravel and dark mud. Plucked from the dirt, he held it to his face.

'What's that?' Sarellia asked.

A fleck of black glass. Nothing more than a splinter. His eyes searched but he saw no bottles. Nothing smashed, nothing discarded. He flicked it from his fingers and watched it land on a broad triangular leaf. Frowning, he replied, 'Dunno.'

'So?' she said.

He wished she would stay quiet, keep that flapping gob shut. Too many questions, too many noises in his mind. But the coin was good. Concentrating, pushing away his agitation, he said, 'So, *what?*'

Kneeling beside the print, he heard her sigh. Forced, it was an agitated breath cut short. He smiled, understood that Sarellia's patience had snapped. For Jerune, it was a small victory of wills; the country-boy defeating the city-girl.

She said, 'I know you think I'm a spoiled useless bitch, but you can stop being such a grumpy little shit.'

He stood, turning to face her. Sarellia's stance spoke volumes, her fists slammed on hips, accompanied by a smouldering stare; annoying but beautiful. Insanely beautiful. The coin, think of the coin. He nodded, clicking his tongue. 'Yeah, I do think you're spoiled but that's not the cause of my irritation.'

Frowning, she replied, 'Then what?'

'I'm a scout. A tracker. My life is all about quiet and patience. You don't learn that in the streets of Anka.' He needed to appease her. Some sign of humility. He pressed his hands flat and held them in front of his chest. 'Look, I'm used to being alone. Company messes with my focus.'

11

'Especially spoilt bitch company?'

An involuntary nod. Too late to retract, he had to acknowledge it. 'Your words, not mine.'

She sighed, a softer exhalation this time. Pointing to the scuff marks, she said, 'Do you think there were two groups or is that single print proof of one man?'

It was proof of *a* man. There could have been more. But he understood her impatience. She had hired him to find the Great King Baza'rad. An old legend, older than the city itself. He doubted her hero was real, an embellishment of history. Sightings were worse than dubious but they had led him here, far from Anka. Stories of giants; tales of gargantuan hammers. And here, niggling his doubt, there was an over-sized footprint and a decimated bandit crew. But still, he was hunting a myth. A rich girl's game.

'Sarellia, you can't really believe the King still lives?'

She nodded, an expression of complete faith.

'He'd have to be ancient. An old man.' Pointing to the bodies hidden in the forest, Jerune said, 'You think he could do that?'

'You don't think he's real?'

'If he was, that was over a century ago. But now? If alive, he'd be an arthritic hunchback.'

Her eyes glared. 'Not Baza'rad.'

The dark skin, her perfect complexion; a supremely attractive woman. Of course, a Bruhadian. The same ethnicity as the fabled King she sought. Though, Jerune understood that nation's sun had set long ago, conquered before the last great war. Scattered across the world, the people of Bruhada no longer held the respect or distrust they once had. It prompted a question, Jerune asking, 'You're a pureblood?'

'In spirit. And I believe in our spirit.'

'Belief doesn't forge truth.'

'And doubt doesn't destroy it.' She paced over to him. 'I descend from those who fought alongside the man who was King. Baza'rad, the name, died in Bruhale. In exile, he became another.'

Jerune knew the ancient stories. Old tales confused by their own myth. In the time of the Terrible Queen of Kalleron, Baza'rad had defied the Butcher, Te'anor. Routed a legion, they said. He alone with his royal Warhammer, Bruch'ail. Epic stories to impress naïve minds. No man could be so invincible. Still, Sarellia had stopped asking stupid questions. His turn.

'So, who'd he become?'

'You swear a secret?'

He wasn't five years old but he wanted to know what she thought she knew. 'You want a pinkie swear?'

She glowered. Sarellia suited anger. He'd be happy to keep her that way.

'Fine, I swear.'

'This isn't a game, Jerune. If I tell you this...'

Her frustration was real. Palpable. That was intriguing. He wanted to know why. 'I promise.'

Looking up and down the trail, though it was clear they were alone, she spoke in hushed tones. It wasn't a whisper; he didn't need to lean in to hear. Yet he did, to be closer.

Sarellia said, 'After exile, Baza'rad joined Petra and the Cult. But he had found a new identity. A simple sailor, Argan.'

Jerune recognised the name. 'The Argan from Anka?'

Sarellia nodded.

'He disappeared when I was a child.' He could picture the man. Or some hobbled memory of him. A quiet type, lived on the outskirts of the city. A recluse. The children too scared to taunt the giant. 'Dead now, surely?' he said. 'Besides, he was no King. I recall a mucky hermit.'

'Argan was Baza'rad. And it was he who killed Kalle at Stranghame.'

Another myth. A battle too good to be true. Hyperbole for history. Shaking his head, Jerune said, 'Listen, things that happened nearly a century ago can be hard to understand. Armies fought and Kings died. We always want to immortalise someone. And you're a Bruhadian by blood, it's no surprise you want to deify Baza'rad, or Argan.'

She appeared offended. A perfect pout with which to express her anger. 'And what are you, mongrel? Who do you idolise?'

Mongrel. It was a fair comment. His line ran as far back as his whore mother. And though she may have loved him; he had left her as soon as he could hunt. Spreading his arms wide, gesturing to the forest, he said, 'I worship this. Nature. It gives and it takes, but it never judges. My god lives and dies with savage indifference. But it doesn't require worship, or respect. I exist within it, and that's all I need. As for my heritage? Too many fathers to count. My mother had straw hair and sallow skin. Nothing as pure as you.'

Nodding, evident she was shocked by his self-deprecation, she said, 'Well, Bruhadians follow the bloodline. We protect our lore.'

'Elementalism?' He wished it were a religion but it wasn't. More real than life itself. More dangerous than fickle human gods. 'Where does this fit in with Argan, or Baza'rad?'

'The royal line—Baza'rad was the last—is bound to the Elementals, Earth to be specific. I don't know the ritual, or how, but it's true. I can see your disbelief but hear me out. When Petra left An'Korathall, who appeared in her place?'

Jerune recalled. Frightening times for a child. An aura that smothered the city. It was good that he lived beyond the reach of stone. He said, 'Kor'A. The old Queen of Kalleron came back.'

'And she is the Elemental Earth, correct?' She nodded, prompting him to agree. He did so, felt foolish. Sarellia continued, 'Well, we know Petra kept Anka safe. For almost three-quarters of a century she protected it. Nobody would dare insult her treaty of peace. No blood to be spilled. But Kor'A didn't return to keep us safe—only she knows why she came back. Yet, her very presence was a ward against attack. Nobody's suicidal enough to stand against the Elementals. But Kor'A's left us, her aura has gone. The city is starting to change. You must have noticed it? Haven't you felt it?'

He had, offered another involuntary nod.

13

Sarellia, frowning, said, 'Once the other nations realise this, they will scheme. Spies have always come to An'Korathall. Come to see when the white city loses its guardian. Who do you want, Jerune? Who would you rather see march across these free lands? Fire from Laria, or the Fury of Kalleron?'

Sarellia had been a novelty. A rich urbanite spending coin on a whimsical quest. It seemed that was not the case. Things weren't so childish, so easily dismissed. What she said made sense. Terrible sense. He hadn't signed up for it. Though, it did explain the coin she had promised.

'So, you seek Baza'rad. Why? What can one man do?'

'Against the Elementals? Nothing. But it's who he can find.'

Cryptic words. He was sure the answer was profound. 'And you want to find him, so he can find someone for you?'

'Yes.'

'Who can he find? Someone to fight the Elementals? Because that's nonsense.'

Sarellia smiled. 'Petra. The Queen of An'Korathall. Queen of Stone.'

He frowned. Thought the conversation was glaringly circular. 'But you just spoke about that. Petra left, Kor'A returned, and now she's pissed off too. I don't understand; why would Petra come back? Everyone said she slinked away in the night, never to be seen again. Is she even here in the Northern Lands?'

Sarellia nodded, cast her eyes all around. When she spoke, there was a strange melancholy in her tone. 'She'll always be here. Can't ever leave... But you know enough for now. More than anyone beyond my line ought to. Remember, you swore this to secrecy.'

'Nobody would believe a word of it anyway.'

Pointing to the single surviving print; that giant foot, she asked, 'So, can you track that?'

'Yes. Easy.' He could track a man that large through an ocean. But the other print. So small. The chip of glass. Too much talk of Queens and stone. He wanted another look, moved to the broad leaf where the flake had landed. Gone. Dropped into deep litter and lost. 'Shit.'

'What?'

'Nothing, let's go track your ghost.'

Chapter III

A fortress had been her home, her world. Yet in these days with Goddard, away from the walls of marble and granite, she had experienced a new reality. Mother had taught her much of their world, told her of men and women, of lust and war. Spoke of things she did not understand. Chara had experienced nothing of those lessons; feared much of it. Her mother had said to be afraid. To be wary of human deceit. Though she had never told her to fear the Sisters. They were kin, unlike the mortals of flesh and bone.

And now Chara stared at a babbling brook, this creature of flowing crystal crossing her path. Splitting the green of the land, it appeared uninterested in her affairs, the Sister gave no hint of intrigue as to why a child of stone walked with a man of flesh. Caught in her own thoughts, Chara twitched her head. Had someone called her name?

'Chara?' It was Goddard's voice.

Stolen from her thoughts, noting his concern, she nodded. 'I'm fine.' She pointed, 'I've never seen her until now.'

'The stream?'

'No. Water.'

A pause before he replied. 'Surely, just a stream?'

Perhaps he didn't understand? 'No, *Water*. As mother is Earth.'

His eyes flickered recognition. 'Is Water not the vastness of the oceans?'

Mother had said humans lacked logic. Odd creatures bound to a thing called emotion. She would show him. As Goddard approached, she reached to him, and taking his hand, she asked, 'Is this you?'

A frown was his reply.

She squeezed it. 'Your hand, you feel that?'

'A tickle,' he said.

Chara squeezed harder but he laughed. She asked, 'That doesn't hurt?'

'You wish to hurt me?'

'I'm sorry...'

Goddard laughed. Chara wondered if he was trying to fool her?

She frowned at Goddard's game but decided it would be better to continue with his Elemental education. 'Mother said humans are complete in their form. As long as this is attached,' she wiggled his hand for emphasis, 'it is part of you. Just as this stream connects to a river that flows to the ocean. It is part of Water. But unlike you, she is all of her form, not a part of it. You understand?'

He remained quiet. Were her words too clever for his human mind? He appeared confused, though his expression was unusual; a thing she thought might be sadness etched upon his face.

'Goddard?'

A huge sigh and a nod. 'I understand.'

'Are you...sad?'

An unconvincing smile appeared on his lips. 'A memory.' He looked to the stream and asked, 'You can cross?'

Of course, she could cross, she was kin. Nodding, she strode to Water.

Stop!

Alarmed by Goddard's command, she ceased and turned. 'Why?'

He appeared perplexed. 'Why what?'

The voice. Not his. There could be only one other. Turning to her kin, she asked the sister, 'Why must I stop?'

The Oath.

'Oath?'

'Chara?' Goddard came to her side. 'Who are you talking to?'

Make him silent.

A feeling inside. Was it guilt? Looking to him, she said, 'She wants you to be quiet.'

She expected Goddard to grumble. He often did. Perhaps unleash the hammer. But his eyes narrowed and he nodded. He tipped his head to Water and backed away. Turning to her kin, agitated by her rudeness, Chara said, 'He's my friend.'

He is insignificant. They all are.

He wasn't. Kor'A had spoken of him. More than any other man. 'Mother didn't think so. He has purpose.'

That which ceases to be is insignificant.

'I don't understand?'

You are insignificant.

Chara knew the word. Mother used it to describe life. That which could die. Water's words were apt. Chara asked, 'I am insignificant because I am mortal?'

Yes.

She had a reply. One her kin would not understand. Something mother had taught her about the human way. 'I exist; I am significant. And I will be remembered. Life is to be remembered.'

As you say. There was a pause. Had the sister flowed away with herself? The voice returned, confirming she remained. *Tell me, are you bound as we are? Or free, as them?*

Chara did not know. She sought Goddard for help but he was distant. 'Bound? Free? I am free, am I not?

Can you leap, child? Can you leave her touch?

She had never tried. Did not know how. 'How do I leap?'

16

I am narrow here. Leap across and you are free. Stand fast, and you are bound. The oath is bound. You are of Earth. I wish to see your insignificance; I will not part for you.

From the citadel she had watched human children play. Observed their movements, never copying them. Leap: to jump. She gauged Water to be narrower than she was tall. It would be easy—if she was free. With a concerted effort, she copied the children and leapt into the air.

You are bound.

Chara looked down to see one foot had stayed firm. Touching her mother Earth. A hop of sorts. Yet, she was certain that she was free. Could not feel the bind that held her down. She was to be as them, the humans. And human children adapted with practice. Observation over countless passing Suns had shown her. Mimicking a deep breath, she leapt again, this time pitching her weight forward.

She left Earth. It was terrifying. Dizzying. Dislocated from the essence. Flying as high as the moons of Noctyrne and Ambyr. The panic rose and collapsed as she fell back into Water. A surge of panic—something said of an oath? But as she sat in the stream, her kin laughed and flowed away.

You are a free thing, child. Unbound by us. Do what they do, be as them; you will live and you will cease. You are insignificant.

'Chara!' Goddard came rushing over and plucked her from the stream. 'What happened? Did she attack?'

But all she could do was laugh, and when he put her back down, Chara jumped back into the water and splashing all around, called out, 'I'm free, Goddard, I'm free!'

The sun was setting, not yet lost to her vision. Far from the trail, a thinning wood provided ample shelter. Another fire burned in a pit. Chara thought it curious Goddard could create fire. He sat close, his leathers steaming in the heat. His eyes fixed upon her. An intense gaze she thought might suggest he was irritated.

'I didn't mean to soak you,' she said.

Shaking his head, he said, 'I was a sailor, once. Damp is fine.'

'You're annoyed at me?'

'Curious.'

She grinned. It was good to be a mystery, though she was happy to invite Goddard's query. 'Of what?'

'You're not like Petra.'

'Is that bad?'

'No, not at all. But when she was... changed by your mother, she became bound to her. She could no longer cross the seas. Couldn't leave the land.' He patted his damp legs. 'Let alone frolic in a stream.'

Chara looked around, searching for the Sister but they were far from Water. She said, 'There is an oath.'

'Oath?'

'Until today I thought I was bound to Earth.' Sat on the ground, she touched it. Hand flat on the soil. It was cold, indifferent. 'But I'm not. Water said I was either bound or free. If I could leap, I was free.'

'Is this why you're... not so strong?'

That pause; Goddard almost said *weak*. He hadn't. Chara knew that was kindness. But it would have been true. Kor'A had told her she would be weak and mortal. It was how humans experienced existence. The only way to understand them was to be as them.

She said, 'I was created to know life. Through me, Kor'A would learn more about your kind.'

Goddard shook his head and displayed his palms to the sky. 'But where is your mother? What happened, Chara?'

She thought of that day. Another cycle, the sun rising. Kor'A was gone. She had felt it, rather, *not* felt it. Yet, in the previous day, her mother had seemed different. It was unknown, her character; not as it ought to be. Perhaps Goddard could help to understand it.

'Mother would explain things to me. Tell me of the world of humans. We would sit, and she would talk. I would listen. I would ask questions. Then I would sleep. On the next cycle, we would do the same again. On the last day, she was different.'

'Different. How?' Goddard asked.

It was better to demonstrate. She stood and moved to him. He was too large to do it properly but she put her arms around him; at least, as far as they would go. Which wasn't far—the man was a boulder slipped from the slopes. She stopped, placing her arms by her sides.

'Like that. But she could encircle me. You're too big.'

Goddard didn't say anything. His face softened. She saw his jaws clench. He asked, 'Just once. She did that once?'

'Oh, no. All that day. She kept doing this.' She repeated the action. This time, she felt Goddard's arms wrap around her. It felt safe. Secure. Wriggling free, she asked, 'What is this?'

He sighed. Didn't answer straight away. The pause was exciting. She was fidgeting when he spoke. 'A hug, Chara. A human thing. Your mother was hugging you.'

Noting the sun was about to disappear, she moved back to her side of the fire. Sitting, preparing to sleep, she asked, 'What does it mean?'

The sun set, and though his mouth moved and she could see it all, her world became still. Sleep, as Kor'A called it. The quiet time; sheltered in silence, alert to few sounds. Soothed by her waking rest, she smiled. What was a hug, she thought? And why were Goddard's eyes sad?

Chapter IV

H is heart was pounding. Sword hand shaking. The damn storm didn't help. The night sky ruptured by crackling blue light. A bad omen. But they'd planned the raid for weeks, it was too late to pull out. The castle on the hill. Everyone knew it contained riches beyond belief. Guarded by a witch, they said. But witches weren't real. The Elementals were the only real powers, every fool knew that. Nonetheless, Dekka couldn't control his fear. Staring at the silhouette of the fort, he yelped when a hand fell on his shoulder.

'Dekka, stop shaking, you miserable maggot.'

It was Achallon. She had instigated the whole damn thing. A mercenary as scary as the legend of the witch. As she peered down at him with her one good eye, he realised she was the rock, and this was the hard place.

'I'm not shaking, I'm cold.'

She laughed in his face. Bitch.

'Seriously, the wind's fierce.'

'Whatever you say, Dekka.' She leered at him.

How he wanted to smash out her crooked teeth. Wishful thinking—he was no match. Besides, her crew were nearby. Dekka had provided the local knowledge. A Farenian lowlife, he considered himself on the rise. This job would do it, help him get away from the squalor of the port town, perhaps travel west to Venhyne. He had thought Achallon's arrival in Farenhyne a blessing. Not so sure now as her fingers clawed into his shoulder.

'The basement?' she asked.

That was the word. He nodded.

'Better be. Lead the way.'

He moved off without complaint, better to placate her mood. She had brought three others, all faceless hired goons. He knew of Achallon, they called her the Frigid Hand. Cold to all, loyal to none. It was said she paid well; the reason she was renowned. A contrast of morality. Dekka hoped that rumour was true; dreams were expensive things to furnish.

Moving past crumbled wall and overgrown bracken, he reached the keep with ease. It had long stood atop the plateau overlooking Farenhyne. A relic of the old wars, the lone tower was all that remained intact. Among the ruins nothing stirred but the wind which was accompanied by the distant rumbling. The storm was coming closer. Damn sorcery. No. The witch was myth. He needed to remind himself. Otherwise, why was he here? *Nobody* would cross the Witch of Anka.

Achallon close behind him; she whispered, 'The door?'

He pointed to the stairs leading down. A well of dark descending into nothingness.

'Go,' she urged.

Fuck. He was shaking. Something wasn't right. But what was worse; the possible witch in the castle, or the very real bitch on his back? Either would kill him, but he was certain which carried more threat. Legs of sluggish lead brought him to the basement door. Reaching into his pocket he retrieved the picks. Fumbling in darkness, he started to work on the lock. Merciful for the storm, his scratchings were lost to the wind and thunder. The lock was child's play and he nodded to Achallon, her eye glinting in a flash of lightning. Maybe *she* was the witch?

'Open it.'

The latch snapped open in a dreadful silence between gale and rumble, Dekka cursing his bad luck. Another crash of thunder removed the silence and he pushed the door open. A nod from Achallon and he ventured inside. She followed, shadowed by the mercenaries. Darkness greeted their entry, nothing visible in the gloom. Lips pressed close to his ear.

Achallon said, 'Nobody's home. Light it up.'

From his belt he withdrew the torch. No ordinary wrap of oiled rag, it was a Kallerye flare. He had stolen a few from a trader. These were special; Drohendrian Darkwood with a chemical tip. They burned with a blue flame, subdued and cold. An unusual effect; green being the normal hue. Expensive torches—Dekka considered only a fool would be stupid enough to trade for one. He struck the end against the ignition block, a small cube of alloy; the sudden illumination revealing great disappointment to his eyes.

'It's empty,' Achallon said, too close to his cheek.

His mind scurrying for an excuse, he replied, 'There's three more floors. I saw no lights from outside. Nobody's home.' He wasn't sure he believed that. But Achallon was real; her sour breath suffocating his senses.

A prod in his back and he was moving to the stairs. Floor by floor, he found nothing but empty space. Elegant vaulted ceilings mocking the vacant riches. Each flight upwards brought him closer to despair. One more floor and the metal point in his ribs had all but promised his death. Dekka found himself longing for the witch. To die by legend was better than a stab in the back. Slowly, he ascended. His breath shallow, his steps mute. The uppermost floor came into view.

Madness.

'What is this?' Achallon asked.

It was obvious. And confusing. A ship's cabin built inside a castle. Wooden timbers curved upwards from the stone floor. Windows, circles as though portholes, graced each wall, and a modest chest claimed the centre of the room. Or was it a cabin? A bed, immaculately made up, filled the space at one end. All of this was delivered to Dekka's view from the erratic lightning stabbing through the portholes. His heart sank; this was not a treasure trove. This was the folly of myth.

Dekka came close to laughter—there was no witch. Perhaps an eccentric artist? Why else decorate a keep with the innards of a ship? He felt foolish. Allowed a sigh. He turned to Achallon. 'Shall we?'

She smiled. He felt the pain. Sharp ice in his ribs. 'Sorry, love. Not enough to share.'

'You...'

'Bitch,' she said. 'I know.'

Achallon moved past as Dekka slumped down the stairs. He could still flee. Wasn't sure if she wanted to finish him off. The others moved past, one smashing a knee into his face. Blood gushed from his nose and he slid down the rest of the flight. His jerkin was damp to the touch. No way of knowing how much blood was soaking through; Achallon had taken the torch, his injuries were hidden in the dark, the pain suppressed by fear. Above, he heard their voices. Furious words cursing his name.

He knew he couldn't escape, not on hands and knees. One floor further and he found an alcove; dark in between the stabs of lightning. If he could hide, they might think he had fled. Crawling into the confined space, Dekka made himself as small as possible, hoped they would rush past. They took longer than he had thought and he rued his mistake. Basement below, his flight a scramble away. But now they were coming, the blue light dancing down the steps. Horror gripping him, Dekka realised his alcove was poor cover.

Her grin was wicked. 'There you are.'

Achallon's flare lit the room. Something else. Dekka's eyes flicking to the basement stairs. His heart hammering hard. Saw the ghost rising from below; a phantom come to haunt them all. Rock and the hardest place. Achallon relegated to his periphery, he saw *her*. Ascending the stairs and stepping into the room, her body wrapped in a cheap cloak; it was the Witch of Anka. It had to be. Her skin reflecting the blue as only white could. A face of marble cast in a human visage. Eyes of sapphire and diamond sparkled in the dark. Her beauty was ungodly.

When she spoke, it was a human voice. 'Come for my treasure?'

For a moment, silence. Then Achallon replied. 'You have none.'

'I need none.'

'Legends are always based on truth. This castle, undisturbed. There must be something?'

The witch sighed. 'And if there was treasure, you think you'd take it? From me?'

Achallon sneered. 'I've fought monsters before.'

Laughter from the ghost. Real and infectious. Dekka smirked though his pain was seeping through to his senses. And although she was the Witch, she was everything she was not meant to be. Glorious and gentle, the sound of her mirth was music.

'I'll cut out your tongue,' Achallon said.

'Hmmm,' was the witch's reply. She was smiling. 'Tell me, the monsters? Fangs and tentacles? Claws and slobbering madness?'

Achallon moved her free hand to the pommel of her dagger. 'Don't test me.'

The witch appeared unimpressed. 'Child. I'll allow you to leave. I shouldn't, it's clear you're a sewer-dwelling rat. But I've had my fill of murder and death. Enough for lifetimes.' The witch stepped to the side, gestured to the basement stairs. 'Your path is free. Go.'

Dekka watched, his vision blurring. He didn't want this. He wanted to be outside, to be away. Maybe there was still time. Lurching from the alcove, he fell on his side. The pain was excruciating. From the floor he saw the witch stare down upon him. He lifted a finger to accuse Achallon.

'No honour among thieves, eh?' she said to him.

Her voice. Her tone. She cared? He tried to reply but his ribs wouldn't comply. All he could manage was a gurgle and a sigh.

'Well thief. On my ship, I had a rule. No bloodshed. And this is my ship now.' The Witch pointed at Achallon. 'Does she deserve mercy?'

With all his might, Dekka forced a wheeze from his lungs. Pushing his tongue to the roof of his mouth, he said, 'Nnn....'

Without warning, Achallon lunged at the Witch, a low scream rumbling from her lungs. From his foetal position it was hard for Dekka to see. He swore the blade pinged off the white body. An impotent sound. Furious, Achallon hacked at the Witch but the woman in the cloak did nothing. Her rough fabric robe disintegrated under the attack and it fell to the floor. Dekka realised the mercenaries had backed off. None offering their support to Achallon. Wise men, he thought.

Achallon was panting, exhausted by the effort. The Witch stood firm.

Glancing at her tattered cloak, she said, 'This is why I don't wear nice things.'

In a movement too fast to comprehend, the witch's hand was around Achallon's neck. The mercenary struggled but it was obvious there was no escape. Dekka expected a speech from the woman of stone, but it didn't come. No time for false grandeur. A castrated screech from Achallon was followed by her head ripping from her neck, torn off in one terrifying swipe of the witch's hand. The ugly skull bounced against a wall, then to the floor and rolled toward Dekka. Disgusted, he tried to move away.

'And you, mercenaries, you wish to fight?' the Witch asked.

Out of view, swords clattering on wood, the men shuffling past. They descended the stairs and he heard the basement door swing open. Sweat dripping into his eyes, he saw the witch approach but he held no fear. Death was coming. What could she do but hurry his path? He blinked; his vision faltered. She was lowering herself, sitting beside him. She covered her modesty with a shred of the tattered cloak. In the encroaching grey, he felt his hand being taken into hers. It wasn't as cold as stone. It was gentle.

'Does it hurt?' she asked.

He sighed, a slight nod.

'I will stay with you.'

A nod. A tear. He forced out the word on a frail breath. 'Why?'

Her voice changed. Such melancholy. 'I've watched all my friends die. A hundred years of death. I'm cursed to see it, never to know it. I long for it. She did this to me,

22

and now I'm alone. I'll stay till your end, but know that I envy you. This is the treasure I seek. You fear it, you call it death.' She paused; he heard a longing sigh. 'I call it life.'

Dekka blinked. Thought he saw stone cry. A diamond falling in the dark. He gripped her hand tighter and she returned the touch. He shut his eyes and exhaled.

Chapter V

An'Korathall. An effigy in stone. Legend told two truths of its creation. Brought forth from the ground to mimic the splendour of the great city of Kalleron; the Queen's salute to her old master across the sea. That was the Kallerye opinion. Bücka knew that to be a lie. She saw a canvas of granite and marble, coloured by human expression. The city was steeped in legend, the stories passed down from her grandmother, Thelia, the woman who had raised her. Tales told at bedtime to fire her imagination. The white city—An'Korathall—built by the Queen of Kalleron for the new Queen of Stone.

Walking through the streets, climbing the central avenue, Bücka noted the forms created by the old Queen's hand. She knew more than most. Understood the oddity. This was the product of an Elemental power, and there were subtle hints for the keen eye to see. The ground fused seamlessly with each building. There were no bricks or mortar; nothing so mundane as a tooling mark or a stonemasons motif. Her grandmother had told her, in its first days of creation, the city had been a sterile place. A ghost of a city. But time had changed An'Korathall; the cold stone long since furnished with human enterprise. Every open portal held a wooden frame, the structure battened inside with fine precision. From these, shutters swung on the breeze, or panes of glass blocked the wind. Doors provided security in a city that had needed none. There were flowers of saturated hues hanging from baskets suspended from rooftop beams Those wooden posts lay unsecured, anchored by their own weight. There was a theme to Anka's carpentry—nothing was nailed into the white mineral, not a mark upon the white stone. Bücka knew why. An'Korathall was the skin of Earth, a city risen from the Elemental's essence. To set foot in Anka was to stand upon the flesh of a god. Though, just days past, rumours had reached Bücka in Wederhyne that the god had left. Bücka had doubted that. But marching through Anka, she knew it to be true. Saw it in the faces of those she passed; frightened eyes staring. Staring at her; Bücka, the infamous mercenary. And though she was no cold-blooded killer, she could not refute the title. Two swords hanging from her belt, one a relic from ancient Bruhale, the other forged in a Larian furnace. Underneath a grey cloak, her steel bodice wore the colours of old Kalleron; red and black. A skirt of long metal plates over leather boots, chiming as she walked.

An'Korathall, city of peace no more. Anxious faces asking her to leave. Retreating figures slinking back inside. She wondered if the city had any fighters. There could be refugee soldiers from the foreign wars but none were visible. Swords and anger dropped in favour of the protection of Anka. Such a mistake. Gods are fickle. The Elementals more so. But Bücka wasn't here for blood, she had come for family. She had to see the tomb.

Anka was anarchy. As close to the concept as could be. No council, no courts. Living in the shadow of a god removed such human need. People traded and worked; arguments rare, always settled without blood. That had been the rule under Petra; no bloodshed in An'Korathall. Draw a sword and suffer her wrath. Bücka had never seen the Queen of Stone. More tales passed down from her grandmother. But she had seen a glimpse of Earth, the Elemental whose domain was the Northern Lands. It was of little surprise the peace remained when she had returned to Anka. A human god replaced by her inhuman creator.

All those stories—Bücka had learned them from Thelia's tales. Regaling her with the world of Kor'A, once the Terrible Queen of Kalleron. She was the pawn of a devious King, and she was the abominable power that turned cities to dust; great nations such as Arkallon brought to ruin by her will. Yet that destruction had fired off momentous events. All because one great woman had lost a lover to the Queen's senseless slaughter. One death from countless thousands and the world changed. One woman rising to claim revenge—Petra, the dashing Captain that had secured Thelia's safety. Taking her and her sister, Thelissa, from the hands of slavers. Petra the brave; Petra the fallen. Her death and resurrection at the hands of Kor'A should have been a myth—a tale so far-fetched it shouldn't have been real. But it was. Oh, so very real. Bücka now standing among it all—this city called An'Korathall. Created, Thelia had said, in a moment of monstrous guilt; a gift from Earth to the woman whose world she had destroyed. Bücka, staring at the house of Great Tombs, shivered at the thought. If Thelia's story was true, it was a mountain of guilt.

Inside the citadel walls, it appeared as everything else. Not built, projected from the surface of Earth. A mausoleum of shining marble. In the noon sun it was painful to observe, the mica dazzling, the light blinding. A simple block higher than a townhouse, a domed roof to cap it off. Two pillars flanked an open portal beyond which a slab of darkness was relief from the glare.

A breath. A pause. The house of Petra's closest allies. In the reign of the two Queens, the place was forbidden. It was Petra's solace. Those whose own lay within the tomb were allowed to visit. Nobody else. The fortress gate shut to all others. Decades of closure. Lifetimes of grief. Thelia had told of the first passing, her old eyes watering as she recollected the life now gone. Too young, Thelissa, her own sister had passed.

Fifty years was not enough. Though, she had told Bücka, most all of it was lived under the shining light of Petra's presence. More, she had found sanctuary in the company of Shadow, her father by all rights. No man had ever matched his soul. Saviour, protector, clown. Bücka recalled Thelia's story with a swollen heart. Recalled her grandmother's tears. After her sister passed, it was Shadow's death that took Thelia away from Anka. Never to come back. But Bücka would right that wrong. In a bare plot in Wederhyne, Thelia lay. For years Bücka had wanted to return her to An'Korathall to rest with her sister. Under Kor'A, the citadel had remained shut. Colder than Petra's reign. But when those rumours had come to Bücka that the second Queen had left, there was only one thing she could do.

'For you, grandmother.'

Into the gloom and cold air, she strode. A fitting place for death. Three sarcophagi spaced across the floor. Bücka moved with trepidation, her careful steps reverberating, returned to her tenfold. A powerful echo. A moment of hesitation. The Queen was no more; she had to believe it. It was a blessing for her purpose, not so for the city. Standing in Anka's only tomb, Bücka knew hers would not be a lone interest. Proof given to her on the long journey. The clumsy shadows following her since Wederhyne. There was time enough before they came. Time to investigate Thelissa's place of rest. To secure Thelia's final home.

Each massive marble block, raised on three tiers of concentric circular steps, was topped by a smooth dark lid. The casket merged seamlessly with the floor, another projection of Earth's essence, though this had been created by Petra. The lids were Drohendrian Darkwood; it seemed a strange touch, something warm among the cold stone. The three pristine blocks were identical but for the size. One massive block stood in the centre, flanked by two smaller sarcophagi.

Their names were engraved in native scripts. It wasn't fortune that Bücka understood them all. Well-travelled, she knew many languages, had spoken death in so many tongues. On the left lay Shadow and Kallisa. Angels; what Thelia had called them. Curious, Bücka stepped to the plinth. Wanted to see their faces; understood that the ravages of time were kept at bay by Petra's magical touch. Inside, she knew she would find the bodies sealed in quartz. Funerary benefits of Elemental friendship, Thelia had once said. Hands on the wooden lid, she pushed. Some grunt was required, Darkwood being notoriously heavy. And expensive. Casket partially open, the dim light failed to illuminate inside. She pushed again, a prism of colour reflecting within. Two sleeping shadows deep in the unnatural glass. Poetic. But unfortunate.

'Damn.'

The quartz was level to the lip of the stone. No way to place another inside. Staring at the silhouette of lovers, she felt a pang of regret. Wished she had known such heroes from before the wars. Ironic, though—what Bücka knew. It was their actions a century ago which had brought calamity to these shores.

A salute. A nod of respect. 'Goodbye Shadow, Kallisa.'

She would leave Thelissa's casket until last. Didn't want those tears yet. Best to keep hope on a longer leash. Instead, she turned to the middle tomb. It could only be

Argan. Thelia had always described the man as an enigma. Her words had often seemed confused; Bücka assuming old age had addled her grandmother's mind. That Argan had secrets was no surprise. Petra's entire crew, it seemed, was a mystery of sorts. But the man Thelia had described as a mountain with legs stood out above the rest. Literally. Bücka stepped to the lid, the huge dimensions matching her grandmother's outrageous stories. Once more, hands firm on the Darkwood, she gave a push. Nothing. Not a surprise—damn thing was massive. Frowning, a deep breath released with a grunting force, she tried again. Not an inch.

'Come on, dammit!'

A final heave of effort and the lid budged open. A howl as the pain stabbed inside her shoulder. *Really?* It was always the bloody same; how many battles had she endured? From how many had she walked away with nary a scratch, only to strain her muscles in rare moments of peace? Cursing under her breath, rubbing her shoulder, Bücka peered inside. Once again, the gloom did nothing to aid her view. But she knew empty. Different from the previous stone casket. No quartz to defeat time. A ghost of nothing coming from the depths.

'Where the hell are you, Argan?'

Perhaps not yet dead? But he had been a man when Thelia was a child. By her wrinkles, though she never could recall her own age, that woman was *old*. And gone, more than fifteen years. Impossible. Even in the Northern Lands, in Anka, where death came later because life was good—nobody lived that long. The puzzle was a welcome prize. If Thelissa's casket was a block of quartz, Thelia could rest in Argan's empty bed. He wouldn't mind. Would he?

Careful with her shoulder, the empty casket was sealed. One more. Tentative steps carried her to Thelissa. Inside lay the doting sister who had given everything for her younger sibling. Bücka recalled the day she learned the grim truth of how Thelissa had spared Thelia from the abuse she had endured under the slavers. As a child, a fresh bruise on her cheek, Bücka's luck had run out. Thieving was fine. It was capture that wasn't. And this man had been different. Leering, suggestive. His words as sickly treacle. Words used she didn't know, gestures she thought appeared violent. A hand upon her. Places not welcome. His mistake; the knife in his thigh a good lesson. Her pride sullied, her face caught as she fled, she had run home to tell Thelia. She had never seen grandmother so angry. Coughing with rage, she was. Bücka thought she'd get a whipping. Instead, she had learned of her grandmother's salvation. How she had come to be with Petra. An alley in Kalleron, so long ago. Thelia and her sister, another trade, another man. It was to be Thelia's first time. For years, Thelissa had shielded her. Bore the brunt of what sick men wanted. In that alley, the man had turned to her grandmother. It was meant to be her first touch. It wasn't. Unsullied, she killed him, a slash to his neck with a blunt blade. Bücka recalled the story as though it had been told yesterday. How Thelia's face lit up when she spoke. Their handlers had remained guard at the end of the alley; the sisters knew they were finished. Killing a customer was death for a slaver's girl. But then *she* came. Petra, a fierce and magnificent woman. An avenging angel. Killed the slavers, took her and her sister away from that world. And because her sister protected her, Thelia had never known that vile abuse. After that, Shadow became their shield. Life had been good.

'I never had the nightmares my sister suffered,' Grandmother had said. 'Her sacrifice allowed me to dream. And in time, I found a good man. I think he always feared Shadow.' With fondness, Bücka recalled Thelia's wicked chuckle. 'Any man that touched me would fear my father. But you exist because I could love. Something Thelissa never did. That was taken from her. I owe the chance of my daughter and you, to her.'

In her mind's eye she held her grandmother's tear-stained face. Beneath the lid lay Thelia's selfless sister. And though Argan's casket was empty, she wished for Thelissa's to be free of quartz. One push, a grumble from her shoulder, and the lid slid over. Inside, in glass, one silhouette. Not moving, Bücka remained. Tears not useful, her throat tightened. Jaws clenched. No, Bücka wouldn't cry.

Sighing, a tremble in her breath, she said, 'Thank you, Thelissa. Thank you for Thelia. For my mother too.'

She slid the lid shut and backed down the steps. With one final farewell she stood still, soft steps diminishing in the chamber. Long after her own echo died another arose. From outside, footsteps approaching. Bücka turned. Four silhouettes appearing in the open portal.

'You can't spill blood in Anka,' she called to them.

Too dark to discern features, one tapped a sword against the pillar. 'Nobody's home, Bücka. Can't hide behind legends now.'

She nodded. But she wouldn't do it here. Not inside the tomb.

Chapter VI

B etter days.

    Lost in time, obscured by distance and shimmer. Goddard stared out across the ocean to the land he couldn't see. Laria. A frigid land, far removed from the heat in Bruhada. But the stories all said Fire had come to those shores and Goddard understood the Laria he knew would be gone. His last visit a century ago; the inn at the harbour—never recalled its name. A night of merriment, drinking and dancing. Who knew he could dance? He remembered Shadow's expression, priceless. Of course Kings could dance; though, back then few knew his truth.

Better days. The next they had sailed, and Petra would never again return home. None of them would. Loyal to her, she in turn forever bound to the Earth, his fate had been sealed. And now he had found her. At least, where he thought she would be.

'This is it?' Chara asked, a tug on his hand.

The keep was intact but the rest of the fortress was derelict, a sight made pretty for the roses and flowers crawling across crumbled ramparts. A relic from the early days. Built on the peninsula west of Farenhyne. The work of General Aracyse and his engineers; fortifications to keep the Northern Lands safe. Aracyse, the legendary Kallerye general that defied his King. Memories coming back; the General falling on the fields that bore his name. Goddard, as Argan, facing Kalleron's mighty King, Kalle, the false immortal. A human god crushed by Bruch'ail. A day of blood and Fury, victory and loss.

Another tug, pulling him from his memories. 'Goddard, is this it?'

He grunted his reply.

'But it's...' Chara's words trailed away.

Goddard thought he knew why. All Chara knew was the white city. Their journey had passed timber huts and shacks but nothing of stone. Nothing to match Anka's sublime grace. This fort was built by human endeavour, the practicality of defensive engineering hardly affording it an aesthetic touch. It lacked the unnatural fluidity of the Elemental city.

'This is what we build with stone. A fort. What you see remaining is the keep.'

'It's ugly.'

He laughed. Compared to An'Korathall, most things were.

'Will the Queen be home?'

'Only one way to find out.'

Leading Chara along ancient paths, he scanned for life. Not that of his old friend. He sought thieves and vagabonds. His mistake was made leaving An'Korathall—years of solitude muddying his mind, not thinking things through. Chara was unique; a literal gem. Her nakedness was natural but her existence was anything but. Some had seen her—it explained the bandits. He wasn't sure how many others knew but if Chara remained visible things would be difficult. The child couldn't be seen again. Her onyx skin drew too much attention. He needed her to be Petra's ward. Then nobody would come for her.

Climbing over the collapsed outer walls, he looked at the dark glass on the flanks of the keep. The windows revealed nothing, no glimmer of stone beyond the panes. It was futile to approach the main gate; boulders blocking the entrance. Rocks too heavy for men to lift. Placed with precision by an unnatural hand. Moving to the lower entrance, the basement, he passed two graves. Fresh, one marked with a clean marble stone. A long cube, rounded and precise, it was unnatural. On top lay a single gold coin. The other grave bare, anonymous. A pit for necessity.

'What is it?' Chara asked.

Who is it, Goddard thought. It couldn't be family—Petra had none. He shrugged, shaking his head, and led Chara to the stairs.

Locked. The wooden door would cave in with a punch. That would be rude.

'You don't have a key, do you?' he said to Chara.

Her face expressed concern. 'Should I?'

Such a curiosity. Shaking his head, he said, 'I'm joking.'

'Oh. Should I laugh?'

He dismissed her with a wave of his hand, pointed to the steps. 'You wait here, don't move—all right?' Moving past Chara, careful not to step on little fingers, he saw her eyes following him.

'Where are you going?' she asked.

Scanning the area, he sought a vantage point. He needed to keep Chara away from prying eyes. Goddard pointed to an outcrop of wall with views across the grounds.

'I'll be there. Make sure nobody sneaks up on us.'

Nodding, she asked, 'What will I do?'

He would say sleep, but he imagined that wasn't built into her behaviour. Not until sundown. 'I don't know. Think of what to say when you meet Petra.'

Chara smiled. Such an obedient child. A perfect mimic, too good to be true.

The sun was falling close to the horizon. He could see Chara, patient on the stairs. An occasional glance came his way and he would wave. In the shadows he couldn't see but he knew she was beaming. Her body twitching; he had noted, she did so when content. He hoped Petra would come. Wanted her to see the child before slumber. The sea breeze was refreshing, though it had become colder. A chill to the air. Bruhale's evenings were golden sunsets and warm gusts. He could still hear the banners rippling in the majesty of dusk. The northern ocean glistening under the moons of Noctyrne and Ambyr. Bruhale before Te'anor. Bruhada before its fall.

The hand was lightning fast. His position impossible to flank. It reached around his mouth, silencing him. He grabbed the air behind, caught the arm. Solid. Not flesh. Stone? Then she laughed.

'Argan!' Petra cried out. Her arms wrapped around his shoulders. 'It's been so long.'

He hugged her arms tight. More memories flooding back. Those better days. He looked to the stairs. Chara was on her feet. 'Petra, yes, too long.'

She released him and with one hand on the rock, Petra leapt from the wall, landing to face him from the ground. She was as petite as he remembered. A slip of a girl. But even before her change, she was a fighter. One of the best. Her white face glowing, those diamond eyes sparkling. Her immortal body was covered by a tattered grey cloak.

'Too long, too long. *Too damn long,*' she said, smiling and shaking her head. Radiant. Then a frown. Her eyes flicked to Bruch'ail leaning against the wall. 'Why now?'

His hands spread wide, he asked, 'I'm not welcome?'

She slapped his knee. An impact as hard as a hammer. He tried to hide his surprise—too late. She frowned, shook her head. 'Ach, you'll live.'

One hand on tomorrows bruise, the other pointing at her, he said, 'Not if you keep hitting me. Lay off an old man. Mind young lady, I'm still your elder.'

'Yes, you are,' she said. He saw the hesitation. Conflicted thoughts in her mind. 'Thank you for putting me in my place, grandpa.'

A glance past Petra to see Chara patient on the stairs. He fixed his friend with a stare. A sigh to prepare the news.

'What?' she asked, her smile untroubled.

'It's better you see for yourself.' He waved at Chara. 'Come on over.'

He wondered how she would respond. Petra was unique. The only mortal he knew to be altered by an Elemental's touch. Of course, his royal lineage had given him the constitution of stone. But his mutation was ritualistic, opportunistic. A meddling of sorts; of things that should not be. Petra was of Kor'A's design. Saved once, then reborn. And now there was Chara; so different. Both unique, two lives created by Earth.

Petra stared at Chara. A quick glance to him. 'What? *Impossible.*'

He spoke so Chara could hear. 'Petra, this is Chara. Chara, Petra—The Queen of An'Korathall.'

A quick scold from Petra. 'Don't call me that.'

Chara came close, stopping a pace away. Silence from both.

'Well?' Goddard said to Chara. 'Did you think of what to say?'

'I had. But she's more beautiful than I thought.'

Petra looked to Goddard. So many questions in her eyes.

He pointed to the keep. 'We should go inside.'

To age with an empty soul was a torment. A great void he had never known until Anka. Yet now, trailing behind Petra, walking into her home, that hollowness had diminished. Not completely gone. An in between state; a sense of belonging anchored to the past. But it was a comfort he hadn't known since she had left. Looking around, noting the keep was bare, it was what he had expected. Never a woman for needless possessions. No trinkets or charms to clutter the walls. Petra lit lanterns as she went, Chara staying close to his side. He could see she was transfixed. Her gaze never leaving Petra. Nearing the next flight of steps, he passed a dark stain on the floor. Then another.

'You had uninvited guests?'

'Most years,' she replied, moving from lantern to lantern, climbing more stairs. 'Folks can't imagine anything other than a keep full of treasure. No matter how many never return or leave empty-handed.'

Ironic. A humble woman in life, she was now legend. Her treasure imagined by wishful minds. It made perfect sense. He said, 'You know fine well; myths endure longer than truth.'

She blew away a short laugh. 'Why can't myths be about poverty?'

'Too dull.'

He climbed the last steps and stopped. A sudden jolt within his mind. The surrounds so familiar, he had arrived in the stateroom of the *Melody of the Sea*. A facsimile of Petra's old cabin. Surprised, stupefied. To encounter the lost past; to be among his own memories. Her ship obliterated by cannon in Venhyne. Long gone. But here it was real. Chara shuffled to his side. His hand fell on the girl's shoulder. Pulled her in close. There was more than a familiarity about the place; there was belonging.

Petra turned to face him. Her expression sealing his fate. Perhaps the long years. Old age making him soft. He blinked, rubbed a hand across his eyes. These were the better days. Before so much loss. Petra came close, stepped into his one-arm embrace. Muffled in his chest, her voice was soft.

'You recognise her?'

A tighter hold to say yes. Didn't want to speak.

'She's almost the same. No crew to annoy me, though.'

Petra pulled away. A glance and a frown at Chara. She moved to a window. A porthole in a castle. Goddard followed. She pointed to the dark beyond.

'The ocean. I can sit and watch the sea. It's like being in harbour. The gulls, the wind coming off the water. I watch the world turn.' She smiled, nodded at Chara. 'You must think me rude? A guest, evidently, a special guest. Welcome to my home. Chara, was it?'

No response from the girl. Nerves? Goddard prompted her and said, 'You can speak to Petra.'

'Hello,' said Chara.

Petra smiled, gestured to some crates scattered around a reinforced but ordinary chest. Goddard ushered Chara and she sat down. He took position beside her. Petra sat on the chest, facing them both. She stared at Chara. Goddard hadn't known what to expect. Thought there would be a bond. Something wasn't right.

To Petra, he said, 'When you left Anka, Kor'A returned. Chara followed.'

'Followed?'

She ought to know. But her confusion was evident. 'Kor'A made Chara. She made a child. You didn't know?'

Petra shook her head, her eyes scanning the girl of glass. 'A daughter?'

'Kor'A is my mother.'

'How?' Petra asked.

Goddard watched Chara. So still. He could sense her discomfort. No fidgeting to show her enthusiasm. He said, 'Chara came to me when Kor'A left.'

Petra frowned. 'Left?'

Things *had* changed. Or was it his memory confused by events too long ago? He asked, 'You know none of this, do you?'

She shook her head. 'You know why I left An'Korathall.'

He did. The same terrible things that had hollowed his own soul. Just as Petra, he had watched his friends age and die. Death, it was how life was meant to be. Unless you were corrupted by Earth. A change to all that is mineral. A curse, not a gift. He nodded, understood her pain.

Petra said, 'I thought you left the city. I made you a tomb to bury Argan's legacy. But you stayed close? Why? Rebirth needs new memories.'

'I settled in the hills above Anka. Minded my own business, stayed away. A good place to grow old and die.'

Petra nodded, leaned in, elbows on knees. She spoke to Chara. 'And how did you meet this big lump?'

A glance to Goddard. She was seeking permission. It was easy to forget how timid she could be. A girl of glass. Was her mind as fragile? He said, 'We're very old friends, Chara, you can tell Petra anything.'

'But she's the Queen.'

Petra laughed. She gestured to the cabin. 'My palace? I knew An'Korathall for many years. I lived in the citadel but I was never a Queen. Never ruled. Just a name given to me. In my home, aboard *The Melody*, you're free to speak.'

Chara bobbed in her seat. Goddard felt the grin creep onto his face.

She said, 'Kor'A told me of the man in the hills.'

'When?' Goddard asked. He hadn't been in Kor'A's presence since the old days. Though everybody had *experienced* her return to Anka. That sense of suffocation.

Chara continued. 'She knew you had gone there. Said that she felt every footstep on her skin. Mother warned me of men, said they were born to deceive. But she didn't say that of you.'

'And she told you to go to me?'

She shook her head.

Petra asked, 'So, why did you go to him?'

'With mother gone, I had nobody else. I thought I should go to a friend, at least somebody mother considered to be safe.' Chara nodded, 'And you have kept me from harm.'

It was colder than he realised; Chara's story. Kor'A had left without any instruction. Abandoned her daughter. He looked at Petra, shook his head to explain he never knew. Her diamond eyes sparkled with a strange brightness.

'It's what she does. Just walks away,' Petra said, her voice low, bitter. 'How long ago was this?'

He had lost track of the days. Preoccupied with his ward. 'Not a month ago.'

Goddard recalled Chara's tale of hugs. It was a riddle. But it was becoming clearer. And it was cruel. Kor'A's sudden display of emotion; was it guilt or regret? A quick glance and he could see the sun setting through the western window. It was good timing. He wanted private words with Petra.

'Do you have a bed?' he asked.

She pointed to the east wall. 'Decoration. I don't use it. Tired?'

'Not for me.' Another frown from Petra. He knew there would be many more. Wondered if stone suffered wrinkles. He said, 'For Chara. I'll explain when she's comfortable.' Turning to the girl, he said, 'It's sundown, best make yourself comfortable.'

Chara hopped from the chair and moved to the bed. She patted it, squealed a pleasant squeal, and lay down.

Goddard called to her. 'We're going outside. We'll be close. You'll be safe.'

She didn't reply. Just blinked. The riddle.

In the light of the moons, full in the clear sky, Petra's face was radiant in red and blue. She looked as she had the day Kor'A brought her back. The day she destroyed a legion; the day Aracyse declared her Queen. Tugging on his beard, Goddard knew he hadn't aged so well. Wasn't a fair comparison. He was flesh and blood. Mostly.

'The crew. You never stop missing them, do you?' he asked.

'No. You?'

'I hope for senility to help. But most nights their ghosts walk my dreams.'

'And Chara? What has Kor'A done?'

He recalled the day. A simple morning, as were most. 'I was in my hut, wrapping the binds on a new harness for Bruch'ail. She just walked in. I literally fell off my chair. A walking shadow comes into my home squeaking words at me.'

Petra laughed. 'I'd have paid good coin to see that. What did she say?'

Any other person he wouldn't tell. But Petra already knew his secret. The terrible realisation had occurred to him after her resurrection—he knew that she would see the others age and die. Him, not so. Courage and necessity had brought him to confession. He had told Petra of his corruption; the touch of stone. A rite of the Bruhadian Kings.

He said, 'She pointed a little, skinny arm at me and said *stone will help stone.*'

Petra's eyes widened. 'She knows then. I mean, Kor'A. She must know of your... constitution.'

'Possibly. Suppose it shouldn't be a surprise. Well, Chara introduced herself, said her mother had gone and that was it.'

Petra shrugged. 'And, what else? Nothing more?'

There hadn't been. No scroll of declaration. No baggage or kit to carry. An exceptional and awkward day. He said, 'I asked her what she meant. She didn't say much else. I assumed you knew of her. Thought you'd feel her. Obviously not. But, she's not like you.'

Petra craned her head to the tower. 'She sleeps?'

A finger raised in the air. Shaking. A device to help him focus. 'Not exactly. She's been in my company a few weeks. I've learned a little. She sleeps at sundown, wakes at sunrise. But she's awake—she watches. I don't think she hears, maybe alert to sudden noises. But... it's a riddle, Petra.'

'I'm already lost.'

That night by the fire. She had awoken with a start. Even though she was watching. He scratched at his beard. How could he explain?

He said, 'She's mimicking everything a child would be. Sleeps but she's aware, although I believe she thinks she's asleep. It's like an illusion. She can smell food, appears interested but doesn't eat. And physically, weak. Made by an Elemental yet suffers human traits.'

Petra nodded. Goddard noted something in her expression. Knew she would have better insight. When she spoke, her voice was haunted. 'An illusion. I understand that, perhaps more than you realise. When you saw Kor'A bring me back, I think you witnessed one. An illusion, a trick. I remember my death, the blade coming toward me at Venhyne. I felt it. I died, Argan. The blade, that was the last I saw.'

Goddard recalled the day. A hideous memory that had not faded with time. The upstart Captain betraying Aracyse's orders; he had come to them with cavalry. That day he had picked up Bruch'ail, and close friends witnessed Baza'rad's return to war. If Petra only recalled the sword, then she never saw Shadow's desolation. The distress caused by her murder. A small saviour—Shadow's grief had been insurmountable.

Petra continued. 'I awoke in An'Korathall. Kor'A was gone. But I felt her, inside me. A silent whisper. A reflection in glass, one you turn to see and it's not there.'

She paced away. Goddard sensed unease. Magnified by his own confusion.

'Petra?'

The reply was instant. 'I'm not Petra.'

She was. Yes, she was stone. But he knew Petra. Knew the woman. 'Of course you are.'

She turned, raised her arms to the side. The breeze ruffling her cloak, revealing glimpses of what lay beneath. A woman of stone. A living statue. An effigy of the woman he had known.

She said, 'I'm a copy of her. Memories, thoughts. My body? Argan, look at it. It's the same as her. Like Kor'A.' She gestured toward Chara, safe in her slumber. 'I'm like her. This isn't human. I'm not human. Just memories written in stone. An animated carving of another woman's life.'

He couldn't grasp what she was saying. Too complex. Impossible. A hand reaching to her, to prove she was wrong. 'But... We saw you rise. Kor'A healed you.'

Her words came. He heard. But he dismissed them. Shook his head to clear the insanity. But she said them again.

'Kor'A tricked you. Tricked you all. That was Kor'A at An'Korathall. It was she who killed Oriset and his men. She never left. She became me. Stole my memories. My friends. Lived inside the shell of me.'

Miracles weren't real. Not as he believed them to be. As much as they had all accepted Petra's miraculous rebirth, he had known something wasn't right. Humans didn't come back. Necromancy was a myth, a campfire tale of ghouls and full moons. But better to reject death in the face of the impossible than grieve a lost friend. Yet still... she was every mannerism of Petra. Every essence of an old friend. She wasn't the trick of a god. Couldn't be.

Goddard said, 'But... everything you said and did. How could Kor'A be you?' A terrible thought. 'Is she still you? Are you Kor'A?'

'No. I don't understand what's happened but she is gone from me now. At least, I feel that. What memories and thoughts she stole; she has left them in this body. Whatever I am, I'm still bound to her. But I exist separate to her will. A discarded prisoner, free to roam.'

One question to ask. Pertinent given the circumstances. 'Why? Why would she do that?'

Petra glanced to where Chara slept. 'I think to understand us. What better way to learn empathy than exist among us? I think she learned all she could from me. Watched on as I grieved for Thelissa. For Shadow. Thelia vanished, then we watched Kallisa slip away.'

A realisation. A change of the guard. Goddard said, 'We discussed my death. You built Argan's tomb. You left Anka. Then she came back. Hadn't seen her for seven decades. Not since you...died.'

He didn't want to believe it but his own words made sense. One woman of stone replaced by another. Goddard shook his head.

Petra touching her chest, said, 'She abandoned this.'

'So... she finished with you. Created Chara?'

A nod. 'Perhaps. I left Anka when she left me; when that shadow inside faded. Those memories I had, suddenly I could feel them. Alive within me. Without her watching over me, I could grieve alone for friends that haunted my dreams.' Petra gestured to the keep and said, 'I came here, found some peace.'

'But Kor'A couldn't grieve? Those memories weren't hers.'

Petra shook her head. Frowned. 'There was sadness. Tears, many, many tears. But she couldn't understand them. I cried but it felt as though... as if another person was holding my sorrow. It was horrible, Argan.'

'I'm sorry, Petra. I never knew.'

Shaking her head, Goddard saw the anger. He felt the ground tremble. A god's wrath. Simmering, Petra said. 'She never understood death. To her, those memories were just an echo. She fed upon my tears. But they gave her no sustenance.'

It was horrendous to hear. Petra's body host to a symbiotic, emotional leech. Yet, no matter how much she professed to be different, to Goddard, she was still his Captain. He had no doubt; this was *his* Petra. But the riddle of Chara remained. Though it was unravelling. He looked to the keep where she slept.

He said, 'Those memories of death. Just the end of the journey. She had to see the start. Understand all of it.'

'I know what she is, Argan. That poor girl. Chara's another experiment. Just another thing to learn. I was her lesson in empathy. Chara must give her something new.'

Chara's embrace. He recalled the story around the fire of how her mother had held her. He said, 'Cold feet.'

'What?'

'There's more. Chara told me. Their last day together. Kor'A wouldn't stop hugging her.' Petra shook her head, didn't appear to follow. Unsurprising, it was hard enough for his own comprehension. And yet, he hadn't told her the harshest truth. Pointing up at the window, he said, 'She's mortal, Petra. She knows it, speaks of it. Chara can die.'

Petra's face broke into a grimace of pain. The expression evaporated as a thunder rumbled across the land. She was still the Queen of Stone. The quaking ceased and Petra looked to the moons.

Shaking her head, she said, 'She made Chara mortal—*just to watch her die.* To know the death that she couldn't find in me.'

No more riddles. Goddard sighed. 'And she can't bear the thought of it? An immortal bound to a child that will find death. Kor'A's too scared to see it through. Is that why she left Anka?'

Petra sighed, hugged herself, though he knew she felt no cold. A simple act. Reinforcing his belief. Gods didn't know empathy. No matter what she had said, no matter how much sense it made; she was still Petra. He couldn't see her any other way. Reaching to her, he grasped her shoulder.

'I can't imagine how you feel, what it's like. Her thoughts inside your mind. But I know this, Petra, you're still the woman I knew a hundred years ago. Those eyes may be diamond and sapphire, but I see *you* behind them, not Kor'A.'

She shook her head. 'I stopped being Petra,' she displayed her marble palms, 'when I became this.'

A test of heart. Something too painful for a soulless god to feel. 'Then, before you... before you became that, you wouldn't remember Felicitra, not with passion.'

Her eyes scolding, she said, 'I will *never* forget her.'

'And what do you remember of Felicitra? Of those times.'

Petra looked back over her shoulder, her gaze cast to a lost horizon. Goddard knew what she sought. Faraway Laria. In the moonlight, he saw the sparkle of a solid tear glinting on her cheek. Confirmation of his truth; Gods don't cry.

To the dark ocean, Petra whispered, 'Felicitra, my love. The best of days.'

Chapter VII

'**Y**ou're impressed. Aren't you?'

Propped against the rock, her legs crossed, Sarellia was smiling. A damn victory grin. She had wanted to press on when he had suggested they rest. The break wasn't for Jerune; he had the constitution for the journey. But he had doubted hers. Yet, she had proven him wrong; her smug, pretty face gloating. *At him*. It was worse than losing a fight. Jerune had misjudged—that was rare. Nor had she flinched at the sudden tremor that had rippled across the earth. It was becoming clear to Jerune; Sarellia wasn't the damsel he had thought her to be.

'Don't be pissed,' she said. 'You see the rich girl, spoiled and useless. You don't see my life. You judge me for how I look, the wealth I have. I'm not what you see.'

'You're no scout,' he quipped.

She huffed. 'I can't be everything. Why d'you think I have need of you? Think I enjoy your company?'

Jerune didn't answer. He walked to the edge of the rock, leaving Sarellia in the shadow of stone. The sun had set but they had found their quarry. Perhaps not Baza'rad but certainly the man whose tracks he had followed. Points of warm light dotted the walls of a keep, a silhouette against the darkening sky. Old ruins lay around, skeletons from the century old War of Kalle. Beyond it, Farenhyne nestled in a sweeping bay, the welcoming lights of taverns bringing a taste of ale to his mouth. Sarellia's purse would be consumed by the tankard.

Observing in silence, the noise was obvious—Sarellia creeping up behind. Jerune smirked, tried to stifle his humour. The rich girl moved as though a goat trampling across dry grass and brittle twig. An astounding feat considering the ground was yielding underfoot.

Eyes fixed on the fort, he said, 'I told you. You're no scout.'

'Fuck. Really?' She came to his side. 'I couldn't hear my own steps.'

Despite the hard trek, she smelled of expensive perfume. Sweet spices and exotic orchids. Her breath was still heavy, rasping in his ear.

'Truly, was I that loud?' she asked.

No, she wasn't. But she had bought the best and for that she deserved some credit. 'No, not really. I told you; I'm good at what I do. Sounds, sights, and smells. Since I was a boy, I knew I had a gift. I hear things others don't. See what eagles spy from afar.'

'And your gift brings us here.'

Looking at the dark keep, Jerune nodded. 'I never promised you Baza'rad. Still doubt you'll ever find him. But the man who killed those bandits is in there.'

'Not in the village beyond?'

He shook his head. The peninsula was steep to the south. The fort was approached from the north. They had come from that quarter and his eyes would have picked out tracks moving away. Everything led to the keep. Though, that raised a question. This was no hunt. Sarellia was no assassin and there was no bounty on this mythical king.

'What exactly do you plan to do now?' he asked. Jerune wished she were less attractive. The job was done. He could leave. Something compelled him to stay. Unprofessional thoughts.

'Bruhadian's welcome one another,' Sarellia said, 'No exceptions. I'll go right up to the door. I'll knock.'

A shiver tickled his spine. It was a ridiculous plan. 'And if it's not Baza'rad. As it's not going to be. What do you say when the man who massacred an army of bandits answers the door?'

She appeared surprised. 'You're here. You'll step in.'

'I'm a fucking scout. I track in the shadows. I remain quiet.' Clutching his soft leathers, he said, 'You think this is armour?'

Smiling, clearly playing with him, she said, 'I thought you lot were like rogues. You know, flashy sword play, bows and arrows?'

He was being emasculated. By a bloody city-girl. He could fight. But not as she thought. 'You get those ideas from some ponce of a bard you conquered in the sack? Singing songs of heroes for you? Tickling all your fancies?'

Sarellia grabbed his face, squeezing hard enough that his lips pouted. She brought her own in close and said, 'Wouldn't you like to know?'

Yes. Please. Slapping her hand away, Jerune screwed up his face and wriggled away from her temptations. 'Get over yourself. I prefer my women....' He couldn't think what to say. Sarellia was perfect. What wasn't she? What could deflect her focus?

She grinned, usurping the moment. 'Tell me rogue, how *do* you like your women?'

It was all he had. The word coming forth without thought. Jerune said, 'Earthy.'

Her laughter was instant and loud. A squeal of delight at his stupidity. It was difficult to resist her infectious giggle, Jerune trying hard to suppress his own. But their humour was less than discreet. He moved in close, bringing his hand to smother her mouth.

Jerune's face was pressed against the back of his own hand. Sarellia's eyes staring into his. He was rested but his heart was pounding. So was hers. He could feel it through his body; a powerful shudder of flesh. Did his contract preclude these impulses? Forbid touch? Letting fate play the moment, he removed his hand. An inch between their lips. Sarellia didn't pull away.

'You're a contract,' he whispered.

'I can be more.'

The noise was sudden. A clatter of wood against rock. A door banging open and shut. He pulled Sarellia down, moving back behind the rock. He felt queasy. The moment had pushed his heart to his mouth. The door had caused alarm. This was why women were bad for his focus; at least, a woman as beguiling as Sarellia.

'Stay down,' he said, moving to gauge the threat, peering out from the cover of the rock. Nothing there. He waited. Sought the dimming of lights; the tell of eyes peering from darkness. Every portal still bright against the shadows. Above the breeze no sounds stirred. Peering hard into the gloom, he saw nothing move. Nobody approached. He turned to Sarellia and she screamed. As did he.

The ground beside them was erupting, something rising from the earth, a human flower blossoming in the moons. Naked, clothed by the hues of Noctyrne and Ambyr—she was unmistakable, she was legend. The Witch of Anka, the Queen of Stone; there was nothing else she could be. The witch looked at Sarellia still huddled against the rock. Then her gaze came to Jerune. A thought, irreverent. She was shorter than he imagined a queen to be. Regardless, fear pinned him fast to the earth.

The witch spoke in a soft voice, Jerune surprised to hear it sound so human. A tired tone, disarming and gentle, she asked, 'Have you too come for my treasure?'

Sarellia shook her head. Jerune looked at her. Was his stare as wild as hers, eyes wide open, full of dread? He wanted to be strong. Wanted her to see it. What was there to lose?

To the legend, he said, 'We want to see Baza'rad.' He glanced to Sarellia, who nodded her awestruck confirmation. He realised that wasn't the truth; recalled the king wasn't the true quarry.

'Say that name again,' the witch who was once Queen said.

'Baza'rad,' Jerune replied.

From the ground, Sarellia said, 'King Baza'rad.'

Jerune was canny enough to know deception, even from stone. The Queen wore a mask of feigned ignorance but she had given away her secret.

'Leave,' she said. Her eyes scanned his attire. 'Scout?'

A nod.

She tuned to Sarellia. 'You're paying him?'

Sarellia appeared confused, nodded with a questioning frown.

The witch said, 'Whatever it is, he's not worth it. Your journey's over. Go home.'

Not the best idea to argue with fearsome legends but Jerune was going nowhere; he had to prove his worth. Be the rogue his client desired. Be the man Sarellia could admire.

With a nod, Jerune said, 'I wasn't sure.'

'Sure?' asked the Queen.

Pointing to Sarellia. 'She seeks Baza'rad. I thought it futile. But he's here. I don't know what sort of power you have...' He held his nerve, said it with confidence, 'but you're a poor liar. I know he's here.'

All for Sarellia. This stomach-churning bravado. He wondered if she could see him quaking, holding things together just enough not to flee. The Queen of Stone was legend. Becoming the Witch when she left Anka. Tales of compassion and brutality, a tormented hybrid lost in the darkness between flesh and stone. Which of her two faces would she show to him? A terrible silence caused his mind to err toward death.

Rising to her feet, Sarellia spoke with struggling confidence. 'If Baza'rad is truly inside that keep, then I must speak with him.' She paused. Jerune sensed her trepidation; the city girl stumbling to address the creature she had sought. But it was clear, in the Queen's presence, Sarellia's courage was evaporating. Yet from nowhere the city girl found her faith, Jerune surprised to see Sarellia rally her resolve.

Stiffening, standing tall, she said, 'A Bruhadian cannot refuse another's company. A King cannot deny his people.'

Turning to her, the Witch of Anka replied, 'Bruhadian or not, there is nothing for you here.'

Sarellia's eyes caught Jerune's. An apology. Fleeting, but there. Frowning, he quizzed her in silence but her gaze moved away.

She said, 'I descend from a line of great women. I am beholden to their truths. I know Baza'rad was friend to Kallisa. She passed her secrets…'

'Kallisa?' The Witch's words came as a startled sigh. 'And you are?'

'Sarellia. Melody, my great grandmother was daughter to Shadow and Kallisa.'

'*Sarellia.*'

Jerune watched as the Witch paced a step backwards, her face turning to the ground. Sarellia's words had impacted the woman of stone. From a deity of power, she now appeared fragile, lost. But she was quick to compose herself, though any deception was dropped from her tone.

'Your name, Sarellia. Do you know why?' the witch asked.

Jerune was puzzled. Whatever was happening, he was ignorant of it all. It was clear Sarellia shared a common knowledge with the Queen. Of what, though, was a mystery.

Sarellia replied, 'As is the way of the Bruhsa, Kallisa's life was shared. Her stories passed down to each new generation. A history of spoken words. I learned mine from my grandmother, my own died in childbirth. It was she who named me. A story she knew of the Sarellian Plains. A story once told by you, to Kallisa. A treasured memory of your love, Felicitra. In times before the Cult. Before the wars.'

Jerune watched as the witch faltered. He was mesmerised to see the transformation as the legend became a woman called Petra. Almost a human. It was painful to observe. Sarellia's words appeared as swords, stabbing at things lost in time. Bringing not blood, but a flood of memories. Petra's expression told him enough to know she was hurting. And though she fought to maintain her composure, tears ran down her marble skin. Drops of grief becoming diamonds that fell to earth. He stared at Sarellia; certain he appeared as shocked as she. A gesture to her and she came to him. Hugged into his body. Together they stared and waited for the Queen to recover. To say something. An inferior mind might think her weak, but Jerune understood the strength of the creature that stood wrapped in her own turmoil. The Witch of Anka remained an ungodly power.

42

When she spoke, her voice was calm. The emotion gone. 'I think you've earned the right to see your King.' She pointed at Jerune. 'But he stays here.'

Sarellia stepped forward. A small step for a human but a great stride in the presence of the immortals. Sarellia said, 'Jerune comes with me.' He felt her hand grab his. A reassuring squeeze. She said, 'I own his silence. And Jerune of Venhyne is no rogue.'

The Witch nodded. 'Very well. I think you know what happens if you cross me.'

Chapter VIII

W here was the honour? Bastards hadn't allowed her to leave the tomb. Ugly but effective, kicking, punching, and dodging her way past, Bücka had scrambled into the citadel grounds. Bruhadian and Larian steel drawn from her belt, she faced four mercenaries: three men, one woman. She would break the rule of Petra, blood would be spilled, but it was a necessity upon which her life depended. At least she wouldn't sully the tomb.

'So,' she said, as they circled her, 'I don't suppose you wanna come at me one at a time?'

Bücka took their silence as a rebuttal and without response, they began to close. Scanning her foes, she sought the weakest link. Found him. White knuckles uncomfortable on the hilt of his sword. Holding it as though waving his manhood at a parlour girl. No time to waste, Bücka charged, roaring her battle cry—a well-rehearsed scream of aggression. He reacted as she had expected, a startled hand pulling back to strike. Bücka had judged the distance to perfection. He had not. She ran him through, his chain-link armour useless against the Larian Rapier. On impact, his sword arm clattered against her as he tumbled to the ground; a sting of his blade kissing her cheek. She turned, the thrill rising within. Three was a better fight. She wiped the blood from her face and taunted them to attack.

They did so with more vigour than she had expected; the leading mercenary bearing down upon her, a contortion of hatred upon his face. A quick glance to the fallen. A family resemblance? Younger, but similar features. Bücka expected a hail of abuse to come with the attack; his blows raining down with furious screams. And though she was spared from a verbal tirade, it was clear that anger had grabbed her adversary. It would be his undoing. Bücka had been trained better, knew that the red mist obscured a warrior's vision. It created mistakes. She parried the first strikes with ease, her eyes alert to the others who were closing in. Another flurry of flashing steel and Bücka leapt away, catching the third assailant off-guard. Her accuracy was her strength, the tip of the rapier needling into the woman's neck before she could react. Arterial rain splattered upon the white marble and she fell clutching the terminal wound. Bücka was halfway there.

But the fourth backed away, his eyes wide and wild with fear. Whoever hired them for the job hadn't told them the truth. Their quarry, their adversary—Bücka, the mighty warrior. He shook his head, spoke an inaudible apology to his companion, and turned on his heels.

'Just you and me,' Bücka said, returning her focus to the last man.

His sword extended towards her; an obstacle to pass. She tapped it with the rapier. A test. He didn't pull away, the blade remaining in place. He had reigned in his anger.

'Who are you?' he asked, eyes glancing at the bodies.

'You weren't told?'

A shake of his head. Beads of sweat flicked into the light of the sun.

'Bücka.'

Nothing registered in his eyes. 'Bücka? Should that mean something?'

Foreigner? Everybody with a sword for hire knew Bücka. 'Ah, outsider, eh? Kalleron? Laria?'

'No. Dreyahyde.'

Bücka knew the region; the far west of Kalleron. 'You travelled a long way. For me?'

He nodded. 'A good contract.'

'One you'll never finish. Why me?' She asked, but it was a redundant query. She was no better than he; both for hire and often without question although she retained a modicum of morality. Nonetheless, Bücka had made many enemies, too many on which to keep tabs.

'Why not you,' he replied. He waved his sword. 'Let's finish this.'

A brave mercenary. Too rare. 'You don't have to. I'll let you walk.'

Hesitant, he glanced at the body of the downed man. 'My cousin. I can't walk away. One of us must die.'

Bücka understood his words, a nuanced acceptance of defeat. A nod to the man. Polite, with heart, she said, 'I applaud your commitment.'

And he charged.

Mercenary work paid well. Defending oneself from others, not so. Bücka rose from the woman, pocketing the last few coins. She wore pretty earrings, but you never took what was personal. Not from the glorious fallen. Bücka didn't know if there was an afterlife. Didn't seem likely with ignorant Elemental gods. Best leave the dead unsullied. The coins, though, they were fair spoils.

The ground was a bloody mess—a brutal stain on the pristine marble. It would take a flood to wash it away. Surprised they had fought without an audience, Bücka stared up at the citadel. Visible for miles around, it seemed even taller standing so close. In the time of the Queens, the outer wall was sealed off, nobody ever came so near. Yet, here she was, Bücka the victor in the shadow of gods. She didn't need Thelia's tales to understand the power. The aura was impressive. Overpowering. A mountain masquerading as an elegant white tower. Bücka felt she could reach out beyond what she saw and the citadel would be there. Everywhere.

A thought crossed her mind. Reckless. Kor'A was gone, those rumours coming from Anka had whispered it. Scared faces in the streets had reinforced it. The tomb had confirmed the fact. The old Queen of Kalleron had left her city. Was there even anybody in the citadel? Above her head the tower stood in silence. The breath of the wind was a song of loneliness. A few paces toward the massive entrance, a hesitant stop to stare. Between Bücka and the interior was a huge archway that drew into a tunnel. The walls sparkled white in the shadow—an uncanny illumination. At the end of the tunnel there was a wall of light. So bright. So magical. Gazing into the arch, Bücka stood transfixed. Hair the colour of autumn fire lifted on the breeze. Nothing scared her. Nothing. So, what was *this* feeling?

'Come on, Bücka, just walk.'

She spoke it, but her legs disobeyed. It was mesmerising, a tunnel of soft shadow, walls glittering without sun; the cool wind, a melody of melancholy; and the light at the end, shining bright, concealing secrets. The house of the Queen. The domain of Kor'A. Not for mortals.

'Come on, Bücka. It's only stone.'

A lie to tell herself, she knew it was more. It was Kor'A's flesh. The Elemental would know.

Damn it. Defeated by doubt. Bücka shook her head, turned on heels and walked away. She would return. Give it a few days, keep an eye on the city. Then, back for family. Brave the absent Queen and bring Thelia to rest with her sister.

Chapter IX

U nguarded. It was a rare experience for Goddard to feel vulnerable. He and Petra, deep in conversation outside the keep when laughter rang out from nearby. Too close. He had returned inside, almost battering the door from its hinge, huge lunges swallowing the steps to reach the top of the tower. Looking down upon his ward; Chara's eyes, black diamonds on a pretty onyx face, were open. Or were they? Goddard stared. Daylight gave more expression to her countenance; the glint of the sun animating her features. In the pseudo-gloom where she lay in bed, Chara's expression was an unfathomable mask.

'Chara?'

No answer. Then a blink. He wondered if her designed routine incorporated reaction. He recalled the the night she had awoken when he had jostled his own armour. Why wake then? There had been no threat. But tonight, there had been a sudden noise; the laughter. The basement door had slammed hard against the wall. His mistake, a clumsy hand. But she lay content, undisturbed. Another blink and he knew she was watching. *Asleep*. There were still riddles to solve.

'I'm going downstairs. You're safe here,' he whispered. He waited for a blink. None came. With a sigh, he moved to the basement.

Petra greeted him at the open door. She pulled her cloak over her shoulders. Glancing behind her, she said, 'We have guests, Argan. A girl and a scout. She's Bruhadian.'

To mention his heritage wasn't a courtesy. It harkened to the old ways. Hard to deny his culture, even when lost in time and conquest. A thought crossed his mind. Why invite random guests? Unless there was nothing coincidental about another Bruhadian in Petra's home.

'Who is she?' he asked.

Petra frowned but behind her mask Goddard saw the emotion.

Now his turn, his brow crumpling. He asked, 'This isn't chance, is it?'

Petra shook her head. 'I don't know her story, but she seeks you.' Her face brightened, a smile across her white lips.

'What?'

No answer given, she turned to the door and beckoned to the darkness beyond. A pretty woman appeared, jet black hair and strong features. Dressed in tastes more suited to old Thania than Bruhale, it was clear she was wealthy. Obvious that she descended from a robust Bruhsa line. Behind her, another figure appeared. A man, the scout. Hair the colour of straw, a weathered but young face. He didn't appear warlike, though even those few steps informed Goddard of his talents. Silent as the dead. But not of interest. His focus returned to the woman. Something familiar. She curtsied; a flourish added that would be unfamiliar to most. Clear to Goddard, it was Bruhadian etiquette for the royal line.

'King Baza'rad,' she said.

There was no point lying. Goddard said, 'Once, but no more.'

A glance at Petra and the woman raised a hand to her bosom to introduce herself. 'My name is Sarellia. My line follows Kallisa of Bruhale. You knew her.'

He did. Further, he recognised the likeness, though he tried to conceal an old bond of friends. 'Almost half a century has passed since she faded. Yet I can see her features. What generation are you?'

'I am a fourth Bruhsa.' Her face wrinkled. 'My grandmother, Kallisa's second Bruhsa, said you vanished?'

Her words sent his mind back in time. When he had been Argan. Many long nights were spent with Petra in the cliffs above Anka. Staring at the stars. Discussing the endless universe. Counting the years as age stalked their friends. Watching their bright lights blink out, one by one. Kallisa lived the longest. Left the world in good spirits, no regrets. But her passing had weighed heavy upon he and Petra. That was the last he would face. He had been glad of Petra's company, knew he wouldn't have to watch her die as he had the others. But to spare her that same pain, he had left Anka's walls. On request, she had created a tomb for Argan, something within which to bury the myth of the man who killed Kalle, the last King of Kalleron. Argan's passing was the birth of Goddard.

Sarellia spoke again. 'Why did you leave us?'

He would be patient. But he was not a book to be read. 'I don't need to explain myself. But as a courtesy to Kallisa's line, know this; I am no King. Baza'rad is long gone. Your Bruhsa accepted that; even she called me Argan. And now even he is gone. I live as Goddard now. My life is my own.'

'Goddard?'

'Yes.'

She smiled. 'You gave yourself that name?'

Kallisa's Bruhsa or not, her questions were grating. Petra appeared to notice.

She said, 'Sarellia. Goddard and I are old. We seek our peace. I gave you this audience out of respect for your line. But Goddard owes the world nothing. What is it you seek from him?'

The girl nodded. Perhaps it was Chara? Come for the onyx wonder. But her eyes shifted, drawing away from him, falling on Petra. A truth to come, not what he was expecting. She didn't want *him*. He took a step forward, curious of her intent. The scout stepped back but Sarellia remained.

Goddard asked 'Why are you here?'

She nodded; eyes fixed on Petra. 'I came to speak to you. I knew Baza...Goddard would be able to find you. You are linked by Earth's touch.' She pointed to the scout. 'Jerune tracked Baza'rad to this keep. I never imagined you'd be here—I thought those rumours to be nothing but bait for tourists and thieves. But you are here. This is the hand of fate.'

Goddard felt Petra's quizzical stare fall upon him. The Bruhsa was not seeking the line. Sarellia hadn't come for him. Was that his pride that rumbled? No, a fear. Why Petra? What would drive a mortal to seek the Queen of Stone after all these years?

He frowned at Petra, spoke to the girl. 'You sought me, to find Petra?'

'Yes.'

'Why?'

Sarellia inhaled and exhaled. Goddard considered it a prelude to darker things. She nodded as though urging herself to speak. 'I think I can trust you. Both of you.'

A pause. Was she waiting on his confirmation? He gave her silence in return.

Sarellia continued, a flicker of embarrassment across her face. 'You knew the Cult in Kalleron. Your sacrifices freed the Queen. Stopped the King's conquests.'

That was not a secret. The Northern Lands were established under that dubious victory. Their intervention had stopped one war and begun another. Not something of which to brag.

'Those are open truths,' Goddard said.

'Yes, but the Cult lived on. A network of spies across the three continents. My family line kept the word in the north.' Her attention returned to Petra. 'But with you in An'Korathall, there was little to fear. After Baza'rad...Argan killed Kalle at Stranghame, Kalleron descended into terror and catastrophe. Poor Laria fell to flame. But not here, not under your reign. For decades you remained, then without word you left, and although Kor'A returned, the protection she offered was nothing but a shadow to repel the fire.'

Petra frowned at Goddard. He understood her unspoken query. It was a secret known to so few; a truth of dangerous indifference—Kor'A had absolved herself of mortal ways. And though she dwelled behind those impenetrable walls, she was not Anka's guardian. The Elemental didn't care for life. Kallisa's Bruhsa, her family line, would know this. Sarellia's grasp on that reality was a sign of her knowledge. To the ignorant masses, however, Petra's flight and Kor'A's return marked a continuity of sanctuary. It was a reliable lie to keep the white city safe from harm.

Goddard was curious; how certain was Sarellia of her story. He asked, 'You doubt Kor'A's protection?'

Sarellia nodded her head, an obvious confidence in her eyes. 'I am Kallisa's Bruhsa.' She waved a flowery hand toward Petra. 'It was recorded that Kor'A disappeared after your rise. Kallisa noted the change. You all agreed upon it—Kor'A sought to distance herself from human affairs, never again to take a mortal life—no matter what their intent. Kallisa informed us that your plight bestowed guilt to her immortal soul. With your resurrection, she left us alone.'

A glance at Petra, a test well passed. Sarellia knew the fundamentals, though ascribing a sense of guilt to Kor'A was misplaced romanticism.

'I give you this, you understand more than most,' Goddard said. 'But you've not told us why you've come to find Petra.'

Sarellia nodded. A gesture of preparation, perhaps an inner prompt of confidence. She said, 'All right... all right. The spies from Laria; they returned to us with grave news. A fleet of ships assembling in the north. Possibly naval. But worse—the Seer of Fire is rising after years of quiet. We believe he has once again harnessed the weapon of the Great Destroyer. Just as Etherus reaped the Fury from the Wind, he has reclaimed the Seed of Fire.'

'Seed of Fire?' Goddard asked.

'An orb of flame. He has the power to wield it. Legend says it is what he brought to Laria so long ago. It was how he brought King Edramus to his knees.'

Petra asked, 'And what of this seed? Why does this involve me?'

Sarellia's eyes lingered on Petra. An impassioned, silent plea or awestruck wonder? Goddard couldn't tell. Her eyes fixed on the stone face, the Cultist said, 'There is a Covenant. That's what our sources have gathered. The Seer's inner circle spoke of a Covenant with the Elementals.'

Petra shook her head. 'A Covenant *with* the Elementals? I've never heard of such a thing.' She looked at her hands, turned them over, clear for Sarellia to see. 'And though I know little of their ways, I can claim to understand more than most. I know my limits, that of my element, Earth. I am bound to these lands by Water. My range ends where Earth meets her sister. I was...' Petra paused, clear she had doubts about her thoughts. With a grumble, she continued. 'I was given the freedom to travel this land but the ocean is too great a barrier. It is hostile to me. Is this the Covenant of which you speak—the opposition of the Elements? If so, there's nothing to fear in that.'

The Cultist shook her head. 'It is more than that. Those spies closest to the Seer's inner circle heard word of a great change.' She shook her head. 'It's too much of a coincidence.'

'What is?' Goddard asked. He found Sarellia's trail of thought difficult to follow. 'You say the Seer is rising; rising for what purpose? You mention a fleet in the north, a weapon of Fire. A Covenant. Please, offer sense to my old ears—what is happening?'

Once again, Sarellia appeared to perform an inner ritual, composing herself to deliver the news. Several nods of her head, a worried play with her delicate digits. She said, 'Kor'A's disappearance, her aura diminished. Within the week, the spies reported back with news of the Covenant. Word that Fire had abandoned Laria. Those closest to the Seer spoke of Fire's gift being complete. Once again men hold the weapons of the Elementals. And the Elementals in turn will stand aside. The new Covenant.'

Goddard noticed Petra's reaction. Confusion. He asked, 'Stand aside?'

'Don't you see?' Sarellia said. 'Just as Kor'A has left An'Korathall, so too Fire has left Laria. It can't be a coincidence.'

Goddard knew something of stone. But of Fire? Nothing beyond folklore. Sarellia's fanciful story should have been just that—a story. Yet, the sudden disappearance of

Kor'A, something he had presumed linked to Chara's fate, could now be explained by other means. After all, why wait so long to abandon the child? Kor'A would have understood what she had done. Perhaps there was merit in Sarellia's message. A Covenant to call the sisters away; to once again watch humanity wage war with itself? After all, a century past, Kor'A had destroyed nations. These were unfathomable creatures with unimaginable ways.

Petra appeared intrigued. Her brow furrowed, she said, 'You believe Fire intentionally gifted a weapon to a human? And left him to his devices?'

'Nobody knows what Fire did; nobody but the Seer, and our spies never saw him,' Sarellia replied. 'But we do know the line of the Seer is beholden to flame. The weapons are real and they are without doubt of Elemental power. And with the Covenant in place, he will bring that fire to the Northern lands. That is why I sought you. The Northern Lands need the Queen of Stone now more than ever. The destruction of Fire is coming.'

Hands on hips, Goddard sighed. Another campaign against his adopted home. Long ago, when General Aracyse and Petra had agreed to defend these lands, he had thought peace would follow. But Kalleron had come, one final battle for its immortal King. A war ended by his own hands. Bruch'ail triumphant on a new dawn. The Northern Lands had finally become the sanctuary it was dreamed to be. All to change again.

He asked, 'The intelligence from the spies. It's reliable?'

Sarellia nodded. 'I trust our agents.'

'How long do we have?'

'I'm unsure. The mobilisation is recent news. We may have weeks, possibly a month or so.'

A cold chill gripped Goddard. The girl. Chara would need to be made safe. Taken away from the immediate harm. Laria lay directly to the south, across that angry sea. This was not the place to hide a mortal child of glass.

He said, 'I'll need to return to Anka.' A discrete nod to the floors above. 'Her safety.'

Petra agreed. 'Yes. All of you return to An'Korathall.'

Sarellia frowned. 'You're not coming?'

Petra turned away, glanced through a window to the south, the view obscured by broken walls. 'I will remain here. I want to see what comes my way.'

Noting she was about to protest, Goddard waved a hand to Sarellia. She had no right to question Petra. He shook his head and said, 'You can rest here but in the morning you must go back. I will join you afterwards.'

'But...'

Quiet until now, seemingly content to listen, the hand of the scout reached for Sarellia's shoulder. 'Come on, we'll leave now.'

Sarellia's eyes resisted but the scout's hand moved her to the door.

A hurtful expression on her face, she said, 'You'll not abandon us.'

Sarellia disappeared through the doorway, a forlorn look to her King. A shallow chord played inside his heart, a memory stirred from long ago. The door shut with a solid clunk. He stared at it, Sarellia's final words playing over in his mind. With a sigh, Goddard turned to Petra who was peering through a dark pane.

She said, 'Do you have any fight left?'
About to reply, Goddard realised Petra was speaking to herself.

Chapter X

It was a surreal scene to behold; Goddard watching as Petra stroked Chara's shoulder. Marble on glass, the two unwilling daughters of the Elemental Earth. His thoughts were clouded by the underlying anxiety—what had Kor'A done, what was coming their way? Those thoughts were banished as Petra turned her attention to him.

'Do you sleep?' she asked. 'You may be flesh but like it or not, you're part of this twisted family.'

'I doze. Occasionally.'

Petra smiled. 'Like an old man at his fireplace?'

He was an old man. 'Like a tired man in a new world.'

Petra continued to stroke Chara's shoulder. Goddard didn't need to understand immortal stone to see the affection. Kor'A's firstborn gazing down at her second. Both abandoned, neither linked to the creator. Was this a bond appearing?

'She really can't hear?' she asked.

'Truly, I don't know. But I don't think so. She'll awaken if something disturbs her but her sleep puzzles me, it doesn't follow our rules.'

'Your rules,' Petra replied, waving a finger at him.

'You never sleep? After all these years?'

Petra shook her head. Slender shoulders shrugged, dismissing the thought. 'Can't say I miss it.'

Thinking of the slumbering world and the coming of a new dawn, Goddard was reminded of Sarellia's warning. Of Laria and the return of Fire. It seemed improbable, though worryingly, not impossible.

'What the girl said, what do we do?' he asked.

'About your Bruhsa's warning?' He nodded and Petra continued. 'You should return to Anka, as I said. You'll find safety there.'

'You think they'll not threaten the city?'

'I've been detached from Kor'A for a long time but I understand enough. An'Korathall is her essence. And she ceased killing when we showed her the deception of the King. But she knows what she did to anger me when she destroyed Arkallon, when she took Felicitra from me. And though I doubt she'll ever understand it, she knows what guilt is; she's left that inside my memories. I know that city was built to keep us safe, to apologise for her crimes. She'll not raise a finger to help, but An'Korathall will remain a sanctuary from whatever threat comes to these lands.'

Those words should have offered comfort. Yet Goddard had seen troubles in Anka. Kor'A's eyes were no longer on her creation. The more he considered it, Sarellia's news of the Covenant appeared more urgent. 'The city is troubled, Petra. I've seen violence go untested. I'm not so sure it offers the protection you say.'

A frown formed on Petra's brow. One-hundred years and still it amazed him how stone could display such nuanced expression. Malleable and organic—unnatural but wonderful. Chara was similar but her skin appeared harder, as though molten glass.

Shaking her head, crystalline hair moving as though fibres of platinum, Petra frowned. 'So many decades without blood. Why now?'

'The Covenant? Could it be that?'

'Argan... Sorry, I really ought to call you Goddard,' she smiled. Warmth gifted in her gaze. 'If the Elementals have truly decided to leave our affairs—and I'm not certain they care either way—then we've nothing to stop human aggression crossing the sea. There are still small garrisons on the coast, well-defended courtesy of Aracyse. But if Laria or even Kalleron come with *gifts* from Fire or Wind, these lands have nothing to reply.'

Goddard noted the reluctance in her tone. Petra could stop much of what was to come but she had offered scant reassurance her powers would grace the battlefield.

'You don't want to be a part of it, do you?' he asked.

'Do you?'

A fair response, if cheap. He had forgotten war; long since forsaken any dream to return to Bruhada to restore its glory. After Aracyse fell to Kalle, and Goddard had avenged the General, he had found his peace. Disliked it at first. Hard for an old King to lay down his weapon. Though, in time, he had learned to accept it. For Chara, he had once again picked up Bruch'ail but that was to swat away bandits. In truth, he could defeat them armed with a bundle of wheat in his hand. Armies weren't so easy. Elemental sorcery was wicked. It would be dangerous. Kalle had brought the Furies; Goddard had witnessed their power. He shivered at the memory. Felt the tingle in his fingers. A whisper of stone. It surprised him. An ancient sensation; a call to arms.

Looking at his hands, open on his lap, he said, 'I'd forgotten what my heritage gave me. I bemoan the quiet fading of the light. Not a Bruhadian way to die. Yet, I'd convinced myself I no longer yearned for war. But now...'

'A calling?'

Close enough, he thought. More of a battle-cry. 'I'll return to Anka. Take Chara. You're staying here?'

Petra's hands were clamped between her knees. A strange position, a confessional. She spoke but kept her gaze on Chara. 'She's definitely mortal?'

'She believes so. But I now wonder, did this Covenant take Kor'A away, or did the fear of losing Chara accelerate her departure?'

'Without addressing Kor'A directly, we have to assume the worst. In which case, Chara needs to be protected. We can't risk her life. If the girl is an experiment in death, there's no telling what grief will do to Kor'A. If you are to fight again, you ought to do it in Anka.'

'What about you? The city needs its... guardian.'

Her eyes met his. An intense stare coming from sapphire and diamond. It should have been beautiful but it was cold. Petra said, 'I've seen too many friends fall, Goddard. I may be immortal but my mind remains human. And it is troubled enough by loss and grief.' Her stare unrelenting, she asked, 'Don't you suffer it? The centuries of death you've survived?'

A phantom breeze or a chill, whatever it was, Goddard shuddered. He huffed a humourless laugh. 'My breeding taught me to honour death—the warrior's code. I see the glorious fallen. At least, that's what I tell myself when the sorrow comes.'

Petra nodded. 'Kallisa was just as pragmatic. Until...' She stopped and Goddard saw her struggle to compose herself. He understood what thoughts darkened her mind. The death of Shadow. Petra's right-hand man, confidante and soul mate. How such a brutal soldier could touch so many gentle souls had always perplexed Goddard. Even so, Shadow's passing had been a hammer blow to Kallisa and Petra.

He reached across, squeezed her shoulder. 'I understand.' Giving her time to gather herself, he asked, 'Then what will you do?'

'I will stand here, watch the southern shore.' She placed a palm on Chara's head. 'Use Bruch'ail to summon me. But only if the girl is in danger. You can handle Anka.'

'Summon you?'

Her face softened, the old Petra returning. 'I'm a sensitive soul. You know that. Three knocks on the earth, and I'll feel it in my core. But... Goddard, don't strike the ground of An'Korathall. Whatever forge that hammer came from, it created something more than steel.'

'What if we're trapped in the city? If I can't get away?'

'You must, whatever you do.' She smiled, offered him redundant advice. 'Don't get trapped. Don't strike the essence of Kor'A.'

Time passed all too fast; a novelty for him. He considered the same would be true for Petra. Memories and laughter of olden days shared between them. Stories of heroes and fools, lovers and friends. The serious discussion sparked by Sarellia had been relegated to the periphery. A glow had crept into the cabin in the castle, turning dark wood to amber fire. Patting the wooden chest upon which he sat, he called Petra over. 'Watch,' he said.

Huddled close beside him, so small and slight, Petra leant forward. 'How does she...' He felt Petra jolt as Chara awoke. The little black body rising without warning. Goddard laughed. 'Told you.'

'Hello?' Chara said, rubbing eyes that required no attention. No sleep to wipe away.

'It's amazing.' Petra said.

'What is?' Chara asked, standing and stretching.

'You are.'

She stopped, her hands still reaching for the ceiling. 'Me?'

Petra laughed. 'Adorable.'

A face of glass quizzed Goddard but he shrugged. 'I think you're a nuisance.'

'You don't,' Chara said. 'What did you talk about last night? I watched it all.'

Goddard didn't have to turn his head to feel Petra's eyes boring into his skull. 'We spoke about how you sleep. How you watch but don't listen.'

'It's rude to listen.'

Petra said, 'Why don't you close your eyes when you sleep?'

'So I can see danger.'

'Well, I suppose that makes sense.'

Goddard peered at Petra. 'Does it?'

She didn't answer. Bit her lip and frowned. Clearly, it made no sense at all. To either of them. Standing, Goddard said, 'We have to go back to Anka.'

'All right,' Chara said.

Complete acceptance. It was unusual. Especially for a child.

'Are you coming with us?' she asked Petra.

'I need to stay here.'

'Why? It's ugly.'

'Chara!' Goddard said. A swift rebuke.

'It's all right,' Petra said, gesturing to the wooden walls. 'It's not to everyone's taste.'

A nod to thank Petra's courtesy, Goddard reached out his hand and Chara came to his side. Tiny glass fingers wrapped around his. It was impossible not to feel for her. A child so fragile she could literally smash to pieces. It empowered him. Provided the motivation to summon his strength. He looked up, Petra's beaming face staring.

'What?' he asked.

She shook her head. Still smiling. 'It is good to see you again, Goddard.'

Her words were warm. Sweet sadness lingering in the air. He rested his free hand on her shoulder. 'I hope I find danger so that I can see you in Anka.'

'Don't wish for calamity. I'll always be here. You can travel to me anytime.' She knelt and took Chara's other hand. Stone upon stone. 'You listen to what he says and you'll always be safe.'

A thought came to Goddard. Words of safety and travel. 'A cloak, do you have anything for Chara?'

Petra motioned to the chest. 'Feel free to rummage. Might need some adjustments.'

Chapter XI

S arellia squirmed. Holding her down, Jerune was conflicted by his feelings. Hands on her shoulders, he was trying to reassure, not oppress. Undeniable, his excitement was both unwelcome and invigorating. Sarellia's charm was growing on him. Though, he doubted he could ever be her equal. Not him. He was just a lowly scout. Dreams of something more where just that. But to spend more time with her was an opportunity come by way of chance. He had persuaded her to wait for dawn. An idea to track Baza'rad. Throughout the conversation brought by Sarellia's revelation of Fire, he had listened, watched the silent exchanges between a human god and a forgotten king. He had never been in the presence of such legends. But still, his instincts would not rest.

Wriggling, too eager to move, Sarellia spoke. She probably thought she was whispering; to his ears it was a hiss. 'You're sure about this?'

Sunrise painting the walls, the keep was a solemn monument to past wars. He was convinced. 'Positive.'

'Someone else?'

'It was well-hidden but they were hiding someone, or something. Didn't you hear his last words?'

'Was it, *get out?*'

'Do you have cloth ears?' She turned, her eyes beautiful and scolding. 'Don't answer that. Baza'rad said, *her safety*. He didn't mean Petra—she was right there.'

Sarellia's expression was a blank. 'I thought she meant the city? Do you think...a person?'

He couldn't tell. Not a single noise had come from above. Not the slightest squeak of a floorboard. If someone had been listening, he would have heard the gentle tell of weight shifting on old wood. Or a scrape upon flagstone. There had been nothing. Possibly someone asleep but who would slumber during that commotion? Who required protection, or secrecy, while they slept?

'Sarellia?'

'Uh-huh?'

'Stop breathing so hard.'

Contorted, squashed behind the rock, she turned. With a whisper shouted through clenched teeth, she said, 'I'm not being noisy.'

She was. But he knew it wasn't intentional. Anyone else and the contract would have been terminated. Sarellia was worth the irritation. He could train her; show her the ways of silence. Jerune could learn to endure her clumsy city manners.

He held out his hands, keen to placate her agitation. 'Just breathe slowly, please.'

'He's not going to hear!'

'It's not about him. It's about everything else. We make the slightest noise and birds fly their roosts. He won't hear us, but he'll see the disturbance.'

Those dark eyes squinted. So close and fiery. He wanted another excuse to draw nearer. Now was not the time. She relaxed, her posture visibly softening. The slightest nod and a smile.

'All right, Mr scout man. I'll try.'

Focusing on her sublime features, he startled when the basement door opened.

'He's leaving.'

Jerune had chosen a safe vantage point farther up the hill than his previous location. Assured their presence was distant enough for security, he watched as a huge figure stooped under the doorframe and emerged into the late dawn. A trick of perspective, the keep appeared smaller when the old King stood beside it. But it wasn't the legend that took his attention. It was the tiny flutter of fabric that trailed by his side. A rough cloth cloak that covered limbs and torso. A hood drawn up, presumably to conceal the face.

He nudged Sarellia, pointing. 'A child?'

Her silence, welcome as it was, told him she was as clueless as he. She leaned into his side, placing an arm around his shoulder. Her cheek drew close to his. Too close—her proximity caused his heart to race. With the slightest turn of his head, he said, 'I need to focus.'

A quick kiss on his cheek. Sarellia whispered, 'Do I distract you that much?'

She was a ruthless tease and her actions were a fog across his senses; his faculties under assault on too many fronts. Sarellia was as near perfect as a woman could be. Their quarry was as good as a god. This was a contract without compare. In the middle of it all was Jerune, and what was he? A simple scout; the best, but no myth of the ages. Not a wealthy Bruhadian beauty. Not a king. Perhaps he was nothing more than a plaything. He wanted to follow his human instinct but years of solitude and experience stifled his passion. With a gentle touch, he moved Sarellia into deeper cover.

'We can't lose them. You mentioned nothing of a child; whose is it?'

Sarellia's playfulness gave way to pragmatism. She said, 'There is no child. None that I know of.'

'Is it his?' Another thought, too obvious to keep quiet. 'It can't be hers, can it?'

Sarellia shook her head. She peered out, the tension evident in her posture. Drawing back into the protection of the rock, she said, 'We follow. Lead the way.'

Alone he could track at close quarters, moving through the undergrowth with minimal effort. With Sarellia by his side, he kept out of visible range. Several nights had passed and they were close to Anka. The next day would bring them home. He was confused by the King's travel. As though clockwork, they would move at dawn and bed down at dusk. The first night he hadn't seen it. But the second, he had almost stumbled into them. That mistake rectified by the wind which had picked up, covering their hasty retreat. Without fire to keep them warm, each night Sarellia slept by his side. He had wanted nothing more than to lay with her but meditation kept him alert. Cross-legged, hands on his lap, he would remain motionless as Sarellia lay curled against his legs. Fortune had smiled upon them; no bandits had come their way. Every morning she would wake and smile up at him. He waited for it. Watching her as she began to rouse. That had been his sunrise.

They spoke little of life, tracking too important to disturb with small-talk. The King and the child walked the path at day but slipped into the forest before dusk. He and Sarellia moved within the treeline, sheltered from view. Immersed in the forest, their own sounds would be mistaken for any beast or bird. On occasion, he would move back to the trail to gauge the tracks. It was all too easy, a man as big as the King. Sarellia had even ventured forth to check the prints. She had returned, her face a treasure of delight. He hadn't the heart to tell her a blind man could follow their target. Sarellia's achievement had made her more determined to appease him. She had said so. Wanted to be a help, not a hindrance. Reminding her he was being paid, she had shrugged and smiled. It didn't matter, she wanted him to be proud. But one more day and Anka would loom before them. She would go back to being a rich city-girl playing her game of Cult and spy; he would return to the woods. He knew his game of prince and princess would end. Reality would return. Queens and commoners.

Dusk had come again and the King and child had moved into the forest. A thought born of curiosity had occurred to Jerune. Would the secret be lost in Anka? The King would surely enter the citadel. Not a place he could follow. There was a splinter in his mind he could not remove; Jerune wanted to see the face that lay beneath the cloak. Who was the legend escorting? Through dark columns in a black forest, the glow from the King's fire was masked. No beacon of light to give themselves away, though Jerune could see the signs; the trunks lit with the dullest glow. The King and the cloak sitting close to a pit of embers, or perhaps a shallow fire. To get closer Jerune would need absolute stealth. He would have to go alone.

Explaining his plan to Sarellia, she said, 'You're leaving me here?'

'Don't you want to know who the child is?' he asked.

In the darkness he could see she was seeking the King's location. 'Where are they?'

He pointed, his arm barely visible.

She said, 'I can't see a thing.'

'They have a dim fire. I can see the surrounding trees are brighter.'

Silence, he imagined she was straining to see. 'You can see that?'

He held her shoulders. There was no danger to her. This close to Anka there were few predators. The wolves that had taken the bandits roamed farther North. Even then, they would stay clear of so many humans; the fire a beacon to avoid. Savouring the air, Jerune noted the scent of the forest was nothing but undergrowth and decay. Not even the acrid stench of a wildcat's piss had bothered his senses.

'You'll be safe right here.' He coaxed her to sit down. She did without fuss, though her hands held his forearms as she sat. Her breathing was calm. Her grip remained. 'You'll need to let me go.'

'How long will you be?'

'It's not far. I just want to see. Clap your hands once if you need me, if something is wrong.'

'Clap? Shouldn't I make a bird noise?'

He doubted she could. 'Can you?'

'I don't think so.'

'A clap then.'

He felt the movement through her grip, the nodding of her head. Sensing it was appropriate to do so, a caring and protective gesture, he leant forward and kissed her forehead. He pulled away but her hands clawed onto his face and dragged him to her lips. Days in the forest and she still smelled so sweet. Her lips soft and warm. She broke away, still holding his face.

'You better come back,' she said.

His heart was pounding. But he wanted to stay aloof. Jerune said, 'Of course I will—I still need paid.' He felt a fool for saying it, thought how callous his attempt at humour would be perceived.

In the dark he saw the faintest aura of her smile. Sarellia replied, 'Oh, I was considering offering you a bonus.' A pause. 'As long as you come back.'

A silhouette moved into shadow and he was gone. Jerune was unlike other men. Softer, quiet. It was evident he had the pride of a typical man but he wore it with discomfort. She admired that; a sense he wanted to be himself but had to erect some semblance of a façade to hide it. Sarellia had known other men, teased them, coaxed them—ultimately rejecting them. Her heart was not impressed by strength and aggression as so many men believed. Even in Anka, where peace had prevailed, it was a weekly routine of swatting away muscled morons and swaggering traders. Jerune was opposite to those fools. Nothing to prove beyond a typical male ego. A man of the earth, happier to listen to birdsong than the clash of steel. A lover, she hoped, not a fighter.

Sitting in the forest, the moons hidden by canopy and cloud, her world was featureless. Her eyes quickly accustomed to the dark, yet all she saw was more of it. Varying shades of nothing, hiding behind a veil of gloom. The more she focused, the more she strained. Defeated by night, and with nothing to see, she shut her eyes. The sounds were clear; the breeze, the distant creak of a tree. A smiled appeared on her face.

A game to play. Could she hear Jerune? She knew his direction, that was easy; he had set off away from her. Head bowed, tilted to one side, she concentrated. Felt muscles she rarely used tense behind her ears. His words in her mind; her noisy breathing—Sarellia inhaled and released her breath in a controlled escape. Held it with empty lungs before drawing air again. She heard nothing from where he had gone. He was a phantom walking the woods.

A sudden sound caused alarm. A crack of wood—a twig underfoot. The muffled sharpness; it was a clumsy noise she would make. Another brittle thing crunching. Far away, but coming closer, opposite to Jerune's direction. On the breeze, a whisper came to her. Two voices. Perhaps more. Heartbeat quickening, her game of scouting over, Sarellia's excitement was banished. Jerune had told her to clap but that would give away her position. The voices could be friendly. Why create alarm? Sarellia pulled her knees closer to her chest, waited for more noise. They could be moving past, farther away than she realised. But why move through the forest when there was a track? The sound of trampling came closer. Now three voices, muted but audible; words spoken with secrecy. A shiver through her spine. They were coming straight toward her. She turned her head to look, expected nothing but darkness.

The hand and a gentle hush were instant. And though she startled, Sarellia knew it was Jerune. How on earth had he come back so quickly? Truly, a ghost. He was magnificent. But the voices were still coming closer. Yet, somehow, with Jerune by her side, she knew it would be all right. She felt gentle pressure pushing her to lay down. The log she had sat against made a perfect hollow with the ground. Pressing flat, she squeezed into the narrow space. Jerune vanished as the voices hovered above. Words spoken, a foreign accent; something about Anka and easy spoils. The log moved as a boot thudded into it. As a grumbling storm the strangers passed over, many more than she had realised. They continued on, their noise fading. Jerune appeared at her side. Her heart was hammering too fast to allow another fright.

In the softest whisper, silk on the breeze, he said, 'You're safe.'

She nodded, held him.

But Jerune was agitating. 'They're heading straight for the King.'

Her grip tightened. She couldn't let him leave her again.

His hand came to hers, tried to prise it free.

'Please, no. Don't leave me.'

His body relaxed; she felt the tension wash away. 'I won't,' he said.

She had found her true guardian. Burrowed into him. Wrapping her arms around him, he reciprocated. Though slight, he was strong enough; his hold confident and secure.

'Thank you,' she said.

He replied with a squeeze of her body. She understood he was listening to the sounds moving away. Jerune focusing on the enemy was in contrast to her selfishness. A curse in her mind to chastise herself. Sarellia was better than this.

'If you need to go...' she said. Sarellia didn't want to appear as the spoiled bitch from their first few days. He needed to know she was a better person. And though she was loath to do so, she pulled away from the embrace. 'Go, warn them.'

'Too late,' he said, standing, taking her with him.

Not sure what he meant, the sound came to her. A distant disturbance, something heavy moving among the trees. A girl screamed and Jerune was off. His stealth was such that she only noted he had left her side. Not a sound came from his flight. What to do? He would come back for her. Besides, she would be useless in a skirmish. Blind and defenceless, nothing but a liability. Sarellia jumped. The forest groaned as something massive struck a tree. In her mind, that was all it could be. Or the ground itself. Again, the thunder shook the forest. The girl screamed a second time. A man howled as another sound bit the night. A crunch of bone. More shouting coming from the dark. How many had there been? Blind, she stumbled forward, morbid curiosity usurping her decision to stay. The sounds continued, terrifying and powerful. Storms in the forest. She imagined she knew what it was. The howling in the air was the hammer of Kings, Bruch'ail. An unearthly slab of Elemental steel. It roared and the forest trembled. Men screamed again but the girl did not.

Sarellia leapt with fright when Jerune returned. She clawed at the dark to grasp him. 'What's happening?'

His hand settled on her shoulder. Jerune said, 'Don't be scared.'

Seldom did those words work as intended. She asked, 'Of what?'

Her hand was grasped by his. Pulled down to fall upon rough cloth. He said, 'Sarellia, meet Chara.'

The child. She knelt as her hand traced the girl's shoulders, her body still cloaked in secrecy. 'You're safe now,' Sarellia said.

The girl replied, 'Of course I am. I'm with Goddard.'

Confused, she moved closer, reached for the unseen face. Her hand touched a cold, smooth surface. Not flesh. A mask? Of glass? A countenance impossible to behold. Sarellia pulled her hands away. Not fear.

Jerune said, 'We know a Queen of Stone. Why not a child of glass?'

The words made sense, even if the moment did not. '*An Elemental?*'

The girl, invisible in the dark, replied, 'I'm mortal, like you. I'm not like my mother.'

Mother? Sarellia was lost. The Covenant was real. The Fire in Laria, the Wind in Kalleron, and Petra: they were the toys of the immortals. There couldn't be a fourth. About to question the miracle child, she stopped. The forest had become still but for one sound. One large beast coming their way.

To Jerune, she said, 'Does he know you took her?'

Before he could answer, the girl called out. 'We're here, Goddard.'

An agitated voice rumbled back. 'We?'

Sarellia looked to the darkness and sighed. This was not how you impressed your King.

Chapter XII

It wasn't meant to be like this. The journey should have been noble, solemn. Not a bloody comedy. Fucking cart. Bücka lashed out, sending the fractured rim spinning off into the meadow. It disappeared from view, lost in the long swaying grass. Thelia's coffin lay atop the open wagon listing on a crippled axle. To the northeast, mere hours away, the gleaming citadel of Anka beckoned. So close. Shang'si snorted her discontent at the unbalanced load. Her flank was a shining shadow in the sun. A thoroughbred and obedient Western Star; not even she would pull the cart another inch.

It rose within; the predictable anger. Bücka wanted to contain it. Show herself she had matured. Looking to the track she saw nobody on either horizon. All alone on the road to Anka. She had to try to control the rage but gritted teeth and a seethe of breath did little to arrest her fury. One glance at a stubborn Shang'si and Bücka stormed off into the grass. Eyes turned up to the open sky, she let howl a scream of rage. Heard her futile cry echo away, diminishing on the slight breeze. Still fuming, she returned to the cart and set about releasing the harness. Once free, she leant on the casket. Shoulders slumping, the anger softened to frustration. Tears would come next. This wasn't how it should be.

Sword in hand, the flat edge of the Bruhadian blade, she creaked the lid open. Every jarring crack was a protest from the dead.

One look to Shang'si. 'What?'

A snort. The stamp of an iron shoe.

'What else do I do? Drag the coffin? You want to do it?'

Shang'si turned away.

'Exactly. So, we take Thelia... Oh gods, I can't believe I'm saying this. Take out gran and you carry her home.'

Removing each rusted nail, Bücka lifted the casket lid. Thelia, none the wiser, lay within, cocooned in a silk shroud, the purple fabric still vibrant under a sheen of fine dust. The stench, sweet death; herbs and spices laid with the dead. A gift to pass on to the next life. A mask to hide the truth of decay. Uncertain how to handle her, Bücka placed tentative arms under Thelia. Prepared for the effort, Thelia's weight was a shock.

'You're just bones. Gods, you're just bones.'

Disjointed bones. In one lift, the woman beneath the shroud collapsed. Horrendous. Bücka had sent many to their death. Standing here on this lonely track, holding it in her hands, a terrible truth was brought home. To die was the end. The return to dust. Just bones and silk.

'I know this isn't you. I know you've gone. But I'm still taking you home.'

Struggling to maintain the shape of what was once beloved, Bücka moved Thelia to Shang'si. As though the bundle was a sleeping child, she laid it with affection across the saddle. Secured by the reins, Thelia was tied in a silk roll. Head down, Bücka led the way, Shang'si following without command. A loyal horse. An intelligent mare. She was her only true friend.

Walking along the main avenue, Shang'si close behind, Bücka saw few changes since her last visit. She hadn't summoned the guts to intrude into Kor'A's home. Her curiosity was a poor match for the citadel's oppressive aura. Never knowing if the Lord of the Earth was truly gone. Not a house against which to trespass. Not without absolute faith. True, the streets still eyed her with suspicion but if Kor'A was absent why was Bücka, the great warrior, hesitant? She knew no fear. Bücka the brave. Bücka the insolent. Not Bücka the mouse.

The rise to the tomb was a strange journey. A warrior. A Western Star. And a shroud. It made perfect sense. But not for Anka. The tomb of legends was not for people such as she. But it was for Thelia. A funeral procession that brought people from their homes. Some pointed at her. Others shook their heads. Yet, in all of their stares, Bücka saw the respect. There was still a soul in An'Korathall, the city of stone. At the top of the main avenue, she paused. Looking back, she saw the faces watching. Confused, curious. They wanted to know who she had brought to the tomb. She had nothing to explain to them. Owed strangers no due. But Thelia deserved the attention.

Loosening the straps and removing her with care, she held the bundle in her arms. To the crowd, she said, 'Thelia. Sister of Thelissa. Ward of Shadow, friend of Petra, Queen of Stone. This is my own blood.'

Young eyes stared back without knowledge. Old eyes twinkled, solemn nods to accept the return. To those with wisdom, Bücka bowed her head. She moved under the grand arch and toward the tomb, Shang'si left behind, content to graze on a hanging lunch of herbs and flowers.

The tomb, cool and gloomy, welcomed her return. She brought Thelia to the middle sarcophagus—Argan, the giant. Glancing at Thelissa's casket she imagined Thelia resting on top. It wouldn't look so bad. They would be closer. But Anka's open doors were a threat. Bücka imagined Thelia's shroud being stripped away. No dignity. Not what she deserved. Laying her down, she pressed against the Darkwood seal. Recalling her initial difficulty, she summoned her strength and pushed. Nothing. Patience was required. A pause, a deep breath; this was not the time for frustration or anger. Palms against wood, body tense, Bücka shoved hard. *Movement*—but it was hers. Her feet sliding away from the sarcophagus; the lid remained tight shut.

'Don't lose it. Stay calm.'

She collected herself. Took another breath and tried a third time, this time not giving up until she collapsed onto the stone casket, her energy spent. The cart falling apart; the long hot trek to Anka. It had all taken its toll.

Bücka had to control her emotions; this was not the place to repeat her childish tantrum. A deep breath and she said, 'Rest Bücka. Just rest.'

She closed her eyes, sat against the stone and focused on her breathing. Trembling with effort and frustration, she kept her eyes tight shut. The marble cooled her hot skin and the echo of her breath calmed her senses. Rhythmic and steady, the sound was soothing.

'Try again soon. Just rest.'

Nestled close beside Thelia, Bücka drifted into a peaceful slumber.

The dagger from her boot swept into darkness, a disturbed dream fading away. The hand on her shoulder fled; the blade catching air. Leaping to her feet, Bücka ran her other hand across her neck. No blood—the assassins had failed. Everything still a haze, she dropped the dagger and drew her swords.

'Whoah!' A man called out. It was more of a shriek.

She focused on him. No weapon in hand, leather too soft to offer protection. He had moved fast. Quicker than any man ought to. His eyes were wild and wide, a restraining hand thrown her way.

He spoke again, 'Steady—I'm not here to harm you.'

Damn sure. Bücka glanced to the open portal, three shapes in a block of blinding light. His friends? The strangest troupe she had ever seen. A child, a woman, and a colossal man.

'Allies of yours?' she asked the thief. Or scout, she couldn't be sure. Often the same thing. Similar to her mixed profession: warrior and mercenary.

'Friends,' said the thief, squinting at her. Then he smiled. The most unusual reaction.

'What? What's so funny?'

With his warding hand, he pointed to the tomb behind her. She saw his eyes glance to Thelia. He said, 'Looking for a home?'

'None of your business. You or your friends. Go, get out.'

Another glance to the exit. That huge frame. She'd like to think she had fought bigger, but she hadn't. He'd probably be slow, most behemoths were. Stupid too. If the fight became a chore, she could always run. No cowardice to live another day. The dead don't earn coin.

The thief said, 'There's only one person who actually has the right to be here.'

A frown, confusion. What was he saying? Did he mean Thelia? She looked to her grandmother, that small bundle. It couldn't be. She didn't know this rogue.

'You know Thelia?' she asked.

'Thelia?' he shrugged. 'Who?'

Her sword pointing to the shroud, she said, 'Thelia.'

A voice boomed. Loud, but soft. 'Thelia?' It was the colossus.

She turned. He was approaching. His footfall as thunder. As he passed from light to gloom, she saw him. An impossible man. Heavy strapping across his chest, a hefty weapon on his back. A hammer. A massive hammer. His one word, that tone, it laid claim to memory of her grandmother. Impossible. But there could be no other.

'Argan?' She barely heard her own voice. So quiet.

He came close. She stared at eyes she imagined knew no fear. He said, 'Once. Another life.' He looked to the purple shroud. His eyes lingering. Bücka saw sadness. 'This is Thelia?'

Bücka nodded. What was happening? Perhaps the lightning-fast rogue and Argan were a dream. What else could it be?

'My grandmother,' she said, expecting to awaken.

He pointed to Thelissa's sarcophagus. 'Her sister.'

'I know. But the quartz fills the casket.' Thumbing to his empty grave, confused, Bücka said, 'Yours? It's empty.'

He sighed. It filled the tomb with an echo of the wind. Such detail in the dream. Too real. Bücka understood. This *was* Argan. A man never defeated in battle. Legend said in the time of the Queen of Kalleron, he defied the King. Single-handed he routed an army, sending the Butcher, General Te'anor, scampering away. They said he even faced down the evil Queen, slapped her immortal face. Though, she doubted that was true. Men were men, gods were another thing. But he had killed Kalle, the King of Kalleron, on the fields of Stranghame. He was more impressive than she could have imagined. But still, Thelia deserved to come home.

A softer voice. Not a plea. She repeated: 'Your casket's empty.'

He said nothing and moved to the sarcophagus. With giant hands, he grasped the Darkwood lid. She stood, stunned. Her swords clattered on the marble. Argan lifting the Drohendrian seal, placing it to the side. The weight of a cart, he put it down with ease. The ground chimed an anthemic note as the lid settled on stone.

'Please,' he said, gesturing to Thelia. 'May I?'

Bücka stepped backwards. Nodded. Her vision blurred. Didn't know why, then she sniffed. Tears, her nose leaking to match her eyes. Wiping a hand to them, she watched him stoop to the tiniest bundle of beloved bones. Shovel-like hands scooped Thelia with grace and he bowed his head. Bücka crumbled as one legend buried her own. Falling to her knees she sobbed. Argan said something to the others. She didn't hear it but they left, leaving her alone with him.

'Do you wish to say goodbye?' he asked.

She did. Bücka rose, leaned over the lip of the sarcophagus. It came without invite but she felt no guilt. A laugh. It was preposterous. Thelia, in her noble purple shroud, little more than a cloth lying in Argan's place.

'She's tiny,' she said.

Argan moved to the Darkwood. Hefted it into his hands. 'She's home.'

Bücka stood back and Argan replaced the lid. He handled the Drohendrian slab as though it was hollow; made the impossible appear trivial. No matter how large he was, no man had that much strength. That power only belonged to gods.

Looking to him, she said, 'I'm sorry.'

'Sorry?'

'For this. For trespassing.'

His smile was warm. His eyes, honest. 'Your name?'

'Bücka.'

His smiled widened. More than a pleasantry. She thought she knew why.

He said, 'Thelissa had a dog. Kept her company to the end. Bücka, I recall?'

It was true. Thelia had raised her, often spoke of Thelissa's dog; how it had given her comfort and purpose. So important to her sister, she had named her granddaughter after him. Bücka nodded. 'Yeah. A loyal mutt.'

'Just like you?'

More tears. 'Just like me.'

Chapter XIII

C ould it finally be true? War was coming again? Goddard had lived the best part of a century without its threat. There had been rumours, but nothing so grim had ever come to pass. This time though? Too many convergences to be a coincidence. With Chara by his side and Sarellia seated opposite, he glanced to his left. In the vast funnel of light that was the inner citadel courtyard, Bücka and the scout had been relegated to the literal periphery. Sarellia had asked for his ear, and his alone. The Cultist appeared content with Chara's presence, her onyx skin an invitation to all Elemental talk.

Goddard, the child, and Sarellia, sat upon two of six marble blocks. Arranged in a broken circle, they enclosed a dark granite pillar. As tall as he, the column was a mystery. Uncertain of its function, but knowing of its creator, it was sure to serve some purpose. He doubted the feature was decoration. Gazing around the cylinder of marble, there were few traces of a human touch. A spiral of stairs wrapped around the interior wall. Every thirty-foot, a darker band encircled the citadel; ten balconies offering views down to the courtyard, their circular corridors leading to simple portals. Human-sized arches that opened into plain spaces, in turn those blocks constituted the exterior wall. There was no element of thoughtful habitation. No halls, no kitchens, no grand distinction of design or class. A tower of boxes. That was how Shadow had described it a century ago. A god's empty closet.

Jerune's voice floated across. A mumble buried under Shadow's ancient words.

'Did you call?' Goddard asked.

Low down on the steps, Jerune waved. 'Yes.'

'What?'

Before he answered, Bücka, two steps above, shoved him. Jerune, unbalanced, leapt to his feet. He pointed at the warrior. 'She wants to try the hammer.'

Bücka hissed at Jerune. Her tone sharp, her scowling face evidence of displeasure. Try the hammer? Serious times. War was coming. Yet a smile crept onto Goddard's face. He had learned much from his trials. The greatest thing to preserve in catastrophe was humanity. And comedy, intentional or not, was a light to dispel most gloom.

Standing, he said to Sarellia, 'Excuse me.'

She smiled, shook her head. 'You'll let her wield it?'

A memory came to him. A young Thelia swinging around on Bruch'ail as though it was a festival pole in Bruhale. Bücka, a splinter of time in his long life, had already displayed many of Thelia's traits. It felt right that he allowed her the chance to embarrass herself. She would not lift the hammer.

'She can try,' he said.

Picking it up from the ground beside the marble seats, he carried it over, haft resting upon his shoulder. The provenance of the weapon was lost in time. An impenetrable fog of mystery. What was known, though, was simple. Stone knows stone. As he approached, Bücka's eyes cast daggers at Jerune.

'I only said I'd love to hold it, I didn't ask. But this idiot,' she pointed at the scout, 'just flaps his mouth like a loose tarp in a storm.'

Jerune held up his hands. 'I only wanted to help. You've been going on about it the whole time we've been sat here.'

'No harm done,' Goddard said. He placed Bruch'ail down, hammer on the marble. 'Be my guest.'

It would be a miracle if she moved it. A genuine miracle. Many had tried. Of all his friends, he had imagined only Petra would be able to accomplish the feat. Yet she had never shown an interest in doing so. That had always been her way; another person's business was their own. In many ways she was more serious than he. Her games never involved other people's cultures. Never had she mocked, or made light of, another person's world. One day he had asked her, as a curiosity. Had said he wanted to know if the legend was true: did stone know stone? Could she, Kor'A's reluctant Queen, wield it? With a polite smile Petra had declined, no effort made to touch the hammer. Her words had troubled him. *Argan, I can feel Bruch'ail across the plains—I don't know what that is, but it has no love for me.*

Bücka frowned. Her words bringing him back to the present. 'You're sure?'

Dismissing Petra's prophecy, he gestured to Bruch'ail. 'Please.'

Bücka nodding with confidence, grasped the haft in preparation. Two upside-down grips, ready to upend the mighty block. This was where all failed. Bücka would be no different. A tug. Then another accompanied by a mighty groan. She let go, quizzing Goddard with her eyes. He smiled.

'What did you do?' she asked.

'Do?'

'You've done something. It's... stuck.'

Jerune paced forward. His frame didn't suggest strength. Lithe, sinewy—built for his own purposes.

'May I?' he asked.

Goddard nodded.

But Jerune didn't grab the haft. He knelt low, put his face to the marble and stared at the head. He blew at the ground. It was an unorthodox technique.

Goddard asked, 'What are you doing?'

Jerune stood. 'Since we met in the forest...'

'When you stalked me.'

He nodded. 'I explained that's a scout's habit. It's better to track than be tracked. But I noticed how you handled the hammer. You never lay it flat. Always this way.'

'Easier to grab when disturbed.'

Jerune appeared to accept his words. 'I've never seen it topple. I saw Sarellia bump into it that night in the forest. It didn't waver. Solid, as if it's got roots.'

'You think my hammer has roots?'

'No. But it's as though it's bound to the ground.' He smiled. 'Like Petra.'

Goddard's smile dropped. A frown to replace it. What Jerune said was true, a peculiarity noticed by few. Petra's literal connection; bound to Earth the immortal. She was required to touch the essence of her saviour at all times. He thought of Chara at the stream, how she had leapt those few monumental inches. Mortal, not bound, she could leave the prison of Earth. Not Petra.

Impressed by Jerune's deduction, Goddard asked, 'When did you notice? Petra, I mean.'

'After she caught us at the rock near the keep. We followed her. Tracks fascinate me. I always watch people's feet...'

'You're a weird one,' Bücka interrupted.

Jerune nodded, 'I get that a lot. But it serves me well. I saw how she moves, watched closely. The earth binds to her when she walks. Which makes a lot of sense, I mean, she's the Queen of Stone.'

It didn't explain his thoughts on Bruch'ail. 'But why think this is the same?'

'Look, I know folks think I'm dumb. Just a country-boy rogue playing scout. But I need to listen to everything, react to small changes. I see what others don't. You, the Bruhadian lore, a hammer without a single scratch on its surface.' Jerune reached and grabbed the haft of Bruch'ail. It was clear he was relaxed, no effort in his grip. 'I couldn't lift this if I was a hundred feet tall. This is *hers*, isn't it?'

'Kor'A?'

Jerune nodded. His eyes squinting.

'No,' Goddard replied.

'No?'

It wasn't Kor'A's—that much was clear. The lord of the Earth had no need of a human weapon. No more than a fish required a boat. Jerune's conclusion was easy to understand but it lacked comprehension of Kor'A, the Elemental.

'Why would she need a hammer?' he asked the scout.

Bücka answered. 'To crush her foes?'

He pointed at her. She should have known better. 'And did Thelia tell you this?'

'Well, no. But that's what hammers are for.'

'Men and woman wield hammers. Not Elementals.'

Jerune appeared dejected. His theory debunked. 'You're sure?'

Goddard paced to Bruch'ail. One hand lifted it from the ground.

'*Damn!*' Bücka said.

Holding it out, he offered her the chance again. She frowned.

'I can't. You saw.'

'It's very heavy. Use two hands. Don't swing it, you'll not manage.'

Her features a portrait of distrust; it was clear Bücka's curiosity was greater than her fear of humiliation. She came to him and grabbed the haft, her arms close to her body, her stance ready to receive the weight.

'Ready?' he asked.

She nodded. With care, he relinquished his grip. He watched as her shoulders trembled. Her knuckles white as the marble floor, hands shaking with effort. Her face was exquisite. Aspects of duress, triumph, and wonder.

'*Oh, by the gods!*' she said, straining with effort.

A thought occurred to Goddard. Petra's warning and a moment lost to the years. A time he had slammed Bruch'ail into the ground of Anka. 'Don't drop it,' he warned.

Nodding with furious intent, or perhaps shaking with seizures, Bücka lowered Bruch'ail as best she could. With a dull thump it contacted the earth and she reeled backwards. Flinging her hands in the air, she leapt with joy. Her grin was delightful.

Jerune asked, 'Heavy?'

Bücka laughed. It reminded Goddard of Thelia's cheeky giggle. Music. She pointed at the hammer. 'If he can swing that bloody thing, he doesn't even need to use it.' She focused on Goddard. 'If you're that strong, you must be able to punch through houses.'

Nodding at her, he excused himself and returned to Sarellia. Now the children had played with Bruch'ail, he could hear more of what the Cultist had to say.

Baza'rad. That was his name. It was hard to see him as anything else. The King that wielded Bruch'ail. Watching him return from Jerune and Bücka, Sarellia saw the human behind the legend. His strength undisputed, the poise without comparison. But the humility he wore was that of a normal man. A man of whom her Bruhsa's had spoken. Argan, now become Goddard to live his last years. He sat down beside Chara, the girl of glass smiling and shuffling along. A sigh from his huge lungs. Raised eyebrows and a smile.

'Sorry,' he said. 'As you know, I knew her grandmother. I treasure that bond.'

'Never apologise to me, my King. That's not the order of things.'

He shook his head. 'The day chooses the order, not the past. I'm not your King.'

The reluctance to dwell on his own myth was painfully apparent. Sarellia relented, she would respect his commoner façade. 'Goddard, I'm going to meet with my contact from Laria tonight. If they followed the plan, they should have stayed hidden within Anka.'

He frowned. 'After Kalleron, Kallisa spoke of the Cult. Secret doors and hideaways.' His hand gestured to the tower. 'There is nowhere in Anka to hide. No tunnels or hidden rooms. Just what Kor'A designed.'

It was true. Anka held few secrets. The reputation of its Queens was enough to dissuade those that wished harm upon others or those that might seek to topple the order. There was no need to fear discovery. The Cult had hidden in plain sight. Trust and integrity were the walls behind which to conceal their activity. She realised the irony. Opposite sat the greatest living legend in all history. The King who routed the Butcher on the Battle of the Bridge became the common man who killed the immortal King of Kalleron. Two heroes; one heart. Hiding in plain sight. Just as she had.

'How did you manage it?' she asked.

'Manage what?'

'What we did—stay hidden.'

The King shuffled, leant great big elbows on his knees. Sarellia noted how Chara hung on his every word. So quiet and well-mannered. Unlike any child she knew. Her black eyes, visible only for the highlights of her lids, followed his every movement. The occasional blink to remind her of life. Sarellia thought back to the previous night; the bandits in the woods. Jerune leading Chara. She had expected anger from Goddard but he displayed none. Told little of Chara, except for the obvious. The child was Kor'A's creation. Sarellia wondered what role the impeccable girl of black glass was to play in the looming dawn of war. She would speak to her in time. But for now, Chara's attention was fixed on Goddard's reply.

'We all fought with plate and helm,' he said. 'Heavy metal conceals much of a man and I fought many battles, sent many men to their end. I never knew any of them.' His eyes widened, his tone changing. 'Your history, Sarellia, the Cult. I never knew.'

Confused, Sarellia questioned him with a frown.

Goddard huffed. 'We stay hidden behind our masks. Even Te'anor.'

'The Butcher?'

The old King smiled. It was without humour. He said, 'Yes, you know Te'anor.'

How could she? The man was a barbaric legend from another time, a sadistic killer of her own people. 'I know of his myth,' she replied. 'His brutality.'

Goddard stiffened. 'You don't know, do you?'

Sarellia shook her head.

'Te'anor became Kastane.'

Her reaction was an utterance of a laugh. His words were confused. The Butcher who was Te'anor, and the old Cult leader, Kastane, were not the same man. Could not be the same man. The Bruhsa line would have told her of such a contradiction. Te'anor, an evil monster, Kastane a hero. Shaking her head, she said, 'No, you must be mistaken. Kastane led the Cult, not the Butcher.'

Goddard shook his head. 'You should know this, Sarellia; your Bruhsa line should have told you. Truth is tradition.'

Confused, Sarellia replied, 'There's nothing to know. Kastane wasn't the Butcher. He died at Venhyne, your ally. You were there, I don't understand.'

'*Ah*,' Goddard said, the reply becoming a breath. Something hidden underneath.

'Ah, what?'

Nodding, Goddard said, 'Kallisa. It was her.'

Kallisa, four generations before. Infamous, incredible; friend to Petra, lover of Shadow. Sarellia was about to question Goddard's statement when she thought of the history. Kallisa was Kastane's loyal General. Loyal to the end. Of course, there had been rumours but Kallisa had denied them. Settled them using the Bruhsa narrative, the oral history of truth. But for a Bruhsa to lie was heresy; to manipulate history was wrong. Her loyalty to a man wouldn't usurp Bruhadian tradition.

'She wouldn't have done that,' Sarellia said. 'Why would she do that?'

Goddard looked to Chara. Cradled her head in his huge hand. To her, he said, 'Can you let me speak to Sarellia for a moment? Go and join Bücka and Jerune?'

Chara blinked, glanced at Sarellia, brought her gaze back to Goddard. 'I will, for you. But why?'

With a sigh, Goddard said, 'Because I'm going to talk of death and war, and it'll not make you happy, little one. What I have to say is not for sensitive souls.'

'I have a soul?' Chara asked, pointing to her chest.

'More than most.'

With a smile, she moved away. Sarellia could see the affection Goddard had for the girl. His eyes following her. She was caught off guard when he called out, his voice a resonant thunder. 'Bücka, Jerune—look after her. No games!'

Blank stares and confused nods were the reply as Chara hopped over.

'She's an Elemental, yet you seem very protective,' Sarellia said.

'Chara's not like her mother. I'll tell you more later.'

More mysteries. But she could wait. 'Kastane then, what don't I know?'

'In Bruhale, everyone was in heavy armour. Te'anor, the Butcher, was no different. His soldiers came first, then the captains. He joined the last rush. I never saw his face. We fought. Over the bridge he went, injured, defeated. The last man, nobody came after that. Though, I knew if I continued my campaign, the Queen would come. Not such a glorious thought. So, I left Bruhale. The King that was Baza'rad died the day the Butcher fell.'

Sarellia watched as he appeared to shrink, shoulders slumping, spine curving. It was clear the memory was a terrible weight to bear. He folded his arms, hands tucked close to his chest. It was a cold, lonely embrace.

'It cost you—that victory?' she asked.

He nodded, stared at the ground. 'Victory? I fought for my pride that day. Not my people. I sealed their fates when I presumed to stand against Kalleron.'

'You stood for Bruhada.'

'Myself. I did that for myself. Stubborn, foolish.' His voice simmered with resentment. He raised his eyes. She felt his gaze; a thousand horrors.

'Then what happened. After that?'

It was empowering to observe; his posture recovering, a king returning, though, of course, it was no king. It would be Argan.

'Petra.' He spoke her name with a devotion hard to fathom. 'Free of my armour, smuggling Bruch'ail aboard, I became a sailor. Well, I suppose we were well-mannered pirates, mostly. But all good people. All escaping our pasts. That was her way; *the Rules of the Melody*. New beginnings.

'It was then we fell into the path of the Cult. Petra's desire to avenge Felicitra's death. Much happened but when everything appeared to be going wrong, I was reacquainted with Te'anor. Of course, now he was Kastane. Reborn to lead the Cult. Petra told me it was penance. And... I believe it. Kastane gave his life to defend what he had built with the Cult. An irony, his last battle was as my ally against an old master.'

If true, and she could see no reason why Goddard would lie, it was a tale of redemption. Why hide it? Sarellia said, 'Kallisa spoke only of Kastane's heroism. Never of his past.'

'You are separated in time from the man I knew as General Te'anor. And in time, even monsters lose their fangs. The blood spilt by history is diluted—people forget. But, Sarellia, Te'anor massacred thousands of my people—your people. No matter what he became, I doubt Kallisa could colour his past any other shade than red. I suppose she thought it better to maintain the myth of the Cult than to crush it with the truth.'

To be made to feel hollow. Numbing. That Goddard's story had carved that hole made it a particular type of emptiness. One legend destroying another. History being rewritten. Now she felt her own body slump. Her enthusiasm escaping on a long, expired breath. Staring at her feet, she felt his hand fall on her shoulder. She sought support but his words were sharp. They cut deep.

'Don't idolise people, Sarellia. It never ends well.'

A contradiction coming to mind. Not brave enough to look into his eyes, Sarellia asked, 'And what of Petra?'

His grip tightened. Just enough to tell her it was fine to judge. He said, 'When you watch your friend die twice, see her create a city of peace and stand against nations—not even then do you idolise them. But when you understand they're all you have left of what was once good, you treasure them. That's what Petra is to me.'

'I'm sorry.'

His hand lifted from her shoulder. Felt his fingers under her chin. Her head lifted, he leaned in. Furrows and wrinkles; a wisdom of centuries. Those were his eyes. Emotional, intelligent, and tired.

'Sarellia. What you do is noble. What you will do, is unknown. But don't look back and judge the past. You live now—you treasure the moment. The days of Bruhale are over. My days are over. What is about to come may be dark. You'll face it. And you'll face it with my help. Now tell me, tell me of your Cult.'

Chapter XIV

I t was a strange end to the day. Jerune lifted his hand, raised two fingers and pointed to the table. Opposite, Bücka sat with her arms folded, lips pouting. His junior, though not by much, she was a grown-up child. Her physical prowess was clear; he understood she could kick his backside up and down Anka. An oddity hard to define, Bücka maintained a social naivety he associated with someone far younger. For all her travels and blood spilled, she appeared to be backwards. Not dumb. *Different.* As though a child had picked up swords and shown an impossible accomplishment in dealing death. Playful, cold, impatient. A domesticated wild-cat. Jerune stifled his humour, didn't want to offend the warrior. But she was opposite to Sarellia in almost every way, and that tickled him.

At the edge of Anka, they sat outside the first inn of many: *The Long Rest.* As all Anka's structures, it was a clean marble block, decorated by plant pots and baskets suspended from rooftop beams. A scattering of tables and stools bathed in the glow of dusk. A cool breeze descended from the mountains into which the city nestled; the forest shielding it from the *Falla*, the temperate wind that dusted the southern coastal plains. There was a tension in the air, palpable without Kor'A's aura to suppress it. Ironic, it was that which gave rise to the unrest. In his immediate vicinity, Jerune observed the surreptitious glances cast Bücka's way. Warriors, once unwelcome in Petra's city, were now more frequent. It wouldn't be long until there was more blood on the streets. He had already noted the stain near the tomb. No bodies, just the remnants of death, most of it washed away in the rains. Anka was changing.

His thoughts interrupted, he thanked the bar boy, a juvenile with a scraggy mop of blonde hair, and pushed one of two ales across the table.

'I don't know if you drink?' he said.

Bücka took the wooden tankard. Stared at him. 'Why did they send us away?'

'They told us why.'

Sarellia had a meeting with a contact; she couldn't allow their presence to be known. Goddard had remained with Chara in the citadel. The old king had muttered something about *stone knowing stone*; wasn't sure the tower was safe for he and Bücka. Whatever the truth, Jerune was happy where he was. Close to the forest, ale in hand.

Bücka huffed. 'I could help guard them.'

Jerune smiled. 'Goddard and the child?'

'Or the pretty woman.'

Sarellia. Keen eyes had picked up on Bücka's interest. Jerune hoped the Bruhadian only cared for his advances. She had carved a space in his desires, didn't want competition from a fierce warrior.

'You like Sarellia?' he asked.

Bücka's glance fell away. 'So?'

Jerune lifted his ale. Hops, alcohol, and a crispness to match. Best in the house, he could afford many more; Sarellia had paid him well. That had been a disappointment. He had wanted an excuse to remain close to her. The Cultist liked him, that was clear, but was he a keeper? He wouldn't presume it to be so.

'So, I like her too,' he said.

'She yours?' Bücka asked. She was clearly curious, not combative.

'I don't own people. Nobody should. Sarellia can choose her own suitor.'

Bücka nodded. Sipped the ale. Her face expressed approval.

'It's the best,' he said.

'How much do I owe you'

He smiled. 'On me.'

She leant back on her stool, her eyes tracking the modest crowd. Jerune noted how she fixated on specific individuals. It was obvious Bücka was seeking trouble. The type of trouble that might be searching for her.

'You've a bounty on you?' he asked.

Her eyes lit up. A disarming grin appeared on her face. 'Have I!'

'How many? Or, better, what's your worth?'

'I've counted five contracts across three regions.' She leaned forward, elbows on the table. 'Folks have even come from Dreyahyde.'

'Impressive. What'd you do to deserve that?'

Bücka paused. She looked down, a frown on her forehead. 'Maybe the Astran contract, or...no, could be Fennig. One of them, I guess. All of them?'

The names meant nothing. He was glad. Bücka was entertaining. He didn't want to know if she was a soulless, murdering mercenary. Some contracts were moral obligations, retribution for crimes, others were not so ethical.

'What you gonna do now?' he asked.

Bücka appeared confused by his question. 'I'm staying.'

'For?'

'I'm going to help Goddard. He's as good as family to me.'

'You're not going back to Wederhyne?'

She shook her head. 'Thelia's home now. Besides, Shang'si likes it better here.'

'Who?'

Bücka's smile threatened to split her face in two. She stood up, said, 'Leave your coin, bring your ale. I'll show you.'

'A horse?'

'Yes, a horse,' she replied.

Not far from the *Long Rest*, five minutes west, lay the stables. Anka was large, but the city wasn't built for animals. Grass didn't grow on those white streets. Along the southern perimeter, grounded on natural earth, there were numerous equine houses. Jerune noted Bücka's choice was of a higher class.

'You know your horses?' she asked.

'Like you know swords.'

Leading the way, she turned to glance at him. 'Like feet, eh?'

'I'd be a shit tracker if I couldn't follow a horse. What's yours?'

'I'll test you.'

Fair challenge. Bücka's weight had been appraised, a solid frame but nimble. She had long legs, and from her various seated postures, Jerune had noted she could straddle a meadow. Her armour was mixed-plate, that would necessitate a heavy breed.

'Do you fight horseback?' he asked.

'Never. I think it's cruel.'

Unlikely it would be a Tormelorian Grey. He had two breeds in mind, but as she led him to the stable door, he was stunned. It was neither.

'This is Shang'si,' she said.

The horse nuzzled Bücka's face. A black mare with white flecks on its flank and a clean white mane. On its face was a perfect star, not a brand; a mark of nature. An exceptional breed.

'You have a Western Star?'

Her pride obvious, Bücka tried to downplay the value of such a specimen. 'To me, she's Shang'si. The breed doesn't matter.'

'You can't buy them, Bücka.' A thought crossed his mind. Spoke it without thinking. 'You steal it?'

'No!' Her reaction was more than impulse. He recognised the tone; it was experience. He regretted his words but before he could speak, she continued, 'You think I'm a dirty mercenary, I can't afford the coin or respect to own a Western Star?'

Hands raised, an apology. 'Bücka, I'm sorry, it's...'

She cut him off. 'No, I get it. I'm poor Wederhyne trash. And no balls to boot. You know how often I have to deal with that shit? Think if I had a cock, I'd get these fucking questions? Is that it? I'm a girl? Fucking men, you're all the same.'

'Bücka...'

'Piss off. Go on.' She threw her tankard to the ground and hugged the horse's head.

Jerune stood. Impotent. Hadn't felt such redundancy in a long time. Him and his stupid mouth. He tried again to placate her fury.

'Bücka, please, I'm sorry. I didn't mean anything.'

No reply. It was better than more scathing hatred. Stooping, he picked up the tankard and thought it made a strange sound. A reverberation of wood. It hadn't come from the falling vessel. A shaft oscillating after impact. *An arrow.* He glanced up, twenty paces west, still quivering in the wooden frame of another stall door.

'Bücka!'

He launched at her and felt the impact. Sharp and deep in his back. Tumbling to the ground, on top of her, he felt the darkness creeping into his periphery. Heard her voice. Thought she was pissed he had lunged at her. What did she say?

'Jerune!'

For a slight man he was surprisingly solid. Crashing to the flagstones, she saw the arrow glinting in the amber flame of the lanterns. Idiot. Why had he taken the impact? Her armour would have shattered the damn thing. He was in soft leather. Typical bloody man. Perhaps a good man. Though, not a time to judge. Time to act.

Scrabbling to get out from under his weight, she felt the breeze as another arrow flew past. Too close. Important sign. Whoever it was, they weren't stupid. They wouldn't approach until she was dead. Free of Jerune, one glance at his wound, she hissed and rolled across the stable courtyard. Without attention, the arrow could be fatal, blood already seeping into the grids of flagstone mortar. A cart laden with bales of hay gave her immediate cover. Splintering shrapnel cracked the air as an arrow smashed apart on the ground at her feet. Straight through the spokes. This was not good. Another blast of speed and Bücka was through the door of a vacant stall. Not stopping, she leapt through the open portal at the back, landing in the grass beyond.

She knew to move. Shift position until she had eyes on the enemy. With night as cover, and the long grass swaying in the breeze, she crouched low. Flanking back, plotting the trajectory of the arrows, she stopped at a low wall bordering the stables. The archer. That was the target. She knew there could be more. On other days, she would hope for it, but with Jerune down, time was not on her side. Waiting, patience a poor ally, she struggled to see the assailant. Bücka needed to move to the open.

Breaking into a sprint, she charged across the track. Her cover was the bushes overlooking the courtyard. Ahead, a rustle in the foliage. Shadows moving faster than the breeze. Instinct raised an arm to her face and she felt the impact; her vambrace deflecting the arrow. She had seconds. Bücka charged, swords drawn, and leapt at the bush.

Falling through the dark green, she hit a moving mass. In a clatter of darkness, she rose to her feet. A quick glance to the surrounds, she spied just one figure. *Nobody else?* No time for questions, she launched at the shape but her foe pulled away leaving Bücka flailing at the air. The sound of a sword emerging from a scabbard was followed by steel upon steel. The assassin was goading her, trying to lure her to the trail but Bücka knew the undergrowth gave good cover. Out there, she was vulnerable to other enemies. Her turn to taunt the assassin, Bücka's blades tapping together. But no reply came her way. The shape opened up; arms spread to the side. *She was to attack*. No, Bücka wasn't so naïve, she'd not fall into the trap.

Another tactic. In one movement, she dropped low, released the Larian rapier and snatched the dagger from her boot. In that instant, she saw the bow close by, discarded and harmless. Bücka rose, flicking her wrist and sending the dagger to the enemy. The sound was clear; a puncture of flesh, a gasp of breath. Now to attack, but reaching down for her rapier, she fumbled, clumsy hands at the wrong moment. Straightening up and raising her guard, Bücka stared into the darkness where her foe should have been. Nothing there but shadows in the gloom; the bastard had fled. She thought to give chase but recalled something more pressing. *Jerune!* Stooping to retrieve the bow, she charged back to the stables, scanning all quarters for the assassin or his accomplices. With no threat in sight, and her heart pounding, Bücka reached the scout.

The blood had not spread farther—a good sign. The shaft of the arrow likely stemming the flow. She could help him, but she needed somewhere safe. A place nobody would dare assault. Looking up, it was obvious. Amber and blue in the light of the moons, the citadel beckoned. A wise King would shelter his friends. Releasing the latch to Shang'si's stall, Bücka placed Jerune across the mare's flank and threw her kit bags alongside.

'You stupid man,' she said. And though she meant it, she understood his heart was good.

Chapter XV

It was difficult to gauge time. The citadel courtyard was bathed in a gentle glow, yet the sky above appeared as a dark orb. A trick of the light, a contrast created by Kor'A's elemental magic. Seated on the marble stones, Goddard marvelled at the spectacle. It had been many years since he had gazed up at the dizzying funnel. The light emanating from stone was an impossibility that defied nature. But this was not nature; this was Kor'A's living skin. As was all of Anka. The city's otherworldly radiance kept an uneasy peace. That glow; the reminder that the city was more than cold stone. If the light ever dimmed, he knew what would follow. There was an uncomfortable truth to the place. The design bereft of a human touch, empty of empathy. Patting the stone block upon which he sat, he quizzed Chara who was sitting patiently by his side.

'When you slept, where was it?'

'Anywhere.'

She wasn't a dog. He couldn't imagine Chara simply lying down on stone. 'No, I mean, you have a room, or a bed?'

She shook her head. Smiled.

Pointing to the ground, he said, 'Would you sleep there?'

'Do you want me to?'

'No, but when Kor'A was with you, would you?'

Chara appeared hesitant to answer. A first sign of non-compliance.

'Chara, what is it?'

'Mother would say sleep. She knew when the cycle was ending.'

'Sunset?'

'Yes. The light cycle. A day.'

She had evaded the question but he sought the answer. 'And you would sleep, anywhere?'

She shook her head. 'I don't remember.'

He again peered up at the sky. So dark against the glow. Something wasn't right.

'Wait here, Chara. I'll return in just a moment.'

Returning to form, she nodded.

The sky was too dark. The day had been long. Sunset was past; it had to be. Yet Chara was awake. She had said Kor'A would send her to sleep. Without sight of the sunset did her body-clock trigger a reaction? He had thought it was an instinct. Instead, he felt a growing unease her behaviour was a neurosis. A thing she was compelled to obey, not a mechanism she was bound to follow. At the great archway the night sky revealed itself. Ambyr and Noctyrne settled high above, though invisible from Chara's eyes. He sighed and returned to the child. Goddard had no wish to mislead Chara but he needed to know.

Strolling toward her, he felt a sense of guilt; Chara beaming at his approach. He had thought to expose the truth of Kor'A's false sleep, tell Chara her slumber was a fraud. It seemed so harsh; to remind the child she was far from human. Instead, he would observe her reaction to an innocent lie. Sitting beside her, he pointed to the sky.

'The sun is setting. You should sleep.'

'Oh, I did think it was dark.'

As though a dog, she curled up on the slab, nestled in beside him and shut her eyes. Then opened them. Kor'A's nocturnal lie.

He placed a hand on her shoulder, then looked to the entrance of the courtyard A sound coming to his ears; a strange noise for Anka at night. A horse. Reaching for Bruch'ail, he moved to the archway, curious as to who would approach the forbidden ground of Kor'A's domain.

It was Bücka on a magnificent Western Star. A large shape slung behind her. A worrying expression cast upon her face. Distress or fear, he could not tell, Goddard strode toward her. Holding out Bruch'ail, he pointed to the tomb; he didn't want her to disturb Chara. Bücka turned direction, did as she was told. He came to her side as she dismounted, a bow clutched in her hands. Goddard was shocked to see Jerune slumped over the horse's back.

'What happened?' he asked.

'Ambushed at the stables. Arrow's in his back.' She paused and appeared agitated. 'The bastards fled but I got one good.'

Goddard nodded and plucked the scout from the horse. He moved into the arch of the tomb and sat Jerune down, mindful of the arrow. Bücka approached, her eyes darting around.

'We pull it out?' she asked.

Years of war were a medic's best mentor. Baza'rad and Argan had known their fair share. The arrow was too high for his lungs but to pull it out would be dangerous. A barbed head would do more harm. It had to go through.

'Get some padding. And a belt.'

As Bücka rummaged in her bags, he held his fingers on the shaft of the arrow. A glance at the scout to see he was oblivious to all. With a growl of apology, Goddard pushed the arrow through. The tip emerged, a shaped metal cone, the same diameter as the shaft. A rare design, specific for plate, good news for Jerune. Goddard snapped off the flights before removing the projectile from his chest. As Bücka came to his side, he held it to her face.

'For you?'

She squinted. 'Larian plate arrow?'

A shrug. Goddard hadn't fought Larians. But the business end was intended to pierce metal. 'You wouldn't shoot this at leather. Waste of good steel. It's designed for plate.' He tapped it against her breastplate. 'Like yours.'

Bücka ripped open Jerune's shirt, padded the two wounds. 'Hold him,' she said, moving to wrap the strap around his torso. 'The blood's good. He's lucky.' She looked around, asked, 'Where's the child?'

'Sleeping. But I should return. I'll take Jerune.' Goddard had supplies in the citadel. Herbs he could use. 'Keep an eye out for Sarellia, she'll be returning soon.'

Bücka nodded as he stood with Jerune held in his arms.

'Show me that bow,' he said.

Holding it out for inspection, she asked, 'You recognise it?'

He didn't but it appeared well-crafted. A recurve bow with an exceptional build. In the night it appeared as though a snake. He shook his head, thought of the Cultist. 'I'm sure Sarellia will know. I'll take him inside, see that he's comfortable. Stay at the main gate. Come back when Sarellia arrives.'

Bücka nodded and moved to the gate. Watching her go, Goddard presumed she had been the intended target. Why else use such an arrow? Certainly not a bandit's weapon. A professional mercenary, no doubts. A contract of retribution? There was another possibility, something more pertinent to the moment. But Sarellia could confirm that. Though, he hoped she would not.

The clatter of footfall came fast. Goddard rose, Jerune propped against the inner wall. Chara lay undisturbed in the centre. He didn't want her to wake. In time she would see suffering. Better to keep it at bay. Predicting the reaction from Sarellia, he held out his hand to her, a warning finger to his lips. Arriving with Bücka behind, the Cultist shrieked; the squeal stifled by her own hand.

She knelt beside Jerune. Took his hand in hers. She looked to Goddard, her eyes wild with panic. 'What happened?'

'An ambush. For Bücka, I think.' He nodded as Bücka approached. 'It's a clean wound, he'll recover. The arrow was for armour, not flesh.'

Goddard watched as Sarellia fussed. Her fingers raised to stroke Jerune's cheek, quickly returning back to his hand. He noted how her affection was troubled by anxiety; it reminded him of long-lost souls. He had never courted after Bruhale. Losing a Queen was one death, his daughter, the second. A pain worse than a blade through flesh, or hammer smashing bone. He had persuaded himself it was better to be alone than to suffer such loss again.

'*Jerune!*' Sarellia said.

His attention piqued, Goddard knelt down to join her. The scout's eyes flickering open. His pale face smiled.

'That hurt,' he said, then grimaced. 'That too. And that.'

Sarellia said, 'So stop talking you damn idiot.'

Jerune nodded, his eyes tracking to Bücka. Discomfort etched on his face, Jerune asked, 'You got them?'

The warrior paused. Goddard sensing the moment, he imagined she considered her actions to be a failure, perhaps something of which she had little experience. He said to Jerune, 'She brought you back here. Saved your life.'

'He took the arrow,' Bücka said. Then, with a softer tone, added, 'Damn fool.'

'Idiot,' Sarellia whispered to Jerune.

Goddard sought to avoid the drama. Standing, he held the bow to the Cultist. 'Do you know this design?'

She took it, turned it over in her hands. Looking at Jerune, she said, 'The arrow came from this?'

Bücka replied, 'I took it from an assassin in the bushes near where we were ambushed. I bled him but he fled.'

Goddard felt Sarellia's eyes upon him. 'What?'

'The arrow?'

He pointed to a pile of bloodied rags. The arrow lay beside them. Sarellia picked it up, handled it as though it were made of gold.

'Important?' he asked.

Her voice, distant, she replied, 'No. Not important. Terrible.' She rose to face him. 'The bow is a Fire-song. Larian, after it fell to flame. The arrow is rare. We've seen only a few on our shores.'

Bücka asked, 'Why attack me?'

Sarellia turned to the warrior, Goddard noting the change in her poise. The rich city Cultist discarding her pretence. He was reminded of Kallisa: courtier, spy, and Cult strategist. A fearsome and brave woman.

She paced to Bücka, Sarellia's posture of confrontation met by the warrior's indifference.

'You've done something,' Sarellia said. 'Or seen something.'

Bücka, unfazed, replied, 'I'm just a warrior. A mercenary to some.'

'But you've taken a contract on Larian soil, haven't you?'

'One.'

Sarellia pressed. 'Where?'

Goddard watched as Bücka hesitated. What had she done? He raised his head, spoke to the soldier, not the mercenary. 'Bücka. Answer.'

'The furnace. The Larian Forge. I fulfilled a contract to... recover something.'

Sarellia's voice was a hiss. 'What did you steal? What was it that brought them here?'

Bücka's expression shifted and from her fugue she found a smile. She said, 'I can show you.'

She watched. Still as a pebble. Earth was all around but she was not here. Goddard fussed over the scout; fabric removed from within his clothing. What was white had become dark. It was how they deconstructed—blood—they called it. Chara had none. In her days since finding Goddard, she had observed his flesh. Soft, yielding; unlike her own surface. He had been polite, kind, called it skin. She knew he had done so to make her feel more *human*. A gesture not lost on her gratitude. Kor'A had spoken of the humans, of how they had friends. Goddard was a friend, a thing to trust. Chara never pried but mother had inferred Goddard's uniqueness. Stone knew stone, though nothing more had been said of it. Chara called it *the silence*, to be as quiet as a stone—for a stone had no words to tell. That silence was a fragment of dust scouring inside her mind. Watching, admiring Goddard tend to the fallen, Chara wanted to speak of everything she knew. The secrets of stone; reflections inside glass.

Her thoughts fractured as the two females returned, dark and light. People were as though rocks, different shapes, colours, and sizes. Mother had not explained why she was onyx, why not marble, as she? Petra, the beautiful Queen, was white as the citadel walls. But all was stone. Were humans the same? Did their differences matter, or did they create function? Goddard and Sarellia were dark—she thought that might make the woman a warrior. Though she was not. Bücka was, though her colour was subtle. Jerune was light, a scout. A poor decision to be light, she thought, harder to blend in with shadows. It confused her; why be a colour that could hinder his task? She could do better. It was a puzzle; it appeared their colour spoke nothing of their ability.

Watching without sound, she observed Sarellia react to the scout with a different expression. Human faces—Chara found them to be a strange language. This reaction she saw was not happiness. She imagined a chasm in a mountain; a void pulled apart. That was what she felt watching as Sarellia touched the scout. Goddard rose and showed the bow to the woman. Chara knew it to be a bow as Goddard had kept one in his hut. A thing to send arrows at speed. He had said it was used for hunting to gather food. Was he asking Sarellia to get food? No, she did not leave, she reacted in a strange manner.

Sarellia had altered her structure. As though she had become a pillar, tall and solid. She spoke to Bücka whose expression was difficult to understand. But then she smiled and moved away from the others. Goddard and Sarellia faced each other, pointing at Jerune still sitting against the wall. Chara wondered if he had stopped deconstructing. Imagined he had, otherwise, surely something would fall apart.

All the while, Chara trying not to see it, the hammer lay close beside Goddard. Bruch'ail, he called it. She did not know what that meant. Her silence forbade her to ask. Though she knew it was not a weapon made by mortal hands. There was an energy beneath the strange metallic surface; an aura of something more. And that aura was not the same as her mother's—it was more vibrant, more powerful. It was why she feared it. Surely Goddard didn't know. It was why she closed her eyes when the hammer was swung. What could be more powerful than Earth? It reminded her of when she had asked her mother; *who created you?* Her mother had smiled without answer. Though that smile was a chasm across the earth. Confused by Kor'A's silence, she had persevered; *Don't you have a mother?* And her mother had looked to the dark sky, pointing to the moons of Noctyrne and Ambyr. *We all have mothers, Chara*, she had said. *And mine is crueller than all.*

Chapter XVI

They were whispering. The King and Sarellia. His thick rumble mingling with her velvet voice. A stream flowing around boulders. It was surreal. Jerune wasn't sure if the pain was numbing his senses or if the herbs Goddard had applied to his skin were altering his consciousness. Abstract thoughts detached from his body. He knew the sensation; the forest was a bounty of hallucinogens and stimulants. A scout needed to understand the flora. He had an *interest* in the chemicals, dabbling enough to understand the effects. Medicinal or otherwise, Jerune appreciated natures gifts. So too, it appeared, did Goddard. His hand on the padding, Jerune pressed the wound. It throbbed but he had known worse injury. He'd suffered greater ills. Not wishing to sit around, useless as an unstrung bow, he rose to his feet. One hand on the wall to steady himself, he was content his movements did not alert the whispering duo. How close could he get?

Facing away, King and Cultist looking to the tomb. There, Bücka's hands in her horse's rear. His vision was hazy. *Saddlebags.* Bloody saddlebags. She wasn't pulling things from the horse's arse. Shang'si, the Western Star. Recalling the stables, he thought of the tankard thrown down in Bücka's huff. Had he not caused offence; he may not have had the chance to save her. Jerune laughed, foiling his stealth.

Sarellia turned. 'Jerune?' She came to him, hands on his body. It was pleasant. 'Why are you up? And why're you laughing?'

His finger waving at Goddard, he replied, 'Rude. Whispering.'

Goddard frowned. 'Not for your ears.'

Cupping his own, Jerune said, 'What?'

'You're a fool,' Sarellia said.

'I'm a high fool. My King, what herbs did you apply?'

'Yverelyn.' A grumble. 'I'm not your King.'

Yverelyn. That explained it; a most versatile extract. Known commonly as Ambyr Dust. A potent narcotic. Explained why his muscles were loose and fluid. He smiled; tried not to giggle. 'Thank you.'

Sarellia fussed, her worried touch persuading him to sit. 'You need rest.'

He found her hands, so soft, held them with authority. Looking into her eyes, he felt a rush of desire. And though it was real, he knew the Ambyr Dust was amplifying his emotions. He didn't care. Pressed his lips to hers. Expecting a slap, he was exhilarated when Sarellia reciprocated his touch. Pulling his lips away, too soon but aware of the moment he said, 'I'm glad I didn't die.'

She smiled. 'As am I.'

'Touching,' Goddard said. A flat dismissal of their moment in his tone.

A cheap interruption but nothing could spoil the moment. His vision beginning to stabilise, probably from the rush of blood in his veins, Jerune noticed Bücka returning. Not wishing for her to see the embrace, he pulled away from Sarellia. She glared at him, a silent question.

Nodding to Bücka, he whispered to Sarellia, 'I'm not your only admirer.'

She frowned. Then, glancing at Bücka, said, 'Oh! I see.'

'Should I worry?'

To his horror, Sarellia shrugged. It was clear she saw his reaction. Grinning, she said, 'Don't give me a reason to make you worry.'

'Yes, Ma'am.'

Goddard's voice broke their play. 'Bücka, what is that?'

Jerune looked to the warrior. In her hand she carried a silver sphere. Similar in size to a cannonball. As she approached, he saw the object more clearly, illuminated by the citadel walls. Not silver, it was glass or quartz.

Bücka, seemingly unimpressed, holding the object to her face, said, 'This is what I retrieved from near the Larian Forge. Well, somebody else handled it, I was to bring it to the contact.'

Sarellia's demeanour changed. Jerune was sad to see it; passion giving way to something more pressing. She moved to Bücka, reached for the sphere. 'May I?'

Bücka nodded, relinquished her grip. 'You know what it is?' she asked.

'You don't?' Sarellia replied. 'Why didn't you give it to your contact?'

A shrug from the mercenary. 'He was dead. I didn't get paid, so I kept that as a memento.' Bücka smiled, a frown to accompany her grin. 'Why? You look troubled.'

Sarellia turned to Goddard, her expression pained. 'You know this?'

He shook his head. 'I've seen similar. Not as small.'

Confused and pained, the effect of the herbs diminishing, Jerune leant against the wall. 'What is it?'

Sarellia didn't reply, she squinted at the sphere, holding it close to her face. She growled, moved the orb closer to the wall, presumably for more light. Jerune startled as she let out a huge sigh. Her features relaxing, Jerune sensed something terrible had been avoided.

She said, 'It's empty.'

'Of?' he asked.

'Fire. It's the shell of a Seed of Fire.'

Goddard said, 'This is what you spoke of at Petra's fort?'

Sarellia nodded. 'Yes. Inside, she places a seed of her essence.'

'Does it work like the Fury?' Goddard asked.

'Not from what I know. It doesn't attack flesh; it's not malevolent like the weapons of the Wind.'

'I don't understand. What then?'

Jerune watched as Sarellia hesitated. She shook her head. 'You've not seen Laria since the fall, have you?'

Goddard shook his head but Bücka came forward.

'I have,' she said.

'The Plains of Desolation? You saw them?' Sarellia asked.

Bücka nodded. Pursed her lips. 'It's a volcanic region. Isn't it?'

'No,' Sarellia said. She placed a hand to her bosom. 'My name comes from Laria. Old Laria. I was named for the Sarellian Plains. A place dear to Petra.'

Bücka shook her head. 'Not familiar.'

'But you are. They became the Plains of Desolation when the Seer attacked.' Sarellia held the sphere for all to see. 'Legend says he released many of these. They opened huge chasms in the earth, brought Fire to the surface.' Turning to Goddard, she said, 'A Fury pales in comparison.'

It appeared so innocuous. A pretty ball of quartz, not smooth but with hundreds of facets. Jerune imagined in the light it would look magnificent. His mind tracked back to the stables: the arrow, the bow, was this to do with that assassin?

'I took an arrow for that?'

Sarellia turned to Bücka. 'No. I think *she* was sought for her knowledge. Or, to erase it. You know where it is, don't you? The Forge in Laria?'

Bücka nodded.

Jerune sensed the moment turn. He felt a cold wave of reality wash over him. An intense chill. Sobering, robbing him of the last joys of the Yverelyn.

Sarellia said, 'This is good fortune. We can't let them bring these to our shores. This is what we feared for so long. Once here, not even Petra could help. With those, the Seer could destroy all of us. There's only one way to stop that from happening.'

'But it's empty,' Jerune said.

Sarellia stared, promptly turned to Bücka. 'You were to retrieve an active weapon?'

Bücka shrugged. Pointed at the sphere. 'I was told to get that.'

'Yes,' Sarellia replied, 'fortunate for you it was an impotent seed.'

Goddard spoke. 'And if not impotent?'

'As I said,' Sarellia replied, 'we have no defence should they reach our shores.'

The King frowned. 'You believe they're bringing more? The Cult have this knowledge?'

Sarellia nodded. Her face animating with a myriad of emotions. Jerune thought it impossible she could look more beautiful. Sarellia was striking; perfection found in all the masks she wore. Her gaze fixed on the King, Jerune felt compelled to wait on his response. Goddard's face crumpled in thought. Jerune understood a tormented mind. He feared what the legend might say next.

Goddard sighed. 'We need to find that Forge. Destroy it.'

Jerune tried to speak. Events had moved with frightening pace. He wanted to arrest the conversation. Instead, Sarellia's soothing voice said a terrible thing.

'We need to go to Fire. We must go to Laria.'

In the entrance to the citadel, the companions sat as though children scolded by parents. Jerune, for his part, was happy to have Sarellia by his side. Opposite him, Goddard and Bücka were a fine contrast of size. Chara slept undisturbed within the courtyard. Goddard had expressed his wish that she not be privy to their plans. Such plans could be grave. Jerune recalled that prior to the attack at the stables, he had been politely dismissed from the Citadel; now, he and Bücka were most welcome. Grave plans indeed that required both scout and mercenary. Sarellia had told them of her contact's reconnaissance. There was no word of Pitbombs or Fire-seeds. None had come from Laria. *Not yet*, they had said. It was probable they would come with the fleet. And those ships were far from ready to sail. Time was on their side, but only if they moved with speed. A ludicrous plan had been devised. At the very least, reckless. At best...

'It's suicide,' Jerune said.

Goddard nodded. It wasn't the response Jerune wanted to see.

Sarellia repeated her plan. 'We don't have time to organise the numbers to assault the Forge. We'd need months to amass those allies. And even then, who would stand against the Seer? We need to strike as a single arrow, not a volley of cannon fire.'

'I'll not risk Chara,' Goddard said. Jerune noted he would not raise his eyes. The old King appeared aggrieved at his situation. 'I can't go to Laria.'

'We'll protect her,' Sarellia said. 'Won't we, Jerune.'

It was the safest way. Goddard and Bücka, a lightning strike against the Forge. Bücka knew the way, and Goddard was invincible. He nodded, agreeing with Sarellia. 'She'll be safe with us.'

But Goddard was adamant. 'No. She is my ward.' He brought his eyes to meet Jerune's. A nod before turning his attention to his Bruhadian kin. 'You must know why, Sarellia. You know my line. My ancestry—those rites. I am bound to protect Chara.'

Jerune wanted to suggest to take the girl with them. Couldn't understand why an Elemental's child could not face a human foe. But there was something he had not been told. In the two days he had been in their company, the girl of onyx had appeared as fragile as glass. At least, that was how he had observed Goddard's focus around her. Careful, considered. This very day the King had warned them, his tone sincere and concerned. It was clear he feared for her. But why?

'I'll still go,' Bücka said. 'I know where it is.'

'That won't be enough,' Sarellia said. 'Our spies have told us the Forge is well guarded; But Goddard would be the battering ram. No man can stand against him, not with Bruch'ail in his hands. Without that power, Bücka, you'd not get past.'

Jerune thought of an alternative. A standard observation for a scout. 'Nothing is built with one entrance. It's got to have a weak spot? A back door.'

Goddard grumbled. It was a gentle laugh.

'What?' Jerune asked.

The King pointed to the single entrance to the citadel, then back to the enclosed courtyard. 'This has only one way in and out.'

'Fair point.' He turned to Sarellia. 'The Forge though, built by human hands?'

She shrugged. 'I don't know. Etherus in Kalleron was.'

Gesturing to the walls, Jerune said, 'Elementals can't build shit. Humans have need of multiple access points. It's a forge, sure. But what powers it? Who works the mechanics? Who transports the goods? Because I doubt an Elemental lord would do the manual graft.'

Sarellia said, 'I can find out. In a few days another spy will return. They're landing at Port Aracyse in Wederhyne. They had contacts within the place, they should know.' She sighed. 'I still don't see how that helps us if Goddard isn't there.'

'It's nice to feel important,' Bücka said, a hyperbolic sigh puffed from her lips.

'It's not like that, Bücka,' Sarellia said.

Goddard shuffled. It was clear he was uncomfortable with his recusal. 'I wish I could. I'd bring the whole thing down.'

'You can lend me the hammer,' Bücka smiled.

'You can take the strapping,' Goddard joked.

Watching it, the camaraderie between warriors, Jerune felt helpless. He could survive a barfight. Maybe defend with a knife. With a bow he was a sure shot, but bows were useless in a melee. A thought occurred to him. A stupid idea.

'I'll go.'

The warriors stared at him.

Sarellia took his hands. 'No.'

'I can figure out the best way in.'

She protested. 'You've not even seen it.'

'Your spy will tell us what we need to know.'

Goddard spoke, his tone cautious. 'Can you fight?'

'That's what Bücka's for. I sneak, she fights when that fails.'

Across the space, Bücka grinned. It warmed his soul to see the acceptance in her eyes. Hoped his clumsy words at the stables were forgiven. But Sarellia wasn't pleased; her agitation palpable.

'You're not like them, Jerune. What if you... what if...'

He turned to her, placed a hand on her arm. 'I'll come back. Bücka owes me a drink.'

She stared. One look and he knew what was happening between them was not a throwaway moment. For an instant, he regretted his decision. Sarellia was a rare woman, a princess beyond his reach. But across from him sat the greatest living legend of all time. A week ago, Jerune had thought him a myth. The next day, he had stood with Sarellia, watching the King speak with the Queen of Stone. His world was changing. Jerune didn't believe in fate; a fickle human nonsense. But this *was* fate. A simple woodsman embroiled in a moment of history.

No words of comfort came from Sarellia. Just her anxious eyes and a shallow nod. She squeezed his hands, hard. It was as though she was saying goodbye. Lost in her beauty, Jerune was brought back to the present by Goddard's voice.

'Well, we can discuss this tomorrow. Bücka and I will guard Chara tonight.' He waved a finger at he and Sarellia. 'You two should go somewhere. I'm feeling queasy.'

Bücka laughed and Sarellia snapped out of her sadness. She stood and Jerune followed, his hands still encased within hers.

'Where we going?' he asked.

She smiled, 'The contract isn't fulfilled. We need to sign it off.'

He *had* been paid. His frown must have pleased Sarellia; she laughed and winked.

'Oh!' Jerune said. 'My bonus.'

Chapter XVII

'It's strange,' Bücka said, gazing at Chara asleep on the marble block. 'You said she doesn't listen?'

Goddard shook his head. Chara hadn't moved an inch. An effigy of a sleeping child, carved in onyx.

He replied, 'She said it was rude to listen.'

Bücka knelt closer to Chara. Goddard observed, wondered if the child would fidget with the warrior's gaze so close, so intense. But Chara did not stir.

'But she's watching us?' Bücka asked. 'While she sleeps? How can that be?' Bücka frowned, turned to Goddard. 'I don't mean to be rude, it's just I've never met a creature that...'

'A girl,' Goddard interrupted. 'She's a girl.'

Bücka nodded. Though, he didn't think she fully grasped his meaning.

'You called her a creature. Is that how you see her?' he asked.

'I don't know,' Bücka replied, a frown appearing on her brow. 'Isn't she? A creature, I mean?'

'As opposed to a human?' Goddard asked.

The warrior's discomfort was clear. Her fidgeting and hesitation spoke of her reluctance to counter Goddard's words. Bücka sighed and said, 'But... she's not really human, is she?'

Perhaps he expected too much from the warrior. So young, so naïve to the strange world to which he belonged. He had witnessed Petra's resurrection. Tended to her as she turned. Knew her flesh had gone, transformed into immortal stone. But it never replaced the woman. Had not diminished her nature. Yet Chara was the opposite; something created to mimic a human; a choice not of her own choosing. And from his brief time with her, Goddard found it impossible to think of Chara as anything but a wonderful little girl.

He said, 'Chara knows she's not human. But Kor'A can't create flesh. Yet she did create a child.' Goddard nodded to Chara. 'What do you see? Creature, or child?'

Bücka's eyes widened. 'Oh... I see a child.'

Goddard nodded. 'Yes, Chara is a daughter to Kor'A. A copy of what she has seen. What she sees us to be.' He waved a hand to the sleeping wonder. 'She knows this, Chara understands what she is. She understands she's a copy of a girl but it doesn't diminish her status; what it is she was created to be. What she believes herself to be.'

'As human as you or I?' Bücka said.

Chara's unnatural sleep was recognisably more human than his own slumber. She feared violence, was all too aware of death. Curious of the world and things he took for granted, in contrast to his ways, she was more human than he. Goddard nodded and said, 'More human than most.'

Bücka grinned. 'Did you see her when she was little?' She giggled, pinched her thumb and forefinger together. 'Was she a pebble?'

'From what she says, she's always been this size. I think near to three decades.'

'So strange.'

It was. But Chara's uniqueness had grown on him with every passing day. He imagined life would be a dull shadow without her hopping along by his side. Though, he feared what might happen if her days overtook his own. Perhaps Bücka could take on that mantle if Petra would not. Not the thoughts to have for now. Something else required discussion, a detail that had not escaped Goddard's attention.

Pointing to her swords, he asked, 'Your blades. Trophies? Heirlooms?'

Bücka patted her weapons. She sighed. 'I thought you'd ask. You want to know about the Bruhadian steel?'

It had caught his eye. Old, from Bruhale in better days. He nodded, made sure to express curiosity, not suspicion.

'Well, I took a contract in Bruhada.' Bücka held out her hands. 'Don't worry, not one of yours. But while I was there, I came across an old market. I'd been paid, didn't really need the coin—I'm good at what I do. I make a lot. But I don't need much stuff. Got my horse, had the other blade.' She unsheathed the sword, passed it to him. 'I saw this and the crafting spoke to me; I'd never seen a blade like this before. It's magnificent.'

It was. All royal weapons were. To Bücka, he assumed it was a sword. The Royal Guard used them as daggers. A heavy and double-edged blade which tapered at the tip to a piercing point. The Drohendrian handle was inlaid with cubes of marble, the pommel a rounded sphere of steel. Passing it from hand to hand, he smiled. Memories of old times. Before Te'anor had come to destroy his world. The golden city came alive in his thoughts. The Palace, the bridge, the streets below; so many arches over rivers of shiny cobbles.

A sigh, uninvited, passed his lips. He held the tip of the blade, passed it to Bücka. She took the handle but he held onto it tight. She frowned. He didn't want to ask yet he had to know. Connected to Bücka by the dagger, he asked, 'Bruhale. What's left?'

Bücka's eyes fell away. His fingers relinquished the grip. Let it go. Let it all go.

Looking up, she said, 'You can see it, I think. What it once was. Like an old painting. There's strength in the beauty, you know? Behind what Kalleron spoiled you can almost taste the grandeur.'

Goddard realised Bücka was too young to appreciate the true beauty of Bruhale; what it was to walk its colourful streets, tree-lined avenues and golden lanterns. Apart from Petra, there was nobody else alive that had experienced its glory before the fall. He wanted to ask Bücka of the Palace, the Great Library, and the Halls of the Kings. But he was certain they would have been desecrated by Kalleron. Wondered if they had found the *Pillars of Bruch'alma*; the Rock of Kings. What would they have done to it? Would they even understand it? Probably not, more likely in pieces. For the best. This curse of his lost in time.

Bücka said something. Hadn't heard it, his thoughts lost in memories of stone.

'What?' he asked.

'You've never been back?'

Not once. He shook his head.

'Not even after you killed Kalle at Stranghame? You killed the King of Kalleron, destroyed the myth forever. You could've taken the war to them.'

Her enthusiasm was childish. Not something to scorn or reject. But it lacked comprehension of conflict. How dreadful war between nations could be. Bruhada, undefeated in battle, unprovoked for decades. Decimated by the inevitability of Kor'A when she had been Kalle's pawn. Kalleron had taken Bruhale, raped her soul. Tarnished by such grotesque hands, the golden city could never be restored. He imagined those streets. Those eyes that might ask, *why did you leave?* To stay, to defy the Elemental power of Kor'A, would have condemned them all to death. That fate had befallen Arkallon; the capital, proud Arkalla, crumbled to dust. Baza'rad had blood on his hands. Guilt within his soul. A kingdom could not be resurrected on such foundations. Kalleron won the war the day Baza'rad defied the King. How to tell a child? How to tell the eager warrior some battles were lost before they had begun?

'Kingdoms don't last forever, Bücka. Nothing does. You can only move forward with what you have. You can't reclaim the past. Those that do—and I've seen them—they wear the ghosts of memory. I won't be haunted by that.'

Bücka nodded. 'I think I understand.'

She fell silent, hung her head. Bücka was an enigma of sorts; this fresh-faced mercenary whose age he found hard to judge. A seasoned and skilled warrior, that much he could tell from her poise and armour. Goddard had seen the frauds. Braggards with virgin blades, not a single bite of bone etched upon their edges. Bücka was different, she was battle-hardened. A fighter who spoke her confidence in silence.

He asked, 'How many contracts have you carried out?'

Her brow creased, she looked at her fingers, shook her head. 'Lots. I stopped counting when I ran out of fingers and toes.'

'All bounties?'

A nod. 'I know what you're asking. I'm waist deep in other people's blood. But I made a promise to Thelia. I never take a bad bounty.'

'Ever taken a bad hit?' He was curious. She presented no signs of injury. Finger tips all in place, walked with grace. Even her skin, where visible: upper arms, neck, around her knees—not a single scar.

But Bücka nodded. Appeared unhappy with herself. She stood, fiddled with the buckles that sealed her chest plate. Lifting it above her head, she placed it down with care. Lifting her soft leather tunic, without shame she showed him the scar. It was impressive, a long gash running from navel to left breast. He ushered her to lower her vest.

She paced back, sat down and patted the metal chest plate. 'I started wearing plate afterwards. It was a lucky shot but it cut deep. As much as it was bad fortune, someone smiled on me that day. Lost a lot of blood, but I didn't die.'

Goddard smiled. 'Clearly.'

She leant forward, elbows on knees. 'What about you?'

Scars. He had many, though none were visible. His body healed better than most, the benefit of the curse of kings. His wounds were carried in his memories. All those faces of allies lost in battle; family, lost to Kalleron; and those dear friends, taken by age as he soldiered on. He shrugged.

'Got a few.' He tapped his temple. 'But up here is where the worse ones are.'

'You got hit on the head?'

'No, I...' He started to explain when Bücka smiled.

'I *know* what you mean.' Her grin faltered. 'I see them too.' She looked over her shoulder, thumbed in the direction of the tomb. 'Did you see the blood outside?'

He had. Figured some small skirmish had occurred. Feared it to be the first of many with Kor'A gone.

'That you?' he asked.

She nodded. 'A contract on me. One ran, I killed three. But the last, I offered mercy. Wouldn't take it. I'd already cut down his cousin. Said someone had to die.' Bücka paused and Goddard saw it. The regret. The necessity of her path—their path.

He said, 'Bücka, people like you and me, we pay our dues with the pain we carry forward. I've never met a true warrior untroubled by their actions. Some hide it. Bury it so deep it appears they've no heart. But it shows in other ways.'

'Thelia once told me something. A thing Shadow had said. You remember him?'

She didn't have to ask. Larger than life, a joker until the end. Shadow was the rock upon which Petra had built her sanity. It was his passing that inflicted her greatest heartache, even more than Felicitra's death. But he was also a murderous man. Goddard knew Shadow harboured a darker secret, one buried when he became part of Petra's crew. A secret exposed one fateful day on *The Melody*. He wondered what Thelia had said to Bücka. What bleak truths had she learned?

'I remember him well,' he said with a smile.

'Gran was destroyed when he died. I could see it when she spoke of him. But one thing he said, she recalled. A strange thing.' Bücka's expression faltered as though she tasted something unpleasant. 'He'd said: every life you take, the face stays with you. The only way to get rid of it is to kill someone else. Keep the ghosts away by feeding them more.'

They were words Goddard could easily imagine Shadow speaking. But he didn't want to trouble Bücka with such truth. He said, 'I'm sure that was said in jest.'

She replied with an unconvincing smile. 'Yeah.'

Goddard craned his neck, peering to the stars above. The early hours. He required little rest. Bücka would need more.

He said, 'You should sleep.'

'Here? Am I allowed?'

'The marble's not the most comfortable but you're more than welcome.'

A smile to accept and Bücka said, 'I'll get my things.'

Bücka stood and moved to the outer courtyard, presumably to Shang'si. Goddard hoped she knew not to bring the horse inside. It didn't seem right. He looked at Chara, moved to where she slept. Placing a hand on her shoulder he sat down. He wished Petra had come back with them. There was no other person he could trust to keep her safe. With Petra restored to Anka, he could travel to the Forge; he could wreak havoc with the Seer's plans. Bruch'ail would swing to the glory of the Northern Lands and keep this world safe. Protect Chara from harm.

'Keep you safe,' he said, stroking her glass shoulder.

He thought she might stir but Chara remained at peace. Her eyes blinked. The glory of battle would wait. For now, his place was by her side. *She needed him.* And as the thought spun in his mind, he smiled, heartened by it. Bücka has spoken of old Bruhada, of thrones to regain. But only one thing mattered now, one purpose restored to his old life. When once there were thousands to protect, now there was one. Chara was the last kingdom for which he would go to war.

Chapter XVIII

It was a strange place. Jerune, lost in thought, was staring at the wall. The same as the other walls. All gave off the same blue glow; a gentle aura emanating from the stone. The sun was rising and through the open window the colours mingled as though fire dancing on crystal water. He had thought that Sarellia, the city-girl, would have an opulent mansion and although his time in the city was extensive, he had never considered the jarring uniformity. *There were no mansions*, nor were there hovels. One hundred years ago, Kor'A had created a city of equals. There were deviations in form and size but nothing that could be considered regal or ramshackle. Only her citadel stood above it all.

Sarellia's bedroom was neat and tidy. Wooden beams that spanned floor to ceiling provided the anchor for hanging tapestries and paintings. Anka had been ingenuous with its décor. Nothing could be nailed into the stone. It was impervious to harm. Jerune, still sprawled on the bed, reached out and touched the wall. The skin of an Elemental. A shiver ran the length of his spine. He smiled. It was beyond a miracle yet what had followed—the human touch—was equally impressive. Timbers brought from the forests and cut to precise size had been hammered into positions to create frames and interior skeletons upon which to build. Life had crept into the place, created a community and built a city of hope.

Kor'A's creation was not without its problems. The immortal mind from which it was conceived had not thought of human needs. It was said, in the very beginning, it was a colossal sculpture, devoid of living space. Bücka had told him a story of Thelia's—that she had been there the day Kor'A hollowed out the living spaces. On a whim, she had said, a great rumbling had taken hold of the land, and Anka, as they now knew it, had been born. Though, it had been without sanitation or resource. It was the legendary General Aracyse's engineers who had brought water to the city, building viaducts that carried water from the mountain streams. Clay was used to construct waste pipes. Following Tormelorian design, those pipes channelled waste into dense, tiered reed beds. The odour from those fields was pungent but the water that seeped into the river was clean.

As much as he respected the city, Jerune preferred the forest cabins. To live among nature and beast. Anka was too harsh for his taste; though, it had its attractions. The greatest of which now approached; Sarellia, ascending the stairs. She held two cups of glazed, white pottery. Not local craft. Jerune imagined they would be expensive imports from places far away. She breezed over, a smile upon her face, and sat beside him.

'Tea?'

Jerune propped himself up. Grimaced. A stabbing pain in his chest.

'I warned you last night,' Sarellia said, 'we could leave it. What with your injury.'

'And I said, it was rude to decline a lady.'

'I'm a lady now? Thought I was a city bitch?'

She played the part well but he knew she was nothing of the sort. 'You fooled me.'

'We spies are good at that.'

He took the cup. Aromas of clove and cinnamon rose from the dark liquid. He moved his free hand to the padding wrapped around his torso. The night's activities had masked the pain. Though, he had to admit, Goddard's battlefield medicine was exemplary.

A thought crossed his mind. Probably best not to say, feared it might sound boastful. 'Was worth it.'

Sarellia laid a hand against his cheek. 'Saving Bücka?'

Jerune frowned. 'No, last night. Bücka was reflex, not really a choice.' He put his hand on hers. 'This was a choice.'

'I'm glad.'

She tried to hide it but he saw a miniscule crack in that glorious smile. 'What?'

Sarellia shook her head. 'No, it's nothing.'

Jerune scowled. 'You can't do that, Sarellia. Your face betrayed a thought. I saw it.'

'That your scout's intuition?'

'It is, actually.'

She sighed. Nodded. 'The thought of you leaving for Laria.'

'Miss me?'

The smile vanished. 'It's dangerous, Jerune. You need to understand that.'

He understood his offer to accompany Bücka to Laria would put him in harms way. But Jerune didn't want to make assumptions that it was his safety for which Sarellia showed concern. Though, it would be reassuring if she was worried about his welfare. He feigned ignorance, hoping he'd be corrected. 'You're worried we'll fail? Bücka and I won't be able to do it?'

Frowning, Sarellia said, 'No. Well, there is that.' She stood from the bed and paced to the window. The golden sun cast a glow upon her skin. Her beauty defied description. All Jerune could imagine was a goddess. A smiling goddess. She turned to him.

'I never knew I wanted one,' she said.

'One what?'

'An idiot. Like you. Never knew how useful you could be.'

Her tone was warm. There was no mockery. Sarellia was being evasive, clear that she valued him, certain she wouldn't say as much to his face. She was strong of will. Stubborn. A trait of hers of which Jerune was strangely fond.

'I suppose having an idiot by your side makes you look more competent, eh?' he said.

'Exactly. And I need my important friends to see me in good stead. So, it's wise for you to be around.'

'What's in it for me?'

She came back and sat down. 'Prestige. People can gawp and wonder how you did so well to have Sarellia of An'Korathall on your arm. I'll make you look like a prince.'

She was satirising herself. Her expression was exquisite. Jerune considered he had a suitable reply.

'That's very generous, dear lady. But I'd settle for sex and tea.'

He squinted, waited for her response. Sarellia burst out laughing.

'We'll see. We'll see.'

It felt uncomfortable, the eyes upon him. People stared as he and Sarellia walked the treeless avenue to the citadel. In any other city or town, the abandoned marble tower would draw attention; those curious to see the life of a Queen, or those seeking treasure. In Anka, everyone knew that there was no bounty beyond the wall. Neither Queen of Stone, nor the Elemental Earth had need of trinkets of gold or silver. Jerune wondered if that could be another reason for such peace? Without a fabled trove of precious gems and coin, Anka was less attractive to those who would dare try to sack her wealth. The true riches of the city were to be found in its legendary peace. A home for the soul, not for the purse. It did have wealth; though, as Sarellia's abode had shown, it wasn't worn as a symbol.

'See?' Sarellia said.

'Huh?'

'All these people looking at you. They're amazed I'm by your side.'

'I wish it were so,' he said. 'You can feel their unease.'

'True. You can hear their breath, hear the questions on the tips of their tongues.'

Looking around, Jerune saw the faces; mouths forming the shapes of words. Silent curiosity, too polite to ask. 'Poor souls,' he said. 'They need a leader, or at least, someone to reassure them.'

Sarellia hummed. 'With Baza'rad staying here, they have that, and more.'

It amused Jerune that she found it difficult to adapt to the King's new identity. In truth, he found Goddard a more relatable name. Neither comfortable with myth nor idols, it was easier to think of him as just a man. Not the slayer of immortal kings.

'You'll have to call him by his other name, you know.'

'I will. In his presence. And around others.'

Although she stopped talking, Jerune knew there was more to come. He wondered if the life of a Cultist made it awkward to speak freely. In their short time together, he had noted how often she would withhold even the most trivial information. As he had expected, Sarellia continued.

'He's the king of my family line. Each Bruhsa passes down their own knowledge. Obviously, as time passes the distance to the truth increases but still, Jerune, the man is legend.'

'True. But a legend he wishes to forget.'

Walking through the massive open archway of the citadel outer wall, Jerune stopped. Bücka's horse was gone; perhaps she had taken it inside the tower. A cruel thing, he thought, no green anywhere. At least in the streets the horse could plunder the odd flower box.

'You think they're waiting on us?' he asked.

'Let's see,' Sarellia replied.

He strode through the citadel entrance, noting the shape of Goddard seated at the centre of the courtyard. Moving closer, he saw no sign of Bücka or Shang'si. Just the old King and the child of glass.

Goddard raised his head. 'Morning.'

Chara copied his word. Her voice was a chirp.

Jerune waved at them both. Sarellia repeating the spoken greeting.

Curious about Bücka's absence, Jerune asked, 'Bücka?'

Goddard was about to speak but Chara sprung from her marble seat. Jerune watched as the girl approached. Illuminated by the funnel of light, her features expressed more than glass should allow. Mesmerised, he had to focus to hear her words.

'Did you know horses eat grass?'

'Um, yes. I do,' he replied. He glanced at Sarellia. She raised her eyebrows, appeared to accept the oddity of her question.

'And,' Chara added, 'they make a terrible mess.'

He scoffed. 'That I also know. Is that where Bücka's gone?'

Chara nodded. Then without another word, she turned on her heels and marched back to Goddard. Jerune followed, sat on the adjacent marble block. Sarellia sat beside him. Closer than she had the previous day.

As the child sat beside the King, Jerune observed his features soften. Chara's effect on him was clear. As though children had come home safe from a night in the dark forest. The king nodded, inhaling deeply.

'You slept well?' he asked Jerune.

Placing a hand to his chest, he replied, 'Your physician skills are remarkable.'

A smile upon his face, Goddard squinted. Jerune was certain he saw a mischievous glint in those dark eyes. 'I trust you rested *all* night,' he asked.

Hesitating, Jerune found it difficult to reply. Sarellia spoke, a hand falling on his thigh. 'Don't worry, I saw to his needs.'

Goddard laughed. Chara looked up at him and asked, 'What's funny?'

The king shook his head, patted hers. 'I'll tell you one day.'

A sound came to Jerune. Footsteps. He had memorised the aural signatures each of them made. On the marble floor it was easier. Bücka's pace was efficient, a medium stride carried on strong thighs. Her armour was distinctive, the manner of how the plates on her skirt chimed as she walked. It was melodic. A curiosity of Bücka, he thought; a fine woman, strong features but attractive, her hair a natural auburn blaze. Her body, honed and lean, was graceful. Yet, for all she was a woman, Bücka had the mannerisms of the eternal child. Where Sarellia had mischief hiding behind her sophistication, the warrior was bereft of such social graces. She was endowed with an endearing immaturity, beneath which lay the mentality of a killer. Jerune imagined it to be a unique expression of being that would cost a naïve trespasser his fingers.

Bücka sat down on the adjacent block. He turned to greet her. She glanced at Sarellia, wrinkled her face, then asked, 'You fuck?'

'*Bücka*, language!' Goddard said. 'Children present.'

Chara, clearly ignorant of such terminology, looked at Bücka, and asked, 'What's that?'

Jerune replied. 'None of her business.' He looked at Bücka. Made sure his gaze was loud and clear.

Bücka shook her head. A rapid and fleeting movement. 'Just asking. Did you?'

'That's not for me...' he said, when Sarellia interrupted.

'We did. Shall we move on?'

Jerune wasn't sure what was happening. Was that jealousy? And was Sarellia stamping her authority. It would have felt different if he were the common object of desire. But it was Sarellia. A thought occurred to him, one which wasn't pleasant. He considered his forthcoming journey with Bücka to Laria could be awkward.

But Bücka smiled. 'You're a good match, the two of you. I see these things.'

Goddard cleared his throat. 'Sarellia, you said you had a contact coming in to Port Aracyse?'

'Yes, that's correct.'

'When?'

'It should be tomorrow night.'

Port Aracyse was due south, a small distance east of Venhyne. On the main track, setting off at dawn, a good horse would be there for dusk. Jerune wasn't averse to four-legged travel, though for his method of tracking it was always better to be close to the ground. He assumed from Sarellia's words that the Port was as far as the contact would be going.

'Are you to meet them there?' he asked.

She nodded.

Bücka said, 'You'll need an escort?'

Another effort to impress on Sarellia? Jerune regarded the offer with suspicion. Not for the threat on his ego, rather, Bücka's intent.

He said, 'I can go.'

Bücka shrugged. 'I was just thinking that if anything happens, a warrior by your side would be of help.'

It wasn't coincidence that Jerune's wound throbbed. He straightened up, tapped the injury, and said, 'It's you they're after. You could drag them with you, lead them to Sarellia's contact. That wouldn't be wise.'

'A fair point, Bücka,' Goddard said. 'We can't risk drawing attention to Sarellia.'

Jerune could see her squirming under his words. They were as good as orders. Such an irony, it appeared the reluctant King's word was law.

Sarellia said, 'I appreciate the offer, Bücka. But Goddard's right. The assassin who attacked you may still be following. Likely knows you're in here. I don't want an arrow in my back. Besides. I travel best alone.'

'What? Not a chance,' Jerune said.

She gripped his thigh, glanced at Bücka. 'I'm sure you saw the other Western Star in the stables?'

Bücka nodded. 'Oh, is that yours?'

'Yes. She rides well. Fastest I've known. I'll travel tonight.' She looked into his eyes. 'You'll escort me to the stables. See me off. I'll return in two or three days. I'll have my contact provide any details of the Forge they can. A plan if possible.'

He still wasn't happy. Realised the contradiction. He was to sail to Laria. To help a warrior destroy a Forge that made Elemental firebombs. And here was Sarellia riding not more than a days travel to a sleepy coastal town. To make a map. Not the most perilous adventure. But still, his heart ached.

He nodded. 'Alright. I can do that.'

Jerune watched as Bücka stood from her block then sat down, squeezing in beside him. 'What the...?' he said.

Her arm fell around his shoulders. A solid limb. Bücka said, 'Don't worry, I'll look after you.'

A plea from his eyes to Goddard, Jerune willed the King to call Bücka away. Wanted his support; he received none. The King stared and smiled, mischievous old eyes twinkling.

Devoid of allies, Jerune removed the invasive arm from his shoulders, smiled at Bücka, and said, 'Try not to get us killed then, eh?'

Chapter XIX

Beyond the funnel of marble, the sky was a dark and brooding amber. Goddard stared at the circle of dull fire. Dawn had arrived. Chara still slumbered. He turned his gaze to look upon the child of glass. Within the citadel, shut away from a view of any horizon, time had no place. How did the girl wake under Kor'A's motherhood? The previous day, she had caught him off-guard. Standing at the citadel entrance, the grand arch, Goddard had stared at the rising sun. Bloated, surrounded by haze, it had appeared. Watching it, he had been reminded of Bruhale; how the ocean turned to flame in the dawn light. Ripped from the present, transported a century in time, he had once again become Baza'rad, standing on the balcony of the Royal Palace, his daughter by his side; his hand cupping her skull, holding her close. Yesterday, a tap on his arm had arrested that memory. Brought him back to now. Looking down, he had seen that head of black hair. For that brief moment, his heart had soared. But those hopes collapsed, the girl not his own but a child of black glass. Chara had stood where once his daughter had, her innocent eyes gazing at his own. His own, less than innocent. How had she awoken?

That fright; the wrench of reality had troubled him. Not for his loss but for his gain. He had noticed it; Chara looking upon him with the adulation only a daughter could offer. To a child, the parent was God. Invincible, indomitable, and eternal. A folly of the infant mind. Yet he knew that was how she saw him. He felt it. He understood it. Chara believed he was there for her. And Goddard knew it was how it was meant to be. What had been lost was gone. What was now, was his to protect. Observing the sleeping enigma, he wondered what she thought. Dared to imagine the consciousness she possessed. What thoughts and emotions directed the mind of an immortal's experiment in death?

Dispelling his recollections, he reached to her shoulder. Shook her with gentle care. 'Chara?'

Her eyes already open, she blinked.

'It's morning, Chara. The sun is up.'

She smiled. Didn't move. He wondered if she had heard, shook her again.

'I'm awake,' she said.

'It's hard to tell.'

'Do I smile when I sleep?' she asked.

He thought about it. No, she didn't. He shook his head, smiled.

Chara said, 'I'm comfortable here.'

'On the marble?'

'Beside you.'

It was strange. The feeling. In his time with Petra, surrounded by others, he hadn't felt so attached. The sisters, Thelia and Thelissa, as wonderful as they were, as mischievous as they had been; he had not developed this bond. Chara, a creature not born of flesh, had become entwined with his soul. It was ironic. He glanced at Bruch'ail, the mantra repeating in his mind. *Stone knew stone.* It didn't matter how detached they had become from Kor'A; her children, those of her skin, were as one. He had noticed a change. A connection to the child. More than what humans knew. A primal bond. A belonging born in creation itself.

'What?' she asked.

Confused, he replied, 'I didn't say anything.'

'Your face. It speaks without words.'

'It does? What does it say?'

Chara raised herself to a seated position. Her cheerful expression became a wrinkled countenance. 'I don't know. I'm not yet clever enough to understand.'

What to tell her? Explain the truth. Or better to stay detached?

He said, 'I wonder how you would wake if nobody was here to tell you the sun had risen.'

Chara looked to the sky above. She shook her head. 'I don't know. Yesterday, I saw you awake. The sky was lighter. I assumed it was day.' She paused. He could sense her agitation.

'What is it?' he asked.

'What happens if I wake too early? If I stop sleep before sunrise?'

Goddard thought he knew the answer. A simple response. Although, to speak it would strip away her human façade. It would undermine her experience as a mortal child; she didn't need sleep at all.

'I don't know, Chara,' he replied. 'But as long as I'm here, I'll wake you at dawn and remind you when dusk is near.' He looked to the floors above. Away from the courtyard, there were rooms that faced east and west. 'We could move to the upper floors. From there we could watch the sunset. Together.'

Chara beamed. 'I'd like that.'

'Tonight then. We'll do that.'

At midday the sun shone overhead and the inner courtyard was awash with a painful explosion of white. Goddard, escaping the searing glare, stood at the citadel wall looking down upon Anka. The colours and shadows, set against the marble, provided a much welcome contrast. Chara had remained perched on her marble block in the cauldron of light. It didn't seem to bother her. But for his eyes the intensity was a harsh reminder of Kor'A's ignorance of human comforts. Bücka had spent the morning away but now she was returning, moving with elegance toward him.

'Come to greet me?' she asked, a broad grin on her face.

'The courtyard's become a light trap. Thought I'd stretch my legs. Where's Jerune?'

She shrugged. 'Last I saw he was waving off Sarellia.'

Young love, Goddard thought. He'd be reflecting on her journey, worrying unnecessarily. 'Well, there's not much to do until she returns.'

Bücka frowned, shook her head. 'No. There is. There's likely still an assassin in Anka. I need to find him.'

One man seemed a trivial concern. Though, of course, Goddard understood the possibility he would come again. That was why Bücka was welcome in the citadel. It would be a rare fool that threatened those walls. Goddard had warned the young warrior of the threat of ambush—the risk she took stabling Shang'si. She had smiled, dismissed his concerns. He had expected an explanation for her lack of caution. She had given none. As if proof of her confidence, she was here, still breathing.

'Perhaps you scared him off,' he said.

'I hope not. I'd like to finish what he started.'

About to warn her away from such thoughts, he saw Jerune ascending the avenue steps. It pleased him to see the scout wasn't moping in false distress. To Bücka, Goddard said, 'Speaking of such things, here comes your pin cushion.'

Jerune stopped a few paces away, a typical behaviour of the scout. Goddard had underestimated his tactical awareness. It was rare that he came within range of the edge of a blade. He'd be difficult to surprise at close quarters. Always a safe distance from immediate threat. It reminded him of when Jerune had troubled Bücka at the tomb, his defence timed perfectly to avoid her blade.

The scout shook his head, raised a querying eyebrow. 'Pin cushion?'

'You heard that?' Goddard was surprised.

'Ears of a wolf.'

Bücka said, 'I didn't want to say. They're a bit furry.'

Jerune smiled. 'Better my ears than my face.'

Goddard waited for Bücka's retort but none came fast enough. He said to Jerune, 'Thought you might be staying in the forest?'

'Had something to check.'

'What?'

Jerune looked at Bücka. 'There's a killer on the loose. And after seeing off Sarellia, I thought I'd have a look around. Of course, the stables were a royal mess. Stables are to tracking, as water is to fire. But I recalled what you said, Bücka. About the bushes.'

The warrior put her hands on her hips, straightened her spine. 'What'd you find?'

'At first it was easy—lots of disturbed undergrowth. But he moved to the city. At least, had the gait of man. I had to double back plenty, tracking using his blood.' Jerune appeared impressed, praised Bücka. 'You caught him good. Bled heavily in the woods, stemmed the flow before moving onto the white streets. They knew what they were doing. Knew how to disguise their path.'

Goddard assumed that sounded final. 'Did you lose him?'

Jerune's tone was clear, offended at such an insult. 'Give me credit. That's why I'm here.' He turned to Bücka. 'I figure you might want to come along? I'm no match for an assassin.' Jerune said to Goddard, 'I'd ask you but a man of your size wouldn't do well at sneaking; besides, I thought you'd need to stay with Chara. Bücka's the clear choice, she practically glides along on those thighs.'

As Bücka grinned with delight, Goddard acknowledged his stature would be detrimental to the task. Jerune was right. Bruhadian King's didn't sneak. And though he had shaken off the mantle of Kingship, he couldn't diminish his stature.

'You're right,' Goddard said, 'I'm not really the stealthy type.'

Jerune cocked his head from side to side. 'I mean, if there's a damn nest of them, I know I'll be running straight to you.' He waved a hand to him. 'Hide behind Fortress Goddard.'

'I'll not run,' Bücka said.

Jerune shrugged. 'Yeah, you absorb all the blows while I get *dad*.'

She frowned, 'He's not your.... Oh. I see what you're saying.' Bücka giggled, pointed to Goddard. 'Dad.'

The thought in his head was a warming one. *Children*. Hiding his smile, donning a serious countenance, he asked, 'Jerune, you know exactly where the assassin is?'

He nodded. 'Trail goes stone cold. Only one house it could be. I've looked all around, no blood on the open windows or walls. I'd wager they're still inside. Again, given the blood loss—far more than me—I'd imagine they're in no state to fight or flee.' He paused, seeming to ponder a thought. 'If they're even alive.'

'So, we go now?' Bücka asked.

'I'll take you there.'

Goddard had faith in Bücka's resilience. Appreciated her prowess. She had completed many contracts; she required no advice. This new family, for which he had never asked, was growing on him.

'Be careful of the surrounds,' he said. 'You'll need to keep eyes on Jerune in case there are others. It's all well and good killing one assassin, but what good is that if in the moment you're distracted? Be cautious.'

'I know how to watch my back,' Jerune said. 'And I know Bücka's capable.'

Two truths. Two unique talents. He thought he would feel more anxious about them. But he didn't. For all his years in peaceful Anka, he had imagined he had softened. As his hair had greyed, perhaps his nerve had also blunted. It had not.

Goddard scanned the city below, noting the shadows had shifted, dissolving away under the noon sun. Nowhere for a scout to hide. He said, 'You're not going now, are you?'

Jerune shook his head. 'We'll head close, keep an eye from higher up where we can see the door and windows. They can exit from the west door and north facing-windows.

I can get us close, stay hunkered down northwest. We'll see all movement, then we... then Bücka can go in at dusk.'

'Sounds good to me,' Bücka said.

Goddard nodded. One final thought. 'Where is it, roughly?'

Jerune pointed to the southeast. 'On the edge of the Cotton District. Closest to us.'

Thinking of dusk, of Chara's needs, Goddard was troubled by his predicament. She would need to sleep. To maintain the cruel illusion of humanity. And if she slept, he would not leave her side. A silent thought, a harmless curse on Petra. Why hadn't she just come back? She was the perfect surrogate mother for Chara. More stone than he could ever be. What if he was needed elsewhere?

He sighed, considered the skills of the scout. 'You have fire arrows?'

'Signal flares?'

Goddard nodded. The same thing. Identical chemical ingredients, used for two different purposes. As an axe was for splitting timber, so too it could split bone. That Jerune referred to fire arrows as a 'signal' said much of his trade. Combat was not his concern. Somehow, Goddard was comforted by that. Perhaps a safe pair of hands to have near, better for Chara's welfare than another sword-wielding warrior.

He said, 'If you come to trouble and you can't get away, send a... signal to the night sky. I will come.'

Jerune grinned. 'That would be something.'

Goddard shook his head. 'Please, don't let it come to that. Keep your wits about you... both. Let's not play that hand unless necessary.'

Bücka said, 'It'll not be. We'll be back for supper.' She stopped, scratched her head. 'I've not seen you eat. How can you be so big and not eat?'

An impulse. Uncontrolled, Goddard burst into a fit of laughter. Bücka stared, her confusion a tell of inexperienced youth. Composing himself, Goddard reached out, grasped her shoulder. 'Child, I've lived more than four of your lifetimes and you question my *diet*?'

Her confusion remained. It amused him. Thought it better to put her out of her misery. 'Herbs. Stimulants. I eat when required. But I have the literal constitution of a king. Gifts of my youth make things different for me.'

She frowned. A reluctant acceptance of his obfuscation. 'If you say so.'

He looked at Jerune. 'Signal me if you must.' To Bücka, he said, 'Otherwise, bring me some meat for supper. Come back safe and find out what you can about your assassin. It would be wise to know what the enemy does, and why they're here at all.'

Chapter XX

Anka had its problems. For Jerune, cover was the greatest. He had thought a house overlooking the target would suffice but none were vacant. The rooftops were out of the question, exposed by the rising tiers of the city. In the Cotton District, lower down, he had few options. He had settled on a last-ditch spot, a narrow space between two marble blocks, one tier above the target. A strange feature in Anka—a fault—such as could be observed in natural terrain. Neither alley, nor shelter, it was cramped and uneven but it offered shadow and secrecy. One drawback. The space confined and intimate such that he and Bücka were intertwined; their legs knotted as though lovers in bed. He had endured worse positions throughout his career but always on his own. Bücka was gleeful, revelling in his social discomfort. Adjusting her position, for the umpteenth time, she poked his shoulder.

'Think Sarellia would approve?' she said, winking.

He looked at her foot nestled against his groin. His reply was a silent stare, one eyebrow raised.

She grinned.

'I'm sure she'd be amused,' he said.

'You really like her, don't you?'

It wasn't the conversation he wanted to have. Preferred silence and contemplation. Bücka, the warrior child would have none of it.

She pressed. 'You do, don't you?'

'We should be quiet.'

Shaking her head, she said, 'I'm whispering. I'm not an idiot. You just don't want to talk about her.'

'Is that so unusual?'

'I just want to know.'

She'd probably not stop until he answered. 'Yes. I like her a lot.'

Bücka nodded. She appeared to be thinking, contemplating a deeper issue. The sudden change in her demeanour was curious. And although he didn't want to pry, didn't care to know other people's business unless it was his business, he considered it shallow to ignore her introspection.

'You alright?'

Her eyes met his and for the first time he saw sadness. Bücka said, 'I had a girlfriend, once. But it didn't last.'

'Why?'

'Dunno. She just left me.'

'How long were you together?'

Bücka frowned, counted three of her fingers. 'Not long.'

'Weeks, months?'

'I'm not that bad,' she sighed. 'Am I? No, it was three years.'

'That's a long time, Bücka. Best I've managed is two. You don't know why she left? You must have an idea?'

'I travel a lot. The job, you know?'

He did. The greater renown he gained as a proficient scout, the farther afield he had been asked to work. Jerune imagined Bücka's lot was similar, likely far worse. He knew she'd travelled to Dreyahyde in the far west of Kalleron, and as far east as Laria. Crossing the world to kill.

'Our skillsets don't afford much homely stability,' he said.

Bücka smiled, murmured a humourless laugh. 'My path leaves a trail of the dead. Not so good for one place.'

'It's ironic, I've followed such trails. Not yours, I think. You think she left because you were absent so much?'

'I suppose.'

It would be an awkward question. Perhaps too invasive. But it seemed apt to ask. 'Did you love her?'

The slightest nod. A breath of a whisper. 'Yeah.'

'I'm sorry, Bücka.'

She smiled. It was warm, genuine. 'I know I act dumb, or childish. Well, I *am* childish, but it doesn't mean I'm not a whole person, you know? I deal in death so lots of folks think me heartless. I'm not. It's just... it's difficult to get close to someone when they know you've murdered more people than they've had lovers.'

Jerune had never thought of it that way. Considered it a necessity to deliver justice as Bücka dealt it. Keenly aware of her sexuality, he hoped his thoughts would be received as intended.

'I don't see you that way. Sure, you can be a pain in the ass, but your swordplay doesn't make you less attractive. What you do isn't ugly. It's other people that have the problem. Not you. In another world, I'd cross the floor of a crowded inn to be closer to you. You're... *unique*.'

'You know you're not my type?'

'Well, yeah. You like Sarellia. Women.'

She laughed. 'You're such a man. Apart from that, I prefer dark skin.'

'Oh. Can I ask why? I mean, beauty is beauty, is it not?'

'Thelia used to tell me tales of Kallisa. Described her vividly. I think I fell in love with the image I pictured in my mind. A dashing, dark and glamourous spy.'

Jerune formed a mental image. Conversations with Sarellia had informed much of his knowledge of the past, those heroes from Petra's golden days. He imagined Bücka's lore was painted with romanticism. What Sarellia had told him came from a more stoic source; Bruhsa business, formal knowledge not to be exaggerated. A history not soiled by epic myth. But still, he understood Kallisa to be a formidable presence.

In the cramped fissure, he didn't need to reach across to tap Bücka's shoulder. 'You'll find love again. Or, it'll find you.'

'Until then, I guess I have you to annoy?'

'Well, shit, you got that right.'

At dusk, certain neither he nor Bücka were visible, Jerune crawled out from the gap. With a progression of stifled groans, they emerged into the gloom between structures. Leading the way, he cringed at every step Bücka took. She was silent. But her armour clinked as though fabricated from tone-deaf windchimes. It was difficult but he had to remind himself it wasn't her fault. His senses were tuned to detect everything and in truth he knew her noise was minimal. Yet still, the sound was grating. He turned, using his hand palm down, he signalled for quiet. Bücka nodded, clear she was compliant, not offended. They moved slowly, her noise dulled enough to blend with the ebbing bustle of the city. Pointing, he indicated a window above ground level. An easy climb against a shuttered portal; it was the most sheltered point of entry. Jerune paused, holding Bücka at bay.

'What?' A whisper in his ear.

The smell. Faint but ever present. Not blowing away on the breeze. Without words, he flicked his eyes to the house, sniffed the air. Bücka reacted, inhaled. He wondered if she would taste it, a sliver of a scent. Her brow furrowed; she shook her head.

As quiet as he could, close to her ear, he said, 'Death.'

'Inside?'

He thought so, nodded to confirm. But caution was best kept close, there could be others beyond the walls. He pointed to the upper window. Receding into shadow, he ushered Bücka on, watched as she moved to the wall, reached for a ledge and pulled herself up to the low roof. Jerune was impressed; how she moved as water, fluid and unbroken. No gruff pulling or sudden grasps. He was reminded of the Hill Tribes, those to the east living among the cliffs and bluffs. Confident and assured, it was a skill most had to learn. Not a warrior's training. Those were questions for later—he was intrigued.

Bücka reached the window and kept low, her focus coming back to Jerune. She appeared to be waiting for a command. He signalled to her to open the shutter. Instead, she waved her hand across her face, back and forward. An unmistakable gesture, she was wafting away an unpleasant stench; she could smell the death from within. Jerune moved from the shadows and in seconds had climbed to her side. The odour was horrendous. He reached for the shutter, pulled it open enough that a bloated black fly buzzed past. Swiftly followed by more. Bücka grimaced, he imagined it was a reflection of his own disgust. It was a good sign though; in all his years tracking, it was rare to find anything alive near such death. Anything other than the creatures of decay. Humans wouldn't tolerate such a putrid environment.

'Cover your mouth,' he whispered.

Inching the shutter open, he peered into the subtle blue-white gloom. From within he heard nothing beyond the droning chatter of the flies. He started to move through the window when Bücka pulled him back. She scolded him with a stare and moved inside. Jerune thought to protest, realising that was the plan. *His* plan. A scout wasn't meant to breach the assassin's lair, that was the warrior's job. Shaking his head, he followed Bücka.

Inside the room, she stood motionless. Jerune followed her gaze to see a figure slumped against the wall in the corner. The right hand trailed the floor, a bone needle close, black twine with beads of crusted blood beside it. Jerune followed the thread with his eyes. It crossed the body to an exposed abdomen. There, half-sutured, a deep gash, black in the blue light. Rags of cloth, darkened by innards, lay across his legs. Discarded near his feet, his armoured tunic; rigid leather with chain links. It appeared a brave, if not futile, effort to heal the mortal wound.

Jerune noticed Bücka draw a breath, a preparation to exhale a spoken thought; something he considered to be noise. Her head turned but before she utter a single letter, he raised his hand to silence her. She frowned. He waved a finger then held it to his lips. His other hand pointing to the floor, asking a question: what lay beneath? The body was too fresh to be the source of putrid death. The clothes, the armour, the recent wound; this appeared to be Bücka's assassin. There was an older death in the house, somewhere the maggots were feasting. He gestured to the stairs.

Bücka nodded, moved to the top step. She stopped, her eyes on his. He understood, she was seeking permission to descend. Jerune nodded, following behind. As they climbed down, the origin of the cloud of flies became clear. A muddled downstairs, a chaotic collection of furniture and crates, and the body. An older woman. Throat slit, eyes gone, sockets staring. Nothing else of obvious interest; the scenario was clear to Jerune. Why pay board when you could stay for free? He imagined an assassin wouldn't hesitate to cut out the landlord. He moved to the back room, empty wooden pales on the floor, splashes of blood on the walls. No other souls. He returned to Bücka, tapped her shoulder and began ascending the stairs, returning to the first corpse. Removed from the worst of the stench and assured they were alone, he considered it was safe to speak.

'That your assassin?'

Bücka looked at the body. 'Maybe?'

Jerune thought it a good match for her description. Besides, he had tracked him here. It had to be the same man. Peering down, he saw a flash of silver. He knelt close, moved a stiff arm away from the far side. He reached over, plucked the bloodied blade from the floor, stood and showed it to Bücka.

'Yours?'

'Oh, thank you,' she said, and took the knife.

'You'll wash that, right?'

She nodded. Placed the dirty blade back in her boot. Glancing down, he saw the hidden sheath tucked tight to her shin.

'Well, at least that's one less bastard to worry about,' she said, nodding to the body.

It was. Assassins were awkward foes, though, not this one. Jerune moved to the discarded tunic. He searched the lining, sought the typical thief's pouch. Assassins, thieves, all the same; they required a secret place for the priciest gems and illicit orders. Nothing. He turned to Bücka.

'We need to search him,' he said, 'Search this place. Find any parchment, contracts.'

She nodded and moved to the body, her hands reached to his boots, removing them without care. Jerune watched, amused. She looked up at him.

'What?' she asked.

'Really?'

'It's where I put my contracts. Wrap it in leather, inside my boot. Handy things, the old plodders.' She smiled, pulled a slim package from within. 'See!'

'And I had the foot fetish?'

'Fair point,' she said as she stood, passing to him the folded rag.

Jerune removed a waxed parchment from the patch of leather. A small note, a few lines of careful script. The style was decorative, a flourish of symbols. Artistic as it was, it didn't help.

'Damn it,' he said.

Bücka leaned in, looked at the parchment in his hand. 'Oh, that's pretty.' She looked at him, appeared to wait for the great reveal. He was sure to disappoint.

'I can't read it.'

Bücka frowned. She said, 'It could be Sanhe, you know, the old Larian script.'

'I don't know,' he replied, surprised by her knowledge. 'You read it?'

'Sanhe? No. Thelia used to scribble with sticks in the dirt. Said it was Petra's language but I don't think gran knew what she was drawing. I just recognise the shapes.'

'Well, we can take it back to Goddard. If he doesn't know it, maybe Sarellia will?'

Jerune nodded. What precious time he had spent with the Cultist, he knew she was well read. It was her business to know other people's stories. When she returned from Port Aracyse, she'd have some answers, of that he was certain. A flicker of anxiety troubled his mind. Pushed it away—the vulnerability of attachment. But it stirred a thought. He looked down at the assassin. Something was out of place. He pointed at Bücka, his finger agitating in the blue gloom.

'You took his bow, right? I was high on Ambyr Dust, I can't recall.'

'Yeah, I took the bow. Why?'

'His sword? Quiver?'

She shook her head. Turned to look at the body. 'Oh yeah, they're not here. Hang on.'

Bücka moved to the assassin, unceremoniously hauling him from the wall. He fell to the side, bent at the waist, death's grip still in control of his muscles. The warrior shook her head. 'Nope, he wasn't sitting on it.'

'So, where'd it go? He had a sword, right?'

Bücka nodded. 'Definitely. Two. You think someone took them?'

'There's not even a weapon belt. We need to check downstairs. If it's not here, there's got to be another. Then we get back to Goddard.'

She nodded, screwed up her face, lifting her arm and pressing her nose into the crook of her elbow. Waving to the stairs, she said, 'After you.'

Jerune took a deep breath, gagged without retching and descended into the hellish stench.

Chapter XXI

It arrived as the sun set over Farenhyne. A glorious ship. A terrible omen. From the crumbling fort walls, Petra watched the Larian yacht draw into harbour. Never had she been troubled to see the elegance of her homeland. Now, knowing what she knew—Sarellia's revelations of Fire—every ship from the south was a possible harbinger of doom. She focused on the figures that set foot upon the boardwalk. Too distant for human eyes to see, her diamond gaze brought the view to bear as though a sea eagle spying the harbour rats. Robes, flowing as fire; they were the colours of Larian conquest. Red, black, and yellow. No effort to conceal the arrival. Three brazen figures. Walking tall, they momentarily stopped and turned. Petra stepped to the cover of the wall; an old reaction imprinted on reflex. On the pier they stared. Looking toward her, surely unseeing, their gaze upon her keep. She revelled in the sensation. Intrigue and anticipation of the fight; a rare thing to experience after all her long years.

'You've come for me?' she said to herself.

The robed figures moved again. She tracked them as far as she could, losing them in the muddle of Farenhyne's chaotic streets. Pacing along the wall, she waited for another glimpse. Was it her imagination? Had they come for her? She laughed at herself.

'Pompous cow. Not every significant thing is yours to covet.'

They appeared again. Never stopping to savour the town's rustic charms, the trio approached the tower. A chance they might yet travel onwards, though without horses and unencumbered by backpacks, it was unlikely; they were not equipped for distance. Petra moved away from the wall. Walking, as she most often preferred, she moved to the basement and ascended the stone steps to the cabin at the top of the keep. Kneeling beside the old chest, she lifted the lid. What to wear for her new guests? Rummaging inside, she retrieved the robe she sought. Standing, holding it to the candlelight, Petra smiled.

'It's been a while,' she said.

Swinging it around her shoulders, frowning at the small holes of disrepair, Petra adorned her family cloak. A black velvet embroidered with an intricate golden thread. Letters of Sanhe bordered the robe, speaking whispers of her ancestral line. An action reminiscent of mortality, she brought her nose to the fabric, a false inhalation to imagine the scent her curse forbade her to know. Comforts of another time. Petra recalling with fondness, the day Shadow had returned to Anka, bringing with him this present for her. Smiling, she pulled the material across her breast, raised the hood and moved to the window.

'So, you do come for me?' she said, watching the figures turn from the main path.

Closer they came, lost to her view as they drew near the wall of the keep. The door. Would they knock? It amused her, the idea of a delegation. The past century had shown her many things. Dealt many blows. Yet Petra remained true to herself; whatever memory that was of the woman she was meant to be. And rare moments such as these, unforeseen novelties—these were worth the wait.

The knock came. Three heavy thuds on the basement door. Petra smiled. You can wait, she thought. If those who had conquered her homeland wished an audience, they would suffer her protraction. She clapped, joyful in her surprise; the basement door pushed open without invite. It clattered against the wall. How to react? Storm downstairs and test their resolve, or wait, regal in her cabin? Better to be a frightening figure of calm, than some angry witch. Petra moved to the east wall, settling down on a dusty wooden chair. A poor throne for most, perfect for her needs.

She listened as they climbed the stone steps. Comical. Noting their hesitation, sensing their trepidation. Petra understood the dictum of such visits, the words would be formal, the tone, officious. The illusion of calm was shattered on hearing their uncertain approach. No matter how brave they would show themselves to be, she knew they were anything but.

The first head appeared, rising step by step. The hooded robe framed a golden mask. A skeletal visage, unpleasant to behold. Cold, mechanical in appearance, it would cause a mortal to pause. Odd it was from Laria, the appearance reminiscent of the clockwork engineering of old Kalleron. The figure stopped, not yet clear of the steps. Those hollow eyes surveying her. Heavy breaths betraying the air of control.

Petra smiled, waved to the cabin. 'You've come this far. Please.'

She observed as the three figures shuffled into the room. By their movements, she judged one to be a woman. The curve of her breast visible as she walked across the flagstone floor. All the same height, identical masks staring; Petra could not discern who was the leader.

A century ago, as a mortal woman, she would have killed them where they stood. Shadow by her side, they would have revelled in the revenge. Those who had sacked her homeland, turned ice to fire. But the power Kor'A bestowed upon her was not to be used in anger. To kill with impunity was evil. The thief from before had attacked; the defence was just. These robed fools sought an audience. Their lives were not hers to end. She would play with them until she knew their purpose.

'How is Laria?' she asked.

One stood forward. Not the woman. A man replied, 'Laria is well. Though I'm sure you don't care to know the truth?'

'The truth?'

'We know the lies and deception spoken of our land. But Fire and ice co-exist. It is not as the rumours and ill-informed gossip suggest.'

'Gossip? Is that what you call it? Then, I ask you, did Fire not destroy Larastra, defile the temples?'

A sigh from within the mask. 'Religions are petty. The Seer revealed the true power of our world.'

The Seer. Petra knew of him. A rare survivor of Arkalla's fall. The tales that followed him were infuriatingly incomplete. Once the spiritual protector of proud Arkallon, his city had been crushed by Kor'A when she was Queen of Kalleron; the same fate had befallen Petra's love, Felicitra. Yet that monstrous act had instigated an unforeseen consequence. Few understood why, Petra wondered if any knew at all, but the Seer, his mind broken and twisted, had left Arkallon to seek the Elemental Fire. All understood that his quest was fulfilled and Laria had suffered his wrath. Few knew why he had chosen to attack Laria rather than Kalleron which had ordered his country's demise. It was an enduring mystery.

Of the Seer, Petra said, 'And what power did the Seer wield? The power to kill innocent people?'

'Innocent? Had Laria not already declared war on Kalleron? Is that innocence?'

The things Petra forgot. Rather, things she wished not to recall. It was true. Her actions, and those of the Cult; to free the Queen from captivity—it was that strike against Kalleron that had given Laria the confidence to attack. Put events in motion that had brought great destruction to both continents. Petra and her Cult had emancipated one Elemental, only to release the wrath of another.

Referring to the war, she said, 'That conflict never truly came to fruition.'

'Because Laria underestimated Kalleron. So too, it misjudged its reticence to aid Arkalla. Your noble and proud Laria, Arkallon's *ally*, stood by impotent as the Queen tore the Seer's world apart.'

'Your ignorance impresses me,' Petra said. 'You come here from Fire and suggest Laria could have stopped the Queen. You think Larian weapons could stop the Lord of the Earth? Flesh can never conquer stone.'

The mask nodded. 'True. But there is more to friendship than blind military allegiance. Regardless, one day I hope you learn of the Seer's true story. If you knew our truth, you would not consider us so hostile.'

'The only truth I know is the madness to worship Fire.' Petra shook her head. 'It is folly. The ancients named her *The Great Destroyer*, yet you find it meaningful, moral, to idolise her?'

The emissary replied, 'You believe we worship Fire?'

'Is she not your god?'

The mask glanced to his left and right. Silent words to his companions. 'She is the power but she is no god. Not as you describe it. She has granted the line of the Seer the means to carry her seed. For that, we are grateful and loyal. But it is no different to the Furies of Etherus.' He raised his arm, gestured to her. 'Or perhaps An'Korathall. Gifted to you, Petra, the Queen of Stone, daughter of Earth.'

'I had a mother. Of flesh. Earth was not she.'

'Perhaps, but your form; it is of stone. As is the white city. We carry Fire, Etherus tames the Wind. But Earth,' he shook his head, 'nobody has tamed her essence. What she left is a far greater legacy. Your city is more powerful than any Fury or Seed.'

'You speak as though An'Korathall is a weapon?'

The mask hesitated. 'Not a weapon. A power, unlike any other. A weapon is to be wielded. A weapon is without free will. What Earth gifted to man is a sanctuary. A place free of conflict. A place that flourished for decades under your reign. Your stewardship of Earth's essence is a glory to all.'

His tone appeared as though reverence. Petra wanted to doubt him, think him insincere. But she knew he was not. She found it disturbing, an undercurrent of menace to come.

'Why do you seek me? You didn't come across the sea to bring pleasantries.'

'To deliver a message. A message from the Seer.'

Curious, she leant forward, removed her hood. 'Why would he wish to send a message to me?'

'To ensure you understand the Covenant. That you must remain apart from it all.'

The *Covenant*. Sarellia's information. How did it affect her, she wasn't an Elemental? Petra understood her power paled in comparison. To protect the Cult, to deny her knowledge, she played dumb.

'I know of my own limitations. Water keeps me here. You may tell the Seer; he need not fear me. So long as he remains in Laria.'

'That is not the Covenant. At least, it is not the one of which I speak.'

'Then what?'

The figure paused. Petra sensed unease. A moment of hesitation betrayed by anxious breaths hidden behind the mask. She waited but another spoke. The female, stepping forward as the other paced back. From within her robe, she brought forth a crystal orb. Petra stared. Flames flickered within. Burning without air. Sarellia's warning rang in her mind—the Seed of Fire.

'You know of this?' the woman asked.

It was beautiful. More alive than fire, the interior of the orb had a depthless aura. It reminded her of the malevolent glory of Etherus's Fury trapped inside the glass. The Elemental weapons were remarkable. In whichever guise they appeared, they always had a dark beauty about them. Begrudgingly, Petra nodded.

The woman continued. 'We have many. When the Queen of Kalleron sacked Arkalla, the Seer sought the sister. His driving belief: Why should one man covet the essence of the Elementals? There has to be balance in such power. This is the balance, Petra. A gift to the Seer's line from Fire herself. Kalleron has the Fury, Laria holds Fire.'

Petra said, 'The seer sought his death, not power.' Though she spoke her own words, she found little credibility in them. What happened to Laria was proof enough.

'In a sense he found that death,' the woman replied. 'By laying to rest the ghosts of human deities such as Arkana. This is better than God.' The hand raised and moved the orb closer to Petra's face. She didn't flinch. It was fascinating. A dull heat touched her skin. A smile rising upon her face. *Warmth*. She hadn't felt it since she had become one with the Earth's essence. No natural flame could bring heat to her elemental skin.

'I can feel it,' Petra said with wonder.

'Fire is power.'

Petra blinked. Dragging herself away from the hypnotic flicker, she knew what the woman said was truth. How could a flame burn within a crystal sphere? How could it deliver warmth to her stone flesh? She had no doubt. This was a Seed of Fire—the Elemental's essence. A sobering realisation; the weapon presumed to have sacked Laria, mere inches from her face.

'The Covenant?' Petra asked. 'What of it?'

'The Seer has been gifted an arsenal of such seeds. And Fire has rested. So too, your Earth has left An'Korathall.' The woman paused as though seeking Petra's confirmation. Cautious, she remained silent. Behind the mask, the voice continued. 'We know she has. It is the Covenant. Earth will not stand against her sister. And Fire will not defend Laria. We have been left with what they gifted to us.'

Petra considered the woman's words. Laria had the seed. Etherus had the Fury. She recalled what the other had said. His reverence to An'Korathall. An unease settled in her mind. The prize of the Elementals, Fire and Fury. At no point had she been portrayed as the gift of Earth. Did they not know? She had the power to manipulate the white city. It was *her* weapon.

Petra said, 'Our gift in these lands, what is it?'

The woman gestured to the other who had spoken. 'As declared—the white city.'

'What of me?' she asked. 'What is my place?'

'You have none. The Covenant is clear. Elementals shall not interfere.'

'I am no Elemental.'

From behind the woman's mask, a sigh was released. 'You are stone. You are not human. The Covenant of Fire is sealed.'

'You expect me to stand aside? To watch war come to these lands.'

'That is the will of Fire.'

Impossible. Petra shook her head. 'Fire does not control me.'

The woman shook her head. 'No, she does not. She doesn't need to. But understand, Petra, if you seek to affect the balance of power, you will break the Covenant. If that happens, the Great Destroyer herself will come to these lands. If the daughter of Earth is to be the shield of man, then Fire will be the sword that strikes him down. The Covenant is sealed, Petra. Do not be foolish. An'Korathall is the gift to men in these lands. It will stand unattested.'

'I am to cower in a city?'

'A city that will survive whatever comes.'

Petra glared at the woman. 'You've come to tell me to stand idly by and watch these lands burn?'

'We came to warn you of the Covenant.'

Petra rose from her chair, the emissaries shuffling in place. Behind those masks she imagined anxious faces staring. Turning away from them, she paced to the window. In the reflection, stark against the dark beyond, the three figures remained motionless. In their ghosts, the city of Farenhyne slumbered.

'Petra?' the woman said.

Focusing through the glass, she replied, 'What?'

'We adore you. We praise you, daughter of Earth. But you must see Fire to understand the Covenant. You must witness the truth.' The tone of the woman's voice altered. A subtle shift but Petra recognised it. A hint of fear in her confidence, as she said, 'You must witness the power to understand you have no option but to obey.'

Disturbed by the words, Petra glanced over her shoulder. Saw the orb in a raised hand. Gloved fingers opened and the sphere rolled to one side. It happened without time. The immortal clock. The sun never moving across a dial; the drip of ice ascending to be solid once more. She stared. The seed fell. Thudding heartbeats filled the room; a rush of anxiety and destiny. Petra could hear their fear. What she knew to be a second, she observed as dozens. The crystal cracking upon the flagstones and planks of her resurrected cabin. As sand flowing through the hourglass, wood became ash, and stone crumbled to dust, cascading inward, a sinkhole of matter spiralling ever downward. The moment accelerated beyond Petra's senses and she saw the figures vanish into the expanding pit. In the flap of a hummingbird's wings, it would take her. The ground beneath her feet disintegrating, her body falling, she slammed her hand through the cabin wall, reaching the stone beyond. Coupled by rock and mortar to the foundations, Petra channelled her essence through the minerals of Kor'A's creation and fled the fort. Not knowing where she would rise, she appeared on the hills overlooking the old ruin. What she saw filled her with dread. It was a revelation of Fire.

A vast pit awash with fire and smoke engulfed the plateau overlooking Farenhyne. A sweltering haze corrupted the sky and the noise of the inferno crackled in the air. Petra strained to see but the circular chasm was a calamity of light—she couldn't see the depths. Though, she knew to where the seed had gone. Back to mother. Stunned, Petra fell to her knees. Mesmerised and awestruck, she watched as the destruction drew crowds from the coastal town. Her gaze cast to the harbour, she saw the tall ship that had brought the emissaries leaving dock. Did they believe her dead, the suicidal pact of their brethren complete? Duelling thoughts troubled her mind. Was it an attack, or a demonstration of what would come should she break the Covenant?

An unwelcome realisation dawning as a bitter and cold sun—no matter what the intent; to come to her with Fire was a prophecy she could not ignore. She placed her hand to the earth, stopping as she realised she should no longer commune with it. The risk was too great; her flight from the fort hopefully masked by the destruction wrought by Fire. Petra had no choice but to heed the Covenant; at least until she knew better. But she had to warn Goddard. Looking to the West, she knew Anka was a few days travel. She would relish the walk but not the delay in reaching her friend. A sigh, one last disbelieving shake of her head and she stood. First to Farenhyne, to secure fabric for her modesty; she couldn't travel naked, then to Anka, to tell of terrible things to come.

Chapter XXII

All those years living as a hermit. Goddard had forgotten the simple pleasure of company. Bücka and Jerune gone to catch a spy, Sarellia meeting her own. Left alone with Chara, it was a strange day. A welcome reminder of beloved ghosts from the past. To fill the time, he had found a new role. World historian. At least, a history of what he knew. The sun was setting, not yet gone. Standing with Chara by his side, he looked out across the Northern Lands. He had climbed to the highest floor of the citadel. The view had drawn his breath away. As high as the eagles that soared above the forest. Looking to the shimmering southern horizon, a fiery sky peppered with cloud framed the view.

Within the room, a large space of nothing, the portal that opened to the world was a precarious feature. No balustrade to offer safety, it was neither a window nor a doorway. Goddard considered it a lack of wall. A poorly conceived balcony, or a panoramic suicide ledge; regardless, it was another hint of Kor'A's startling ignorance of mortal ways. He stood away from the edge, one hand warding the glass child from her curiosity. She pointed to the unseen distance, her finger waving at the far west.

'That's Bruhada?'

'It is,' he replied.

Her finger moved east across the view. 'Kalleron?'

'Yes.'

'Where mother was a captured Queen?'

He had told Chara. Thought it wise to let her understand the devious nature of men. The power of lies; enough to fool even an immortal. Nodding, he replied, 'But released with the help of Petra.'

Another swipe of her finger tracking farther to the east. 'And that's Laria hidden beyond the horizon?'

'Well done.'

'You were King of Bruhada, capital Bruhale. You fought a man named Te'anor, sent him home. But you left Bruhale before mother came, you travelled to Kalleron where you met Petra. That's right, isn't it?'

'It is.'

She had recalled his words well, omitting his melancholy when speaking of Bruhada. He had spent hours pointing to the horizon, telling her of Petra's adventures in the main continent of Kalleron, named for its city-state and once imperious King. Before the days of the Cult, when the *Melody* had traded from East to West, it had been a simple life, a pleasant life. He had regaled Chara with a sanitised version of what had followed. She had learned much of the world that her mother had destroyed.

A tug on his finger. 'Goddard?'

'Hmm?'

'Why are you stone when you are also flesh?'

A sworn secret. Petra his only confidante. Stone knows stone. Yet, it seemed pointless to withhold the truth from the girl. She knew of his curse. He stared at the horizon. Images of Bruhale came to him. The city, the Royal Palace; all the art and culture lost a century ago. Still fresh in his memory, the aroma of the herb markets, the sound of the smiths. The city of gold, a mixture of ochre stone and burnished copper. Though they were colourful ghosts, they haunted him.

He looked down at Chara. Knelt beside her and smiled. 'Your mother's a strange one. She creates things she doesn't seem to understand.'

'Like me?'

What to reply? Tell Chara her purpose was simple? Besides, the girl knew the truth and she faced it with an unnatural stoicism.

'Actually, I think she knew what she was doing with you. But scattered across that world,' he pointed to the south, 'are pockets of strange she left in her wake. Long before Bruhada was a kingdom, there were others who called it home. They came long before us. Left remnants. All across what is now Kalleron, there were temples to all the Elementals. Some of them were quite bizarre.'

Her brow furrowed. A crease of amber reflecting in the dark. Goddard glanced to the sky; the sun was setting.

'What's a temple?' she asked.

'A place where humans worship what they don't understand.' Goddard chuckled. Those were Petra's words. He winked at Chara. 'Humans are just as strange as your mother. What is strange or unknown, we deify, or we destroy.'

'What's deify?'

'To raise something beyond human reach. What we've always done with things that defy our understanding.'

'Why not try to understand?'

He beamed. Her words were so innocent, naïve, yet so correct. 'You know, Chara, if all humans thought that way, we'd not have to worry about war anymore.'

'Then why don't you?'

'We don't work that way, not everyone. I wish we did. But each of us is unique and those differences drive us apart. Kor'A wanted you to be like us, but really, I think you're better as you are.'

She appeared to absorb his words. Nodded. 'The temples. Were they important to you?'

'When Bruhada was settled and the Palace was built, a temple was discovered far underground. Hidden in darkness.' As he spoke of the place, Goddard noted the blue hue emanating from the citadel walls. Night was coming. On the horizon, the fat orb was being swallowed in a haze of fire.

Chara glanced at the disappearing sphere; Goddard saw the surreptitious dart of her eyes. But she said nothing. She stared at him. He smiled, recognised what she had done. Pretending she hadn't seen the sunset; ignoring her bedtime.

She said, 'You were speaking of the temple?'

'Yes, of course.' He would allow her the grace of staying awake. She deserved that much. He continued, 'In the middle of a large cavern there were two rocks, columns, you might say. As the story describes, one rose from the ground, the other right above descending from the ceiling. At first my ancestors thought them hewn by hand but up close they saw no tooling marks. My father told me, as his forefathers told him, it was not natural rock. Between those pillars—as they came to be called—was space enough for a helm.'

He spread his hands to encompass the size. Chara copied, her hands making a small orb. Her scale was off, a child's comprehension. Too difficult to resist, he encased the onyx display between his own hands.

She smiled and he continued. 'In time we would come to call those rocks, *Bruch'alma*, or the *Rock of Kings*. But at first, anyone who placed their hand between the pillars would suffer grave injury. A trap for the curious, or foolish.'

Chara frowned. 'What would happen?'

Goddard considered a white lie. Decided the truth was better. 'A shaft of blue stone would thrust from top to bottom, so thin, yet so strong. Those whose hands were impaled could not break the rock.'

Chara flinched. 'That's horrible. How did they...'

'Escape?'

She nodded.

Goddard reached out with his palm down. Fixing Chara with a grimace, he sharply retracted the hand.

She reached to her mouth. Gasped. Goddard thought of Sarellia's reaction to Jerune's arrow. Chara enacting a perfect facsimile of shock. Empathy, real or otherwise, her action was novel.

He smiled at her. 'Indeed. Tore flesh to pieces. The leaders of the first tribes of Bruhada agreed to destroy the rock. But one man thought that rash. They all knew it was a temple. Yet, they thought to destroy it. So, this man, *Doga'rad*, travelled to the temple early in the day. Took his hammer.'

Chara interrupted, a frown on her face. 'Bruch'ail?'

'No. His own.' He paused. Those shadows obscuring his memory. Bruch'ail evading his focus. A shake of his head and he continued. 'When the leaders came to destroy it, he told them to leave. Temples were sacred, no matter who had built them.'

Chara appeared enthused. 'Did he scare them off?'

'He tried but he was overpowered. As punishment, they dragged him to the pillars and pushed his head into the gap.'

She flinched. 'That's cruel!'

'Yes. It was. At first. And rather than destroy the pillars, they left him there, head impaled, as a warning to all. A threat against those who would defy the leaders.'

'Poor Doga'rad.' Chara said.

Goddard smiled. 'Doga'rad became the first true King of Bruhada. *Bruch'alma* released him after one full day. Alive—a miracle—his wounds healed. He grew stronger with every rising sun and he exacted his revenge on those who had sought to murder him. In time, he was crowned, and the temple became the origin of our Kings.'

Chara frowned. 'I don't understand. What does it do?'

Goddard shrugged, wished he knew. He understood the effect. Presumed to imagine it was akin to what had happened to Petra on a far smaller scale. Injected by the essence of Earth. Another experiment, perhaps Kor'A's oldest?

'But why is everyone not like you?' Chara asked. 'Wouldn't all humans want to be as strong as you?'

'Whatever happened to Doga'rad, it changed the behaviour of Bruch'alma. The King ordered it forbidden to all, but some still found a way in. But the rocks no longer pierced flesh. They had become inert. Until, one day, Doga'rad's daughter snuck into the chamber. She ran screaming to the King, her hand torn to shreds. And Doga'rad understood. What had happened to him, would stay with his kin. Whatever had become of his body, was within it, and he had passed it down to his own line. His daughter would one day return to Bruch'alma, complete the ritual and...'

Chara interrupted. 'What happened?'

Goddard tried to recall the history. A fog had descended. Old age again. He shook his head, couldn't find the memories. 'Well, anyway, after Doga'rad, his wife took the throne as King.'

Chara appeared confused. 'Aren't men Kings, and women Queens?'

Goddard smiled, shook his head. 'Bruhada's more sophisticated than that. King's rule, Queen's sit beside. There were three female Bruhadian Kings.'

'Were they like you?'

He had seen the texts, the descriptions of his ancestors. 'Very much so. All Bruhadian Kings are... large. Only the strongest can rule.'

'Are you a man King?'

Her inquisition was delightful, inviting a deep laughter from his lungs. To his confused student, he said, 'Last time I checked, yes.'

'Check what?'

He sighed. Realised his role as surrogate father had taken an awkward turn. It was underhand but he would use the sundown to his advantage. Pointing to the dark horizon, he said, 'Bedtime, Chara.'

She smiled. Didn't seem to care that her question had been deflected. As that obedient dog, she sat down on the bare floor and curled into a ball. One blink from her dark eyes and he knew she was asleep. He could watch that every day until forever and never find it normal. One day soon, he thought, he'd ask her to stay awake longer. Break through the façade.

Goddard looked to the gentle glow of Anka far below. Wondered how things were with Bücka and Jerune. They would find it difficult to locate him among all of the citadel's balconies. He didn't want them to worry when they returned. Moving to Chara, he placed his hands under her body and scooped her to his chest. Not knowing why, his heart telling him to do so, he kissed her on the forehead and carried her down to the courtyard.

Chapter XXIII

The wind had shifted. A high Falla blowing in from the plains bringing the scent of Anka to the citadel courtyard. The expected florals had been usurped by an altogether different fragrance. Though fragrance wasn't the word Goddard would use. His nostrils flared; the odour tasted rank. *What on earth?* He looked at his daughter lying asleep on the marble block. *Daughter?* Goddard rose to his feet, stared at the child. What had he thought? What had his mind said? Chara wasn't his. He gazed upon her and his muscles relaxed. She slept soundly, a peaceful child. He shook his head, clearing cobwebs left by another ghost. What was he thinking?

'Goddard?' a voice called, a man.

He turned, reached for the haft of Bruch'ail.

'Steady!' the voice said.

Goddard squinted. Jerune. It was Jerune. He reached a hand to his temple, glanced again at Chara. A deep breath. It was all he could do to ward away the thoughts. He realised he had been slumbering. A dream of lost daughters, forgotten worlds. Again, Jerune called.

'Are you all right? You look... peaky.'

'A dream,' Goddard said. 'The strangest dream.'

Bücka emerged from behind Jerune. 'You look dazed.'

'Are you sure you're alright?' Jerune repeated.

'I'm fine.' Staring at Chara, he said, 'We're fine.' Another sniff. He looked at Jerune. 'Is that you?'

Jerune plucked at his tunic, brought it to his nose and inhaled. 'Frankly, I can't smell shit. Literally. My nose is done.' He turned to Bücka. 'You smell us?'

Bücka shook her head. 'I want to lie in a tub of fragranced water. I don't know what I smell of.'

'Death?' Goddard said. 'It comes before you. What happened? The assassin?'

'Dead,' Bücka replied. She smiled, her expression victorious. 'I got him. Fatal blow.'

'How so?' Goddard asked.

Jerune said, 'We found him in that house. Half-stitched but he had lost too much blood.' He paced over, handed Goddard a scrap of parchment. 'Can you read that?'

Looking at the grubby paper, Goddard frowned. 'Petra.'

'What?' Jerune said.

'It's the same as Petra's tattoos. Before she became stone. Sanhe, I think.'

The scout looked to Bücka and said, 'You were right.' To Goddard he asked, 'You know what it says?'

Goddard frowned, stared at the pale face of Jerune. 'Do I look Larian?'

Jerune frowned, raising a single brow. 'You're what, a hundred and fifty years old? Couldn't you have learned?'

Was that a barb from the scout? A pause to reflect; an insult or a show of camaraderie? Goddard squinted at Jerune and said, 'You're a cheeky bastard.'

Bücka stepped forward, beaming at the scout. She said to Goddard, 'So you're saying you can't read it?'

A two-pronged attack from a couple of grinning idiots. Looking at the script he couldn't understand, he shook his head. 'No. Petra could.'

Jerune sighed and said, 'Sarellia might know it. She's due back tomorrow night.'

Goddard asked, 'He had this, the assassin?'

Jerune nodded.

'Just the one?'

Bücka replied, 'His weapon belt was gone, sword and arrows too. Figure there must have been another. But we saw no sign.'

Dead assassins weren't a problem. A missing assassin was not so fortunate. A quick glance to Chara, still safe, Goddard said, 'We can't have rogue assassins in Anka.' He looked at Jerune. 'How good are you?'

Tilting his head from side to side, Jerune replied, 'You want me to find the other?'

'If it's possible in a city of stone.'

The scout turned to Bücka. 'Want to be a live target?'

'No,' she replied.

Jerune smiled. 'We can hang out. Drink ale. Well, you can, I'll need to stay alert. See what eyes fall upon us. Might be able to tempt another strike.'

Bücka scowled. 'You want them to try to kill me. Again?'

'It wouldn't get to that,' Jerune said, his hands padding her shoulders. 'I'll sense any danger. Just like at the stables.'

The warrior laughed. 'You want impaled. *Again?*'

Jerune turned to Goddard. 'Help, big fellow?'

Tonight wasn't the night. Tomorrow would bring new chances. Shaking his head, he said, 'Rest for now. See what happens tomorrow.'

Jerune nodded. 'That's fair. I'll return in the morning.'

'Where you going?' Bücka asked. Goddard noted her surprise.

'Home,' Jerune said.

Bücka grabbed his arm. 'Don't be daft. Stay here. I brought spare bedrolls.' She pointed to the pile of miscellaneous rags and fabrics piled at the far wall. Goddard watched with interest. That bond he had observed. It wasn't desire; he had noted Bücka's eyes on Sarellia. This was something else. Something stronger developing. Kinship.

To aid Bücka, he said to Jerune, 'I'd be happier if you stayed with us this night. Your skills would be valuable.' Jerune appeared uncomfortable with the request. Not a surprise. The scout from the woods didn't display an affinity with the city. Another approach perhaps. Appeal to his vanity. 'I'd prefer you to stay with us. I'd feel safer.'

Jerune smiled. Then laughed. He pointed at Goddard. 'I get it. I get it. I do. But please, don't lower yourself to the level of us mortals. I can't imagine what makes you feel safer at night. But I know it's not me.'

'But you'll stay?' Bücka asked.

'Can hardly refuse a legend.'

Goddard sat. He turned his head to gaze at Chara. Her eyes blinked. A thought came to him. No. A feeling. A belonging. Not just Chara, but the other two. Their behaviours so akin to those of two orphans from a century ago. Though older, and far more capable, it was no coincidence that Bücka was a copy of Thelia. An anchor that secured her place beside his. And Jerune, by default, had taken the role of Thelissa. All those years ago, they had fallen under Shadow's wing. Now Goddard had inherited a small family. He placed a gentle hand on Chara's scalp. It had all started with her.

'How is she?' Jerune asked.

Goddard smiled. Kept his eyes on the child. 'She's perfect.'

Dawn was yet to grace the day but for Goddard, the time for rest was over. His old mind was turning; decisions to be made, consequences to be weighed. Craning his head, he peered to the dark circle above, the stars scattered across a perfect sky. The fading night was in stark contrast to the eternally glowing walls. Close by, Bücka lay on her bedroll, her breath steady and deep. Leaning into a marble block, Jerune appeared to meditate rather than sleep. Similar to his own nocturnal rest, Goddard wondered if the scout was aware of his surrounds. Jerune's eyes were shut, his breathing heavy. Goddard rose, as quiet as any man his size could. Nothing from the scout. Careful not to bump the others, he stepped away. One glance at Chara, her eyes seeing him—she blinked. He extended his hand, palm to the ground, and smiled; a silent command to settle. The smallest movement in response, Chara curled tighter into herself.

Grabbing Bruch'ail, Goddard moved to the citadel arch. He continued beyond, stopping at the steps that descended to Anka proper. With his back to the citadel walls, he stood as he had a century before. History revealing itself in his mind's eye. With those old friends by his side, he had once faced another foe. An ambitious Captain, responsible for Petra's death, had chased them to An'Korathall. Impotent against a hail of enemy arrows, Argan had lowered the hammer. A thunder arose. The gates had opened, the Queen of Stone striding forth, and she had taken her revenge. Anka had changed much since then. A marble and granite shell had become home to thousands. Kalle and others had tried in turn, but Anka had never seen their weapons. Defeated on the plains, conquered by might and majesty. Glorious battles. Lost in the haze of peace that had followed. Things seemed different now. Anka was not the bastion it had once been. What was there to stop an army coming to the White City?

He understood the root of his anxiety. She lay asleep in the citadel. A child to protect. He was the only thing that stood between her and the grievous world. And what was he; an ageing warrior uncertain of his days? Goddard couldn't provide the sanctuary Chara required. Not forever. And though he knew she was mortal, it didn't mean she would die as a human. Her body showed no age, not from her own description. Yet she was fragile. Perhaps more important; she was detached from her mother. Chara was a pebble discarded far from the mountain. Without Kor'A's essence, she would be diminished and made nothing by the winds of time. He wondered—worse, he feared what would happen should she be damaged. He sighed, realising the irony. A simple child of flesh appeared to have more resistance than the girl of black glass.

Gazing to the south-east, he thought of Laria. *Time*. Sarellia had said it was on their side. Goddard imagined the fleet waiting to sail. A breath of war sitting across the ocean. Waiting, anticipating. Bücka and Jerune would need to travel with urgency. If the Larian Forge was hindered, if the seeds of Fire could be reduced or destroyed, there was still an armada. There were men and women ready for battle. He could fight an army, decimate and destroy hundreds of soldiers. Petra could do better. But each had a weakness. Away from the ground of Anka, Petra had no domain over Earth. She could travel through it, he had seen it happen—a miracle, an unsettling sight. But she was still a single woman fighting thousands hand-to-hand. As though a field of candles, one by one, she would snuff them out. But many would slip past. The flames of war would engulf them.

He was weaker. He would fatigue. No matter how strong they were together, they could not stop the avalanche of armour that would thunder across the plain. The Northern armies had disbanded long ago; the legends of the Queens of Stone had been enough to deter all serious threat after Kalle's final defeat. A false security; to lay one's fate at the feet of the Elementals. The country he had claimed as home was terribly vulnerable. Defended by a couple of ancient relics, a warrior and a scout. It wouldn't be enough. He had thought to keep Chara safe within the citadel but that too would be overrun. That he would give his last breath for the child was not in doubt. But then what? Chara would be left alone, defenceless. A terrible image in his mind. His dying body, a crowd of zealots rushing past. Chara, hoisted and thrown from the citadel, smashing to pieces on the marble far below. Thieves and murderers ransacking her body for the precious gems and diamond core.

Rattled by his own imagination, he stamped the head of Bruch'ail into the ground. A small movement. Yet the thunder was real. It rippled far away, a terrible percussion in the night. Not waiting for the city to wake, he turned back to the citadel. Marching into the courtyard, Jerune and Bücka had awoken, the scout coming to meet him.

'What's going on?' Jerune asked.

Looking beyond to the marble blocks, Goddard saw Chara still slumbering. He waited for Bücka to appear alongside. With a heavy sigh, he said, 'I'm not staying here when you go to Laria. I'm not waiting for the war to come to our shores.'

Jerune scratched his head. 'Where will you go?'

'I'm coming with you.'

Bücka grinned. 'Amazing!'

But the scout frowned. 'And Chara? I thought she needed to be protected?'

Doubting his own plan but knowing it to be better than waiting for death, Goddard said, 'She's coming too. We're all going to Laria.'

Chapter XXIV

S olitary again. Perched high in the cliffs east of Anka, Jerune scrutinised the city of marble. Eagle eyes searching for an unseen foe. He had managed to persuade Bücka he needed to do this alone. Talk of her being live bait for the assassin had been nothing but dark humour. The task at hand required more than skill. *Patience.* Jerune had begun to enjoy the warrior's company. That familiarity had revealed her traits. As lithe and graceful as her body could be, her mind was far from still. The soul of Bücka the woman was a child of impish nature. Not suited to the silence of waiting and watching.

Leaving the citadel at dawn, he had decided to watch the city breathe. His current vantage point, hidden in shadow on a shallow shelf of rock, allowed him to watch the populace awaken. A common practice. He had learned the movements of the streets. Knew when they would come alive, what characters would appear and mingle. Strangers were easy to spy. The erratic passage through the lanes a stark contrast to the familiar routes of a native. Colours of foreign garb would show subtle differences in hue; even those fabrics designed to blend with the culture lacked the pigment of local dyes. All the anomalies were visible to his keen eyes. He had observed many newcomers, tracked their movements. None so far had displayed the behaviours of an assassin. Jerune smiled, thought of the irony. They thought themselves special; the contract killers. Trained to blend in with the crowds. Taught how to evade the eyes of the suspicious. A fallacy. Every assassin or thief he had tracked—and he had trailed his fair share—displayed the same tell. The glances to their surrounds. A casual demeanour betrayed by the amount of time spent loafing and watching. Jerune had decided long ago; most assassins were morons. A belief he wouldn't share with Bücka.

On a whim, with nothing unusual to take his interest, he descended the rock face and skirted to the eastern edge of town. Close to the river, between the forest and the city, he moved through the long grass. What had once been shaded by the woods was a meadow of stumps, the trees cut down long ago to build Anka's fixtures and furniture. He wanted to track the eastern trail, the road he had taken with Sarellia to find Baza'rad. With no clues to follow, it would provide a fresh perspective on the assassin's accomplice.

Reaching the track, Jerune cursed. The ground was tinder dry; three days since the last rains had blessed the earth. In nature, the only things worse than tracking on dry dirt were sand and rock. Markings left in the mud had been trampled down, those imprints indiscernible. A glance left and right. The path was clear. He knelt down, peering at the jumbled mess. Nothing. To the east, beyond the stone bridge that spanned the river, the forest grew tall. More shade, perhaps a better chance of damp earth. Jerune stood from the path and looked back at Anka. Too many places to get lost, the way ahead one of many. To focus on one route was a gamble and Jerune was resentful of chance, preferred educated guesswork. Farenhyne lay a few days away; the closest port to Laria, certainly more secluded than Venhyne or Port Aracyse. An obvious path to travel for a Larian spy seeking a quiet journey home.

'Are you even going home?' he asked the wind.

Without an answer, Jerune moved to the cover of the forest and started east.

An hour or so of travel had revealed nothing to betray the presence of the assassin's accomplice. Content to give up and head west, Jerune stopped, his attention drawn to a shadow moving through the trees. Distant, it was coming from the east. He moved to a crouch, not fast but slow. A common mistake made by most; to react with haste to find cover. Those sudden movements always picked up in the periphery of the target's view—it was harder to track that which slowly bled into the shadows. Close to a thick trunk, he watched from afar. A single figure concealed in a hooded cloak. Moving at a steady pace, a deliberate approach.

'Who might you be?' he asked the woods.

The trail was too close to his back. If he moved now, still in the target's frontal view, he would be seen against the sparse cover. He'd have to wait. A minute until they passed his line. Then he could track from behind, always out of view. Jerune waited. The extra time granted by his patience allowing further insight. Shutting out the forest noise, he could hear no armour; no chink of metal. The robe moved without hindrance, not snagging on a belted blade. The hood over the head; he could see the fabric flowing unencumbered down the shoulders. No quiver, no bow. An unarmed traveller sneaking through the forest, hiding from the path. A trader? Out of the question—no goods. No backpack. From where had they come?

Intrigued, abandoning his prior mission, Jerune began to stalk the figure. Moving with a steady cadence, their passage created a rhythmic noise. Nothing as obvious as Sarellia. The thought brought a smile to his face. She would return later. It would be good to see her. Butterflies moved inside his chest. A flutter of anxiety and excitement.

'Get a hold of yourself, Jerune,' he scolded through his teeth.

Disappointed at his own distraction, he frowned and focused on the figure. He followed at a distance, gauging cover with every step. Jerune was careful to obey his own rules. Targets were secondary considerations. Remaining hidden was the goal. It was no use trailing a mark if they led you into open space. Better to lose sight of a contract than

130

come face to face with them. Using stump and bracken, trunk and bush, he shadowed the cloak for a hundred yards.

Jerune halted, stayed close to the ground. The figure had stopped. Without the rhythm of pace, the forest became a soundscape of bird and bug. A rustle of the leaves over it all. He peered. Saw the head turn, the hood moving to the left. They were listening. For him?

'I feel you,' she said.

He knew the voice. Had heard it once before. Days past. *Petra?* But he was no fool. Nobody could have heard him. Wait, she had said *feel*. An unusual word to use. Regardless, Jerune knew not to move.

The figure turned. Jerune knew his cover was complete. He didn't move an inch, waiting for her to speak or continue on.

'Scout?' she called out.

She knew it was him? Impossible. Her next words gave away the doubt.

'Bandit?' she said. 'I know you follow me. It isn't wise.'

A bluff? Perhaps she had not heard at all. A guess born of suspicion. Jerune wasn't sure it was Petra. That night with Sarellia, she had appeared at once, a phantom risen from the earth. Surely, if the Queen of Stone wished to find him, she could do so with ease? Experience had taught him well; Jerune erred on the side of caution. He didn't answer, choosing to remain hidden from sight.

'I'm going to continue now,' the woman said. 'Do not follow.'

Jerune watched as she moved off. He allowed her to move away as far as they had been apart, doubling the distance between them. Rising, he checked his own surrounds and stepped out from his cover.

In an instant she turned, pointing at him. He froze, not even the shadows could disguise his position.

'You?' she called through the trees.

Jerune was astounded. How could she see so far? Caught, his stealth defeated, he could at least answer the rhetorical question with his own.

'Petra?'

'Come here,' she said.

'Fuck.' It was as though he was once more the apprentice. His mentor about to chastise him for an amateur's effort. Shaking his head, Jerune huffed and made his way to the woman of stone. He stopped at a safe distance, at least what was safe between humans. With Petra it seemed redundant.

'Jerune, was it?' she asked.

A nod of his head.

She smiled and said, 'You look unhappy.'

It was unusual, her voice. There was a hint of mischief within her commanding tone. 'How did you know I was there?' he asked.

Petra frowned. Pointed to his feet. 'Imagine a fly walking upon your skin.'

'You can feel that? Feel me?'

She nodded.

He asked, 'You feel *everyone?*'

Petra appeared to understand his question. Not the words but the meaning behind. 'It doesn't annoy me as you might imagine. You have to be close. And it's noticeable because there is nobody else around.'

'So, we are alone?'

'Yes.' She looked around, brought her attention back to him. 'You're not tracking me?'

Jerune smiled. A terrible thing to admit. 'I was looking for something else. Saw you, became distracted.'

'Apologies. From what did I distract you?'

He hesitated. She was legend. That much he knew. Sarellia had sought her help. But he was wary of such a power. Uncertain of how much she should know, he said, 'Something happened in Anka. I was looking for a fresh trail.'

'Not something serious, I hope?' Petra paused, then asked, 'Have you finished your business with the woman, Sarellia?'

Trying not to smile, Jerune said, 'That contract has been delivered and paid.'

Petra frowned, Jerune finding the detail in her stone brow fascinating. She said, 'That's a shame. I need to speak with her. And Argan.'

'Goddard?' Jerune asked, not meaning to correct her.

She nodded and smiled. 'Yes, the same. Time has a habit of etching names into the mind.' Her frown returned. 'Can you find him?'

'Is there trouble?'

With a sigh, Petra replied, 'It's all I seem to know.'

Jerune hesitated. 'Can I trust you?'

She leaned forward. Though she was stone, Petra was beautiful. As unhuman as she was, her form was perfection. Her eyes sparkled with a radiance he would see in the stars in the darkest night. Hypnotic.

'You hardly know me,' she said. 'Do you think you can trust me?'

'I want to.' It wasn't a lie.

She looked over his shoulder. A glance to the east. 'For what is soon to follow, you'll need to trust me.'

'That doesn't sound promising.'

'It's not. As I said, I need Sarellia's ear. And... Goddard's.'

Jerune realised a simple thing. If she wanted them, she could have them. This conversation was a pleasantry. He said, 'They're in Anka. Well, Sarellia should return tonight. Goddard stays in the citadel with the child.'

Petra appeared unhappy with his news, a scowl upon her face.

'What's wrong?' he asked.

She shook her head. 'I can't step on Anka. Out here, I'm a fly like you. But in her city, she'll know it's me.'

'I don't understand. It's your city, is it not?'

Petra shook her head. 'My city? No.' She looked away, her attention distant. Jerune turned to see what had taken her gaze but there was nothing. He understood. She was elsewhere, another place, another time. A human trait; the distraction of memory. She continued, 'I never asked for it. No more than I asked to be this.' Petra gestured to herself.

It was difficult to comprehend her inner thoughts. Jerune could make a guess at Sarellia's mood. A woman of similar years to himself. There were a finite number of things a mortal could ponder. But Petra had lifetimes to consider. Her expressions were clear but what lay beneath, what caused her distraction, was a mystery.

'Shall I accompany you to Anka?' he asked.

'I said I can't go.'

'I'll take you to the periphery. I have a cabin. You can stay there. I can bring them to you.'

Jerune's confusion was complete when she pointed to the ground. 'Earthen floor, or wood?'

'What?'

'Your cabin. What flooring?'

'It's a log cabin.' He frowned as she waited on his answer. 'Wood, of course. Why?'

'I'll go to the city's edge. No nearer. You bring them to me, yes?'

Jerune nodded. Thought of his mission. 'Before you, I was looking for an assassin, or an accomplice. Someone tried to kill Bücka. Got me.'

Petra squinted. 'Got you? You appear well.'

'I have Goddard to thank for that. He knows his herbs.'

He felt a mellowing of her mood. She had been urgent, troubled. Mention of Goddard's herbs and she smiled, her stone skin relaxing.

She said, 'He's a good man. One of the best.' She waved toward Anka. 'I have experience of his medicine. Before that place had dwellings, Argan, as he was back then, tended to... a terrible injury. Kept me from death's door.'

'He saved your life?'

'Had he not been there, I am certain I would have died. Then perhaps Kor'A wouldn't have interfered. Yes, I suppose he saved my life and more.' She sighed, appeared to lose herself in those memories. Jerune watched her eyes, if radiance was a distance, she was halfway across the world.

'More?' he asked.

'Everything that followed is on my head. A pact with Aracyse. The final coming of Kalle.' She stiffened; her tone grim. 'But worse is coming. Worse than all of that.'

'Laria?' he asked. She nodded. Jerune continued, 'The assassin was Larian. Bücka managed to wound him. He bled out in Anka.' Excitable, Jerune recalled the parchment. 'You can read Sanhe?'

'Yes. Why?'

He rummaged on his person, cursed when he recalled giving it to Goddard. 'A note on the assassin. It could be the contract, or part of it.'

Petra nodded. 'Then there is much to do.'

A glance to the east. Jerune thought of his missing target. Recalled Petra's words. 'You'll let me know if you sense anyone else?'

She smiled. 'Every man, woman, and rabbit. But as we near Anka, it'll become a blur.'

'Shit.'

She laughed. 'Do I disappoint you?'

He felt the colour drain from his face. Insulting an immortal wasn't a glorious thing to do. It was evident she saw the change in his pallor.

'I jest. And, Jerune?'

He felt uneasy. Outside of his own skin. 'Yes?'

'Whatever you think of me, this body of stone, at heart, I'm still like you. I try to be human. Treat me as an equal, please?'

He didn't see how that was possible. But he nodded. 'I'll try.'

'That's all I ask.'

She smiled, raised her hood and began to walk toward Anka. As she moved, he watched her feet. Fascinated by her stride, her contact with the ground, he heard Bücka's voice in his mind.

'I'm not a foot fetishist,' he said.

'I didn't say you were?' Petra called back.

Further embarrassment. 'Damn it.'

Chapter XXV

I n the citadel courtyard, basking in the fading warmth of day, Goddard awaited
Sarellia's return. Keen to give her news of his decision to leave Anka, he wondered
how she would react; wondered what she would say. Would she ask him to stay to
protect the city? With few hours of light before dusk he saw a silhouette appear in
the grand archway. Not Sarellia. Jerune approaching the courtyard, his normal calm
demeanour replaced with a sweaty brow and wild eyes.

Rising to his feet, Goddard greeted him. 'Jerune?'

The scout glanced at Chara playing on the marble blocks. Bücka standing close,
poised to catch her if she fell. That had been on Goddard's instruction.

Bücka looked to Jerune and smiled. 'You find them, the assassin?' she asked.

Jerune shook his head and for a moment was silent. Then, to Goddard, he said, 'Petra's
here. Where's Sarellia?'

'Not yet returned,' Goddard replied. Jerune's words sinking in, he asked, 'Petra? She's
here?'

The scout nodded. Answered with a rushed reply. 'In the forest. She needs to speak
with you. Sarellia, she's not back?'

Goddard, noting the scout's agitation, said, 'She'll be fine. It's still early. But Petra,
what does she want?'

'I don't know. To do with Laria, I think.'

Peering over Jerune's shoulder, Goddard wondered why she hadn't come to the
citadel. The scout turned to follow his gaze, appeared to read his thoughts and said,
'She's not here. She'll not set foot in Anka. Said something about being noticed.'

Goddard looked back at Chara hopping from block to block. His focus still on the
child, he asked Jerune, 'How far away?'

'Not far. There and back before sunset.'

'Alright. Take us,' he said to the scout then called out to Bücka. 'You stay here, wait
for Sarellia. Chara, we're going for a stroll. Grab your cloak.'

He motioned for Jerune to lead and followed behind. Chara appeared by his side,
fumbling with her hood. Goddard reached down, flopping the cowl over her head.
From the dark recess she peered up, a smile on her face. When did she ever not smile,
Goddard thought? Serious times lay ahead. Petra's arrival couldn't be a good omen, yet

Chara remained a compact beacon of happiness for his soul. The riddle of her existence was in part deciphered but there was more to the girl than he could understand. Perhaps it was better that way.

Jerune led them through quiet streets, places Goddard barely knew. It struck him how his adopted home could feel so foreign. But the scout's ability to find the path of least habitation was uncanny. In the past, that was Shadow's role. A guile thief and brutal warrior to boot. But not as clinical and professional as Jerune. What the young scout lacked in might, he compensated for with his ability to move as a ghost.

As empty alleys gave way to bare ground, the forest loomed ahead. The sky blazed under dull orange, the shade of the canopy casting the woods into an opaque black. A quick glance down, Goddard was warmed to see Chara close by his side. She didn't sing or hum as a child might. Quiet and attentive, her behaviour was focused. He had noted she was rarely distracted when performing a task or engaged in conversation. Given choices, freewill, he wondered what she would choose. Could she even choose at all? Or was she fated to be under the command of another soul for all her days? New riddles. Time enough to solve them, he hoped.

Jerune brought them deeper into the cover of the forest. Ahead, Goddard saw Petra, a shadow among the vertical columns. As he approached, she removed her hood, greeting him with a warm smile. Her face was a gentle glow in the gloom.

She shook her head. 'I keep seeing Argan. I ought to understand change. It's good to see you again so soon... Mr Goddard.'

He came close, reached out with his hand. She took it in both of hers, a clasp of affection. Her marble hands, small and white against his dark skin; they were a façade of fragility. Those delicate fingers able to crush stone. Petra was a marvel of existence. More human than most, stronger than all.

A smile for her, he said, 'Goddard will do, Miss Petra. I feared I'd not see you for a longer spell. But no matter what brings you, I'm happy you're here.'

Petra nodded. She looked at Chara, knelt down to face her. 'And you've come too, how are you, Chara?'

'I am well, thank you.'

'Is this big lummox looking after you?'

Chara craned her neck, peering up at him. She said to Petra, 'He does. What's a lummox?'

Petra said, 'Oh, a big old thing that lumbers about.'

'Oh yes,' Chara said, nodding, 'Goddard's a lummox.'

Petra laughed. Even Jerune sniggered.

'Thank you for the support, both,' Goddard said. The lightness of the moment a fragile thing, he asked, 'Jerune suggested you don't come with good news?'

Petra shook her head. 'No.' Glancing at Chara, she said, 'Possibly not a thing for younger ears?'

Goddard tugged Chara's hood, exposing her head. 'She ought to hear what I must know. It's time to face things together.'

Petra didn't question. Goddard had always appreciated that. Never one to criticise another person's path. It would take a monumentally foolish decision for Petra to object.

'Very well,' she said. 'Though I need Sarellia to hear this as well. For her benefit, for the Cult.'

'She should return tonight. Jerune says you won't come into Anka. May I ask why?'

'It is why I've come. You'll impart this to Sarellia?'

Goddard nodded. She would learn much on her return. He wondered what Sarellia herself would say; what her contacts had spied in Laria.

Petra said, 'I was visited at my keep. Three souls from Laria, from Fire.'

'They came to you?' It was a surprise to hear. Few sought the Queen of Stone on purpose.

'Yes, I saw the ship arrive in port. Watched them. Came straight to me.'

'You said... visited?' he asked. 'Not to attack?'

She shook her head. Looked at Chara; appeared preoccupied with the girl. Was she relevant to the visit? Petra continued, 'They came to tell me of the Covenant. The very same thing of which Sarellia had spoken. Though, they elaborated.' She sighed. 'Came to tell me the rules of play.'

'Rules?'

Chara tugged Goddard's fingers. He looked down. If she were a human child, he imagined she was requesting a leave of absence to wet the ground. An insistent little bob.

'What?' he asked, neither annoyed nor troubled by her interruption.

'Can I say something?'

Goddard looked to Petra, not for permission but for a sense of pride.

Petra said, 'A child as well-mannered as you can always speak.'

'I know of a rule. Water told me of mine. I am free to travel across the sisters; I am not bound.'

Petra's frown was fleeting but Goddard knew her well enough. A sign of worry, though it was not meant to trouble him. She said, 'I wish I were as free as you, Chara. I am very much bound. I can't leave these shores.' Petra shook her head, any glimmer of a smile fading away. 'But that's not the rule of which I speak. They came to tell me not to interfere. My part in the Covenant.'

'Not to interfere? How can that be?' Goddard was perplexed. This wasn't some game. How could Petra be controlled as though a hand on a gambling table?

She said, 'The Seer controls the seed of Fire. Etherus still controls the Fury—no matter how quiet they have been. In this Elemental conflict, it seems we have been granted our own *gift*.'

'Of course. We have you,' Goddard replied.

Petra shook her head, an expression on her face as though she had sipped a sour liquid. 'No. They have chosen An'Korathall. Anka is the power for these shores, not me.'

Goddard startled when Jerune interrupted, his voice a high pitch of disbelief. '*What?*'

'How will Anka defend these lands?' Goddard asked.

'She won't. To be exact, the city is Kor'A's creation. It's to be her gift, her power in these lands. A sanctuary that no Elemental weapon shall cross.' She looked at Chara. 'Rules to which we are bound.'

Petra had come all this way to tell them. Goddard was confused. Why had she chosen to avoid Anka? She could travel through the essence; could come straight to them anywhere in an instant. Why this clandestine meeting?

'What haven't you told us?' he asked.

A slight grimace, she said, 'You know me well.'

He did. Petra of old wouldn't take well to a controlling influence. Always the rebel, ever the rogue. 'What did you do?' he asked.

'Actually, for once in my life, nothing. I told them Fire wasn't my master. Thought they'd leave. But they didn't, said they had to show me something and... well, I saw my first seed of Fire.'

Jerune said, 'We've seen one. Bücka had it, Sarellia explained what it was. But hers was empty. Sarellia said there were none on these shores, not at least that the Cult knew of.'

Petra replied with a slow nod. 'This was not empty. They dropped it in the keep. I watched it devour the earth. I fled and when I looked back the plateau was cratered with a pit of flames. I watched the ship they arrived in leave as the fire raged. I imagine they thought their mission complete—to warn me off, or destroy me.'

Goddard was astounded. 'Destroy you? Impossible.'

'Is it?' she asked. Her eyes darted to Chara; a message too quick for the child to see. Petra glancing at the *mortal* Elemental.

A grumble, a sigh, Goddard asked, 'Fire?'

Jerune appeared lost. 'Fire? You can burn?'

Petra said, 'This is not fire as you know. Fire. The Great Destroyer. I may be of Earth, immortal to men and women. But I'm not a true Elemental. I'm a bastard hybrid. And yes, I can die. This is why I'm here now—to warn you. I can't risk breaking that Covenant. I can't use the power of Earth. I fled that pit of flame but I can't risk further exposing my presence.'

'What does that mean?' Jerune asked.

Goddard understood Petra's predicament. The reluctant Queen of Stone was master of Anka's unnatural essence. She had confided in him; told of the time she had decimated a legion of Kalleron's finest. Able to manipulate the very rock, she had used the earth to impale a century of men. Her will alone could destroy life. An'Korathall was Petra's spear. A weapon of insurmountable power.

He asked, 'Anka, will you be able to...?'

Shaking her head, Petra said, 'No, I must move as you do. Fight as you do. I can't commune with Kor'A's Earth. I can't let her see me. I fear she may expose my existence. I have seen the wrath of Fire, I won't risk bringing the mother of those weapons to these shores.'

A terrible thought. Goddard glanced down at Chara absorbing all the drama. Looking to Petra, he drew silent attention to the girl. Didn't want to speak her name, make her more aware of her fragility. His question; what role did Chara have in this Covenant?

Petra shook her head. Quiet reassurance. She said, 'An'Korathall and I. Nothing else was spoken. But it is clear, I must remain detached from the Earth. I can't interfere.'

Jerune said, 'And if you do. You believe it would... what, break this Covenant?'

'I have seen the Fury of the Wind—long before you were born. I understand the power of Earth; more than most. But for certain, none of us wish to see Fire upon the land. She is not as Earth, or Water; her terrible presence is rumoured to be death. Nothing would survive. And I've seen a fraction of her power, I've seen it first hand—I won't risk it. If there is a shred of truth to this Covenant, I must abide by it.'

The scout sighed. 'Can't you even...'

Petra interrupted, 'You don't understand them as I do. They don't think like us; don't exist as us. As you. This is not a game of risk. It's a line I will not cross. The Elementals are not distant and unhearing gods—they are very real, and to them, life is nothing but a crawling plague upon their world.'

'Then what do we do?' Jerune asked.

'Stick with the plan,' Goddard said. 'Get things done the old-fashioned way; human against human. Go to Laria, destroy the Forge. Make sure they have few weapons to bear.' He said to Petra, 'I'm going to go with them.'

'I thought you were going to remain in Anka?'

'There was a development. We realised, well, Sarellia, proposed it. To go to the Larian Forge, destroy the seeds of Fire. I was going to stay in Anka. But if I'm to die in a war designed by our Elemental overlords, I'll be damned if I'm going to spend my last days in a tomb of their making.'

Another tug on his hand. Her face lost in the darkness of night, Chara's tone was uncertain, verging on hurt. 'What will I do?'

Goddard knelt down. He held her shoulders, squeezed, wondered if she understood the pressure, felt his affection? He said, 'I'm going to look after you. You'll come too. You and I, we'll have an adventure, eh?'

She nodded. He knew she was smiling. The faint sparkle in her black eyes.

Jerune sighed. 'This will be interesting.'

Goddard looked up at him, raised an eyebrow to question his words.

The scout pointed to him. Then Chara. He said, 'A contradiction in a tight spot. You and Chara; hammer and glass.'

In the dwindling light, Goddard watched Jerune playing with Chara at the edge of the forest. In one hand the scout held a branch, a finger of supple twigs decorated with round leaves. Silhouettes, they appeared as puppets in a show, his gentle rapier thrusts being swatted away by Chara. A giggle travelled through the trees, spanning the distance between them. Keen to be clear of Jerune's uncanny senses, he had taken Petra deeper into the forest, a safer place for private discussion.

'Just like a real child,' Petra said.

'More than you know.'

'You've taken to her. More than I saw at the keep.'

'That obvious?'

Although immersed in darkness, he could see her expression. Petra's skin, the same as Anka, emitting a bluish hue in the night. And although her glow was minimal, against the backdrop of the forest, it was enough to reveal her smile.

She said, 'It's a noble heart that protects another's child.'

'You'd be the same. She's unique. Literally, not another child in the world like her.'

'Is she still the same, you know, breakable?'

Goddard sighed. He imagined Petra could use the word easily. She was, after all, stone. But he didn't like the term; the association with something inanimate. 'I had a waking dream; she was thrown from the tower. Smashed at the bottom. She is fragile. I've no idea to what extent.' He glanced at Jerune and his inoffensive sword of twigs. 'I think that's safe.'

Petra laughed, 'That's good to know. And you?'

'Me?'

'You're almost unbreakable. I've never seen you suffer.' She reached out, poked his chest with a marble digit. 'But inside, caring for her. How does that make you feel?'

He understood the unspoken reference. It was a brutal thought. To compare Chara to his own daughter. Lost so long ago, yet the pain would always remain. Time healed, though not completely. And he had been gifted, perhaps cursed, with more time to heal than any other man alive.

'Bri'alla was far stronger than Chara.' He chuckled. An old memory coming to the fore. Frowning, he questioned why he found it so humorous. 'She fell down the stairs once. Playing around with a guard. Gods, I remember *his* distress. So vivid. It was his screams that brought me running. Not hers. I arrived at the balcony, Kur'han, I think it was. He was looking up, Bri'alla on the floor beside him.'

Petra's smile vanished, replaced by a frown, a scowl of horror. 'You never told me.'

He smiled. 'I watched. For that second my heart froze. Then she started to laugh. Giggling and whooping. Kur'han, well, he almost collapsed with relief. Never seen a Bruhadian go so pale. It takes some effort for that.'

'Tough little girl.'

Goddard nodded. Buried his pain. Not tough enough in the end. Chara was brittle in comparison. He sighed, pointed in her direction. 'I fear she'd not survive a trip on some cobbles.'

'Which leads me to ask; why take her to Laria? That's a dangerous journey. *And to the Forge?*'

'Your news makes that decision easier. Last night, I thought of the coming trouble. If they do come to our shores, even without the seeds of Fire, we don't have the numbers.

The coastal defences are old, they wouldn't last long. It wouldn't matter how many we could each hold back. Others would slip past. We were fools to disband the armies after Kalle's defeat. We left these lands vulnerable. It was arrogant to think we could rely on, well... to place that burden on you.'

'You forget you killed Kalle,' she said. 'Destroying the myth of the immortal king once and for all. We had you as well.'

'Even so, and as I fear, the two of us can't stop an army. If I remained in that damned citadel, they'd flood through. You say this Covenant will make it a sanctuary. But that means I must watch our land being destroyed by others. Watch the forest villages burn? I won't be that coward, Petra. You know me better.'

She sighed. 'I'm not sure Anka would be saved anyway. The message I was given makes me doubt its permanence. The Elementals will not cross it, as commanded by the Covenant. But what of men, of women? The Elementals don't play by rules we can understand. I think Anka is vulnerable to mortal desires. Fire will not fall upon it. The Furies won't shred it. But flesh? Humans have always found a way to fuck things up.'

Her appraisal was refreshing. The old Petra. Cynical, pragmatic. It caused a thought to cross his mind. 'You think I *should* go to Laria?'

She frowned. 'Who else?'

'We discussed this at Anka. Bücka would go...' He stopped, realised the importance of the warrior's lineage. Hands on Petra's shoulders, he said, '*You've not met Bücka.*'

'Who's Bücka?'

'Thelia's granddaughter.'

Petra's eyes sparkled. Shining with an unnatural glow. Elemental ancestry betrayed by human emotion. She covered her mouth with her hands. A diamond fell from her eye. Goddard wondered how many she had shed; how much wealth her tears had left in the earth.

'*Thelia?*' she whispered.

He nodded. 'The same. You can tell. All the mannerisms.'

Petra laughed. Her joy apparent. 'I can't imagine Thelia having kids, such a little imp. Let alone grandchildren. What does Bücka do?'

'Warrior. Bit of a mercenary. Damn good from what I can tell.'

'Shadow would be so proud,' Petra said shaking her head. It was clear she was in shock at his revelation. 'But you said she would go to Laria, not you?'

'That was the plan. Until I changed my mind. Now we'll all go.'

A frown from Petra. 'You'll leave the shores vulnerable.'

'There's a fleet sitting in a harbour. If we can disrupt the Forge, we might be able to damage the fleet too. Same way the Rotynians avenged their rare losses—attack the ships in port.'

Petra stared. Her eyes met his. Goddard could sense something was amiss. Another secret to be told.

'What?' he asked.

'The war between Laria and Kalleron. When the Battleships raged against the Iron Cloud.'

'What of it?'

Petra smiled. 'I never thought to tell you. I've never really seen you to let you know. It never meant much, just a lost fragment of history. When you mentioned the Rot, I remembered.'

'Remembered what?'

'They took a Larian Battleship. Salvaged her, kept her afloat. I've seen it, when I travelled to the East. A hidden seasonal port. It may still be there.'

Larian Battleships. Ancient relics; huge hulks of floating destruction. They had met their match against an Elemental siege weapon on Kalleron's battlements. Stories said the rest had fled Larian waters as Fire burned the land. Those rumours suggested they had sailed around the unknown world, forever lost from Larian view.

'The Rot kept one?' he asked. It was an incredible thing. But meaningless. 'The Rotynians don't care for our affairs.'

'They care for wealth.'

'We have none. Not as they would covet.'

Petra knelt down, graceful, with poise. She plucked her tear from the earth. Although she smiled, her voice was melancholy. 'You know how many of these I've shed in a century? Many will be lost to Fire, that fucking pit swallowed everything.'

Goddard felt a great unease. A wretched thing. 'Petra, your tears aren't currency.'

'But they are. I shed them for my friends in Anka. There's a room in the citadel.' She paused. A breathless sigh blown away. 'It was my space. A place for the grief Kor'A wanted to know. It's full of these. But I sealed it. It's open to the winds but not from inside. You wouldn't have known it was there.'

From the edge of the forest, a voice called out. It was Jerune. 'If it's even remotely accessible, I'll get in.'

Goddard turned, incredulous. He called across the space. 'How can you possibly hear from over there? *Did you listen to the whole thing?*'

'Oh, I'm not rude, I wasn't paying attention. I mean, your voice is like a drum beating in a hollow. But I tuned in when I heard talk of wealth. Aye, I noticed that.'

Petra whispered, 'That's not human.'

'I heard that too,' Jerune called.

Goddard looked at Petra and smiled. 'Imagine your Shadow, amplified ten-fold. That's Jerune, without the anger issues.'

'Impressive.'

'Sometimes,' Goddard said.

In the distance, the scout called back. 'Thanks.'

Turning to Petra, Goddard asked, 'What will you do?'

She looked to the mountains. 'I'll keep an eye on things.' She beamed, her mischief returning. 'Where you went as Goddard, in the hills. Was it a shack? Is it still habitable?'

Shack? Habitable? It was his home. Playing to her tune, he said, 'Have some respect little lady. That place is fit for a king.'

Chapter XXVI

O f all the thoughts to have, it was the least morbid. When did Western Stars become so common? Sarellia dug in her heels, in response *Valla* galloped harder. A glance behind, hand tight on the reins, she saw the distance grow. Sure, they had Stars, but she had the best. Ahead, a white beacon against a darkening sky, Anka promised sanctuary. No doubts they would follow but they would find their fate in the citadel. She had to hang on, not falter; Goddard was close, her pursuers would not have her head.

Disappointed, she had left Port Aracyse without a schematic of the Forge. Scant details were given, too vague to create a coherent plan. The Larian sources had proven less reliable than she had thought. A limited map of general topography was all they could offer. Sarellia had asked, was there a problem? Were curious eyes looking back upon them? But the local Cultists appeared relaxed, dismissive of any breach of their ranks. Now Sarellia had proof. They were gravely mistaken; their assuredness betrayed by the men shadowing in her wake. She wasn't sure when she had noticed them. Several times she had glanced behind, spying a distant cloud of dust. Never looming closer, always far away. She had doubted her paranoia; dust trails on a busy track were not proof of threat. That doubt had been resolved with the arrow. One hand on the rein, reaching to her neck, she had felt the damp. It had grazed her skin, flown past. But she bled. The tear in her skin stinging as Valla thundered across the plain. Another glance behind, every burst of speed was now matched. Her pursuers no longer content to be silhouettes on the horizon. The threat closing, Sarellia roared Valla onwards. She had to reach Anka first.

Long shadows darkened the white streets as Valla's hooves clattered onto stone. Climbing the steps to the citadel, her anxiety turned to jubilation. Seconds away she would cross that threshold. The hammer of the ages would swing to her defence. A grin breaking across her tear-stained face, she approached the archway to the outer courtyard. A figure appeared at the citadel entrance. Bücka, no doubts alerted by the din of Valla's iron hooves on the marble.

'Inside, inside!' Sarellia yelled.

Roaring past, the cacophony of noise reverberating in the tunnel, Sarellia eased Valla's speed. Bücka's expression was comical; a mixture of surprise and relief. Sarellia imagined how Goddard would react. She entered the inner courtyard, glancing around, seeking the King. Her smile faltered, she brought Valla around, stared at the empty space.

Fearful, she called to Bücka at the entrance, 'Where's Goddard?'

'They're not here,' Bücka turned, her attention drawn to the approaching noise. 'What trouble comes?'

Sarellia watched as the warrior broke into a sprint. Grabbing her weapons belt, Bücka came running toward her. She cried out, pointing to the stairs. 'Move, go, now!'

Without pause, watching as her assailants appeared at the outer arch, Sarellia dismounted Valla, slapped her flank to enthuse her flight and ran to the stairs. At the steps, Bücka grabbed her arm, eyes wild with excitement.

'How many? I saw six.'

Sarellia nodded, 'I think.'

A push from the warrior, bundling her upwards. 'Go, go, go!'

Sarellia climbed, reaching the first floor—as high as she had been in the citadel. Bücka followed close behind. From the courtyard, the clatter of hooves on marble. Shouts of urgency, a rage of metal and anger screaming in the funnel. Sarellia grabbed Bücka, the warrior pushed her away, rushed to secure her belt and scabbards. Bücka nodded to the next flight.

'Keep climbing, get to the top.'

A nod. 'You?'

Bücka smiled. 'Right behind you.'

Sarellia raced to the next flight, climbing ever higher. The noise followed, echoing upwards against the walls of the citadel. Halfway to the top, she glanced behind. Horror gripped her heart. Bücka was gone. She heard her voice distant below.

'Come on you dirty bastards—it's only women here.'

Oh, Bücka, Sarellia thought. She moved to the inner balcony, careful to avoid the drop. The clash of metal, the cry of effort; the sounds travelled but she couldn't see the warrior. Sarellia wanted to help but the Cult hadn't taught her those skills. Swordplay; it wasn't how you shielded secrets. To be unseen, at least to conceal the truth; that was what mattered. Ruing her own vulnerability, she winced, feared for Bücka alone against six men.

Looking down at the empty courtyard, she cursed. 'Shit, Goddard, where are you?' Then another thought: *Jerune*. Bücka hadn't appeared distressed. They were safe. Surely, Chara too. But to what would they return? One dead woman, two? Certain it was a bad idea, Sarellia began to descend the stairs. Bücka's grunts becoming clearer; a cry of rage and a clatter of steel. A sudden yell; a man. Sarellia peered over the edge, saw a body sprawled on the courtyard. One down. She descended another flight. Bücka came into view. A wise warrior holding position on the steps, her opponents were queued beneath. Four men. One dead. Where was the other? With horror Sarellia saw him. Rushing to the ground level, peeling a bow from his back. He took aim, pointed the arrow at Bücka.

Sarellia cried out, 'Bücka!'

A glance and Bücka spied the threat, turned and climbed the stairs.

'Move!' the warrior roared.

Once more, Sarellia was being bundled higher. This time, Bücka was close behind, her hands and arms pushing against her back. In rapid time, and with her breath rasping, Sarellia reached the top.

In drawn out gasps, Bücka said, 'Arrows... won't reach.'

Her eyes darting around the open balcony, she pushed Sarellia away from the stairs, closer to the wall. Bücka nodded, then began to move down again.

'Where are you going?' Sarellia asked.

'I need to hold the stairs. If they reach this floor, we're done for.'

Sarellia nodded. Knew she was useless to Bücka. Her lack of power was a harsh reminder. Death would be ever closer as Laria's messengers and assassins poured onto the Northern Shores. Then she heard it. A mighty bellow. A glorious roar.

'BÜCKA!'

It was Goddard. The King had returned. For a moment, the only sound in the citadel was the echo of his voice. Sarellia hugged herself, the fine hairs on her forearms standing on end.

Again, the king called for his warrior. 'Bücka?'

Another voice, this time Jerune. 'Sarellia?'

Bücka appeared at the steps. Her face was radiant, she had tears in her eyes. 'This is my dream. I get to fight alongside a legend. You stay here!'

Sarellia nodded, moved to the edge of the floor. Peering over, she saw the shape of Goddard, a small blob by his side: Chara. Jerune stood close, peering upwards. Sarellia caught his eye, waved. She saw him move to the stairs but Goddard's giant hand held him back. He pointed to Chara, then the archway. Jerune nodded, took the girl's hand and moved to the exit, sending the other Western Stars on their way as he went. One final turn, he looked up, saluted. Sarellia smiled. Blew a kiss, felt foolish. And Jerune was gone.

Far below on the courtyard floor, five men appeared from the stairwell. The archer came last, drawing his sword. They couldn't know who Goddard was. More myth than Petra. Baza'rad the Great. Argan the sailor. Goddard the stranger. Sarellia laughed as Bücka bolted into view. Her voice barrelled upwards, her enthusiasm a candle to her humour.

Her language was colourful, if not eloquent. 'You're dead now, fuckers!'

Sarellia's heart soared as Goddard released Bruch'ail from his back. The men fell back allowing Bücka to slip past and stand beside the towering figure. Goddard leaned toward the warrior, said something that didn't travel. She watched as Bücka nodded, took a step backwards. Goddard, stepped forward. This time his voice was heard. In the funnel of Kor'A's unnatural tower, the voices resonated with a deep bass.

'You can leave,' Goddard said.

A reply. 'Not without the Cultist.'

'One chance. That's all I will give.'

A sword moved, held out toward Goddard. The King grasped the haft of Bruch'ail close to his chest. He nodded. 'Make your move.'

The first assailant lunged and the hammer was swung. But the man was agile, ducking and rolling, closing to Goddard, too close for the hammer to threaten. Sarellia's heart leapt to her mouth. A sword was thrust towards Goddard but the King's reactions were unearthly. With an almighty thud, he kicked the foe in the chest. In that moment, Sarellia was reminded of tales of siege weapons; the thunder of the impact a brutal percussion. As a ragdoll, the foe flew across the courtyard, tumbling to a broken heap against the wall.

That signalled the others to launch their attacks and Goddard swung Bruch'ail again. The metal chunk caught two of them, the awful sound reaching Sarellia; a bundle of branches crushed under rock. As the hammer's song split the air, Sarellia noticed the walls of the citadel glow brighter. Intrigued, losing focus on the destruction below, she was mesmerised by the display of light and sound. Another shiver shuddered through her body; the haunting effect causing her to wonder what was more powerful; the man, or the weapon?

Involuntarily, Sarellia raised a finger to warn her friends; one figure was moving to slip past, avoiding the wicked arc of that flashing steel block. But he met Bücka's sword, dallied for a few seconds, a dance of sorts. He fell, cut down by the warrior's ferocious, scything attack. Within moments, there was one soul left facing Goddard and Bücka. He glanced up, Sarellia meeting his eyes. A wild grin appeared on his face. He darted to the wall, reaching the stairs. Bücka yelled, flew after him.

Sarellia had nowhere to go. She cast her eyes to the floor. Realised with some humour that she was safe. One man and herself on a circular walkway. He could chase her all day, she would simply run away. She moved from the stairs, traversed to the other side. From her new position she could see him racing upwards, spiralling with each staircase. And then, he was there. She glanced, noted Bücka close behind. Though now he had the high ground; Bücka was vulnerable.

With an eye on the stairs, his sword pointing to the approaching warrior, he called to Sarellia. 'You can't stop it.'

'You underestimate us.'

He gestured to Goddard. 'We underestimated him.' A frown. 'Who is he?'

She was in no doubt he was going to die. It would be wise to glean information from his tongue before that happened. Though, she knew he wouldn't offer it freely. It wouldn't harm him to know his fate.

'My King. From a faraway land,' she said. Sarellia was disappointed. His eyes spoke of ignorance.

'I know of no Kings, not with such strength. Not like him.'

'A shame, if you had, you wouldn't have come.'

'Fire guides us. The Seer commands us. We will always come.' He pointed to her, glanced again at the stairs. Bücka was halfway toward him on the steps. 'Whatever you think your contact gave you, your power is insignificant beside the flame of Fire.'

'We're going to take that from you.'

He smiled, turned to Bücka. 'Warrior, you fight well but I have the advantage. You'd do well to stand down.'

The assassin returned his focus to Sarellia. She noticed the surreptitious movement from Bücka, the warrior reaching to her boot. She recalled the story of the assassin at the stables; how she used her dagger to injure him. Sarellia needed the man alive. He needed to talk, not die. Not yet.

'Bücka, no!' she called out.

Bücka turned, a confused look to Sarellia. The assassin flicked his head, saw the threat. He lunged, caught Bücka off-guard. Together they tumbled, landing on the floor below, fortune sparing them the precipitous drop to the courtyard. Sarellia feared the worse, noticed neither figure moving.

Rushing to the top of the stairs, she called out, 'Bücka?'

The bodies heaved, and the warrior stood. Brushing herself down, she removed her bloodied dagger from the belly of the assassin. She glared at Sarellia.

'What the hell was that? You could've got me killed.'

'I'm sorry, Bücka. I needed him alive. To find out what they know.'

The warrior stared at the body, frowned. 'Oops,' she said.

Sarellia saw Goddard ascending the stairs. He looked to her, asked, 'Are you harmed?'

'I'm safe, thanks to Bücka.'

The warrior grinned and turned to Goddard. Sarellia shrieked; a lurch from the downed man. Rising, grabbing his sword, he swung for Bücka. Goddard reacted, those uncanny reflexes in stark contrast to his bulk. Catching the assassin in the ribs, he kicked him over the edge and he fell screaming to the courtyard below. Sarellia didn't watch, her eyes transfixed on her King.

Bücka called up to her. 'See, I didn't kill him. But I think he's dead now.'

Sarellia sighed, a mixture of relief and regret, and descended the stairs to meet them. 'I don't know what I've had done without you, both of you.'

'Die, I think,' Bücka said.

Unoffended, Sarellia smiled. 'You have such a way with words.'

Bücka nodded. 'So I've been told.'

From below, Jerune's voice called out. 'Sarellia? Bücka? Goddard?'

The warrior winked at Sarellia. 'That's a higher arc there. See I came second though.'

'Hierarchy,' she corrected. 'I'm sure we're all equal.'

Goddard raised an eyebrow. 'I doubt it.' He leaned over the edge, called down to Jerune. 'We're all safe. We're coming down.'

Sarellia turned to Bücka. She placed a hand on her shoulder. The warrior looked at her, appeared uncomfortable. She knew why, Jerune had mentioned her interest. To Bücka, she said, 'I'm thankful for your sword. I'm in your debt.'

Bücka smiled. 'I can think of ways to pay me.'

Not expecting such a response, Sarellia fumbled her words. Didn't know what to say. Bücka laughed.

'I'm kidding. Happy to oblige.' She turned to Goddard, nudged him in the stomach. 'Besides, I got to fight beside my hero. Who gets to do that?'

Goddard sighed. 'I think there may be much more to come. Don't wish for it so soon. It won't always be this easy.'

Sarellia watched as Goddard turned and descended the stairs. She felt Bücka's gaze, turned to meet it.

'What?'

The warrior appeared anxious. 'Did I annoy him?'

'No.' She didn't think so. 'He's had multiple lifetimes of war. Probably not as keen as you to see more.'

Bücka nodded. 'I never think of it like that. It still excites me.'

'I think it does for him as well. But I know he's lost friends. Family.' She offered Bücka the greatest compliment. 'I imagine he fears losing you too.'

The warrior smiled. 'Thanks. That's a nice thing to say.'

Sarellia clapped her arm. 'Come on, let's get down. There's much to discuss.'

Sarellia settled next to Jerune. She found it difficult to resist an embrace. A need for comfort after the affray. They had agreed to keep things subtle. In the company of friends, it was childish to show such affection. The warm contact was brief but welcome. Two blocks along, Bücka straddled her seat with Chara huddled close, the child asleep with her eyes open. Sarellia turned to the arch, nodded to Goddard returning from his final trip. The bodies now removed from the courtyard, placed on their horses and sent on their way.

'That's the last,' Goddard said, lowering his body onto the block between Sarellia and Bücka.

With Goddard settled, Jerune said, 'Who wants to speak first?'

Sarellia wasn't sure what he meant. She said, 'I have news from Port Aracyse.'

Jerune said, 'We have news from Petra.'

What had happened in her absence? She asked, 'What have I missed?'

Goddard gestured to her. Shook his head. 'You first Sarellia. Our story comes after.'

'Alright, if you're sure?'

He nodded.

She withdrew the parchment from within her tunic, handed it to Jerune. 'This is the Forge, at least where it lies. Our Larian sources weren't so informative.' To Bücka, she said, 'Your contract, the seed—did you go to the Forge?'

A pause. 'Close but not inside. Acquired the thing from a third party.'

'You didn't see the Forge?'

Bücka appeared suspicious. 'From a distance. Why?'

Sarellia sighed, said to the group, 'It's not a building. It's inside a mountain.'

'Yeah,' Bücka said, nodding. 'I saw that much.'

'But you didn't go inside?'

'Didn't have to.'

Her response was blunt. Sarellia realised they had nothing of value with which to work. It was evident Bücka's contract hadn't required entry to the Forge. Shaking her head, Sarellia said, 'Our sources don't have eyes within the place. We're practically blind. Jerune, it's going to be...'

'Dangerous?' he replied.

She nodded, tried to hide her concern. Imagined she failed.

'Well, lucky there's more of us going to Laria,' he said.

She quizzed him with a stare, said to Goddard. 'What does he mean?'

He replied, 'There's been a change of plan.'

'Oh?'

Jerune pointed to the King. 'He's coming after all.'

Sarellia looked from Jerune to Goddard. 'You're serious? What about Chara?'

'She's better by my side.'

Taking her to Laria would be dangerous. Observing the sleeping child, she said, 'It won't be safer. They're still mobilising, heading north to the fleet. There will be movement across the land.'

'And that movement will cross the sea and come here,' Goddard said. 'I can't stop an army once it reaches our shores. Whatever we do, there is risk.'

He was right. Though his change of heart had taken her by surprise. One which she welcomed. Bücka's skill and courage were evident but she wasn't Baza'rad. Goddard was; no matter who he claimed himself to be. A thought occurred to Sarellia. A false hope.

To Jerune, she said, 'And you? Are your skills needed?'

His eyes on the map, little more than a drawing of contoured hills, he replied, 'Judging by this... map, we still need to find a way in.' He lifted his gaze to regard Goddard. 'If what Petra says of Fire is even remotely true, you can't just walk in the front door.'

'What did she say about fire? What happened?' Sarellia asked.

Goddard replied, 'She was visited at Farenhyne. Messengers of Fire, from the Seer. She's beholden to the Covenant. At least, she will hold herself to it.'

'*What?*' She was incredulous. 'She won't help?'

Goddard stiffened. Sarellia felt a fool. His voice restrained, he said, 'She can't help. It's too great a risk.'

Bowing her head, she said, 'I assume she... dealt with them?'

Jerune turned to her, his face grim. 'Not so much. They dropped a seed inside her keep. Not like Bücka's. An actual weapon. She escaped but it swallowed everything. Petra said the destruction was complete.'

She frowned. Believed Jerune, but wanted more. Sarellia turned to Goddard. He offered no reassurance.

He said, 'A huge pit from one seed. Destruction as she'd never seen. Petra understands what will follow if she breaks the new Covenant; the Covenant you spoke of appears to be quite real. And Petra is part of it.'

'But without Petra we're doomed. That's why I sought her. Nothing can stop an army of Fire.'

'Which is why I'm going,' Goddard said. 'Bücka and Jerune are still going to the Forge. What we decide tonight will decide if I do too, or focus on the northern port.'

Confused by the divergence of tactics, Sarellia shook her head. She looked from Goddard, to Jerune, to Bücka; a silent question. What on earth was going on?

Jerune patted her thigh. 'I have a job to do.' He pointed upwards. 'Somewhere on the top floor is a sealed room. Hidden by Petra. I can access it from outside. Climb in.' She questioned him with her eyes. Jerune continued. 'It's lovely really, tragic and epic. A room full of her tears. Sarellia, Petra *cries* diamonds.'

None of this made sense. What purpose did such a tall tale serve? Shaking her head, she said, 'I can't believe any of this. Even if true, what use are diamonds? To furnish us with an army? To buy mercenaries? We couldn't buy enough.'

'A ship,' Goddard said. 'From the Rotynians. Petra mentioned it this evening. The first I'd heard of it.'

Sarellia stared. She wasn't a fool. No ship could possibly sail against the assembling Larian fleet. The Rotynians were fabled pirates. Masters of the oceans, more so after the fall of Laria. But they wouldn't have the numbers. Besides, Goddard had said a ship, *singular*. Not a fleet.

'One ship?' she repeated.

He nodded. 'One of *these* would be enough to cause serious damage.'

A revelation flashed in her mind. Relics of history, something mythical. Frowning, she said, 'No?'

Goddard replied with a grin and a nod.

It couldn't be. Could it? She asked, 'A Larian Battleship?'

A slow nod from Goddard. 'Petra said they salvaged it after the Iron Cloud sent others to the depths. The Rotynians have one.' He pointed to Jerune. 'That's why we need Petra's diamonds. If we can trade for it, even for one journey, we'll have an armada of one.'

Sarellia sat back. Looked to the ground. It was magnificent. Reckless, but magnificent. She turned to Jerune. 'You're going where?'

'Top floor, clamber outside, find the room.'

Madness. Too perilous. 'You've seen how smooth the walls are?'

He nodded, grinned. 'And you've seen how talented I am.'

Bücka laughed, pointing a finger at Jerune, she said, 'Pfft. Humble too.'

Goddard said, 'While I remember.' Sarellia looked to him, the King removing a scrap of parchment from under his armour. As she reached for it, Jerune scoffed.

'Wait, you didn't ask Petra to read it?' he asked.

Goddard shook his head. Sarellia smiled. She had never seen him appear so mortal. So humbled.

His tone defensive, the King said, 'I forgot. I am human, you know.'

Jerune laughed, Bücka too. She said, 'I'm glad you're normal then.'

Goddard smiled, passed the parchment to Sarellia. 'I'm also old. I plan on becoming quite forgetful. Sarellia, it's Sanhe, can you read it?'

She could. Unfurling the untidy scrap, she was disappointed. It wasn't well written, a poor effort at the complex script. Though it was chilling to see the words, to understand what they meant. 'It's your contract, Bücka. The one on your head.'

She squinted, asked, 'How much?'

'One-thousand, two ways. And two names.'

Bücka replied, her voice an octave higher. 'How much? A thousand?'

Sarellia nodded.

'I'm honoured.'

'Well, that's all good. But you shouldn't be. You should be afraid.' She looked up. Spoke to all of them, tapping her finger on one section of the contract. 'This bounty's guaranteed by the Seer himself. They'll never stop coming for you. Clearly, you made an impression in Laria.'

'That doesn't seem to surprise me,' Jerune said.

Bücka appeared unfazed. 'The names?'

'Let's see, Sanhe can be awkward with exact titles.' She looked to Goddard, winked, 'Should've asked Petra.'

'Really? You as well,' he replied.

She smiled. 'Atarius of Lanhain, I think. That's a male name. And... Gisella of Brokenmire.'

'The woman then, she got away,' Jerune said.

'Bastard,' Bücka said. Sarellia noted her tone. Familiarity.

'You know her?'

'Oh yeah, had a contract on her once. Let her live. Devious snake.'

'A problem?' Jerune asked.

'No. She's more a tracker. Not so much the blade. She'd cut *you* to pieces but she's no threat alone.'

'Good to be valued,' Jerune quipped.

'Well, for what we need next, your role is priceless,' Goddard said. 'We'll need those diamonds. If you're up to it, you'll prove your worth and more.'

Jerune nodded.

Sarellia turned her head to the circle of dark above. Looking down they had all seemed so small. It was a great height; a terrifying thought. She grabbed his hand, squeezed it hard.

Jerune leaned in, smiled. 'Trust me. You survived a half-dozen assassins. Think I can manage a little climb.'

Chapter XXVII

W hat had he said to Sarellia last night? Brave words, off the cuff. Jerune regretted them now. This was no easy climb. Peering out from Kor'A's suicide balcony, he saw few places to grab on the exposed citadel flank. A gentle curve of white mineral speckling in the morning glow. A foolish look down to see the spectacular drop to the unyielding marble far below. He had suggested the climb after dusk but the others preferred time to rest, let the nerves of the assault subside. Just yards away, the next balcony contained Petra's tears; the saddest treasure. Jerune had easily recognised the anomaly, counting the inner portals, there was a clear blank of wall; it had to be the concealed room. Tantalisingly close. Jerune's mind was racing. They needed the diamonds. Sarellia had agreed, the Rotynians would show favour to anyone with such wealth. Loyal pirates. Only a few yards between a Battleship and death. Jerune glanced back to the inner wall. Gauging the distance from centre to edge, he clapped his hands.

'An idea?' Sarellia asked.

'Aye, old climbing tricks. I need a rope. A long rope.'

Goddard, toward the inner balcony, one hand on Chara's shoulder said, 'I have one in my hut, in the hills.'

Jerune shook his head. 'I've one in my cabin. Everything I need is there. I'll come back.'

'I'll come with,' Sarellia said.

Excusing himself, he led her away. Once outside, he glanced up to the citadel. Sarellia took his hand.

'I don't like it,' she said.

He agreed but they had no choice. 'We need the diamonds. Besides, I'm more than a little curious about what I'll find. Aren't you?'

She nodded. 'It's foolish. But it's fascinating.'

A sigh to blow away his doubts and he continued on. They travelled through the waking streets, his eyes scanning for anomalies. Anka appeared calm. The first day of many that felt as though normality had returned. He knew it wouldn't last. Reaching his cabin, Sarellia appeared impressed.

'It's pretty,' she said, clearly surprised.

'Why shouldn't it be?'

'I don't know, I suppose I imagined it to be functional. Like you. You know, earthy?'
Sarellia giggled.

A hand on his chest, he shook his head. 'Sometimes, I feel you misjudge me.'

Sarellia laughed. 'I doubt it.'

Inside, he grabbed a hessian sack, bundling together the tools of the task: the rope, a large ball of twine and his bow which he handed to Sarellia. Her expression spoke of the weight, a look of surprise on her features as she held the long bow in both hands.

'Where's this from? It's heavy.'

'It's Drohendrian. Actual Darkwood.'

'It feels like carved stone. I've seen the like before, in buildings, but I've never held it.'

'Not a lot comes across the sea. Not with Kalleron in the state it's in.'

'How did you get it?' she asked.

He wanted to say it was an heirloom. It made it sound special, valued. 'Truthfully, I stole it when I was young. One of my... one of her customers.'

'Your mother?'

Jerune nodded. He had loved her—as a lone child must. But around Sarellia, he found it hard to talk as though she was important.

Sarellia's reaction to his response was clear. She wouldn't pry, instead she asked, 'Is it powerful?'

'It's brutal. I can barely string the damn thing.'

'Goddard could...'

Jerune cut her off. 'I said *barely*, not couldn't. It's bad enough I'm not able to compete with the warriors; I don't need my buckles fastened by a Bruhadian King.'

Putting the bow to the side, she approached, her arm rising, palm placed soft against his cheek. 'Aw, poor pet.' Sarellia laughed.

'Piss off,' he replied with a smile. Pointing to a quiver in the corner, he said, 'Grab that too.'

She passed it to him and he put it inside the sack. He retrieved the bow, hoisting the unstrung weapon onto his shoulder. He paused, noticed Sarellia's gaze; curious glances cast around his home. Her face, relaxed, held a subtle smile.

'I like it,' she said, nodding. 'The scent of wood, the comforts. It's warmer than Anka.'

'It's why I don't stay there.' He thought about the city, the stone. 'You never feel uncomfortable? I mean, it's the skin of an Elemental.'

'Isn't all the earth hers?'

'That's not what I mean. I know the stories. It's literally her essence. Sometimes I imagine I can see goosebumps when the wind blows cold.'

Sarellia frowned. 'I find it magical.'

'Hmm, no doubt. But I'm wary of it.'

Her eyes scanning around again, she asked, 'Where's your bed?'

He lowered the sack. Put down the bow. Jerune walked over to his hammock, bundled the end from the hook on the ceiling.

'I usually just sit there,' he pointed to the soft rug near the wood-burner. Holding the suspended fabric, he said, 'This is for guests.'

She laughed. 'What sort of guests?'

'You could try it.'

Her eyes flicked to the hammock. 'I'll take you up on that offer. Or perhaps, I'll bring a larger rug, we can lay on the floor beside the fire.'

'Either's good for me,' he said. He looked at the hammock in his hand. Sighed, said to Sarellia, 'We need to get back. Don't we?'

'Unfortunately.'

Jerune didn't like the audience. Standing on the opposite side of the inner balcony, he held the bow in his hands. He was thankful for Sarellia's suggestion that he string it prior to coming inside. Just in case, she had said. A good thing, it had been a frustrating wrestle; man versus Darkwood. Now, they all looked on, Goddard, arms folded; Chara, appearing to predict the arrows path with a bobbing head; Bücka, hands on hips, grinning; and Sarellia, close by, her enthusiasm whispered on her breath.

'You can do it,' she said.

Through gritted teeth, as polite as he could manage, he replied, 'I know.'

He drew back the string. The bow, resilient and powerful, made no noise. Not a creak or complaint of distress. Harder, he pulled again, the muscles across his back tensing. Raising the bow, he let loose the string and the thud reverberated around the citadel walls. The arrow flew fast and high drawing behind it the length of twine.

'Brilliant!' Bücka called over.

The coil of rope sat close, the loose pile of twine vanishing from sight. Then, as a snake rising in anger, the rope shot into the air following the arrows path. The weight slowed the arrow and as the rope disappeared over the roof of the citadel, the line became still.

'You think it flew far enough?' Sarellia asked.

'One way to find out,' he replied.

Jerune trusted his aim, knew the path would fall over the accessible outer balcony. From there, he would tie it to himself and with Goddard at the other side they would flick the rope closer to the concealed room. The strongman would anchor him in place and he would wall run. A simple plan.

He entered the room, saw the line of rope hanging down past the open ledge.

'It worked,' he called back.

Moving to the edge, he grabbed the rope, reeled in the end and untied the twine. Jerune dragged up the arrow and discarded it to the floor. Sarellia followed, strolled to his side and, peeking over, held his shoulders from behind.

'Now you do what?' she asked, her concern obvious.

Pointing, he said, 'I tie this on and Goddard takes the slack. Then, we loosen the line and I walk over the edge.'

'The edge?' she said. Sarellia's eyes darted around.

He nodded. 'The edge. I'll be fine. It'll be fun.' Jerune knew it would be anything but.

Securing the rope around his waist, he checked the knot. It was tight. No chance it could come loose. Better check it again, he thought. Perfect. Secure enough to hold an ox. Jerune checked it one last time. He blew a rapid breath.

'You're sure?' Sarellia asked.

'I have to do it.'

Her hand gripping tight to his shoulder, he prised her fingers clear. A hand to wave her away and a confident grin. 'Trust me.' Looking beyond, he could see Goddard peering through the archway.

'Ready?' Goddard called.

Jerune nodded. 'Take the slack.'

He watched as two strong hands began to draw in the loose rope. If there was any man to hold him, it would be he. With enough rope left for the task, Jerune called to Goddard.

'Now tie it around your waist.'

The old King could fight hordes and heal the sick. His mind had absorbed many things in that long lifetime. Had he learned such a menial labour as rope craft? Jerune strained to see what sort of fixing he might use. Would it be a Thanian slip knot or a Bruhadian Granny? He hoped it wasn't the Granny. That knot was a mixture of chaos and hope.

Best to ask. 'That's not a Granny, is it?'

Goddard tugged the loose end and looked up. He signalled to Jerune, a vertical forearm and a clenched fist—the Hammer—a Bruhadian symbol for 'strong'. It was a bloody Granny. *By the gods*. But still, with those hands on the rope, he imagined the knot was a redundancy. Held by no ordinary man, Jerune inched to the edge.

'Jerune?' Sarellia said, her voice trembling.

It didn't matter how she appeared: angry, calm, distressed, she was always beautiful. He recalled the day he had wanted her to leave him be. Those first few days of his contract. How glad he was they had persevered.

He controlled his own fear, tried to calm her. 'You think your King will drop me?'

Sarellia didn't reply. Fixed him with her eyes.

Jerune gauged her concerns, noticed she was shaking. What he was about to do would push her to the limit. 'Go inside, Sarellia.'

She nodded, backed away and disappeared from view. He caught Goddard's eye watching her leave. Another distraction as Bücka entered.

She said, 'If someone has to watch you fall, it'll be me.'

To her he said, 'Thanks,' then called out to Goddard, 'I'm going over, pull in the slack a little.'

Jerune moved to the edge, peered down. The mountains to the north and east rose high above the citadel. It was reassuring, a false perspective of height. He made an effort to stay focused, not look down. The rope tightened and he felt his weight lift.

'Hold,' he called.

Heart in his mouth, he leaned out, feet placed on the edge. His body stopped at an angle; too far gone to recover if the knot slipped. He remained there for a moment gathering his faith in both ends of the rope. It was secure.

With the wind blowing in his face, he said, 'Slack, slowly.'

Jerune leaned further back, watching as the outside wall shrunk and the sky loomed large. Passing the point of no return he lay horizontal, his entire fate in Goddard's old hands. *Strong hands.* Not old. One slow step, he moved down with the rope, his full weight supported. Another. Buffeted by a taunting wind, he peered across, scanning the open void.

Bücka appeared near his feet, a surreal sight. She said, 'Ooh shit, that's high.'

'Fuck off!'

She grinned. 'Can I help?'

'Tell Goddard to hold it tight.'

She yelled back to Goddard. Jerune took another step backwards, felt the rope tighten.

'Now what?' Bücka asked.

'I'm going to run back and forward, get momentum, and hit the open space.'

She frowned. A genuine expression, not a tease. He would have preferred a joke. Some ill-mannered distraction. Bücka offered none. She offered worse.

'Good luck,' she said.

He sighed, the breath leaving his lungs as though a rat from a sinking ship. Jerune started his run, he shimmied to the right, managing a few steps before the rope pulled him back. He moved with the natural swing, using his legs to increase the amplitude. He ignored Bücka's eyes, wide with wonder, as he repeated the traverse. The rope moved above, sliding across the marble. An unnatural thought occurred. What if the roof was covered in blades of steel? Or sharp quartz? It could be fashioned as a terrible crown atop the Queen's citadel. Fear spurred him on and he neared the open portal. On his last swing he caught Bücka's eyes. *She looked terrified.*

One final, huge lunge, his right hand and foot reaching for the vertical edge. The rock was smooth, his position precarious. He couldn't hold it. If he swung back, he would lose his momentum, worse, he'd lose his nerve. Jerune yelled to Bücka.

'Tell Goddard to move left. Left!'

He heard her shout. Felt his fingers slipping. He clawed with his boot, strained with all his might to hang on. The rope vibrated; an angry twang as it was yanked across the roof. Two digits came free, his index and middle finger remained, one last pad of flesh before he came loose. Jerune roared with effort and he felt the rope move again. This time it peeled him toward the open bay.

'Slack!' he cried out.

Bücka echoed the command.

The rope loosened and he began to fall. Foot and fingers scraped stone and Jerune tumbled down into the space. He lay there on his back, staring at a ceiling he never thought he could love so much. Panic grabbed him as the rope tugged. He yanked on it, cried out.

'I'm safe. Give me slack!'

The tension released. Jerune exhaled a colossal breath. Lay still. He wouldn't do that again. Figured how he would get back down. An abseil from this floor to the next. The thought of it relaxed him. An easy way back. He raised himself on legs of blubber, steadied himself against the wall. Lifting his head, he gasped. Everywhere: *diamonds*.

His elation was brought crashing down when he realised the source. Petra. This had been her domain for over seventy years. Seven decades of immortal grief. A terrible solitude of sadness. Every diamond a tear. And there were thousands. Piled in the corners, he imagined scoured by the winds, they lay as though pockets of ice. Jerune, sweeping a few gems away from the ground, knelt down. It was sobering. A dreadful place. He knew sadness. Had grieved for others; imagined in time he would do the same for Sarellia. These stones were not wealth. They were despair. He plucked one from the marble. Holding it to his eyes, he saw no flaw. A perfect gem. In any market it would be worth hundreds. A few could buy a Western Star; assuming you knew the right people. A handful would get you a full stable. The room held more value than most cities. An unfathomable fortune. Yet thinking of the tragic Queen of Stone, it felt as though warm ice. A fragment of grief, frozen forever. In that moment, he felt for Petra, understood who she was; a woman of stone with an all too human heart.

Jerune stood, sighed. With heavy steps he moved to the corner. He pulled the first of several velvet pouches from his tunic and began to fill it. Each handful was a weight of shame, the scales tipping far from a noble ounce. With barely a dent made in the pile of gems, he had five full pouches. Jerune nodded his head and moved to the ledge. Before tugging the rope, he turned back to the room. A tightness in his throat.

'I'm so sorry, Petra. One day I hope you find your peace.'

Five fat pouches. Laid out, side by side on a marble block, they appeared as though plump, ripe fruit. The scout had done well, Goddard nodded to him. Jerune, quiet since his escapade, dropped his eyes, gestured to the treasure of tears.

'That enough?'

'All diamonds?' Goddard asked.

'Yeah.'

Sarellia said, 'That's a fortune.'

'Double a fortune,' Bücka added.

Chara picked up a bag. She tugged it open, peeked inside. 'You're funny.'

'How so?' Sarellia asked.

Chara pinched a diamond in her fingers. 'It's just rock. Like me.'

The irony wasn't lost on Goddard. He had already defended her from dozens of rogue bandits.

He said, 'To me your worth is beyond stone. Priceless, is what we say.'

She beamed, put the gem back and lay the pouch beside the others.

'I need some air,' Jerune said.

Goddard thought it an odd thing to say. The courtyard as breezy as the plains. He considered the scout's mood, reasoned his mind was distracted. His suspicions were confirmed when Sarellia made to follow, Jerune warding her away. She turned to Goddard for support. Her eyes searching for an answer, he frowned.

'Leave him be,' he said, his voice soft and quiet. 'I think I understand. Stay here.'

Sarellia nodded as he followed Jerune.

Beyond the citadel wall the scout stood still as a statue. Goddard approached, imagined his attempt at a quiet pace was futile.

'Just a fraction of her tears,' Jerune said, facing away. 'You knew her. Know her. I can't imagine it. Living with so much pain.'

Coming to his side, Goddard exhaled through flaring nostrils. He had known grief. Seen more death than Petra. But he had always been apart from it. The Bruhadian way. Death was a thing to honour, for most. True, loss of family was always painful. After his own, he had never become so attached. Petra had. Mothered them all, cared for too many souls. Though he knew the scales of her grief were unevenly weighted by just two hearts.

'She's lost a lot in her life,' he said.

'It's strange. You never imagine they cry.'

'They?'

'Legends,' Jerune replied. Now I've seen her, know something of her, it's tragic.'

'Petra isn't tragic. She's strong.'

Jerune turned, shook his head. His brow creased. 'Then, I don't understand. Why so many tears?'

Goddard looked behind, scanned the high cliffs. Out of sight, his old shack. She would be there, unless she wandered alone along the rock. Perhaps she was watching them, wishing to be with them? His eyes only human, the rocks gave no clue to her presence.

He said, 'Petra bonded to all her crew, all her friends. But there were two above all. One was her lover, Felicitra.' Goddard waved his hand across the scope of Anka. 'Without her death, none of this would be here.'

'I've heard the myths, or the whispers of legend,' Jerune said.

'Most likely true when you scrape away the insincerity of history. Felicitra was special. Shadow used to say she had tamed Petra. But she died at the hands of Kor'A when she was Queen of Kalleron. It was one death too many for Petra. Became involved with the Cult, helped kill the immortal King. Everything you see followed that. We followed her on that path, we owed her. Petra gave all of her crew a new life. Those days were golden. Like Bruhale.'

'The other death. It was who you just mentioned, Shadow?'

'Yes.' Goddard thought Jerune's position in the group deserved some truth. He said, 'Shadow was an enigma, almost as much as Kor'A. In the moment, a playful fool, in the change of the breeze, a brutal soldier. He was Petra's rock. The stability she needed when things were bleak. No matter what the sorrow, Shadow always dragged Petra from the depths. So bound were they, most assumed them to be lovers. I had thought so when I had joined her crew. But their bind was beyond what most men or women could imagine. One soul shared between two bodies.

'When he died, she lost her way. She remained in Anka for three decades after his death. They had raised orphans, Bücka's grandmother was one. Thelissa, the other. But she died young, before her time, before Shadow. That hit him hard, his last few years were difficult; Thelissa was as good as his own flesh and blood. Petra watched her rock start to crumble. Age didn't help, too many knocks on the head.

'And then Shadow passed. Petra was distraught.' Goddard stopped. Cursed the reality of an immortal life. A torturous thing for a human heart. Shaking his head, he continued, 'Shortly after Shadow's death, Thelia vanished. We all knew it was too much for her; losing her sister then Shadow. Finally, of the family we had become, Kallisa passed. A strong soul from my own time as King; though, she would've been young—a mere child—when I ruled Bruhada.' He stopped. A moment to remember Kallisa. His jaw clenched. Another sigh to control his emotion. Grief wasn't useful. Continuing, he leaned into Jerune. 'Sarellia is Kallisa's fourth Bruhsa. If you like, in clumsy terms, great, great granddaughter. She had a daughter with Shadow, Melody, named after Petra's ship; Kallisa hails from that line. All but she have passed away. Imagine, Jerune, watching them all die. One by one. All the people you ever cared about.'

'I can barely cope with one,' Jerune said.

'Petra knew a long time ago, after her resurrection, she would watch her friends pass to dust. She told me once, she was fortunate to love women. She would bear no child. Becoming stone sealed that choice. What horror it would be, to know you would outlive everything you created.'

Jerune shook his head. 'I've seen that horror. In that damn room. You know, I didn't really believe it would be real. Maybe, couldn't imagine such a thing. But to see it, to know what those stones are, it's... hollowing. I know we must, but it disgusts me to think we'll trade that grief for a fucking ship.'

The scout's empathy was palpable. Goddard, not one to trip over sombre thoughts, appreciated the depth of feeling he showed for his immortal friend. He could offer a healing word or two.

'You see her sorrow and feel it?' he asked.

'I wouldn't presume to feel her pain.'

'And she'd appreciate that. That was her way. Even with Shadow. Petra guarded her sorrow; kept it from everyone. Why do you think she shuttered her tears away from sight? They're hers and hers alone. If she knew how much you were affected by them, she'd be embarrassed. Petra was a warrior. Not in profession but in her soul. Grief was a sickness; she never valued those that wallowed in it. She wouldn't ask for yours.'

'A proud woman. Guess it's why she's a legend.'

159

Goddard stood tall, raised his chin. 'She is more than legend, Jerune. That woman has endured things mortal men couldn't. I'm honoured to have her as my friend. Humbled. She gave us the insight to use her tears. And when she offered that, in the forest, she never wept. She smiled. You can raise your head, Jerune, stand tall. We will go to Laria and we'll show Petra we're worthy of her friendship. With her blessing, we'll sail a damned Battleship to the Larian coast and annihilate a fleet sent from Fire. The Forge will fall; these shores will be saved. Petra has paid in tears and blood to deliver this moment to us. Don't grieve for her sadness, rejoice in her spirit.'

'Rousing words,' Jerune said. 'You sure you're still not that King?'

Goddard smiled. He placed an arm around Jerune's shoulders. 'My friend, Petra made us equal. But if it fires your resolve and lifts your soul, consider this; you stand with a King to aid an immortal Queen; all the while, we protect a child of Elemental Glass, daughter of Earth herself. The days to come will be full of honour. There is no place for grief in our story.'

Chapter XXVIII

'Where are we going?' Bücka asked.

'To see a friend,' Goddard replied.

'She lives in the hills?'

'She does now,' he said, thinking of Petra's forced migration.

Chara tugged on Goddard's tunic. 'Are we going to your hut?'

Hut? It was a home. Huts were for tools. It was late in the afternoon and he had left Sarellia and Jerune in the city. They had agreed a plan to move east to Farenhyne, then onwards to the Rotynian territory. It would be their last day in Anka and Goddard felt a sense of duty to close a family line. Bücka, so comparable in traits and mannerisms to Thelia, deserved to meet Petra. Goddard considered it a circle of fate that she should meet the granddaughter of the orphan she saved a century ago.

He led them through the roughly hewn pass climbing above the White City. The trail grew narrow, at points the southern edge becoming a sheer drop. Few travelled the path; most knew it went nowhere. A long trek for no good purpose. It was why Goddard had chosen it. Not far from his destination, he stopped, realised Bücka had fallen behind. Turning, he saw her, boot raised upon a rock, staring out across the southern reaches.

He called to her. 'Bücka.'

She smiled. 'You can see everything.'

It was true. The citadel below, a fraction to the west. The open balcony from where Jerune had acquired Petra's tears was visible. The tower, a cylindrical structure with those stretching, perilous windows, was adorned with occasional jutting anomalies. Not quite turrets, not quite anything. Try though he had, Goddard had conceived neither purpose nor access to those incongruous features. He considered them to be as other *faults* in the city; something to show the imperfect hand of its creator. Beyond the citadel, Anka sprawled to meet the lush green of the forest. Farther still, the plains met the ocean. A glimmer on the distant horizon.

He said, 'The view's better where we're going.'

Bücka nodded, hurried to join him. Goddard continued, one last twist in the trail taking them deeper into the mountain. The rocky flanks rose higher, sheltering a staircase which led to an unseen plateau. Incongruous with Anka, the steps were hewn by human hands. His own. To see the erratic tooling marks of manual graft was a refreshing sight after the seamless nature of Kor'A's design.

'Almost there,' he said.

He recalled Chara coming to him at his home. She would have climbed these steps. They were too tall for her to ascend with ease. He smiled, thought of how she would appear, scrambling up each in turn. At the bottom of the flight, he stopped. A sense of pride as he pictured her on the granite ledges. He patted her crown.

'You climbed these yourself?' he asked.

'Uh-huh.'

Bücka said, 'They're mighty big steps for such small legs. How'd you do it?'

Goddard looked at Bücka, caught her wink. She was mentoring the girl, buffing her ego.

Chara shook free of his hand and said, 'Like this.'

Folding his arms, Goddard watched as she mantled onto the first step. She turned and smiled. Pointing at Bücka, she challenged the warrior. 'Your turn.'

Bücka nodded at Goddard and placed a foot on the step. One powerful lunge and she was beside Chara. Bücka reached down, held open her hand. 'Come on squirt, let me help.'

As the girls climbed with giggles and huffs, his thoughts drifted to the past; a memory of the sisters, Thelissa and Thelia. Thelissa, the elder by several years, doted on her sibling. A shield against the worst of humanity, she had protected Thelia from the hideous desires of shallow men. Pawns of human traffickers, they found their freedom aboard the *Melody*. More souls set free by the woman Bücka was soon to meet.

Lost in those days, Goddard looked up. Bücka was calling.

'Come on!'

Her face was a picture as he launched up the steps. Mouth agape at his effortless stride. Reaching the top, Bücka blurted her response to his extraordinary strength.

'You're like seven feet tall. Hardly a fair competition.'

A grumble of satisfaction; Goddard had a suitable reply. Smiled and patted her head. 'You'll grow up one day. Let's go.'

Goddard heard Bücka tutting, revelled in the moment. Ahead lay his home. A great expanse of flat rock, another bluff rising from the plateau. In the shade of the cliff, nestled in a natural cove, a jumble of rocks and wooden beams formed a rough shelter. It was as it was meant to be. A dilapidated appearance.

'That's it?' Bücka asked, coming to his side.

'That's it,' he replied.

'It's nicer inside,' Chara said.

'Wouldn't be hard,' said Bücka. 'So, your friend, they live in this house?'

'She does now.' Goddard assumed Petra would be here. Hoped she hadn't ventured higher or deeper into the mountains.

As they approached, a dark void appeared against the wall of rock and wood; a figure emerging from within. At first concealed in a hooded cloak, two marble hands rose to lower the cowl.

Bücka whispered, 'By the Gods, *is that her?*'

'It is. Go and say hello.'

The warrior paced forward, her steps showing hesitation. Chara came alongside Goddard, her fingers interweaving with his. Bücka continued on, her steps uncertain, a glance back. He wanted this to be right; for the moment to be golden. A treasured memory for Thelia's descendent. He didn't want the moment to be spoiled by an awkward greeting, after all, Bücka's social bluntness was often jarring. Petra hadn't met the woman. No matter how much he longed for it to happen, he couldn't be sure they would bond, though he knew Petra would always welcome family. A rare flutter in his belly, he followed on, greeting Petra with a smile.

Nodding to the warrior, he said, 'Petra, this is Bücka.'

Her diamond eyes glowing, Petra slowly shook her head. She said, 'You look so much like her.'

'Thelia?' Bücka replied.

'Yes.'

'I... know of you...'

Goddard heard the tremble in Bücka's voice. Gone was the mischief. Not a hint of sarcasm or wit. He had wanted the warrior to meet Petra; to see the face of the woman to whom she owed her existence. It was clear Bücka was overwhelmed.

Petra's eyes lifted, met his. She nodded to him. He reciprocated. He was being dismissed for the moment. Before he turned away, he saw Bücka walking forward, arms by her side. Colliding with Petra, she was caught in an embrace of stone. Decades ago, Petra had abandoned Anka, left it to find her solitude and peace. But her family still continued. There was Sarellia, and now there was Bücka. The hopes of her past living in the present.

Leaving one perfect view to survey another, he stood on the cliffs, staring out across the Northern Lands. Beside him Chara shuffled and he felt a tug on his hand.

She asked, 'Bücka won't cry diamonds, will she?'

'No, but her tears are worth just as much.'

Bücka stood inside Goddard's home but she couldn't take her eyes away from Petra. The legend of Anka sat on a rough wooden chair no doubt carved by the old King. A functional hemp robe covered her marble body, her arms visible, folded across her chest. Unlike Chara, Petra's face was human, everything as it should be, all except for the sapphire and diamond eyes and the white marble skin. A priceless visage. Her flesh appeared supple, yet her embrace had felt solid; a sign of her improbable strength. Hair, as fine as silk, flowed down her shoulders. At rest it appeared as though sculpted in form. Though when she moved it was fluid. An impossible thing to behold. She was beyond magnificent. Sitting opposite this legend, Bücka hadn't spoken a word since entering Goddard's home.

Petra smiled. 'It's remarkable. You have your grandmother's eyes.'

Bücka stared. Her heart was in her mouth. A silly thought, she thought she might be falling in love. With a goddess.

'Thelia used to stare like that,' Petra continued, 'when she was lost for words. Tell me, if you may, did she live well when she left Anka?'

Bücka blinked, focused. 'Yes, she did.' She recalled the reasons for her departure. The same, she supposed, that had led to Petra's absence. 'She was happy enough in Wederhyne. Often looked out across the sea.' She smiled, recalling Thelia's affection for the ocean and the ship upon which she had once sailed. 'She loved the *Melody*. She would always go on about how wonderful it was. I don't think she spent long at sea but she treasured the time.'

'My ship became home to many people. All of them I counted as family. Thelia and her sister gave me a lot of joy. I always knew when they were on board, you could hear the giggling.'

Bücka grinned. 'Gran said she was a pain in your arse?'

Petra laughed. 'Never. Well, just a little, perhaps. I knew they'd be bold as brass when I... when we met. That's why I gave Shadow the task of getting them shipshape.'

'What was he like, Shadow? Thelia spoke of him all the time. I can't imagine any man being so perfect.'

Petra's smile remained but Bücka could see the effort it took to hold the façade. It wasn't hard to understand why; Thelia had told of the bond the pair had shared—something she'd never seen again, not even between her and her sister.

'I'm sorry,' Bücka said, 'I didn't mean to upset you.'

Shaking her head, Petra said, 'You didn't upset me. Memories are to be cherished. They guide us, set us right. They can be sad. So very sad. But without them, we'd be hollow people, no better than the Elementals.'

A strange thing to say, she thought. 'You hate them, the Elementals?'

'Never. You shouldn't hate what you don't understand. I don't trust them. Can't describe what they are, what purpose they serve. But I know they are ignorant of love. For that reason, they are all too shallow.'

Bücka waited for more. It didn't come; the answer to her question. No reply of Shadow. Was that a deflection, the talk of Elementals? She thought better than to pry. Besides, she was enchanted by Petra's eyes, wondered what it was to be stone. She knew, though, it would be a terrible thing to ask. Despite her lack of social graces, those of which Jerune was constantly reminding her, she wasn't as insensitive as the others believed. There were times that called for her abrupt nature, her wicked streak. This was not that time. Another tangent, another tale Petra could tell.

'You love Goddard?' Bücka asked.

'As a friend, as family, of course.'

'Obviously, I'm a warrior too.'

Petra smiled again. 'Obviously.'

'But he's the best, isn't he? The mightiest you've ever known.' Bücka leaned forward, elbows balanced on her thighs, knees raised on tip-toes.

'You know he was King once?' said Petra.

'Yes.'

'I've known... Goddard, for a century. But even then, he was Argan. Baza'rad the Great was a legend in my days. Imagine, Bücka, what life he's lived, what battles he's won. It's true, there is no warrior greater than he. Even stronger than General Aracyse, and the bastard King Kalle himself.'

Bücka had heard the names. Aracyse was the General that betrayed his evil master, Kalle. Thelia had spoken of the huge man with the mechanical arm. Always thought that to be one of her tall tales. In her travels, however, Bücka had seen the statues of the General. Every effigy had the arm in pose. Not a human arm.

'Did he really have a metal arm?' she asked.

Petra nodded. 'Oh yes, from his shoulder down. A solid metal fist at the end.'

'Really?'

'Really. He was charged with overseeing Etherus, where Kalleron created the Furies. When Cultists attacked, a Fury was released, killed most of his men. Shredded him, taking his arm. Aracyse always said he'd been lucky. Called it a 'slap in his face' from an Elemental Sprite.'

'Sprite?'

'He called them Sprites. Rarely said Fury.' Petra paused; her eyes turned to the floor. Brought them back up, looked into Bücka's. She found it hard to keep contact with those sparkling gems. Petra continued, 'Those orbs. Inside the glass prison, under the light of the sun, they're beautiful. Imagine, Bücka, the colours of the rainbow, dancing and swirling.' Petra straightened, her tone becoming serious. 'But beware what appears to be a thing of beauty. Once free, when the sphere is smashed, those shreds of the Wind are horrific to flesh. Imagine a room full of invisible blades. All swirling and hacking away. That's a Fury. That's how Aracyse lost his arm.'

Bücka shivered. 'But how did he get a metal one?'

'An engineer at Etherus. A genius. Aracyse respected him but often inferred he was a law unto himself. A man called Anders.' Petra grinned, let out a short laugh. 'Actually, I recall now; Aracyse told me, Anders put the arm on the General when he was unconscious. Never bloody asked. Can you imagine? Experimenting on your own master.'

'No! Really. Did Aracyse have his head?'

'Not at all. To the contrary, he rewarded him. Placed great faith in a man so committed that he could treat a General as any other soldier.'

Bücka recalled what she had been told of the old wars. Thelia never spoke in detail of the battles. She was never a soldier, always far from the real danger. Bücka knew little of what had happened to Kalle on the fields of Stranghame. She wanted to ask Petra but thought it a cheap question. Goddard hadn't brought her here to talk about war.

She asked, 'What was the world like before all of that? Before you came here?'

Petra frowned, gazed around Goddard's home. Rock walls and sculpted logs blended to create an open space. Some furs and pelts lay across boulder and wood. The ceiling, high at the cliff face, sloped down to the doorway. Spacious, it was fitting of a man Goddard's size. Petra motioned to the rustic surrounds.

'Like this. Peaceful.' Petra paused, shook her head. 'But war is never far away; it was never far away, even when I was...' She stopped and displayed porcelain palms to Bücka. 'Before I was this. There was always Kalleron and if that bastard King set his sights on your home you were doomed. Nothing could stand against his Queen. You know Kor'A was the Queen of Kalleron before she came to these lands and made this city?'

Bücka nodded, knew the history. Understood from recent revelations that the Elemental was something terrible in the time before An'Korathall was a beacon of human hope.

Petra continued. 'In truth, Bücka, the world never knew peace. There's no such thing. Humanity will always wage war with itself. Greed and a sense of entitlement to rule have always spoiled the world. But it's what we do in the periods between the rage that matters. Carve a niche, enjoy what you can. I did. I had the *Melody*. We had good days. Even when we didn't, we had each other.'

Those words resonated with Bücka's own experience. In recent days she had found something unique in her life. A companionship of friends. An irony that it was the looming threat of war that had brought them all together. She stared at Petra, thought of the coming storm.

'What will you do?' Bücka asked.

'Do?'

'We're leaving for Farenhyne tomorrow. All of us. You're staying here?'

Petra nodded. 'I'm going to enjoy the comforts of Goddard's home.' She patted a brown pelt on the rock. 'My fort in Farenhyne is a little worse for wear. Not really fit for habitation anymore.'

Bücka thought of the destruction of which Jerune and Goddard had spoken. 'Fire?' she asked.

A nod. Petra tilted her head to the side, scrunched her pretty features into a scowl. 'I liked that place.'

'I'm sorry.'

Shaking her head, Petra said, 'Don't be. Everything moves on someday. I've learned not to become too attached to things.'

It wasn't overt, more nuanced, but the sadness in her voice was clear. A quick question to change direction. Bücka asked, 'So, you'll stay here instead, keep eyes on Anka?'

'From above, yes. I can see farther than most. Up here, higher than the citadel, I can spot trouble before even it knows it's a problem.'

'And you'll sort it out?'

Petra smiled. 'If I must.'

Bücka understood Petra had power beyond comprehension but it was difficult to find anything other than serenity in her ways. Reserved, polite; Bücka imagined her as a Queen ought to be. Dreaming of Queens and palaces, Bücka sat back as Petra stood. The woman of stone held out her sculpted hand.

She said, 'I'd best say hello to Goddard and Chara. Shall we?'

Bücka smiled and took the Queen's hand, warmth flushing into her cheeks. Beautiful, she was beautiful.

Chapter XXIX

D ays of quiet accompanied the journey to Farenhyne, Goddard relieved that his ward drew less attention than before; Chara now concealed from prying eyes in her oversized cloak and hood. He was thankful for the respite, it had given him time to collect his thoughts. Several days out of Anka and with the sun shining down, that peace had been brought to a sobering end. Jerune's keen eyes not required to source the calamity; they had all ventured toward the smoke, a grey plume being blasted by the coastal breeze. He had seen much in his long life but Goddard stood silent. They all did; staring at the crater on the cliff. Sarellia and Bücka had dismounted from their Stars, coming to join he, Chara and Jerune. On his last visit, a ruined fort and proud keep had stood on the plateau overlooking the sleepy town. Nothing was left. Nothing but the vast circular hole, the bottom of which was a black and orange cauldron of subdued fire. He and his companions were not alone. The macabre pit brought many sightseers, Goddard presumed most were from Farenhyne. Across the expanse he could see their expressions. Fear was prevalent, though some gazed with wonder. Looking to his friends, he noted their stares were neither. Anger etched upon each face. All but Chara, who appeared immune to the human trait.

'Laria,' Bücka said.

'Laria?' Jerune asked.

'I've seen areas like this. I thought it was all natural, until I learned of Fire.'

Goddard took a step closer to the edge. A hand grabbed his tunic, a strong tug. He turned, expecting it to be Bücka. It was Chara, a stern countenance glaring at him. Her grip was firm, stronger than he had known.

'Back,' she said. 'It's dangerous.'

More than her grip, her face was fierce. It was a novel display. He stepped away from the edge, watching as her expression softened.

'I'm safe, Chara, see?'

She shook her head. 'Nobody's safe here. It's a bad place.'

An unusual reaction, catching him off guard. She had shown fright at Bruch'ail; he imagined because of its purpose. So heavy and brutal. Yet this was something else. He knelt down, held her shoulders.

'Hey, it's alright. I'm here.'

'And we shouldn't be.'

Sarellia approached, her face a crumple of worry. 'I don't think we should be here either.'

Troubled by Chara's response, he said, 'Get your horses, we're not loitering.'

Bücka said, 'This is what we must stop?'

'Yes, if Petra's story is true, and there's no reason it isn't,' Sarellia said. 'This is the result of one seed. Just one. We have to destroy dozens, perhaps hundreds.'

Jerune moved to the edge, Goddard watched, Chara squirming by his side. She uttered chirping noises, fidgeting and animating. Said nothing but her distress was clear. Another human display. Anxiety?

'Jerune!' he called. The scout turned. Goddard winced. His toes hung over the edge. One slip and he would be gone. He frowned at the scout, a tilt of his head to alert him to Chara's unease. 'Get away from the edge, eh?'

A last glance down and Jerune retreated from the abyss. 'Of course, seen all I need to see.'

'Which is?' Bücka asked.

'A reason to make sure we succeed.' He pointed to the pit, a bubbling hiss rising above the edge. 'These can't arrive on our shores. I don't want my home to burn like Laria'

'We need to know more about them,' Sarellia said. 'But I've no contacts with that knowledge.'

'I might,' Bücka said, though her voice was filled with doubt.

'You?' Jerune asked. 'I mean, not to be rude; you have that sort of contact?'

She shook her head, appeared unoffended. 'Not like Sarellia. My Larian contract. The handler was gone but his reach extended to the place. He had a few friends. They might know more.'

'Where?' Sarellia asked.

She shrugged. 'Laria, near the Forge. Town called Gulda. It's where I got my lead for the orb.'

Goddard nodded. Their plans had been discussed and settled in Anka. He, Chara, and Sarellia would travel farther east. They would trade with the Rotynians. An ocean-faring culture, they viewed the seas as their own. They had few ports to call a capital but those places they landed were a symbolic foothold. Goddard was gambling on a shared value—a freedom to travel. Though, of course, that freedom was subject to Rotynian piracy. The threat posed by Laria was significant; the Northern Lands were considered sacred to the Rotynian people; a rare place to set their boots upon dry land. Fire would challenge that, demand piety. Goddard hoped that would be enough to leverage the Battleship *and* a willing crew.

While that plan was enacted, Jerune would take Bücka to the Forge. Having learned of the destruction from Petra's account, they had agreed they needed to steal one or two seeds. Staring at the pit, Goddard considered one was plenty. They could use it to destroy the other weapons of Fire. The devastation would be immense. And though it seemed an impossible task—to destroy the furnace that created the seed of Fire, there was a precedent. The home of the Fury, Etherus, had been infiltrated by the Cult a century before. No place was truly impregnable. Every castle and every country could fall. Goddard knew all too well that it was rare for an army to topple a kingdom. It was often the will of a few, if not one, that determined the fate of many. It gave him a sliver of hope, something to ward off the magnitude of their task.

To Jerune, Goddard said, 'As discussed, we'll stay the night in Farenhyne. At dawn, you'll sail to Laria's main port on the western coast.'

The scout nodded. 'What's it called again?'

Sarellia said, 'Laria.'

'Oh. How could I forget?'

Goddard smiled. 'The old capital. It was Laria too.'

'Genius,' Jerune said. He gestured to Bücka. 'From there, I guess we set off to Gulda. You can take the lead on that one. Once we know more, I can figure a better way in other than the front door.'

Bücka said, 'It's a cave in a mountain.'

Jerune shrugged. 'Figure of speech.'

From within her deep hood, Chara asked, 'Why don't we travel together?'

Looking at the unknown faces around the pit, Goddard said, 'It's better we don't talk here, we'll settle in town and discuss it then.'

Patting her belly, Bücka said, 'Good. I'm hungry.' She glanced at the smouldering depression, sniffed the air. 'I want something cooked on the flame.'

Goddard raised an eyebrow, noticed Sarellia's response to the warrior's quip was similar. He doubted she was being insensitive. It was just the way she was. Blunt as his hammer. He said, 'Come on, Bücka's right, we need to eat. It'll be a while before we can share a table again.'

Sarellia had paid the innkeeper a generous fee and a lone table was set aside. Goddard, favouring the cover of two walls, sat in the corner, Bruch'ail wrapped in a cloth sheet behind. It had been Bücka's idea. Better hide the beast, she had said. A fair point, there were few weapons such as his. With Laria on the rise, he couldn't risk suspicion. Looking around the table, Chara on his right, Bücka on his left, and Jerune and Sarellia tucked close opposite, he thought they appeared *almost* normal. The barmaid had travelled back and forth with drinks and platters of food. Warm stew from the pot, grilled fish, and fresh vegetables painted a colourful scene on the table. Each visit from the maid came with curiosity. Every serving laid down, her eyes on the child in the cloak. To ward her away, Sarellia had intervened, explained the child was sensitive to noise and crowds; the reason for their paid solitude from the rest of the tavern. Goddard had noted her words worked well, the maid switching her gaze to him. Over his many years he had become accustomed to such attention. Often didn't notice. After Aracyse and Kalle, he had seen few men as tall as he, certainly none larger. But he never considered his stature as a cause for curiosity. No more than others were short. Yet still, the barmaid stared.

Sarellia appeared to notice. Across the table, she said, 'Think she likes you.'

'Don't be silly,' he replied.

Bücka, not helping, said, 'He's rubbed herbs in his beard. He smells nice.' She turned to him. 'You're all ready for a night of...'

Under the table he nudged her with his boot. That was the intent. But the table beams interfered and the whole thing lifted with a solid thump.

Chara startled, sitting bolt upright. 'What was that?'

Goddard scowled at Bücka who grinned with a mouthful of fish.

He said, 'Me, Chara. Just getting comfortable.'

On his words, she settled, leaning back into the chair.

Jerune, poking a potato with a small dagger, said, 'So, tomorrow. The plan?'

Sarellia pointed to Goddard and Chara in turn. 'We'll head northeast along the coast. Another few days. Should get to the Rotynian port Petra mentioned. I can't imagine the sight. I mean, how do you hide a Battleship?'

Goddard realised none of the young crowd would have seen one. Ships of legend, long lost in time. Too expensive to build, not even in his days as Baza'rad could he recall Laria commissioning new vessels for the seas.

'How big were they?' Jerune asked.

'Twice as big as a Kalleron Warship,' Sarellia replied.

Goddard thought she would have known better. The Bruhsa line would have knowledge of the ships. Kallisa had seen one, as had he, on their final voyage to Kalleron. He took a sip of his ale, placed it down.

'Nothing like that,' he said.

Jerune nodded at Sarellia. 'See, told you; no way could it be that big.'

A chuckle from Goddard. Not what he had meant. He put his hands out over the table, Palms facing inwards. He indicated a length as wide as the pot holding the stew.

'Kalleron Light Frigate, this size.' Nodded to Sarellia, widened his arms to his own shoulder width. 'Warship.' With a smile, he reached his arms wide, intentionally putting his elbow in Bücka's face.

'Oi!'

He continued. 'Larian Battleship.'

Bücka, pushing his arm away, said, 'No, you're lying!'

Goddard shook his head, one eyebrow raised. 'You wouldn't believe it, not even if you saw it. Made from forests that were decimated in the manufacture of the hulls. Larissian timber. As strong as Drohendrian Darkwood, lighter than Tormelorian Pine. They kept Laria safe. No fleet could sail against them. They had cannons longer than the girth of some ships. Below decks they had Windspitters, mechanised catapults that knew no equal. Tore sail and flesh to pieces. We all thought those ships unsinkable, until some sailed on Kalleron. Found out the King had devised a way to launch the Fury.'

In a whisper, Sarellia said, '*The Iron Cloud.*'

He nodded. 'Destroyed in the battle that sank three or four Battleships. But it gave Laria pause for thought, hell of a bloody nose. Then, of course, Fire appeared on Larian shores. One man and, now we know, he carried those infernal seeds.'

Sarellia held out her hand, mimicked the size of the Fire-seed. 'What use is a navy when a man in a row boat can carry one of these.'

Jerune said, 'So that's the ship you'll acquire. If it's real?'

'Yes,' Goddard replied, 'Sarellia said her contacts confirmed the Larian fleet isn't supported by anything better than light weapons.'

She nodded. 'It's not a naval campaign. They plan to bring the seed of Fire and soldiers to our shores. Until Petra's news of the Battleship, there was nothing conventional to stand against even a basic fleet.'

'What about the Rotynians?' Jerune asked.

Goddard shook his head. 'They never got involved with the wars, except for paid work. I think Laria once tried to subdue them but their ships are fast; they sailed away. Like swatting flies, they evade you, come back when you're tired.'

Sarellia said, 'I suppose with no homeland like ours, they have no roots to betray?'

'The only truly free people I've ever known,' Goddard said.

'So, that's the ship then,' Bücka said, appearing to wait for Goddard to explain the rest.

Taking another sip of ale, he nodded into his tankard. 'You and Jerune sail to Laria. Fly fast to Gulda, seek your contacts...'

Bücka shrugged, scrunched up her face, indicated she wasn't so sure about their usefulness.

Goddard nodded. 'If they're there; speak to them, see what they can tell you. From there, Jerune can take the lead. Scout the weak points of the Forge. Get inside and...' He stopped. Had no idea what would happen afterwards.

Jerune said, 'I'll find where we can best steal one of those orbs. Figure out how to handle it. Then use it.'

Goddard thought of the pit above Farenhyne. He wouldn't ask. Didn't want to trouble the rest. Petra's story was quite clear. The messengers of Fire died in the pit. It wasn't something you could just throw and be done with. It seemed as though suicide but he had to believe Jerune and Bücka could find a way.

Sarellia patted the table, an anxious smile on her face. 'We do our jobs, then we all come back to Anka.'

Waving a slice of meat on a skewer, Goddard said, 'And prepare for what may come after.'

Chara leaned forward. 'What comes after?'

What else but war, he thought. Raising his eyes, he felt Jerune's gaze boring into his own. The scout smiled but there was a darkness in his stare. A recognition of what the future may hold. Squinting at him, he offered reassurance to Chara. A lie for the rest.

'A celebration,' Goddard said. Staring at the man he thought might not come back; a nod to Jerune, he said, 'We'll all celebrate together.'

Across the night sky, rolling clouds muted the glow of Noctyrne and Ambyr. Leaning against the rickety wooden rail on the harbour wall, Sarellia stared at Jerune's face. In turn, he appeared preoccupied with the invisible horizon, a wall of black to hide the depth. His hair flicked and twisted in the breeze, the edges of his cloak flapping in the erratic gusts. Sarellia knew he was troubled. What little time they had spent together, she had become well-versed in his silent signals. His own words—*I can't take my eyes off you*—telling that they were now so very distant. She knew his task with Bücka would be difficult. More than difficult. Both missions would be fraught with danger. But her knowledge of the changing world made the choice stark. They could abandon it all, ignore the threat and feel secure in a brief illusion of what life they could know. Or, they could risk everything in the hope to find a longer peace. And in that peace, she could savour Jerune's company. As her Bruhsas before, she knew the needs of one were insignificant to the survival of a nation. Not a comforting thought; to understand the necessity of sacrifice. But then, ignorance was bliss until the world turned against you. That was how the common man lived. Not the life for Sarellia.

Jerune broke the silence, though his attention remained on the dark water. 'We're being quite adult about this, aren't we?'

'By not speaking of it?'

'Yeah.' He turned, leaning with his right elbow propped on the rail. 'I'm not a hero, never wanted to be one. But I know this could be a one-way voyage.'

His words were honest. Unwanted. Something she couldn't bear to hear, though she had been about to say the same thing. It was strangely liberating, if not grim, that they both accepted the possible future.

'I've lost people before. Cult members, acquaintances.' She pointed to her chest. 'This time it feels bad before we've even set sail.'

'I've got demented butterflies,' Jerune replied. 'Same ones I had when we almost kissed. You remember, when we were caught by Petra at the fort?'

She could. Thinking of that moment when he had stifled her laughter, she relived the experience, giggled. 'You looked so intense, you know? Thought you would ravage me there and then.'

Jerune appeared certain to protest, say he wasn't that type of man, but she made sure to stop him from spoiling her moment. She continued, one finger pressed to his lips. 'I'd have let you. Been admiring the way you moved on the trail. Watching you. There's a harmony about you; how you interact with your world. I mean, sure, you smell like a forest, all timber and damp, but yeah, I'd have had your hands tracking all over me a lot earlier.'

Sarellia thought Jerune blushed. It was hard to tell. Too dark; the light from swinging oil lamps uneven and dim.

He said, 'To be honest, you *were* a pain in my arse. But if you'd told me sooner, we might not have made it to the fort. I mean, I need my wits to track.'

'Even tracking a man-mountain?'

'Well, you distract me more than most,' he said, grinning.

'Most?'

'Fine. Almost all. You'll have to work hard for that last accolade.'

Distracted by the moment, Sarellia's anxieties briefly faded. The sense of calm didn't last long. A thought: what if they had given up, made for Anka for countless nights of passion? A tingle ran the length of her spine. She felt selfish to consider abandoning it all for such basal pleasures. Scolding herself, she realised it wasn't about pleasure. It was about Jerune. No heroic warrior, just a scout. But not an ordinary man. Not the type she had known. A dislocated gentleman, the forest equivalent of a dashing rogue. She would miss him dearly. Sarellia pushed away another thought. A darker cloud of permanence.

'What will we do after?' she asked.

Jerune sighed. 'Surely, after the medal ceremony, the freedom of the guilds and countless offers of loose women, I imagine...'

She tapped him on the chest. 'Oi! Don't be so horrible.'

'What do you think I'll do? I'll end up following you around like a damned puppy. You know fine well where I want to be.'

In her mind, Sarellia manipulated a great void of time. There was the recent past, a time of intrigue and blossoming romance; there was the present, this very moment on the Farenhyne coast; and there was the future, but it was after everything was done. She could rip the darkest part out, pretend it wasn't there. It was the only way she could smile for Jerune.

'Well, my puppy, may I lead you someplace now?' she asked, leaning in for a kiss.

After the tender moment, lips parting, he replied, 'You can take me anywhere you want.'

Sarellia took his hand, and with a deliberate and slow pace, all to savour their time, she made for the inn. Their own room. A private place for one last night until whatever the fates decreed.

Chapter XXX

F arenhyne, two days past, seemed as though a vague memory. Goddard crouched low, peering over a rocky outcrop. He motioned for Chara and Sarellia, both on their mount, to remain behind. Ahead, lower in the coastal valley and surrounded by towering cliffs, the Rotynian settlement lay hidden from prying eyes. On the shores, difficult to discern, tents of grey fabric blended with the rock. The Rot were renowned masters of camouflage; their ships often given a shoddy aesthetic to conceal their formidable armament. Just as those ships were misleading, so too was the camp. Focusing, peering at the field of canvas tents, Goddard saw more industry than he had expected. An occasional flicker of flame would light the surrounds, flashes of orange to reveal hidden life. As ants, bodies moved around, well-drilled lines of activity; few wayward souls appearing beyond the confines of the hidden town. Yet, for all their ingenious subterfuge, the Rotynian engineers could do nothing to disguise the Battleship. High and imposing sea-stacks dotted the peninsula. A naturally deep inlet flanked by vertical grey slabs served as a natural harbour. Close to the eastern cliff, as near as Goddard imagined such a ship could safely moor, the master of the oceans was a formidable sight. It neither floated nor bobbed; as stable and solid as the coast itself. Five bare masts stood proud on a deck as wide as a meadow. Too far to see details, Goddard noted much of the top deck was swathed in fabric; sail or cover, he could not be sure. But the hull was exposed, the immense size visible for all to see. Portholes closed, the individual decks were lost to the distance but even so, Goddard was staggered by the size. An age since he had last seen one. In all, he imagined that from waterline to tip of the masts, the Battleship was taller than the citadel. A floating castle. Other ships dotted the inlet, each appearing as small as a rowboat. Goddard knew that to be an illusion. Rotynian pirate vessels, they were as large as Larian tall ships. Beside the Battleship they were toys.

He smiled. The thought of such a vessel bearing down on the Seer's Larian fleet, although there was a peculiarity about its condition. Not ready for the sea, unlike the other Rotynian ships scattered around. A strange thing that they appeared unwilling to live or sail in the floating city. Though Goddard imagined the unique nature of the vessel made it the antithesis of their Culture. Nimble, secluded, and often unseen; the Rot ships were everything the behemoth was not. Almost everything, he reminded himself.

The Rot knew how to fight. That they chose not to wage oceanic war was a fortune for the rest of the nations. Though not even their agility on the waves would be a threat to the Larian giant.

One last scan of the settlement and Goddard observed an immediate problem. The Rot had chosen wisely. The steep cliffs afforded few routes down to the shore, none of which were negotiable without tremendous effort and care. He shivered as an image invaded his mind. Tried hard to stow it away; a vision of precious glass falling on hard marble. A treacherous descent, he was certain their movement would be noticed. And once safe on stable ground, what welcome would they receive? With a huff, he returned to Chara and Sarellia.

'Are we close?' Sarellia asked.

He pointed beyond the rocks. 'Very, but it's not ideal.'

'Guarded?'

'Far from it. Hidden, yes, but not fortified. It doesn't need to be, come look.'

Sarellia dismounted, helped Chara down and they came to his side. Her hood removed, Chara observed the surrounds. He thought she appeared awestruck. She hadn't even seen what lay beyond.

She said, 'All these rocks.'

Goddard hadn't considered them. Took a moment to reflect on the brutal majesty. 'Imposing,' he said.

'No, silly,' she replied. 'Welcoming.'

Sarellia gave him a glance. He shrugged. It seemed her interpretation matched his own.

'Welcoming?' she said.

Chara turned to her. 'Uh-huh. Don't you feel it?'

Feel it? That was surprising. Not the words used, rather, the emotional weight. Chara hadn't shown a great affinity to her natural, inert material. Curiosity brought his question.

'What do you feel?'

Chara blinked, turned around. She seemed to be listening. Facing away, her voice became distant. A haunting tone.

'She's here.'

Goddard looked at Sarellia, a frown forming on her brow. She shook her head. He didn't like the context; Chara couldn't mean Petra. The child wouldn't react in such a manner. Someone else. Who else would make her feel welcome when they were not? Who else but Kor'A?

'Chara,' he said. 'Who's here?'

She replied. He heard. Sarellia gasped.

He repeated her answer. 'Mother?'

Chara turned. 'She doesn't speak. But I can feel it. Can't you? You're stone too.'

Sarellia asked, 'Why is she here? How can you feel her? I thought you were... I thought she had left?'

Chara frowned. Goddard sighed with humour as she scratched her head. Another mimicry of behaviour. His own. He imagined she might next stroke invisible whiskers on her chin.

She pointed to Sarellia and said, 'I see how you look at Jerune. You don't speak but he looks at you the same way. Not talking. But you know he welcomes you. Is that right?'

Sarellia grinned, glanced at Goddard. He was impressed by Chara's empathy. He said, 'That's young love, Chara. But you're saying you can feel Kor'A's...' He paused, thought of something appropriate. 'Smile?'

She clapped. 'Yes.'

'You can't?' Sarellia asked Goddard.

'No.' He looked to Chara, said, 'Our bind to stone is very different.'

The Cultist shook her head but said no more.

He shared her obvious bewilderment. It didn't make sense. Nor did it help. Whatever Chara felt, he had noticed no change. Given the urgency to find a way down, he motioned for them to follow and moved to the cliff. He put his hand out, indicated for Chara to hold his hand.

'Careful, it's...'

He stopped speaking. Stared at the view. Couldn't imagine a square inch of his body wasn't tingling.

Sarellia said, 'Look, a staircase.'

She didn't know. Hadn't seen until now. Goddard couldn't find the words. Perfect imprints in the steep face disappeared as dots below. A way down. Created only moments ago. *Kor'A.*

Sarellia, ignorant of the marvel, asked, 'You think the Rot made these?'

Slowly, he said, 'No.'

She smiled, frowned at him. 'How'd you know?'

'It wasn't there a moment ago.'

'What?'

Chara said, 'Mother made it.'

It was true. Too perfect to be carved by hand. No tooling marks. As though a giant square finger had pressed indentations into clay.

'That can't be?' Sarellia said.

He fixed her with a stare. 'Sarellia. They've just appeared. Look at them. Show me what human hand can make something as unnatural as that.'

She didn't look, kept her eyes on his. He saw the flicker of doubt. She flinched. Shivered.

'Chara?' she said.

'Yes?'

'Can you still feel her? Kor'A?'

She hummed. 'No. She's gone.'

A thin smile appeared on the Cultist's face. Goddard was curious to know what motivated the grin.

'What?'

'The Covenant,' Sarellia said in a whisper. 'She's breaking the rules. She's *cheating*.'

Earth had not appeared but she had interfered. Perhaps in a way that wouldn't register with her sisters. What small insight Goddard had into the mind of the immortal, her actions were in character. Since recorded time, those tablets in the temples, Earth had always been drawn to the affairs of humans. A thought occurred to him. One he hoped was paranoia.

'If Kor'A's cheating, let's hope the other sisters don't do the same?'

Chara asked, 'What's cheating?'

Shaking his head, Goddard replied, 'A human thing, a very human thing indeed.'

They hadn't reached the base of the cliff when the welcome party assembled. Goddard led with Chara behind. His insistence she held tight to trailing leather bindings. Sarellia followed after. Though the steps were generous, the descent was slow, care required to prevent any terminal slip. Goddard stopped and Chara bumped into his leg.

'Why are we stopping?' she asked. He felt her peek out from behind his frame. 'They don't look happy? Are they?'

'I don't imagine so.' He turned, loosened the strapping, passing it over Chara's head to Sarellia. 'Wait here.'

She nodded and he descended the remaining stairs. A large crowd had assembled. Spears, swords and bows awaited. Holding out his hands, empty and bare, he said, 'My name is Goddard, my friends and I have come to trade.'

From the mass of fur-cloaked figures, one stood forward. No taller than the rest, she appeared similar to the rank and file. Rotynians were egalitarians; without territory over which to reign they needed no glorified kings or queens. A single sash around her shoulders, a length of chain and gold coloured plate, she appeared to be a leader. To what degree, he could not tell. She removed her hood, revealing her long, tangled hair. Goddard was reminded of Bücka: the auburn colour, her strong features. Her skin was darker, a mixture of ethnicity and time sailed under sun-kissed seas. Piercing green eyes stared at him.

She pointed to the cliff. 'You will explain... that.'

Goddard wasn't sure as to what she was referring; Chara or the steps. Glancing behind, he noted how the stairs jarred against the rock. Each recess a dark pit of shadow against the grey. Just as obvious as the child with onyx skin. It would be foolish to conceal what he knew. Goddard understood enough of their culture to know that, outside of conflict, honesty was a valued commodity.

'Earth created those stairs. For me and my friends.' He pointed to Chara. 'The child is her daughter, I am her guardian. We have urgent business we wish to discuss.'

An expected mumble erupted among the crowd. The woman raised her hand, a clenched fist in the air. The voices fell quiet. Her control was impressive.

Staring at the staircase, she said, 'I'd say you were mad but I watched them appear. As though a ghost was marching down the flank toward us. I feared our time had come. Yet, I feel no threat from you. How can this be? What brings such power to my people? A power we don't wish to see.'

He looked out across the water, noted how the Battleship appeared so much larger from the ground. A doubt crossed his mind. Had they brought enough diamonds? The ship was massive, its size defying all logic. He pointed to it.

'We wish to... sail upon the Larian vessel.'

Dead silence. He had expected a ripple of laughter, his request conceivably that of a fool. The only sound was the wind.

'That doesn't explain the staircase,' the woman said. 'Or the child. Or you, for that matter. That weight on your back.'

Bruch'ail, did she know of it? He said, 'You sail the seas; you must be aware of the Larian fleet in the northern harbour?'

She nodded. 'Sighted from afar. No concern of ours.'

'The fleet will sail for the Northern Lands. The Seer is coming and he brings the seed of Fire.'

Again silence. They all listened, clear that none were willing to break the focus of their leader. She had an authority rare to human ranks. Complete subservience to her word. As the lull continued, he understood it was his place to talk.

He said, 'Those seeds will decimate our lands. Change the power in the North. The Elementals have left us; agreed to see us settle our own conflicts. Earth left her only daughter in my care. But I can't defend her under siege. I need to stop the fleet from sailing. I have friends that wish to stop the seed of Fire reaching these shores. That's why we have come to you—to trade for the Battleship.'

She nodded. 'I see. Enjoy your demise.' The woman turned, began to walk away. Calling back, she said, 'You can return the way you came.'

'Goddard?' Sarellia called down.

All things considered, he thought things had gone well. No violence, no raised voices. It was a good start. The few interactions he had known with the Rotynians always involved an initial refusal.

'Throw me a pouch,' he said to Sarellia.

She tossed a bag down. A large velvet purse, he caught it in two careful hands. Checking the strings, he saw they were secure. Goddard bowled the bag toward the woman, aiming for the ground at her feet.

'An initial trade for your attention. Hear us out, then we can pay more,' he said.

She stopped, stooped and opened the bag. He watched as she closed it, passed it to another and said quiet words beyond his range. Goddard thought of Jerune, his uncanny senses would have been useful. The Rotynian leader turned.

She said, 'You know we're pirates? We can take what we wish.'

'You're not thieves,' he replied. 'And this is land, not the sea.'

Her expression changed, a smile erasing some of her stern appearance. 'Refreshing. You know your pirates?'

'I know a thief when I see one. It isn't a stain I would place upon you or your own.'

She approached, came within a few feet. He noticed it, the squint in her eyes, a question not for the ears of the many.

In a quiet voice, more subtle than a whisper, she said, 'You bring a child of Earth and ask for a Battleship. A man of unmatched stature with a hammer the size of a cannon on his back. Come to us from a slab of rock touched by an Elemental's grace.' She paused, peered at Chara before bringing her focus back to him. 'I *know* who you are. Though, I don't understand how you live in this century.'

Before he could reply, she returned to her people, stood with them.

Sarellia called down. 'What's going on?'

The woman answered. 'We are pleased to accept you to our tribe... Goddard and friends. Please, follow me.'

It had been a curiosity. But now Goddard understood why the Rotynians wore furs in a temperate clime. The tents were breezy, open to the gusts that blew in from the ocean. Few barriers behind which to shelter. Piles of fabrics bundled in heaps were their beds, and wooden planks across boulders were the chairs and benches. It was clear that privacy was a foreign concept, much of the covered space inhabited by several groups. A communal life. Everything shared, Goddard could see little of capital value. He wondered for what it was they used their looted ocean bounty.

He followed the woman flanked by a constantly shifting ensemble of warriors. Chara's hand was tight in his grip, Sarellia by his other side. They moved in silence, Goddard assuming it was etiquette only to speak when spoken to. The woman took them to a large covered space. Inside the decoration was minimal but obvious. There was a single wooden chair, a solid carved lump of timber. Not Darkwood, nor was it Tormelorian Pine. He had a suspicion. The same material from which the Battleships were constructed. The fabrics held more colour than the other tents; hues of red, gold, and green. A subtle show of rank; Goddard imagined it was consistent with the Rotynian way.

The leader seated herself and dismissed the soldiers. Alone with her guests, she directed them to sit. Goddard motioned for Chara to move to a pile of plush red fabrics, not silks, but something voluminous, perhaps cotton. Sarellia caught his eye and he nodded for her to do the same. Goddard found a rock and sat upon that.

'Welcome to my home, for what it is,' the woman said, fanning her fingers. 'I'm Elazra of the *Southern Storm*. I lead this faction and claim the seas of eastern Hallan. Though, you call it, with frivolous imagination, the Northern Lands. You are my guests and you are safe. As is our tradition. Now, explain to me again, without the ears of others listening, what fears have brought you to seek trade with the Rotynian Claim?'

Goddard didn't assume to lead discussions. Looking to Sarellia, eyes raised to prompt her to speak, she shrugged, passing the role back to him. He sighed. There was so much to tell. And with everything to gain and too much to lose, he knew Elazra was not to be misled.

A hand waved toward his two companions, he said, 'This is Chara and Sarellia. Chara came to me in the hills above Anka, told me her mother, Earth, had left her alone. She came to me because I have a history with the events of Kalleron and the wars, too close an association for some. Chara has become my ward. You've already noted the hammer, Bruch'ail, make of that what you wish.'

Elazra interrupted. 'Baza'rad.'

He nodded.

She asked, 'Why aren't you dead? Your time was spent.'

'My years pass slowly, a trait of the old royal line.' He stroked his beard, said, 'But as you can see, age is growing upon me.'

'If you say. I understand your deception; your years should be worn as bone, not flesh. A conundrum for many. Continue... Goddard.'

A strange tone. It was evident that Elazra respected his old name, would defer to his current façade. A personal pleasantry or the Rotynian way?

He said, 'Kor'A didn't send Chara to me but she knew of me. Nobody can presume to know the immortal mind but I think she knew where her daughter would go. But I didn't know how to protect her.' He stopped, turned to Chara. 'I thought Petra would be a better parent, a true woman of stone.

'I took Chara to the fort at Farenhyne, where Sarellia and a scout tracked me down. She informed us of a new threat—the fleet in Laria, the Seer, and a new Covenant between the Elementals.' A thought occurred to him. The ruin of fire that burned above the cliffs. Chara would have died had she stayed with Petra. He couldn't imagine Petra leaving the child; they would have both perished. It angered him. Chance, and Petra's insistence the child stayed with him, was all that stood between their life and death.

Elazra appeared to notice his shifting mood. 'What happened?'

'We returned to Anka, leaving Petra alone. But events have moved fast. The Seer sent messengers to Petra, to warn her to stay out of human affairs. They dropped the seed of Fire, destroyed the entire fort.'

'We saw the flames and the light from the sea,' Elazra said. 'Thought Farenhyne had finally invested in a damned beacon to keep the ships safe at night. I ordered a crew to the port. We saw the pit.'

'Then you know what comes,' Goddard said.

Elazra sighed. 'It comes to land. Not sea. The Rotynian Claim has little stake on the earth. You've seen our camp. We need but a sliver of shore to rest and repair.'

Goddard said to Sarellia, 'The pouches.'

She withdrew them from inside her jacket, secured from prying eyes. Handing them to him, he saw her hand trembling. He frowned, nodding a gesture of reassurance.

Goddard held up one pouch. 'Each one contains the same as that which brokered our welcome.' He threw the four pouches at her feet, a careful lob. Not wise to insult the Rotynians in their own makeshift home.

Elazra stared at the velvet purses. 'I don't doubt your sentiment but I question how you can bring such wealth. I doubt you'd offer me Bruhadian relics?'

A reasonable query. He took no offence. 'Until Chara came to my door, I had few friends. Less treasure. Truth, I needed none. But one soul remained from my long past. These gifts come from her.'

'Of course,' Elazra said with obvious wonder. 'The Queen of Stone gave you these?'

'She did.'

A wide grin appeared on the Rotynian's face. 'A powerful investor in your war effort. I wonder how much more she can plunder from her own kind.'

Goddard had no wish to correct her error. Better to leave Petra's heart apart from the discussion. He said, 'We don't wish for war. We hope to acquire the use of the Battleship to prevent it. And a crew to sail with us.' He pointed to the pouches at her feet. 'I don't ask for change. All of it is yours. Nor do we wish to keep the vessel. We offer a fair trade; an unimaginable bounty of diamonds to sail upon an impossible ship.'

The wind stirred the fabrics and the tent fell quiet. A tap on his thigh. It was Chara.

'Can I speak?' she asked.

Elazra replied, 'You may.'

Goddard smiled when she looked to him for a higher permission. He said, 'This is Elazra's house, Chara, she's in charge here.'

She nodded, turned to the Rotynian. 'Hello.'

'Hello, child.'

Goddard saw the curiosity in Elazra's eyes. She did well to hide it. Just as he, there was a veneer behind which to obscure the human soul. A Rot leader was to be fearless, free of the petty natures of weaker men and women. Yet, he saw it; she was intrigued by the girl of black glass.

Chara said, 'You have to accept Goddard's trade.'

Elazra sat back. Her posture stiffened.

'Chara!' Goddard said. 'That's rude.'

She turned, her expression one of innocence. 'It's not.' To Elazra, she said, 'You saw the steps?'

Goddard waited for the Rotynian to reply. The veneer was crumbling. He understood what Chara was trying to say. He hadn't thought of it; too focused on etiquette. Pointless bartering in the face of the immortals. Why had Kor'A granted them passage but to succeed in their task. That was the message. And Chara delivered it without threat.

She said, 'My mother made the mark in the stone to allow us to come to you. She wishes us to travel. If you deny Goddard's trade; you're saying no to my mother. I never said no to my mother.' She turned to Goddard. 'Did you?'

He looked to Elazra, certain he looked as stupefied as she. Chara's query remained. He recalled the presence of Kor'A at An'Korathall the day she had struck down Petra. A crushing weight of suffocation. Earth's body may have appeared sublime and beautiful but her power was beyond human reckoning. A power to destroy cities, if not worlds.

Thinking of that time, he said, 'No. You can't deny the Elementals what they wish. This world is theirs.'

Elazra pointed at Goddard. 'You didn't intend for this threat, did you?'

He shook his head 'I brought diamonds. To trade.'

Sarellia spoke. 'We didn't know Kor'A would help. She's not meant to.'

'Not meant to?'

'The Covenant,' Chara said. 'They've to stay away. But mother's...' She looked to Goddard, frowned.

'Cheating,' he said.

The Rotynian slumped, appeared to relax. 'The diamonds are still offered?'

'Of course,' he said. 'Without condition.'

Elazra grinned, though Goddard recognised the bitter truth behind the smile. She said, 'It's quite ironic, don't you think? A nation of the ocean is being coerced by the Earth.'

'The unintended existential threat aside, are you favourable to our trade? The Battleship? The sailors?' he asked.

Elazra reached beyond the arm of her chair. She patted a bare surface of rock. 'It seems I don't have a choice. A rare position for a Rotynian. Yet the trade was offered with heart before the mention of... other pressures. Yes, Goddard, the payment is accepted.'

She nodded and stood, motioned for him to do the same. Elazra pulled a small shell from within her fur. Passing it to Goddard, she said, 'Return this to me when you no longer need my service.'

He looked at the iridescent cone, similar in size to one of pine. It was engraved with symbols he'd never seen. Beautiful and simple. Her last words hung in his mind.

'*Your* service?'

Her face gave up the stern pretence, a cheerful expression raising a blush on her tanned skin. With her demeanour transformed, Goddard thought it possible there was a hint of Bruhada in her blood.

Elazra said, 'In your royal terms, consider me as Queen of the Sea. And you will sail, as my King. We'll conquer the ocean with a Battleship on which centuries of honour have been carved. And yes, we'll sail against whatever fleet you command.'

Chapter XXXI

A cold new world. It was a strange thing to see. Jerune staring at a bustle of squat stone buildings nestled at the end of a long inlet; Laria Port coming into view. *The Alahemme*, a rare Kallerye tall-ship, had sailed with good speed from Farenhyne. The passage down the middle of the Larissian Sea had kept scrutiny of the island from his view for most of the voyage. Approaching port, drawing nearer to the barren place, he was greeted by a landscape of snow and ice. Rocky cliffs with patchwork bracken and dustings of powder rose along the coast. Far to the east, beyond the hills and mired in a haze, snow-capped mountains merged with the sky. Scanning left to right, all Jerune saw was inhospitable cold. There was no fire. No plumes of bitter smoke. It was not as he had expected. Not the terrors of which much had been said. Cruising into the narrows of sloping cliffs, he turned to Bücka who was unusually quiet by his side.

'It's not what I thought it would be,' he said.

'You expected it to be on fire?'

It was a foolish presumption. How could a world aflame raise an army? Though, he had presumed to see some sign of the devastation. 'Not on fire. But at least something.'

Bücka shrugged, a cloud had descended upon her. The past day had brought a mournful outlook. Not at all the Bücka he knew. He turned to her, expected her to meet his gaze but she remained focused, her eyes stubbornly staring at the distance. Jerune hadn't seen her this way. Unwelcome given the circumstances.

'What's wrong, Bücka? You've not been yourself the past day.'

He waited for her to respond, watched as she blew a huge sigh into the chill. Her breath was a dense cloud. Appropriate, he felt, as though it mirrored the weight of her thoughts. Bücka's silence was unbearable.

'Bücka? If you don't want to talk, that's fine.'

Without facing him, she said, 'My contract. The Larian contract. It was an unusual one.'

'How so?'

'I had to work with a partner.' She glanced at him, too brief to read her expression. 'Like you, a scout.'

Jerune felt the urge to raise her spirits, throw out a humorous quip. Thought better of it. He wasn't an ass. Reckoned she should be the one to come around considering her unusual mood.

A brief silence before she continued. 'We needed a tracker. You'd think tracking in snow would be easy.' Bücka corrected herself. 'Obviously, *you* don't think that, you know the difference. But the snow was packed hard, the ground is barren. I needed a scout to see what I couldn't.'

Jerune knew the contract hadn't worked out; the orb she displayed at Anka was proof of that. Had worse things occurred?

He said, 'You're down because the job didn't work out? The scout messed things up?'

Silence. She hung her head low.

'Bücka? What's up?' Time for that quip. Nothing to lose. 'Don't worry, I'll not fuck things up. That's your job.'

'You're right,' she said, her voice quiet. With another sigh, she turned, stood tall. 'I fucked up.'

Idiot. Always the wrong moment. The wrong words. Just as at the stables. 'Bücka, I didn't mean it like that. But your mood is... it's not you. Not the you that I know.'

'I killed Anhem. The scout.'

He didn't want to ask why or how. She meant that she caused his death, that had to be it. Not a literal murder.

She continued, 'He was good. Stupid, but good.' Bücka stopped, managed a solemn smirk. 'Like you. On the third night, things were bad—we were proper tense, on edge. We'd been discovered and we'd run, found a place to hide. I had the orb, job done. It was dark and windy and they were searching with bright Kallerye flares. Confusing, you know? The darkness, the white snow... flickering colours; except, it was black, white, and everything seemed on fire. It was... anyway, I was tucked tight beside a cart, concealed. Thought I'd lost the bastards. Figured Anhem had done too, we'd split but he was safe. Had to be. Then I felt it—this sudden stab in my side. I mean, we were being hunted down by those fuckers. And I feel this stabbing in my side. My nerves were frayed. What do you do, Jerune? The fear, the confusion... a stab in your side. What would you do?'

It wasn't a glorious tale. This wasn't Bücka bragging. Jerune said, 'It was Anhem?'

Bücka nodded.

'Shit, I'm sorry, Bücka.'

She wasn't crying but he could see it had broken her. Bücka peeled the winter fleece from her neck and touched the skin. Her eyes were distant. Jerune knew at what memory she stared. Her voice a whisper, she said, 'I turned fast, blade in hand. Sliced right through. Realised straight away.' Her stare faltered. He watched the reflection of light grow in her eyes. Now, the tears fell. An awful feeling to see Bücka struggle. The warrior's strength collapsing. Her inner child exposed.

Jerune wasn't sure it would be accepted. Thought it might make things worse. He hesitated, moved his arms out to the side. Before he stepped forward, Bücka fell into the embrace. He held her. Felt her body tremble.

Into his chest, she said, 'His eyes. He clutched his neck, I did too, clutched real hard. My hands on his. But his eyes, Jerune, his fucking eyes; they went right through me. I saw it all. So much fear. Terror. But worse... I saw the disbelief. I saw he wanted to know why. I couldn't speak. Couldn't say why. He just died there. I felt his heart stop, his last blood on my hands. His eyes, Jerune, just asking, why, why, why?'

Jerune moved his hand to the back of her head, applied a gentle pressure, a secure place for her grief. What had happened was a tragedy. An accident. A heavy price to pay for one moment in time. A debt transferred to Bücka's eternity. Jerune said nothing. Realised words were cheap. Looking beyond, he saw the port drawing close, their mission at hand. For her, he would make sure everything worked out. Do what he could to help mend her wounds. Though he doubted such scars would ever heal completely.

Two days had passed since landing at Laria port and Gulda lay before them. Bücka's mood had lifted, though the temperature had fallen further. Clad in heavy, white winter furs, Jerune was content that the bitter chill was kept at bay. Though, the trail of frozen ground and wind-blasted plains was a painful vision to behold. He had never experienced such an unrelenting contrast of black and white. The alpine mountains in the temperate Northern Lands were colourful in comparison. To add to his sense of detachment, he had yet to see any sign of Fire. The pits and destruction described by Bücka not yet a feature of the landscape.

Gulda sprawled across a shallow valley. Beyond it, mountains rose to the east. A river, much of its surface glazed with ice, ran straight through, a fast current to keep the depths moving. Three stone bridges spanned the water, each with a low single arch. The buildings and homes were wide and low with steep roofs all angled away from the constant easterly that swept in from the mountains. Thinking of Port Laria, a recognisable hub of life, Jerune wondered why anybody would choose to live in such a nightmare of cold.

Leaning in to Bücka, speaking through the scarf across his face, he said, 'Your contact is here?'

'Should be. In the centre of the village.'

Jerune tried to imagine what professions settled in such a place. What could anyone do among the barren wastes. Before he could ask, Bücka trudged off. He watched her moving erratically on the compacted snow. Not a surface for humans. He hated it. Longed for familiar forests of green and soft yielding earth.

Trailing Bücka, he found relief from the elements when they entered the village. The wind dropped and the scour of cold vanished. Looking east, he saw the buildings were arranged such that the wind had no clear path. He imagined the outer structures buffered the gales. Each subsequent rank of buildings further splitting the winds. There was a steady, constant howl, the noise of a frustrated elemental beast. Humanity versus the wind. In Gulda, at least from what he could see, the elements had lost. Deep gravel of pulverised rock was the preferred Larian surface. Frozen in place, it provided grip. The boots he wore were thick, not yielding to the piercing stones. Correcting his assumptions, Jerune considered Gulda had a stubborn charm. A pragmatic resilience to its surrounds. He had to give it some credit and when Bücka pointed, his heart filled with joy.

Looking at the warm glow coming from the windows of a tavern, he asked, 'Your contact's in there?'

'Should be. Remember, I said I wasn't certain they'd be here.'

Jerune did recall. 'You also said they weren't really a contact.' He had a moment of doubt, hoped it wasn't another sorry tale.

Behind her veil, Bücka's eyes grinned. 'A gambling debt owed.'

'Your debt, or theirs?'

'I never lose,' she replied and started off for the inn.

Walking across what he imagined was the town square, Jerune noted few souls venturing outside. Those that did appeared to have hurried purpose. There were no bodies loitering, no beggars in the gutter. No gutter at all for that matter. Despite the oppressive cold, Gulda's soul was warm. An incongruous comfort offered by the glow of burning lamps behind plate glass windows.

Bücka pulled open the tavern door and moved inside. Stepping behind, Jerune was met by a wall of heat. An instant barrage of discomfort. A fire raged against the far wall, a huge alcove of flame, to the left a wooden-topped counter was host to few souls. The barmaid looked up, offering he and Bücka a cursory greeting. The floor was a sprawl of tables, half of which were occupied by men and women. The smell was alcohol and pipe smoke. A staple of any inn he had known. Take away the terrible cold, and Laria was no different from anywhere else.

Bücka grumbled an incoherence and pointed to a table set closest to the fire. Two men sat alone with space for four more. She said, 'Might want to lose the fur.'

Jerune waited as she walked across the floor, her veil obscuring her face. The men were draped in curious furs, dark pelts from another land. On the table between them were a pile of stones, all carved into cubes and flat shapes. Each man guarded a pile of coins, notably one was far smaller than the other. It didn't take a tracker to tell this was Bücka's man. A loser.

She spoke to the figure guarding his meagre prize. A dishevelled man, he frowned, waved her away. Across the space and mixing with the other voices, her words were hard to discern. Jerune smiled, understood a few select phrases. She was pulling no punches. Then the great reveal, Jerune laughing as Bücka removed her veil. The man startled and fell from his chair. This was no lover's reunion. Other patrons glanced, appeared uninterested. Sensing no threat, Jerune moved to join his friend.

'Get on your feet, or at least, your chair,' she said to the man.

He nodded, climbed back to his seat. Said nothing. His eyes flicking from Bücka to the tavern door.

'And you can forget about running,' she said.

'This your man?' Jerune asked.

'Hardly a man. Still losing at Tenkstone? Why d'you even play?'

The man scanned Jerune. 'This your muscle?' he asked.

Flattered but keen to assist, he replied, 'You think she needs any help?'

The gambler huffed and shook his head.

Bücka nodded to a seat. Jerune quizzed her with a frown but she nodded again. He looked at the fire. Too close. He could feel the sweat dribbling down his skin. Hauling the fur from his back, he placed it over the chair and sat down. It was luxury. To sit and be warm without a great white bear on his shoulders. Across the table Bücka sat down beside her contact. She dragged the wooden legs across the floor making it an unnecessarily noisy affair. The other man appeared to lean deeper into his chair as though trying to flee through the back of his seat.

An uncertain tone, he asked, 'Can I leave?'

Bücka asked, 'Do you owe me coin?'

A pause. 'Do I? No. I don't think so.'

Bücka waved him away and he didn't refuse her farewell. Scraping his winnings from the table, he bowed and left.

'Now we're alone, we can get down to it. Jerune, this is Porst. Porst, Jerune.'

Porst greeted Jerune with a timid nod. To Bücka, he said, 'I don't have your money.'

'Now, that's no surprise to me,' she replied. 'But you do owe me, yes?'

Another feeble nod.

She pointed to Jerune, said, 'My friend and I have come a long way to see you. You're not going to disappoint me, are you?'

'Disappoint?'

'You can pay me another way.'

Porst glanced at Jerune. Confused eyes and a crumpling frown. The gambler pointed to himself then Bücka. 'You want me to...'

'Gods, no! Not in a thousand lifetimes.'

Jerune tried to maintain his composure when Porst pointed at him. 'Do your friend instead?'

Bücka shook her head. Jerune scoffed at her rising disbelief. Her face a grimace of disgust, she said, 'What the fuck, Porst? Are you whoring your way out of debts these days?'

He shrugged. Bücka looked at Jerune, her expression was priceless.

Porst said, 'I don't understand.'

'Information,' Bücka said.

'What?'

With tedious emphasis, she repeated the word, dragging out each syllable.

'Oh. What information?'

Bücka leaned in. Jerune imagined she thought she was whispering. It was anything but; her impatience a poor moderator of her volume.

'The Forge, Porst. I need to know how they transport those orbs. Remember the one I got?'

188

Jerune scanned the room, breathed a sigh of relief. No interested parties. No subtle twists of the neck. They probably heard but it appeared nobody cared. Not a surprise given Porst's apparent state of destitution.

'You want more?' he asked. 'That's... but that's...' He trailed off.

'That's what?' Bücka asked.

Porst found his mental footing. 'They'll kill you.'

'Not your concern. You helped once. You do it again... the debt's cleared.'

His eyes widened. 'Cleared? All of it?'

Bücka nodded. She looked to Jerune. Her eyes were hopeful. A thought crossed his mind. Wondered as to the value of the debt. He'd press Bücka later. Tease her.

Porst said, 'You'll still die.'

With a shrug, Bücka said, 'Either way, you're off the hook.'

'I can show you. Will I show you?'

Another glance to Jerune, and Bücka smiled. 'A drink first. Something for the cold. Then, you take us where we want to go.'

It was cold. Too damn cold. The sweat down his back a distant memory, Jerune followed Bücka and the gambler, Porst's dark fur a grubby stain against the white. Two hours out from Gulda, the horizon had once again married itself to everything, a confusion of direction from which Jerune couldn't escape. A maze of hellish nothing made worse by the incessant flurry of powder; all he could discern was a constant ascent. The dislocation from his senses was a hideous disability, a thing which alienated him from his talents. All he could do was trudge behind the warrior and the debtor.

'How far?' he called.

A mumble was returned. Porst's incoherent voice.

'What?'

Bücka turned. Her eyes visible, Jerune saw the concern in them. He thought to look behind to find the cause of her anxiety. He straightened, realising he was the source. She paced over, feet piling deep into the snow. Removing her mask, she leaned in close.

'You alright?' It was genuine, no mockery of his condition. To hear Bücka speak with compassion was enlightening. 'You look miserable.'

How best to answer? Jerune replied, 'This fucking place. It's awful.'

Bücka glanced to Porst, still plunging upwards and onwards. 'We gotta follow him. He's an arse but I need to trust him.'

Bücka's faith was reassurance of sorts. A trail of hope. Jerune nodded. 'You think it's far?'

She smiled. Snow collecting on her eyebrows. 'Dunno.' Bücka paused, slapped him on the shoulder. 'Come on, imagine how brave you'd pretend to be if Sarellia was watching.'

Perhaps the cold numbed his sarcasm. Froze his temper. She was right. Jerune managed a smile.

'You're a cow,' he said.

'Moo!'

Bücka giggled, a serene and welcome anomaly. She turned, waved her hand at Jerune to follow. Warmth crept into his limbs. A positive emotion to fight the chill. He muttered out of earshot, 'A lovely cow.'

Invigorated by his new mood he caught up with the pair. A silent journey shared. Jerune marvelled at the Larian weather; the remarkable speed of its transformation. The blizzard diminished to an illusion of movement and the yellow sun, low in the sky, graced them with its presence. Ahead, a low range of snow-dusted rocks jutted from the ground. Rising a few feet, they ended in an abrupt line above which a canvas of blue spread to the heavens. He recognised the lay of the land, understood it to be a bluff, the drop beyond hidden from view.

Porst pointed at the dark protrusion. 'Over there,' he said, and continued to the rocks. Joining him, Jerune and Bücka stared over the edge.

'Bloody hell!' said Jerune.

Below, a valley of dark grime broke the monotony of the white plains. Jerune squinted, saw something beautiful. *Green.* The deep gorge appeared to be a fissure, not a natural valley. No river ran through it but ponds of water were scattered along the length. From those pits of murk, a green colour painted the surrounds. Few trees, mostly fern and bracken. A mist rose from the depression, the warmer air condensing in the cold. Scanning to the left, Jerune noted the fissure terminated at a substantial, blackened rockface. Swarms of bodies, small as ants, moved around. He tracked back along the gorge, noted the trail of foot and cart. No horses here. Just wheels and effort. The trail stopped at the far right where a zig-zag slope wound its way to the fissure rim.

Pointing at the far wall, he asked, 'The forge?'

Porst turned and smiled; it wasn't the prettiest grin. He said, 'The back way. Less guards.'

Bücka said, 'Less guards? That's still a lot.'

It was. But Jerune didn't care. It was warmer down there, and green. Besides, he had already noticed a crack in the cliff high above where the men were milling around. A wisp of mist rising from its hidden depth. He tapped Bücka's shoulder, pointed to it.

'That's our way in.'

He could see her straining to find the mark. Reaching for her hand he moved it into position and said, 'There, that cave.'

'You're kidding? I'm not a bloody mountain goat.'

She was right. It was a sheer cliff with a difficult climb. Exposed to all below. Not without significant risk to life and limb.

'You have a better idea?' he asked.

Bücka stared at the cliff. He waited for her dry response, something only Bücka would say. Silence was her answer. Not even a shake of her head. Just the slightest slump of her posture.

'It's all we've got,' he said. 'If Goddard was here, I'm sure he'd just smash his way in. I mean, you'd make a dent but there's too many.' Jerune pointed again. 'You want in, that's all we've got. The air's condensing, so it goes into the heat. Could even be intentional—perhaps a chimney of sorts.'

Uninvited, Porst said, 'You'll be spotted. Caught. Probably killed.'

In the snow, his and Bücka's fur were perfect for concealment. Not so on the dark rock. Even Porst's fleece would be noticed scrambling on the face. Success was as close to impossible as he could imagine. A mirror of Bücka, he felt his own shoulders slump, his confidence wither. But as quick as the change in Larian weather, thoughts of failure evaporated. An image in his mind's eye. Sarellia. It was childish, his thought. But it was real. He would do anything to make their future work. A paradox that he was willing to risk his life for that chance.

'I'm not walking away,' he said. 'Not now.'

A sigh from Bücka. To his ears it was a huff. 'I'll fight any man or woman, you know that. But that's a tall order, even for me.' She waved a finger at the rock face. 'And that? I doubt even you can climb that?'

Perhaps she was right but for Sarellia he would climb every mountain put in his way. He said, 'I need a darker fur. Some rope and hooks. Porst?'

He nodded, appeared surprised. 'I can get 'em. You'll still die.'

'We go back to Gulda. Rest. I'll return tomorrow night. Go in when it's dark. I'll figure out what to do inside. I'll work something out.'

Bücka stared. 'You're serious, aren't you?'

'You don't need to come.'

It was unexpected. Her open palm landing on his cheek. She'd pulled her swing, otherwise he would have been sent plummeting into the gorge.

'What the fuck?' he said.

She scowled. 'Don't you dare play hero. Don't you dare cut me out.'

'You're coming? What about the climb?'

'You figure out how to get me inside. But you're not dying alone.'

'Aw sweet,' Porst said.

In harmony, Jerune and Bücka replied, 'Fuck off!'

Chapter XXXII

'**A**re pirates bad?' Chara asked.

Goddard observed Elazra as she pondered the question. Her glance came his way. He shrugged, offered a grimace to apologise, though he wouldn't chastise the child. Standing on the deck of the Battleship he thought it best that Chara should investigate her new world. Outside the circle of companions, she had scant interaction with others. Bandits were the rare and unwelcome exception. In comparison, his novel family seemed a safe place for her curiosity.

The Rotynian leader shook her head. 'I think pirates are misunderstood,' she replied. Pacing to the starboard side, she looked out across the bay. 'We salvage and we charge a fee to those that sail our waters.' Looking to Sarellia, she said, 'You'd call it tax.'

Sarellia raised her hands. 'I've never judged.'

Elazra smiled. 'We all do.'

'Do you,' Chara asked. 'Judge me?'

Goddard folded his arms, keen to hear the woman's response. Chara's uniqueness had been accepted without question by the companions. He was curious to hear an outsider's opinion.

'What is there to judge, little one?'

Holding out her arms for the Rotynian to see, Chara said, 'I'm not like you. I'm made of glass, from stone.'

Elazra pointed to Goddard. 'And he is seven foot tall.' Moved her hand to Sarellia. 'The most beautiful woman I've ever seen. And you, just as rare, as unique. I admit, I'm curious about you. But the Rotynian Claim has long acknowledged our Elemental master. Seen things you mudfeet wouldn't believe.'

What did she mean? In his younger days, Goddard had wondered about the other Elementals. Yet, there were no tales of anything beyond what he knew. Earth was the curious one. Kor'A's touch was the known constant. The others were conspicuous by their absence.

He asked, 'What things have you seen?'

'We spend our lives at sea. Come to the shore only to mend our hulls, hoist new sails. Trade for what we require to maintain our way of life. Out there, among the worst storms, I've seen salvation and mercy from the waves. That's on good days. On bad days,

I've watched the ocean fall in on itself, heard the screams of friends as She swallows them whole.' Elazra pointed to the cliffs from where they had descended. 'Just as Earth manipulates her realm, so too does Water. The oceans are vast, you'd see little on trade runs. But over the years, I've seen Her.' She turned to Chara, nodded. 'Out there, I've seen things as wonderful as you.'

Goddard looked to Chara then Sarellia, certain his expression mirrored that of the Cultist.

Sarellia asked, 'Living creatures?'

Elazra frowned. 'I don't know. But they're not of human form. Whales of surf thrown in the air. Pods of dolphins, transparent as a crystal bay. She plays with her own realm, mimics what is alive.' Again, to Chara, she said, 'Are they as clever as you? I don't know. I doubt it.'

'I never imagined,' Goddard said.

'In all your impossible years you've never seen Water's creations?'

Goddard pushed through the haze in his mind, seeking old Bruhale. So many sunsets watching the water. The glistening liquid fire set alight by the rays of dusk. All those sparkles, so much movement. They had been tricks of the light, had they not?

He shook his head. 'Nothing I could be sure of.'

'Well, they're as real as Chara here,' Elazra said.

Sarellia asked, 'This is common knowledge of your people?'

Elazra smiled. 'The Claim has hereditary lines and immigrants. Those born at sea believe. Those who come from the mud appear to have their doubts. In time, the oceans prove themselves.'

'I can't believe we didn't know,' Sarellia said. To Goddard she asked, 'Why didn't we know?'

Considering his lineage, it was no surprise she sought his wisdom. Yet, for all his days, it seemed he had few answers for the educated Bruhsa.

'I don't know,' he said. 'Elazra, you've kept this from the... from us?'

'Our world is not one we wish to share. What little you know of us, you understand we keep ourselves to ourselves. Our routes, our culture; they are sacred to us. Why give the nations of the land more reason to bother us?'

Chara spoke. 'Does she talk to you, Water, I mean?'

'No. At least, not that I've ever heard. We hear more from the wind than water. The gales and storms that whip across the oceans. They don't speak mind, they howl.'

'Do you think we'll see them, the creatures?'

Elazra tilted her head to Goddard. He saw her wink at the child. 'I think he'll scare them off. Big lumbering brute.'

Chara giggled, looked to him and said, 'You're not a brute.'

Raising one eyebrow at Chara, he laughed when her grin dropped.

'You don't lumber too much,' she said.

'I do, little one, I do' he said, placing a hand on her head. Goddard turned to Elazra. 'How long until the ship can sail?'

Leaning on the deck rail, she replied, 'My father finished the work his grandfather had started. Despite appearances, she is sea-worthy. The Claim has kept her afloat, though by her movement you'd swear she was grounded. She's good to go but we need a day or so to get the sailors ready.' She turned to him. 'To reach Laria, it'll take a few more.'

'As straight-forward as that?' Sarellia asked.

'To sail? Yes. To remain hidden, no,' Elazra replied. 'She'll draw attention to herself. We'll sail at night, anchor during the day. We know what routes every nation sails. Hope for storms and fog to keep us hidden. No matter how distant we remain from prying eyes, this lady's a bloody mountain on every horizon.'

Goddard imagined the curiosity of others. How close would those eyes wish to peer? A thought occurred to him; would anyone even know what it was they saw?

'Nobody's seen one sail in a century,' he said.

Elazra shrugged. 'Not that I know of. Just the Claim but only for sea trials.' She patted the rail. 'Too ostentatious for our tastes.'

Looking across the deck, the tarpaulins covering the cannons, he had another question. He moved to one of the covered weapons, pointed to the canvas. 'Have you tested these?'

Elazra grinned. 'Perhaps.'

It was an answer. The glint of mischief showing in the Rotynian's eyes. 'In anger?' he asked.

'I don't get *that* angry. You can trust in our methods, Goddard. When this leviathan sails to the open sea, she'll perform as those ingenuous Larians intended. Your diamonds will deliver a first-hand account of the power this Battleship holds.'

He shuddered, a tingle running the length of his spine. A rare thing for him to be awestruck by another's words. He looked to Chara who had moved to the deck rail. The cannons would be as thunder. A ferocious display was coming. It troubled him she would see it but there was no other way.

'Chara?'

'Yes?'

'Are you excited to sail?'

She hopped on the spot. Clapping her hands together, sending a chime across the deck, she said, 'Mother never said I'd see the oceans so close. And I know Water will let me pass. I can't wait.'

Goddard nodded. Caught the eye of Sarellia. Her expression matched his thoughts. A wariness of what darkness was to come, hidden beneath her smile.

He nodded. 'Yes. It'll be exciting. An adventure.'

They were better words for Chara to hear. Better than what it would be. A necessary massacre.

'She's asleep?'

Goddard had heard it from every companion. Each one as curious as the next. Now it was Elazra's turn to profess doubt in Chara's slumber. They sat on the shore, the night sky hidden behind the flapping tarpaulin. The child lay beside him, curled up on the fleece covered rock. Sarellia straddled a barrel on its side and Elazra sat on her commoner's throne.

'Her eyes flicker and she sees,' he replied, 'but she says she rests and she cannot hear.'

Elazra frowned. Waved a hand as though to attract Chara's attention. 'She sees?'

Goddard nodded. Smiled at the Rotynian's attempts to distract the child. 'She won't wake.'

'But she'll remember this?'

'Your hand?' he asked. Elazra nodded. 'I've no idea. Some things, perhaps.'

Sarellia said, 'It's not so different from us.'

'It's not?' Goddard asked.

'We may shut our eyes to sleep but do we shut our ears?'

He was about to respond. An obvious answer. But he questioned his wisdom. Thought about it; ears couldn't shut, not physically. 'Hadn't thought of it that way,' he said.

'And do you hear, when you sleep?' Sarellia asked.

He understood her point. Nodded with a frown to accept her wisdom. 'We hear what startles us. What wakes us.'

The Cultist said, 'But we don't really remember the sounds. Perhaps it's as simple as this: Chara sees without sound. We hear without sight.'

Elazra said, 'There's something romantic about that. Poetic.'

Goddard scoffed. Elazra quizzed him with a stare. Holding his hands out, he said, 'Not to be rude, but if you'd met her mother, you'd see the irony in that statement.'

Elazra leaned forward. She asked, 'How close have you been to her? Earth, I mean?'

It was a jolt. To suddenly be there again, one century in his past. A picture vivid in his mind, a ghost that refused to leave him at peace. He felt his grin fade as he began to explain what he knew of Chara's mother.

'In the city she named An'Korathall, we found her after we had taken a contract from old Laria to secure a truth. Find the Queen—as simple as that. Report back to confirm Kalleron was without its weapon. Didn't go as planned. Petra was still raw from Felicitra's death. She reacted... she let her heart do the thinking.'

'Petra, the Queen of Stone?' Elazra asked.

Goddard nodded. 'Not a title she took willingly. But that day in Anka brought the legend you know to bear. Petra was fierce. Underneath that delicate façade was... is... a natural born fighter. Most resilient woman I've ever known.' He paused, not enough of an accolade. 'More than any man. Well, seeing the face of Felicitra's murderer was an insult too far. She charged at her; this petite soul raging against a genocidal monster.'

Elazra, her eyes wide, asked, 'What happened?'

'The great citadel door shut us away, leaving Petra trapped inside with the fabled and terrible Queen of Kalleron.' A pause to hear the sounds. Recalling Shadow's fears and his screams. Shaking his head, he said, 'It is not a good memory; it chills me to this day. We heard every strike. Every yelp from Petra. She was being destroyed. And then the doors opened. The Queen walking forth, holding Petra in her arms.' Goddard mimicked the Queen carrying Petra. 'Just like this. Offering a bloodied ragdoll to us. Shadow took her away and the Queen vanished. Bled into the ground as dust.'

'Petra, she died?' Elazra asked.

'No. But she was dying. Broken inside. We did our best to ease her pain but we knew she was slipping away. That's when Earth returned to us. Days later. She'd been watching all that time. I think our pain, Shadow's especially, caused her... made her doubt her actions. That was the first time she healed Petra. It was brutal. Painful to watch.' He smiled, though the memory was bitter. Thought of the moment; how pivotal it was to the fate of the world. 'Everything you know and live for, even on the high seas, all of it started that day. It wasn't grief that made Kor'A heal Petra. Earth doesn't know romance and poetry. She only knows curiosity, meddling, and death.'

Gesturing to Chara, Elazra said, 'And what of this beauty? Is she not a miracle?'

Elazra couldn't know what he and Sarellia knew. He shook his head. 'Not in the way you think. But to me, she is.'

'Yet she travels with you to Laria? To war?'

'I had resigned myself to stay in Anka. Thought at first she'd be safer there. But if what comes our way passes the ocean, there is no safe place. I need to be there. Need to stop the fleet from reaching our home. Chara's better off by my side; I'm her best chance, no matter where I am.'

'Well, my King, I'll do my best to keep *you* safe.'

He nodded. Elazra's words were honest. Although he had bought her service and that of the Battleship, their trade was bound in honour. The Rotynian Claim lived as free and adventurous a life as any. But Elazra carried herself with a rare regal aura. Not one to wield but one with which to enervate others. A natural leader. As he had once been.

Looking to Chara, he said, 'While she sleeps, it would be best to discuss what will happen when we encounter the fleet.'

Goddard noticed Sarellia shiver. The fur around her shoulders was thick and plush; he knew she wouldn't be cold. Touched instead by the realisation of what must come to pass. Foreboding. He felt the same. A century ago, the Battleships had been repelled by cunning Kalleron. But now a gathering transport fleet lay unaware of what power he would bring. A Rotynian Queen and an old Bruhadian King to terrorise the seas. The shores would run red with blood and the skies would ring with cries of death. There was no glory in what murder they planned. He reached down and stroked Chara's head. What would she think of him? How would she react to the deed that would soon be a dark stain upon his soul?

'Goddard?' Sarellia said. He realised she had been calling his name.

'Sorry, what?'

'What do we do?'

An apology and a promise. Unheard by Chara. 'We become what we hate, to protect those we love.'

Chapter XXXIII

Jerune tried to conceal his disappointment; he had woefully misjudged the geometry of the cliff. It was a fool's error. The entrance he had spied, the chimney on the face, lay beneath a wicked overhang. A dozen feet at least. Sitting hunkered down, squashed in against the rocks, he stole a glance over his shoulder at Bücka. She was nestled behind, her proximity an unusual comfort. She'd been quiet on the return trip. With Porst removed from their company, her silence was more apparent. He thought of the melancholy on the boat, her guilt from the last Larian contract. Under the dark skies, her breath floated past in wisps. He twisted his body to face her, pointed to the overhang.

'That's not so good.'

Her scarf removed from her face, Bücka's expression was clear. She didn't have to speak.

Jerune continued. 'Figure it's a couple of hundred feet down, hard to see in the dark.'

Points of flame moved around the base of the cliff. Dots of fire that moved in and out of sight as they passed into the forge. Protected by dark furs, Jerune knew he and Bücka were invisible. A small grace—the blizzard hadn't yet resumed, just lazy specks of white floating in the night sky. To access the vent, he had planned an abseil from the top. Thought he had been blessed to find the grounding of a suitable rock. Simple enough. A proud plan scuppered by the damn overhang. Accessing the opening would require a great, arcing swing. The amplitude would dislodge the anchor point; at least, he considered the risk too great. He could descend but not swing. No swing, no wall. Nothing more than a hanging target for alert eyes below. But there was another way; he could climb across. Doubted Bücka would. The moons, fat and full behind wisps of ethereal clouds, illuminated the pattern of the rockface. There were holds. Small crimps he could grasp. If he was ten feet from the ground it would be a simple exercise. But as with all climbs, height amplified the severity.

Bücka whispered. The tremble in her tone a crack in the warrior's armour. 'How're you getting in? How are we getting in?'

Jerune looked at the route. 'I'll rope up and climb across...'

Her hand heavy on his shoulder. A vice grip. 'You are not!'

Turning to her, he said, 'I've done worse. You saw me at the citadel, remember?'

'You were on a rope, anchored to a bloody legendary King.'

It was true. Goddard's grip was stronger than rock. Here, there was no such safety. None except for her.

'I'll move across. You dig in here and hold the rope. The distance to the opening is far shorter than the drop. If I lose my footing, you'll have me, yeah?'

She nodded, appeared unconvinced.

As stern as he could, he said, 'Bücka, you'll fucking hold me.'

'Solid. I'll be solid as the proverbial,' she said. 'Then what?'

'Then what, *what*?'

Bücka glared, pointed to her chest. 'Me, you idiot. How'd I get in?'

She wouldn't like it. But it was the only way. Nodding toward the clifftop, he said, 'When I'm in, you'll climb to the top, keep the rope around your waist. There's just enough slack to keep us together. On the cliff, you'll tie the second rope. Big fat rock up there. Secure it on that then abseil down to my level.' Pointing to her waist, where the umbilical rope would be, he said, 'I'll haul you in on our rope.'

'Haul me in?'

'Yeah. You'll be attached to me by the first rope. I'll swing you in.'

Bücka frowned. 'So why don't you abseil first? We can both swing in.'

Jerune imagined her response would be less than enthusiastic. He placed a hand on her forearm. Considered it might placate her fears. She looked at it and her frown creased ever deeper.

Her tone saturated with suspicion, she asked, 'What?'

'The swing. Just a small chance it might...' Jerune stopped as Bücka's eyes widened.

'It might what?' she asked.

Hesitant, he replied, 'It might dislodge the anchor point. Maybe two or three back and forth and it could come down.'

Her mouth hung open. Brown eyes staring at him, she retracted her arm from his hand. In that moment she appeared vulnerable. An unexpected show of fragility; broken all too soon by her response.

'Fuck off! No way that's happening.'

He pleaded. 'Bücka, it's all we've got. Just as you'll anchor me, when...if... the top rope fails, I'll haul you in. I'll have you.'

She turned away from him. Not to the cliff but to the sky. Jerune reached for her again but when she brought her gaze back, he saw the tears.

'Bücka! It'll be alright. I promise.'

Wiping her eyes, she sniffed and said, 'I'm not scared—it's not that. And don't you dare think it is. But this whole thing... I feel useless. I hate it. A dangling doll at someone else's mercy.' A thumb to her sternum, she added, 'And Bücka doesn't depend on anybody.'

He grabbed her, both hands on her arms. 'You're not useless. We're a team. And you're not relying on just somebody else. It's me, and we're doing this for our friends; for Sarellia, Goddard, and Chara. For Petra and the whole Northern Lands. This is us, Bücka. We're going to do this; not me, not you, *us*.'

She laughed. 'I must look the right coward.' A bubble of snot blew from her nose. Wiping it away, she smiled. 'Glamourous, eh?'

'Well, you were raised in Wederhyne.'

A punch to his chest. Swift and sharp. He knew it was delivered with love.

'Bastard,' she said.

'Your bastard,' he replied with a smile.

He held the rope and directed her to raise her arms. Thinking back to Goddard and his bloody Bruhadian Granny knot, he tied a figure-eight and yanked on it.

'Better than a King's knot,' he said and tied his own.

As he stood to begin his traverse, she reached for him. 'Jerune?'

He turned to her, thought to make a courageous quip. Considered he wasn't that much of an arse. Not waiting and without reply, he nodded and moved to the wall.

The night was a blessing; his eyes focusing on the wall, not the drop beneath. A safety net of depthless dark. An occasional glance down to see the dots of flame; easy to imagine as fireflies accompanying his effort. Jerune's one regret was looking to Bücka. He had wanted to look confident; send a motivating message. Yet, each time he glanced, her expression was the same. Terror. The rope in her hand held as though Goddard's hammer. It was a small comfort; her fear held his life with a vice-like grip. She was witness to his predicament, her anxiety multiplied by the drop Jerune was trying to ignore. Inching across, grip by grip, toehold by toehold, the passage of time became irrelevant. The only constant was the rock. It took him by surprise when reaching for the next grip, his hand plunging into a deep recess. It was no hold. He had reached the chimney. With a trembling sigh, he released his nervous energy, a grin wide upon his face. Leaning out, he waved at Bücka lost in the gloom. A shadow moved and he saw her face, a blob against the dark. Standing, she appeared to be smiling. Or perhaps it was his imagination. Jerune pointed to the clifftop and Bücka bled into the night.

Waiting for her, occasionally flapping the umbilical free of snags, Jerune peered down at the spits of orange below. Little fire ants. It was peculiar. Without colours, cast in nothing but amber, the shapes were difficult to discern. The light of the moons was too diffuse to render their true forms. Their movement was hard to decipher. What were they doing? Their direction seemed aimless. His thoughts were interrupted when the second rope snaked past the overhang. It lay still, then began to twitch. Jerune smiled, Bücka's huffing coming to his ears. Hands on the umbilical, he reeled her in, not enough to tug, just enough for security. Looking to the cliff, he saw the warrior appear. Ungainly, her descent was erratic. The rope was sliding through her grip in uneven lengths. In the vast gorge her audible efforts would be lost. A good thing. He didn't want to yell at her to be quiet. She had done well. But the worst part was to come.

Bücka dangled level with the mouth of the chimney. For that brief moment she was quiet. Serene in her place. She exhaled a deep breath, suddenly startling as the rope creaked above. Holding out a hand, Jerune tried to calm her. Ropes creaked. Anchor points groaned. This was all normal. But Bücka was already panicking; kicking her legs, she began to spin, her unforgiving glare flashing as an angry beacon. With haste, Jerune started to haul in what short length was left in the umbilical. Bücka squeaked as the spin was arrested, the tension steadying her position. Pulling, he began her pendulum swing. The rope twanged. Another thought. How much did Bücka weigh? Her muscle, her armour and swords. *The armour.* He hadn't accounted for its weight. It was bloody plate. Cursing himself—a novice error—Jerune hurried his swing and Bücka squealed again. How could he be so stupid? Jerune forgave himself, Bücka moved with uncanny grace. It was easy to forget she was clad in metal, not leather. Damn it.

Then the top rope snapped free.

A surreal split in time. Silence. A terrible quiet as she plummeted on the wrong side of the pendulum. Realising he would be torn from the chimney, Jerune lunged for a crack in the rock, slamming his hand hard into the fissure. Not a moment too soon as Bücka's weight yanked on the rope and he was brought to his knees.

It was as though his wrist was set aflame. But his hand held fast. A blur of violent movement and everything became still. He winced, tried to stay quiet. The pain was excruciating. Not a simple abrasion. Not just flesh. Jerune knew his wrist was broken. Then the rope slackened, Bücka appearing at the lip of the chimney, hauling herself over. She didn't know the cost of her climb; her giggle of relief cut short as her expression of joy slipped to something grimmer. She looked at him. He imagined he appeared in control. On his knees, hand high in the rock.

'Jerune?'

Through gritted teeth, he said, 'You alright?'

'I'm...' A frown. A squint to his hand. 'Yes, I'm...what's wrong?'

'My hand. Wrist.' He nodded to it. Didn't want to look. 'Had to jam it in when the rope went.'

'It's stuck?'

'I don't know. Don't want to try. Think it's broken.'

'Oh, fuck. Really?'

He nodded. Watched in the periphery as Bücka moved to his trapped appendage.

She uttered a drawn-out expletive. A novel combination of the colloquial. He would've found it amusing had it not sounded so severe.

'How bad?' he asked, staring away from Bücka and the hand.

Confusion swept over him. A hand smothering his mouth, tight as an assassin's grip. A moment of doubt; where had the bastard come from? Another hand upon his own stuck in the rock. A flash of terrible pain. Searing. A word from a woman's mouth. It was Bücka. What? Did she say, *sorry?*

The throbbing. That was the first thing. Eyes still shut, Jerune moved his right hand. Couldn't. A stab of pain. His good hand travelled to it. Felt gauze and fabric. Was he in bed?

'Jerune?'

It was Bücka. He opened his eyes and the light flooded his vision. A dark silhouette against the white, she knelt beside him. Beyond the warrior, the valley was lost in a blizzard; though, it was clear night had passed.

'Bücka?'

'I always carry Ambyr Dust. A warrior's best friend. Seems to work well on you.'

He sat up, putting his weight on his left hand. Looked at the bandages on his right. Considered his fuzzy haze and its familiarity to events after the stables in Anka. 'Yverelyn? You did this?'

'I know a little field medicine. All good warriors do. I've reset the bone. Applied herbs and the Ambyr. Did it while you slept.'

A flash of a memory—the hand smothering his mouth. 'You pulled it out?'

Her grin was sheepish, uncertain of its place in the conversation. 'I saw a chance. Took it while you were distracted.'

Bücka was incredible. More than ever, Jerune realised how invaluable she was to have by his side. But he couldn't tell her that.

'You're a bloody maniac.'

She appeared hurt but as his smile grew, her face softened. Bücka giggled.

'You saved me again,' she said. 'You sure you don't fancy me?'

He didn't reply. Wasn't sure what to say. It was natural to find her attractive. Knew she was joking. But she was wonderful in her own way. Not the same as Sarellia. Different realms of beauty. Sarellia, by a single glance, was perfection. Bücka had complexity of depth. Attractive without doubt but as he had grown to know her, he had seen her true face. He was bonding to her in spirit and soul. He thought of words said before. The old legends of Petra's mortal days.

'I think you're my Petra, and maybe I'm your Shadow.' He hesitated, then said, 'Probably the drugs talking.'

Bücka shook her head. Taking his good hand, she said, 'No. I like that thought. But you gotta work on your Shadow. Thelia told me all about him. Boy, you got some way to go.'

He couldn't let her have the sarcastic high-ground. 'Well, you don't have Petra's looks but...'

Bücka laughed. Punched him on his head with a soft blow. 'Arsehole.'

She looked to the back of the cave. Jerune followed her gaze. Revealed in the light of the blizzard, he could see the vent reached deeper into the Forge. Old tooling marks told of its age. The undisturbed layer of dirt and soot spoke of seclusion.

Bücka said, 'When you're not so groggy, we'll go and see what's what.'

He looked at his hand, tried to wiggle his fingers. The Yverelyn was working. No movement, just incidental pain.

'Yeah. I'll sit for a while. Then it's your turn to do your thing.'

Bücka nodded, opened her fur to reveal the scabbards. Patting the belt, she said, 'It's why I brought the girls.'

Chapter XXXIV

G oddard slept. That huge body seated upright, hands upon his lap. A kind face at rest in his strange state of slumber. Chara wondered why they chose to do so. Why they became unaware of everything? They had all been curious of her habits, yet it was theirs that made no sense. Elazra rested upon her chair and Sarellia lay curled under a pile of furs. Wind flapped the cover above their heads and she wondered what noise it made. As ever, when she slept, Chara stared at the hammer. She knew it wasn't as it seemed; Bruch'ail was not the same as other human weapons. They didn't sing. They didn't shimmer with the colours of the moons. It occurred to her—they couldn't see it. They would fuss more if they could, as humans did. All things of curiosity were to be debated and discussed. It was what made them strong. To learn of new things. Kor'A had pressed that upon her; to be curious. And she was. Of the hammer.

The rustling appeared to her senses. The flapping tarpaulin. Then another sound. The whisper of Water, so close, lapping upon the pebble shore. She thought it should be soothing but it was not. She was awakening long before dawn, the world dark under night. Why? A glance at Goddard. His breathing heavy and slow. If she had skin, she imagined she would feel it upon her body. His warm breath of life. A tremble of fear grinding through her core, Chara focused on it all. The realm of night was revealing itself; the sounds of human vulnerability. Goddard's exhalations joined by others. She remembered sleeping in the forest, awoken by Goddard's jostling armour. Nothing had woken her since. Peaceful and certain of her safety. Why now? Still as a stone, she glanced around. Her dark diamond eyes perceived more than the humans could. She saw no threat. Heard nothing untoward.

Except the gentle singing. *The hammer.* Chara didn't look. Just listened. As a human might create a tune, so too did the hammer. As though unaware it was doing so. She had watched Sarellia fuss over her garments; she would do the same, singing an absent tune. No words, just noises. Soft and pleasant. As pretty as this song was, it was eerie. She didn't want to look. Eyes flicking back to Goddard. A mountain of slumber, unaware of the music. Chara wasn't sure if she would be able to move. Tried it. Surprised by her hand travelling to Goddard. Reaching to him, she stopped short, air between her fingers and his skin.

Child.

The song had ceased. The hammer spoke. Chara didn't reply.

I see you, child. Come. Come.

Eyes first, Chara looked to Bruch'ail. In her periphery she strained to see. Moved her head to focus. A frown to reply to the hammer.

Yes, child. Come. Come.

If she moved, Goddard would awaken. He called it meditation. Would hear her skin move against the rock. But she couldn't refuse the call. Careful, she pressed her weight onto her hands. Elevated her body. He didn't move. She peered to the ground; rock and pebble. Chara winced, she was certain it would be a calamitous noise to disturb the peace.

Come.

Looking to Bruch'ail, she saw the shimmer; the colours of the rainbow cascading in a vibrant display. An aura around the steel. Though of course, she knew it wasn't steel. Tentative, on slim arms, she lowered her feet to the shingle. She anticipated the crunch. But the shingle did not compress and grate. It held firm as though one uniform rock. Silence. Another glance to Goddard. Unaware, undisturbed. Impossible.

Yes.

On tip-toes, they said. The human expression. Bruch'ail just a few steps away. Each pace settled on that unyielding and quiet earth. She stood before the hammer.

Child. Hold me. Tell me of your world.

A shake of her head to deny the command. Goddard wouldn't approve.

Do not be afraid. We are... family.

'Family?' she replied, quickly hushing her mouth with her hand. But still they slept. Reassured, she continued, her voice a whisper. 'Family, how?'

Hold me, child. See me so that I may see you.

It felt silly to say it but Chara replied, 'Hammers can't talk.'

I am so much more. See me, hold me.

A new sensation. She wanted to know. Yet, she feared what would happen. Chara wanted Goddard to help. Sought his reassurance. The conflict was a new disturbance. Wracking her memories, thinking of the friends, she found the emotion. The wrench of competing desires, the fear of the unknown. They called it anxiety. Her lack of control over the outcome causing fear.

She turned to Goddard, thought to speak his name but Chara held her voice.

Hold me. Do not fear me.

'What are you?'

The hammer did not reply. It waited for her. She knew it. With one final turn to Goddard and a silent apology, she focused on Bruch'ail and reached out for the haft.

A scream—it was Chara. On his feet, Goddard reached for Bruch'ail. He froze. In the dark, under the canopy, his vision was a blur. His hand far from the hammer. Chara's fingers were wrapped around it. Holding Bruch'ail as Bücka had. Holding it *above* the ground.

'Chara!' he called. She did not respond.

Elazra stumbled from her throne and Sarellia appeared from under the fur. Voices and torches all moving from beyond the tent. Chara stood, both hands on Bruch'ail, the head of it suspended inches from the shingle.

'Chara!' he repeated, stepping toward her.

Bruch'ail fell, impacting the shore with a thunder. Chara fell backwards, Goddard scooping to catch her. On his knees he cradled her, her head rolling from side to side. A whisper from her lips. A confused mumble.

Sarellia came to his side, a hand on his shoulder. 'What happened? What's she saying?'

Goddard strained. Concentrated on the sound. Others had arrived, come to defend their Queen. Elazra came close.

'What happened to her?' she asked.

He shook his head. Chara's words were incomprehensible. Another language? What was she saying?

'Did you see?' he asked, glancing at Sarellia. 'Bruch'ail. She held Bruch'ail from the ground.'

Sarellia nodded. 'That's not possible, is it?'

'You can't trust the Elementals,' Elazra said. 'I told you.'

'Goddard?' Chara's voice reaching to him.

The relief surged. His laughter unprompted. 'Chara. What happened? What did you do?'

In the flicker of countless amber torches, he saw her face. In her eyes, flakes of black glass pooled and rolled down her cheeks. Tears he had never seen. Chara twisted in his arms and buried herself in his torso. Sobs wracked her body and he held her as tight as he dared. His eyes darted to Sarellia. Her own appeared panicked and afraid.

'What in the Gods?' she said.

But as Chara sobbed in muffled bursts, all he could do was shake his head and stare at Bruch'ail.

As Elazra waved away her people, Chara's tears diminished. Goddard released his grip, allowed her freedom to move. Pulling her head from his chest, she looked up at him. Wide, sad eyes and a tremor of her head greeted him.

'Chara, what happened?' he asked.

Once again, the tears pooled and her face creased into a fracture of grief. 'She's chosen you, Goddard. She's chosen you.'

Confused, Goddard glanced at Sarellia who shrugged. Elazra too, all faces disturbed by Chara's behaviour. He tried to soothe the child, stroked her head.

'Chosen me? Who, Chara? What are you saying?'

Her hand raised, a finger pointing to the moons visible between overlapping and billowing sheets of canvas. Goddard stared at the twin satellites. It made no sense. Yet, as his eyes absorbed the amber and blue, something deep within stirred. An old fog. An ancient fear.

'Chara? I don't understand.'

Her voice a whisper, she said, 'She wants you to fix her. She wants you to destroy it all.'

Chapter XXXV

I t was as though it never happened. Dawn breaking on the Rotynian camp, Chara rising with a brooding sun. She had fallen into slumber after her doom-laden words. Elazra and Sarellia remaining alert the rest of the night, as had he. Few words were spoken between them, much of the time spent staring at Bruch'ail and the sleeping child. He had hoped the morning would bring clarity. Feared it might bring worse.

'Morning,' he said to her. Unsure how she would react, he allowed her time to reply.

Hesitant, she glanced around. Her gaze fell upon Bruch'ail and he knew she remembered.

'You're safe,' he said. 'We're all safe.'

Chara shook her head. 'No.'

'What happened. How could you hold Bruch'ail? Why did you say what you said?'

Chara looked to Elazra and Sarellia. 'Stone knows stone.' Her eyes returned to his. Nodded. She repeated her words. He understood. Found it awkward given the company.

To Elazra, he said, 'May we have...'

Before he finished, the Rotynian was already on her feet. She nodded. 'Remember my words, Goddard. Remember my words.'

He nodded. *You can't trust the Elementals.* But Chara was not one of them. Sarellia came to him, placed a hand on his arm.

'Call when you're done,' she said.

Under the flapping canopy, he faced Chara. Unsure what she would say, he was certain it would be a revelation. Before speaking he attempted a reassuring smile.

'What you said last night, what did you mean? Why were you holding Bruch'ail? How were you holding Bruch'ail?'

'It's not called Bruch'ail,' she replied. 'It has another name.'

'Another name? Possibly. My ancestors found it, we never made it.'

'She gave it to the first of men. The first who had seen Earth.'

'She?'

Chara leaned into him. He put an arm around her. When she spoke, her voice was listless, depressed.

'The Allmatta. Noctyrne and Ambyr as one. The moons who created Earth. She made it.'

The name resonated in his mind. Allmatta. He knew of something similar. An ancient word but not that. *All Mother*. A creature beyond the Elementals. Yet the word was only whispered, never found in the ancient Elemental scrolls. Thought to be a myth tied to the four sisters.

'The All Mother?'

Chara's head rubbed against his chest. 'No. Allmatta. She made mother. Only mother.'

Only mother? She was mistaken. Groggy from her confusion and turmoil. 'Chara, that doesn't make sense.'

Her body softened. It moulded into him. Her hands grasped at his fur, seemed to hunt for the flesh between his armour plates. She hugged him harder. It was strange; those little fingers beginning to pinch his skin. A welcome sting.

'Allmatta made mother. She is the only Elemental, *the world*. But she's broken. That's why...' She pointed to Bruch'ail.

Confused, grasping for reason, Goddard asked, 'Then... Kor'A made the hammer?'

Chara remained still. He felt a tremble. A shiver of onyx.

'Chara?'

Her voice impatient, she said, 'Mother didn't make it.'

'But...'

Chara interrupted. 'It was made to heal her. But it will end everything. The first of men failed, mother fractured. She's still broken, she has to be fixed. Allmatta says.'

Her words made no sense. Heal Kor'A, end everything? She had to be mistaken. Such confusion. Just a dream, he thought. She was developing human traits with every passing day. Just a dream, nothing more. Yet, last night Chara had held Bruch'ail. An unfeasible feat of strength. He hadn't dreamt that.

'What do you mean? Heal your mother, what does that mean? And who failed at what?' He heard his own voice struggling to unravel the child's dream. 'Chara, I don't understand any of this.'

Chara pulled away from his frame. She shifted and turned, facing him. Her hands fell on top of his. In other days her stern countenance would cause him humour. Not today.

Shaking her head as though recalling an unwanted memory, she said, 'The Elementals—they're not real. There are no sisters. They are *all* mother. Everything is mother. The earth, the sky, the oceans. Even fire.' Before he could speak, as his frown troubled his brow, she continued. 'Allmatta made her but mother was broken. Imperfect. Allmatta said she had made a mistake. One she couldn't make right.' Again, Chara pointed to Bruch'ail. 'That will fix her but Allmatta said the world would need to begin again.'

Goddard stared at the hammer. His line had known it was ancient. A relic of some lost power. And though he knew Chara would not lie, her words could not be truth. Why would the Allmatta make a weapon for men to wield? If she had created a broken God, she could surely mend it?

'Allmatta gave the hammer to men?'

She nodded.

'To fix Kor'A?'

Another nod.

'Why does that end the world?'

'Allmatta says she has lost control. Mother is dangerous, she doesn't understand. Allmatta does. The hammer will make her new again. It will unbreak her.'

That Kor'A was a danger was no secret. Flesh knew that. Mortals had suffered under the Queen of Kalleron. But Chara spoke of a higher power. Did she mean Allmatta had lost control—or Kor'A?

'Who's lost control?'

'Allmatta.'

Goddard reeled. The creator of Earth had lost control? He thought of the Gods of men; the illusions of perfection imagined to find inner peace. Gods were without flaw, perceived to bring hope to all. The Elementals were fallible. Kor'A had shown that. And if Chara's words were truth, the Allmatta was every part as damaged.

'Allmatta's lost control of Kor'A?' he asked.

Chara nodded. 'It's difficult to explain. Mother was alone. In the beginning there was only Earth. She is everything.' She patted the rock upon which they sat. 'Not just this. What did Allmatta say? Yes, that was it: *fire from dust, rock from fire*. It is all mother; she is the world. Allmatta made her that way.'

'I don't understand. Fire is a different Elemental. Water and Wind too.' He thought to question her reality; the image of Chara holding Bruch'ail a stark ward against his disbelief. Dismissing such logic, ignoring the impossible feat, he said, 'Perhaps you dreamt this, Chara?'

She looked at him, cocked her head to one side and smiled. A small shake of her head. 'I never dream. I long to, but I don't.' Pointing to Bruch'ail, she said, 'That is the essence of the moons. She reaches us through it. You wield the strength of Allmatta.'

He stared at Bruch'ail. On the ground it appeared as lifeless as the shingle upon which it rested. Chara's story was a bizarre and fanciful tale; although; as much as he didn't want to believe it, doubts were rising within. His gaze fixed on Bruch'ail, he wondered if he should ever lift it again.

'How can Kor'A be Fire, Chara. And the other sisters?'

'Allmatta said she broke. Became different. She couldn't cope with what she was. Allmatta called it the burden of being. Fire is her anger, Water is her calm, the Wind is her whimsy and chaos. Earth is what she became to study you. Her curiosity of life.'

'Allmatta, did she make us too?'

Chara giggled. 'No, silly. She doesn't know what you are.'

Such innocent words delivered with certainty. It was chilling. Though, it solidified the belief he knew many held. Humans were not part of the Elemental design. Fleas on a dog's back. Along for the ride. But there were too many questions. Could Chara answer the most obvious?

'Why must the world end?'

Chara looked to the shingle under his feet.

'Why?' he repeated.

'Allmatta said mother needs to rest. To slumber and awaken anew. The hammer will send her to sleep.' Chara paused, looked beyond his arm. She was scanning all around. Absorbing the camp, the hills, the sea. He frowned as she appeared lost in a familiar world. She continued, her eyes brought back to his. 'When mother is put to rest, Allmatta says she will return to dust so that she may become one again.'

'If she is struck by Bruch'ail?'

Chara's frown deepened. She nodded. 'By you. It can only be you. You were made to wield it.'

He had never known her to lie. Nor to fabricate a story. But it was too much to absorb. He knew his legacy was tied to the Elementals; understood they were a race apart, demigods of the world. Yet this new twist was incompatible with what he knew.

'Chara, even if I weren't an old man. I could never stand against your mother. I couldn't wield Bruch'ail against an Elemental. I'm mortal, and mortals can't harm them.'

She shook her head. 'You're not, Goddard.'

He frowned. Her words carried an untold weight. 'What?'

'You're not Goddard.'

Confusion. Not what? He clawed at his beard, the riddles returning. He said, 'Chara, what...'

She cut him off. Her tone sincere. 'Doga'rad. You're Doga'rad. The first to become one with Allmatta. It was you she chose. The day you defended the temple.'

Her mistake. A provable untruth. Doga'rad was ancient, he was not. Goddard could recall his line and it did not run to millennia. And what of his daughter, Bri'alla? His wife? The female Kings of Bruhada? Chara's night terror had been a dream. All this story, a magnificent fabrication from her onyx mind. He had fallen for it. Perhaps he had imagined her lifting the hammer? Not unusual for an interrupted meditation to cause confusion. But he would not chastise her. Not for having a nightmare. It wasn't her fault. Besides, it gladdened him to know he need not destroy the world. All in a child's first dream.

Shaking his head, relief blown away on a sigh, he said, 'No, Chara. That's not right. I'm sorry.' He grasped her slim arms, gave a gentle squeeze to her unyielding skin. 'It was a dream. Your first dream. I'm know I'm not Doga'rad. I wouldn't lie to you about that.'

But she shook her head. Not surprising; her confusion.

'A dream, Chara.' He smiled. 'It's alright.'

'Allmatta said you wouldn't remember. She couldn't let you know the truth. You had to believe your own lies.'

He could never be angry with her but the words were ill-mannered. 'Chara, enough. You can't accuse me of...'

She leapt from the rock and moved across the shingle to Bruch'ail. Her right hand grabbed the haft and she extended her other to him. A determined countenance upon her face, she said, 'You will see.'

'Chara...'

The ground rumbled underfoot. A commotion of noise erupted around the camp. Elazra and Sarellia came rushing back. Not a quake. It was Elemental. From Chara?

'Goddard?' Sarellia called from the edge of the tent.

A hand warding her away, he said, 'Wait!'

He paused before pacing toward Chara, the rumble dissipating as he did.

She said, 'Allmatta will let you see. I'm sorry.'

His hand moved to hers. Stopped inches away. In that fragment of time, he could hear the wind rustle through the camp, the breath of souls upon the air. Thought he could perceive the moss growing upon the rocks. Chara's tiny onyx fingers wiggled for his, so close across the void. Staring at his palm, his wrinkled skin, Goddard felt apprehension. No. Not that. *Fear*. Chara appeared certain of her truth. A truth which would dispel his own world. A world he knew to be true. It couldn't be a lie. His life wasn't a lie.

'It's alright,' she said. A single sound in his world. 'I'm here. I'll look after you.'

Her voice. It shook him to his core. Another memory. Bri'alla at the bottom of the Palace stairs. *It's alright.* The confusion. The midges. Too many damned riddles. His vision blurred, unwanted emotions rising to the surface.

'Bri'alla?'

Chara shook her head. She stretched out her hand and her skin touched his.

Goddard saw her truth. A torrent upon him; a cascade of history pouring into his mind. All the lives he never knew. A vast shadow behind the light; the one immortal King of Bruhada, born of Bruch'alma. The cursed son of Allmatta. He fell to his knees, Chara wrapping her arms around his head. She comforted him as only a child could. His world collapsing, his reality in ruins. And he wept.

Chapter XXXVI

A persistent zinging. How he thought of it; how Jerune could best describe the sensation. He tapped his broken wrist with a finger and it chimed with an unpleasant tingle. Hours had passed and the snow had eased. Beyond the edge of the cliff, the valley appeared picturesque. Across the vent, Bücka tossed a pebble at him.

'How is it?' she asked.

'Useless.'

'Painful?'

'Less than it was.'

'So, we can go?'

Jerune sighed. 'Well, I'm not climbing out, am I? We'll need to find another way now.'

The dilemma hadn't escaped his mind. With the top-rope no longer attached there was no way to ascend. A moot consideration given his useless hand. Whatever happened next, he and Bücka had to gamble on another exit.

'You think Goddard's doing better?' she asked.

'What do you think? Can anything stop that man?'

Bücka grinned. 'Yeah. You're right. Plain sailing for them.'

With care, Jerune moved to his feet, paced to the edge and peered down. Night had passed, there would be no torches. He thought he should see the figures below. Yet nothing moved. The drugs had affected his senses; he'd not heard a thing from beneath.

'Bücka?'

'Uh-huh?'

'Did you hear any noises?'

'When?'

'While I was busy being medically high.' He waved his wrist in her general direction. She grunted and came to his side.

'What's up?' she asked. 'Apart from us.'

'It's more what's down, look.'

'Can't see much of anything,' she replied.

'Exactly. They're gone.' Then he spotted it. Good fortune. 'Ha! At least the rope didn't give us away.' Far out of reach, it was snagged on a sharp outcrop, hanging in the breeze as though a vine.

Bücka leaned forward to look; Jerune placing a hand across her chest. A caution. Her eyes flicked to him with a questioning glare.

'You groping me now?'

'The drop, you moron. Watch the bloody edge.'

She smiled, winked. '*I know*. I was pulling your leg.'

'This high up, I wish you wouldn't.' He put his incapacitated hand to her face. 'I'm not catching you a second time.'

Bücka shuffled backwards, bending from the waist to peer down. 'Where are they?'

He asked again, 'You didn't hear anything?'

She shook her head. 'The wind muffled most things. I've not got your bat ears.'

Jerune scanned the trail leading away from the cliff. The muddy tracks were indecipherable; the snow melted by the heat from the forge forming large puddles that obscured everything. A hopeless endeavour from this distance.

'Where the hell have they gone?' he said.

'Inside?'

He huffed. That would be unfortunate. 'Only one way to find out.' He looked to the back of the vent. 'You ready?'

Bücka moved her fur and drew her sword. He noticed it was the flat blade, not the rapier. She nodded and said, 'Can you lead?'

'Yeah, better that way.'

She stared at him, an expression of distrust etched into her crumpling brow. His words; had she thought he was goading her for previous mistakes—the scout she had killed. That wasn't what he had meant. Thought better of mentioning it and clarified his meaning. 'My senses are coming back, I can see better than you, hear better. But stay close, alright?'

Bücka squinted. Jerune taking the glance as confirmation of his suspicion. He was relieved; for once he hadn't put his foot in it.

Moving through the vent, it was clear a natural fissure had been widened by hand. Tooling marks patterned the rock as though ancient carvings. Guided by a muted chemical torch with a green flame, Jerune scanned ahead. Periodically, a gust of warm air rushing past would agitate the flare. The wind, welcome on his skin, was nonetheless a reminder of where he and Bücka ventured. The passage descended along crude stairs and natural blocks. Cold surfaces were slick with condensation, a verdant glow reflected from the torch. His footing was assured but for balance he leant against the walls. Despite his one good hand, Jerune was aware his progress was quicker than Bücka's. On occasion he would stop and allow her to catch up, her blade reflecting the torch as though a venomous tongue. After a time in that greenish glow, the passage widened ahead. A blaze of red emanated from the floor, a pool of gas swirling in the chamber.

The heat defined their position. Jerune knew the fire was nearby. Bücka came to his side, a hand upon his shoulder.

'Is that a pool?' she asked.

He squinted, listening to the distorted hiss. It wasn't a pool. 'It's a hole,' he replied. 'It's a damn hole, we must be above the furnace.'

Bücka left his side and moved to the cavern walls. The glow from the pit cast her shadow upon the walls, setting her visible armour awash in amber. He watched as she moved to the far side. Bücka stopped and waved. Skirting the pit, unable to see beneath the haze of gas and smoke, he joined her. She pointed to stone steps that spiralled into the depths. Jerune leaned forward, peered down.

'At least they're enclosed,' he said. 'We can descend unseen.'

Her hand on his arm, she asked, 'Will I go first?'

He shook his head. Above the frazzle of fire, he could hear nothing else. Humans made noise, lots of it. And although the furnace was a cauldron of background interference, voices always rose above ambient levels. Distinctive pitches of conversation. Here, he should hear something. But there was nothing.

Shaking his head, he said, 'I'll go. I can't hear anything close.'

'You're sure?'

A nod. A grin to appease the warrior. 'Don't worry, I'll scream like a child first thing I see.'

Bücka smiled. 'Oh, Gods, I know you will.'

He started the descent, Bücka close behind. The spiralling steps were steady and regular, Jerune's stride becoming rhythmic. At times he stopped, reorienting his senses. Such regular movement was a bane to good tracking; monotony of motion inviting a trance-like state. After several moments to refocus, the base of the flight came into view; an arch opening into a space bathed in orange light. He reached behind; his hand outstretched to halt Bücka. This time she didn't comment on the contact. Jerune welcomed her silence. Careful, he moved down the last few steps, inching his view around the curve. A vast chamber, an immense pit. He stepped to the arch, saw nothing moving beyond.

As large as a meadow, at the far end, the cavern floor disappeared over a horizon of light and smoke. A gaping hole on the left side was cloaked in darkness. A tunnel. Perhaps to the outer canyon? There was nothing else. No machinery. No cogs or presses. The absence of bellows was the strangest thing for a furnace. Stepping out with Bücka following, he skirted the wall to the tunnel. A steady rush of hot air fled the chamber, a constant whistle on the breeze. At the far end, a pin-prick of white showed the exit.

He said to Bücka, 'That's the way out.'

She frowned. 'I expected... more?'

Jerune understood her inference. This wasn't a forge. Not a place to construct weapons. The dark tunnel was sure to hold surprises for them. It would be fraught with danger. But it was not the thought of retreat that defined Jerune's fears. It was the cavern within which they stood. This gargantuan crucible of heat. *Empty.*

He pointed to the shimmering horizon where the walls were animated with fiery hues. 'We need to see.'

Bücka nodded, drew the rapier to accompany her flat blade. Jerune shivered, the thought: such things would be useless in the house of Fire. With an exhalation of doubt, he started toward the pit. Edging ever closer, the noise became clearer. The bubbling and hissing of a vast, boiling cauldron. The air shimmered, tortured by the heat. Across the void, the terminal wall was distorted by the haze. Closer he moved until the lip of the pit came into view. It was not the edge. There was another platform farther below. Scanning left and right, Jerune saw zig-zag flights of stone steps descending. Upon that ledge lay the machinations of a forge. Iron blocks and pulleys with chains clung to the far edge. Piles of discarded debris: blackened and broken links, dirty spheres of glass, hammers and picks littered all around. Jerune noted a strange feature. Metal nets raised from the ground. Iron hammocks for unseen bodies. Beyond the lower platform lay a sea of fire. A horror of heat and flame. Its energy and fervour touched the ledge with splashes of red, amber, and white.

At his side, Bücka said, 'The forge?'

'Has to be.'

'I don't understand.'

Nor did he. The metal was broken and twisted; the machinery abandoned. Instinct drove him forward and he stepped to the ledge.

'Jerune!' Bücka whispered from behind. 'Something's not right.'

That much he'd noticed. He turned to her, nodded. 'I need to see.'

'No. This can't be the forge. I've seen it. Before.' She pointed back to the tunnel. 'That goes to the canyon, yes?'

'So?'

'Porst brought us to the back entrance. At least, that's what he said. But where's the front?'

Jerune frowned, looked to the tunnel. How had he missed that? Too much adrenaline? The Ambyr Dust. Always blame the drugs. Bücka was right. This wasn't the forge, not at least what they had expected to find. But what purpose did the machinery serve? About to reply, he saw Bücka startle. Her eyes widening, the whites stark in the amber gloom. Reflected in her constricted pupils, a rising flicker of flame. Bücka's expression was novel; a countenance he didn't wish to know. Terror. Worse, he felt vulnerable, his back facing the threat. Slowly, as though that would help, he turned his head. Saw the source of her fear. And although Jerune had never set eyes upon the creature, there was only one thing it could be.

Fire.

At the other side of the pit. Rising. So far away, she appeared tiny. He wanted to watch, compelled by the terrible beauty. Yet her aura was claustrophobic. A suffocation of air, his lungs struggling to breathe. He glanced to the tunnel, stepped off the staircase and pushed Bücka.

'Go!'

He ran as fast as he could, the rules of tracking relegated by necessity. They reached the tunnel, bolted into its cover. Dark but for the spot of white at the end. Safe, perhaps. He grabbed Bücka.

'Fire,' he said.

She nodded her head. Sharp stabs of confirmation.

'Bloody hell. Why's she here? Sarellia said the Covenant... she's not meant to be here.'

Bücka shook her head, those eyes still wide.

He patted her sternum, pushed her against the wall. 'Damn. Wait here.'

Her eyes narrowed. 'Fuck off!'

'Fine,' he said.

With Bücka's hands on his shoulders, leading her to the edge of the cavern wall, he stared back to the pit. Distant, the obscure form of Fire ascended. Focusing, peeling away the haze, he realised she was spinning. A head was visible, though the body appeared cocooned in writhing flame. Mesmerised, trembling, he watched as the figure floated above the cauldron. And then she stopped. His body wilting at the sight; Bücka's shuddering conveyed to him through her touch.

Fire releasing her wings. The cocoon. Licking out as though a lazy tongue; fields of fire unfurled until they grazed the cavern walls. An entire sky of flame filled the space. He wanted it to be beautiful but it was not. It was everything that terror claimed to be. Impossible, inescapable, and painful. The heat began to sizzle upon his flesh, noticed the odour of burning hair. Before he could react, Bücka hauled him into the tunnel. The relief was instant.

'What's going on? What's she doing?' she asked.

Jerune couldn't answer. There were no words. It was Fire. What was she called; what name did Petra use? The Great Destroyer. Again, he thought—*the Covenant*. Was Sarellia wrong? He ran his fingers through his hair, relief to find it had not been burnt to the scalp. His fur was worse, matted and curled from the heat. An impulse grabbed him, he reached for Bücka, patted down her fur, felt her face, her hair. She was alright. And she didn't fuss, never knocked away his hands.

'I'm not hurt,' she said. 'I'm good.'

Nodding, he said, 'What do we do?'

Bücka glanced to the exit. 'We can't leave.'

He understood. 'A seed of Fire?'

Her eyes closed. A sigh and a nod to confirm the worst. 'We need to find one, Jerune. They have to be here.'

'Alright. Let me peek,' he said.

Jerune inched to the edge and peeked. The heat was bearable for the smallest sliver of time. He withdrew. Told Bücka what he saw. Though it was strange.

'She's flapping her wings.'

'What? Is she coming for us?'

He didn't think so, peeked again, returned to Bücka.

'Hovering. Like a bloody monstrous bird.'

One last look. A moment longer. Held his nerve and felt the skin burn, pulled the fur over his head. Didn't want to be bald. To his mind came an uninvited and irreverent thought; an image of he and Sarellia, drinking wine and ale in a tavern. Her beauty, his hair. Didn't want to be ugly for her. Jerune held his view and he saw the Elemental fan those fields of fire. Clear she was oblivious or uncaring of their presence, his fear diminished. Curiosity took hold. He burrowed deeper into the fur, spied through a pinhole of burning animal hair. Watching, he noticed a change as Fire became motionless, suspended above the pit. All the while, circular drops of fire fell from her wings. *Seeds?* She levitated there, unmoving for a moment, then in a mighty rush, she brought her wings forward in a hurricane of heat. His reaction was instant, diving backwards to the tunnel, covering Bücka with his own body as a wall of flame engulfed everything. Under his protection, she screamed. He thought his days were over. Yet, in a second, the fire was gone. He looked to the exit, saw the light explode into the canyon.

'Jerune?' Bücka's voice called out, muffled under his weight.

He fell away from her, rolling to the ground. 'I'm good.' Uncertain that was the case, he flailed at his clothing. His fur was gone, nothing but hardened leather remaining. But he was unhurt. The cavern was no longer awash with Fire's light; an amber glow replacing the inferno. Jerune stood, bringing Bücka to her feet with his good hand.

'Is she gone? Did she fly away?' she asked.

'I think. I don't know.' A thought came to him. The drops of fire. *The nets.* Waving a finger at Bücka, he said, 'I need to see.'

He turned and moved across the cavern to the upper edge of the pit. The lake of fire was calm, bubbling and hissing as though blissfully content. Bücka appeared by his side. He pointed.

'Look!'

Across the lower platform, spheres of light rolled back toward the pit. The shallowest slope shepherding the curious objects. Yet the orbs moved with uncanny haste not afforded by the gradient; balls of amber and white flying over the edge and returning to Fire. It was a moment of revelation.

'It's not intentional,' he said.

'What do you mean?'

'The fire, the seed. It's as though she shook it from herself. Like a dog from a river shaking itself dry. She sheds fire. And it returns to her.'

'Look at the nets,' Bücka said.

He nodded. His hunch was right. Nestled in one metal hammock, a single orb of flame sat immobile. Removed from the ground it appeared sedate. Trapped in an open cell.

'Like shaking apple trees, caught in a net,' he said. A thought; this was not a gift to men.

He wondered how hot it would be? An indication upon the ledge; the surfaces of the machinery glowing with a subdued orange hue.

'How do they work?' he asked. 'What sets them off?'

'I dunno. I think they hit the ground. That's it. I think that's why it's in a net.'

Jerune puzzled over how they could retrieve it. The heat was fierce. In the furnace of the pit, it would take hours to cool, if it ever did. Scanning the ledge, he was drawn to the glass scattered around. Not glass. Crystal. Hemispheres of angle-cut quartz with mosaic reflections of flame. The shell of a seed.

'Clever bastards,' he said.

Bücka had clearly come to the same conclusion. 'The casings?'

'We need to wait a while, then get down there.'

He thought about what he was saying. How perilous the next step would be. In contrast, the climb and his broken wrist seemed trivial.

Bücka's hand pulled at his shoulder. 'Come on, we should wait in the tunnel. We need to be alert.'

The guards. Jerune wondered if their absence was linked to Fire's appearance. Did they know she would come? It would explain many things. Her tunnel of flame was a death trap. He and Bücka had to be hidden farther down, an unfortunate position in which to be placed: trapped between a living furnace and an army of blades. Jerune sighed and wondered if their circumstances could possibly be any worse.

Chapter XXXVII

C hara's spirits had rallied. It was a good thing—Goddard had his own turmoil to settle, an overwhelming weight under which he now struggled. With Chara at ease in Sarellia's company, he had left them on the Battleship. Their conversation of flowers and pretty things was a fragile distraction from events of the previous night. Sarellia had asked of his trouble but he could not answer. Elazra's eyes had questioned him but he had no reply. Goddard had excused himself, travelling away from them all. Had found himself standing alone, high on the cliffs that pushed back the sea. He stared blindly to a faraway land, looking to Kalleron's annexed territories. One country he sought, Bruhada; its capital, old Bruhale, sitting upon the shore. Invisible to the eye but vivid in his mind.

Allmatta had shown him Chara's truth. His mind wrestled with it. It was as though a black tide was receding, revealing what was written in the sand beneath. Yet he willed the tide to return to cover what he didn't want to see; sought the comfort of the lie he had lived. But he knew who he was. *Doga'rad*, the first immortal. Bruhada's original King. The deception explained much to him; how he had always bled into another life. He was the shadow of eternity living behind the mortal rulers of Bruhale, now masquerading as a common man. But it was the royal line that was prominent in his thoughts. They all suffered under Allmatta's rock, Bruch'alma, but only he had truly been cursed. They all knew his burden. The vision had shown him the truth, how he had sworn them to it. Bruhada's greatest secret. His terrible lie.

That day he had fought off those who would defile the temple of the rock. That day his fate had been sealed. Allmatta had found her pawn. In stabbing visions he recalled the searing pain—each memory causing him to flinch—he knelt to the ground, steadied his balance on one hand. That piercing needle of unknown mineral penetrating his skull. With his past restored, Goddard—*whoever he was*—saw the moons of Noctyrne and Ambyr; their power bleeding into his very essence. One thought to the fore; from where had Bruch'ail come? The knowledge delivered with his mind restored. It had always been there in the temple. Bound within the stone walls, immersed in rock. Yet now he knew—it was not rock—not of this earth. Not of *Earth*. The temple of Allmatta hiding for all those years. A place Kor'A could not go. Her mother forbade it. Goddard seethed at the thought. The Royal Palace built above the temple; it was the one part of the world immune to the power of the Terrible Queen of Kalleron. Perhaps the city above was also the ward of Allmatta? A most unjust and brutal irony.

There was further pain to bear. *Bri'alla*. Goddard remembered her as Baza'rad's own. He now knew; she, as he, had lived longer than most. Trapped in her youth by Bruch'alma's curse, she had never grown older. Not with time. Adopted by the last consort of Bruhale, Bri'alla's secret died as she had. Everything Chara was, Bri'alla had been. It was uncanny. Disturbing. A bitter thought; was Chara a trick? A ruse of Allmatta? He dismissed the madness, recalled Bri'alla's fate; murdered by the butcher's men. A centuries old child, slain by Te'anor's malice. He shivered. A lonely tremble. All that was left of the Rock of Kings was the man staring across the ocean. An agent of destruction. King to none.

His jaws clenched, his nostrils flaring, Goddard retrieved Bruch'ail from its harness. Anger gripping his instinct, he held it in his hands. Held it to gaze upon the block of Allmatta's essence. The power beyond all. A power he no longer wished to control. A century ago, he had fled Bruhale. Used the hammer to defeat Te'anor knowing it would only bring the Queen, the bastard power of Kalleron. Pointlessly excommunicating himself to spare what was left; Baza'rad became Argan to save the shreds of Bruhale from Kor'A's wrath. That wrath he now knew to be impotent against her mother's touch. Anger became fury as he stared at the sheen of the hammer. He could have stopped her. After dispatching Te'anor; he could have waited for the Queen. Struck her down with impunity. Doga'rad, as Baza'rad, wielded the one weapon to destroy Earth. Had he only known. He could have changed the world of men. But that was not Allmatta's design. Kor'A's descent into madness was not yet fulfilled. The twin moons ever-watching over the Earth, waiting to play her pawn. Goddard was the blind instrument of a god. And it was not he that wielded the hammer. It was she, Allmatta, that wielded him. And though her intent was clear, her reason was shrouded in fog. Why was he needed? Why him, why now? It didn't matter. Allmatta had made a mistake. She thought him a pawn when he was a King. An elemental error.

Shaking, he said, 'No more.'

With every ounce of his might, Goddard spun on his heels and released Bruch'ail. It arced high in the midday sun, casting a piercing flash of light as it reflected the rays. He shielded his eyes, the glare too fierce to behold. His palm as a visor, he sought the hammer's fall. Searched the ocean for the tumult of water. There was none. He had missed the impact. Disappointed to have lost sight of it, nonetheless, Goddard sighed. Bruch'ail had been sent to the depths, never again to feel the touch of flesh.

'No more.'

Time to return to Chara. To contemplate their shared ancestry and to speak of Allmatta. He turned. A frightening jolt to his senses. Bruch'ail awaited. One pace away. Pristine, shining in the light. No water. No scuffs. The Hammer of Earth patient for its dual masters. Goddard clenched his fists. Brought them to his forehead. A low growl, willing the thing away but it did not relent. He stared. Grabbed it with both hands.

'We're going to do this until the end of time. I am not your pawn.'

219

Again, with a mighty roar, he spun and released Bruch'ail. Shielded his eyes from the glare as it raced to the sky. Into the blue it disappeared, never falling away to the sea below. He knew where it would be.

Without turning, he said to the hammer. 'Again?'

Swivelling slowly on his heels, Goddard turned. It was there, waiting.

'So be it,' he said. 'You took everything from me. I'll give you nothing more.'

Forcing a grin that came with malice and despair, Goddard grabbed the bastard hammer and roared again.

She had wondered about his mood, Sarellia disturbed by Goddard's sudden depression. She hadn't known where he had gone until she heard the roar from the cliff. Distracted from Chara, she stood and paced to the port side. Leaning on the rails, she said, 'What's he doing?'

Chara came alongside. 'Hurting.'

She peered down at the girl. Frowned. 'Hurting? I know you're not allowed to tell me much but what do you mean?'

'He now knows things. Things that hurt.'

Sarellia looked back to the cliff. Seven foot of man was easily lost along the huge crag. Straining to see, focusing intently, she found him. He held Bruch'ail in his hands. A flurry of movement and he appeared to throw the hammer.

'What in the gods?' she whispered.

'What's happening?' It was Elazra, appearing from stairs. 'The yelling, is it Goddard?'

Sarellia couldn't understand. Had he thrown Bruch'ail or not? Once again, he appeared to hold it in his hands. Another roar travelled from the cliff and he spun, releasing the hammer from his grip. Sarellia tracked the movement, thought she saw the metal fly free.

'I think he's thrown his hammer into the sea.'

'What?' Elazra replied. Another bellow from the cliff came to them. 'That cry. It's tortured.'

The Captain was right. It was a terrible sound. A raging melancholy, a howl of frustration. A quick glance to Chara. Sarellia didn't want to upset the child. But Chara stared back.

'It's my fault,' she said.

'Is this about your nightmare?' Sarellia asked.

'It wasn't a nightmare. I saw things. I had to show Goddard. Now he knows.'

Confused, Sarellia said, 'Knows what?'

But Chara shook her head. An apology etched into her features.

'It's alright. I understand,' she replied. Though, she didn't. Couldn't.

Elazra said, 'I thought you said he threw it away?'

'He did.'

'No. Look.'

Sarellia stared. Bruch'ail was in his hands. Again. 'I know what I saw.'

She peered to the cliff as Goddard repeated the act. The disjointed echo came after.

'I saw it that time,' Elazra said. After a pause, she corrected herself. 'No. wait.'

'You saw that, didn't you?' Sarellia asked.

Elazra didn't reply.

Chara said, 'Sarellia, can we go to him?'

Looking to the child, she nodded. Frowned at Elazra whose countenance was a mask of disbelief.

'Elazra, we'll be back.'

The sun had moved. Bruch'ail flashed in the sky and was gone. Every time he would turn, the reaction was the same. A shake of his head. A snort of laughter, infectious in his madness. The hammer returned. Goddard knew it was futile but what else could he do? One day, after a thousand setting suns, surely Allmatta would end his torment? He grabbed the haft, grinned with hatred, and turned to the sea.

'Goddard?'

The hammer spoke?

'Goddard?'

No, something better. A treasured voice. Bri'alla. He turned. Chara stood with Sarellia.

'I heard...' he said.

He had heard his daughter. Just not Bri'alla. No less special.

'Please,' he said. He wanted to say, *leave*. Realised that was not his desire. Her place was by his side. Company and protection. As fathers and daughters ought to be.

'Are you alright?' Chara asked. As though not wishing to give him time to reply, she added, 'I know you're not but it's polite to ask.'

So human. In every way. Her demented mother had created something special. She was correct; he wasn't well. Conflicted and torn between destiny and death. He wanted the end. Yet Chara's presence brought his selfishness to bear. His life had never been his own. That much was now clear. But neither did the child of glass have any other than he. Bastards of different gods, they shared an ancestral curse.

Looking at Sarellia, nodding to her, he said, 'She brought you, didn't she?'

'She wanted to come. We left Elazra on the ship.'

'Am I going mad?' he asked.

'Mad?' she replied. 'If so, we all are. We've been watching you.' Sarellia pointed at Bruch'ail. 'How many hammers do you have?'

221

His shoulders slumped. Tension flooded out. What could he tell her? To Chara, he said, 'Stone may know stone but I'll not abide by her elemental deceit.'

Chara blinked, said nothing.

'Sarellia, I've seen things. Been shown truths I never knew. This, for example.' He plucked Bruch'ail and without ceremony threw it to the sea. The flash of light. He turned, watched as it materialised before them. Chara's face reflected the rainbow of light as Allmatta reconstituted Bruch'ail.

Sarellia leapt backwards and gasped. '*By the gods!*'

'One god,' he replied.

She frowned. Shook her head. 'One?'

'Allmatta. Kor'A's mother.'

He was gladdened by her reaction. The shock and awe apparent on her stupefied face. He knew his words were taken as truth. The impossibility of the hammer. A child of glass born to an Elemental. His was yet to come.

Sarellia shook her head. Opened her mouth to a string of vowel shapes.

Goddard said, 'And I'm not the age you believe me to be.'

She found her words. 'You're not?'

'I was there when Bruch'alma was discovered.'

'Bruch'alma?'

He was surprised she didn't know of it. The Bruhsa line should have known. 'The Rock of Kings?'

Recognition flashed across her face. 'Of course. The Pillar.' A pause then a gasp. 'What? But that's... you're...'

'Over a thousand years old. I was once Doga'rad.' He shuffled, felt his own features crumple under a heavy scowl. 'I am Doga'rad.'

Sarellia shivered, wobbled and sat on the ground, collapsing upon crossed legs. She appeared dazed. It was understandable. She looked up at him, shook her head asking silent questions.

He grasped Bruch'ail but did not lift it. 'This. It's all about this and what it's for.'

'What's it for?'

'I'm glad you're sitting.' Looking to Chara, he said, 'We're letting her know.'

Chara nodded.

'What I tell you, stays with you. It never passes down the Bruhsa. You understand?'

Sarellia agreed with a single dip of her head.

'I share this, it makes it bearable. We know it, the three of us. And I ask you, as a friend, to keep me grounded. What I tell you, will elevate me to heights I don't wish to know. What you know, will change your world.'

'I don't think there's much left to shock me,' Sarellia said.

Goddard smiled though there was little humour in his soul.

Chara touched Sarellia's shoulder and said, 'Shall I hold your hand?'

Chapter XXXVIII

The end of the tunnel was a penny of bright light and the glow was harsh against the black. Bücka raised her arm to shield her eyes from the glare. In the darkness, she paced close behind Jerune. Blindly following his lead, she had faith in the man whose senses were as the wolf. His steps were silent, his movement graceful. She allowed herself a smile. Reached out to poke his back. A phantom face in her memory, she thought better of it.

'Oi,' she whispered.

He stopped, turned. A finger to his lips, all in silhouette. 'Shh. What?'

Lowering her volume, she said, 'Can you dance?'

No reply. His head turned.

'Can you dance?'

'I heard you the first time,' he said, his voice nothing more than a breeze. It carried no force, no rumble from his throat.

'Well, can you?' she asked.

'Bücka, what in the gods?' He came closer, spoke in her ear. 'What's up with you? We're in the bloody Larian forge. Fire is back that way. Hundreds of guards this way. You're asking: *Can I dance?*'

Suppressing the giggle, she said, 'You move like you can. Probably look good in a dress.'

'Did you take the Ambyr Dust? I swear you're high. Come on.'

He turned and began to move away. She watched. Smiled. Hoped when this was all over, she could get him drunk, watch his hips sway to the dance of Narrahynian guitar strings. Sarellia would love it. Bücka envied Jerune for her affections. Knew he deserved it all.

She followed on, this time maintaining her focus. The orb of white light at the end grew larger. Bücka imagined they were halfway there. Jerune raised his hand against the bright circle, gestured for her to stop. His index finger and thumb raised, he appeared to concentrate on something. She strained to see. Saw nothing. Tried to hear. More nothing, just the phantom breeze from the pit.

'Voices,' he whispered.

His finger tracked to the left, pointing to the other side of the tunnel wall. Against the darkest grey she saw the blackest void.

'Come on, quiet,' he said and moved across.

Bücka looked back to the chamber of the pit, the amber glow a terrible reminder of what lay beyond. Ahead, the cold Larian climes stood in contrast to the infernal heat. The tunnel to which she now ventured was dark as pitch. She placed her hand in front, reaching for Jerune as he was swallowed by the black. She found his leather, what was left of the incinerated fur. Her hand was grasped by his, a guiding touch.

He said, 'Look.'

Ahead, down the new tunnel, a sliver of light scraped the ground. Indistinct but for the contrast, it was the base of a door. Jerune moved forward. Now she heard what he had. From beyond the portal there came a subdued chatter of myriad tones. Too much rabble to decipher a single verse but it was common noise. No fear or despair. Jerune stopped. Bücka noticed the light was close, within reach.

'It's metal,' he said. 'The door.'

With great effort to stay quiet, as though stepping on glass, she came to his side. Pushing her mouth to his face, she whispered. 'What can you hear?'

A pause. In the moment she could feel her heart thumping. Thought she could hear it as though a hammer in her mind. The voices seemed so much louder as she and Jerune focused. There was laughter, a gentle rumble of noise. Occasional words floated above the muted sounds of conversation.

Jerune, still holding her hand, moved her back. She stepped away. Guided by that comforting touch she walked to the main tunnel. There, he let his grip loosen and his breath was released as a sigh.

'I heard them,' he said.

'Me too. Quite a din.'

The outer light cast a faint glow on his skin. She saw his eyes squint. A raised eyebrow. It was the look of doubt.

'Did you hear what they said?' he asked.

'Umm. Something about... you know, whores and beer?'

Jerune's head bobbed. A slow nod. 'Yeah, I imagine that was a different conversation. But no, they wait in there until later. They call it an eruption, what happened; seems it's regular.'

'Regular?' she asked.

'Yeah, why?'

An old contract, west of old Bruhada. A place of mud pools and geysers. Bücka recalled how it seemed so alive, how people worshipped it as an act of life. Others had been more prosaic. *It's just mud*, they had said. She had learned of the workings of nature, how the world breathed. Fire was here, she had no doubt, but did the men behind the door understand. Or did they think the Forge was an act of nature?

She asked, 'You think they know it's Fire?'

Jerune tilted his head, the movement perceptible as a shadow in the dark. 'Don't know.'

'What are we going to do?'

He pointed to the valley. 'We could leave, no fuss. Just run away, escape what guards lie that way. But we need that orb. We have to bring down the Forge.'

'Which Forge?' Bücka asked. This place was new to her. And though she had never ventured inside the other, she knew this was not the same.

'This is where they get them. It has to be,' Jerune said. 'All that machinery, the net; we saw a damn seed sitting pretty.' His hand on her shoulder, she felt herself being guided to the tunnel. He waved to the exit. 'That's the only way out. That and the vent we came down. This doesn't connect to the forge you saw. It can't. Is there anything else you know Bücka?'

What Porst had told her before was enough to fulfil her contract. The orb gathered from another source. Even then she had imagined the sphere was acquired from within by an unscrupulous worker. Her part was to take it from his hands. Never witness to the innards, Bücka struggled to fill the gaps.

Shaking her head and clicking her tongue, she said, 'Nothing. I'm as lost as you.'

Jerune's teeth flashed a smile in the dim light. 'Hey, we're not lost,' he said. 'We've got each other. Two fools must add up to something, right? Let's figure this out.'

His words were reassuring. At least, to Bücka, his words were honourable. She understood their chances were slim. Yet Jerune maintained an air of confidence, something with which she was beginning to struggle. Without combat, without a clear enemy to stand against, her lethal blades remained impotent.

'The guards,' she said. 'There may be more, farther down. We should check.'

A nod from Jerune. 'Stay close.'

Moving toward the light, Bücka felt the temperature drop. The constant breeze from the cavern felt warmer against her skin, the contrast against the cold amplifying the perception of heat. As they inched nearer to the exit, it was clear there were no more guards. A heavy snow had begun to fall. It lay in drifts, mottling the valley floor in a patchwork of light and dark. The melt happened most at the ponds where the green was sprinkled with white.

Standing in the open, face to the cold sky, she said, 'It's so quiet.'

'On another day I'd walk away from this.'

Catching a snowflake on her tongue, Bücka turned to him. He saw it, smiled. She asked, 'You'd walk away? From this peace?'

'It's only peaceful now. Once we figure out what to do, I imagine it'll be less serene.'

'When do we figure that out?'

Jerune sighed. He stared high above his head. 'I can't believe I did that climb.' He pointed upwards, shaking his head. 'And there's your bloody rope.'

Bücka stared. Saw the thing swinging in the breeze. Caught on the jutting rocks. A realisation how close she had come to the same fate. She shivered, said, 'Let's never do that again.'

He nodded. 'If we'd waited until the morning, we could've just strolled right in.'

'You often walk into tunnels full of guards?'

'Well, if we knew then what we know now... Isn't she a bitch?' Jerune said.

'Who?'

'Hindsight.'

Bücka grinned. An old memory, something said to her in her youth. 'Thelia told me Shadow had a lot of weird sayings, liked to butcher proverbs as much as he butchered his foe. He said that if choice had a twin, it'd be called hindsight, and that twin was a self-righteous prick.'

Jerune smiled, appeared to appreciate the wise words. 'That's about right.'

It was surreal. The two of them standing there as though children marvelling at the winter snow. Though, this was Laria and after such exposure to heat, the chill was penetrating Bücka's furs.

'It's cold, and we're no bloody good out here,' she said.

'Cold,' Jerune echoed.

'That's what I said.'

'No. *Cold.*' He waved his finger.

Bücka had observed Jerune's traits. A few had stuck. This excited digit was his thinking finger. 'What?' she asked.

'The snow. We can use it to cool the metal net.'

Bücka tried to imagine the practicality. Couldn't find anything less amusing than what she thought.

'What, we're going to throw snowballs at it?' she said.

'Take off your fur.'

A frown to tell him no.

Jerune said, 'My fur's sizzled. Yours is intact, it'll insulate the snow.'

'Oh, you want to carry it inside?'

He appeared confused. 'You actually thought I meant to throw snowballs?'

She had. Bücka said, 'Don't be silly, I was joking.'

His glare was clear, another raised eyebrow. Her reply had been deciphered into the truth. He giggled.

'Don't you dare,' she said.

'Sorry.' He pointed at her fur. 'Go on, we need it.'

With a huff, happy to escape his amiable ridicule, Bücka removed the fur and they began to gather the snow.

The lower ledge was hotter than she had imagined. The bundled fur was already losing cohesion. A hard-packed shape in the canyon, it was now malleable. Jerune hurried her on, pointing to the iron net. She came close and they paused. The seed sat motionless. An abandoned egg. Bücka thought of the mother bird and shivered. The ironwork was suspended at the height of an average man. It would be impossible to grab the seed without touching the links, and even then, how to grab the damn thing? She looked around, noticed Jerune was scouring the area for something useful.

'Here!' he said.

She came over. Jerune was pointing at two poles linked on a hinge. At the end, two metal ladles sat open. It was a long clamp.

'Put some snow on the handles,' he said.

Bücka put down the fur and it oozed into a pile of hair and slush. With careful haste, she scooped cold handfuls onto the poles. A hiss of angry heat escaped and she continued to douse the metal.

'You think they'd have gauntlets,' she said.

'Probably do,' Jerune answered, his attention drawn to the upper rim.

'What is it?'

He shook his head, faced her. 'Nothing. Can you hold them?'

Bücka knelt beside the tool. The surface of the handle was visibly wet. Where the cold slush had been sprinkled sparsely, she could see it evaporate. It was cool enough. She placed a tentative finger to the iron. Warm, no more than that.

She picked up the clamp, turned to Jerune. 'Now what?'

He had already moved away and returned with a pair of crystal shells. One was held firm, the other rested in the cup of his bandaged hand. With a slight wince, he placed the shells to his chest and said, 'I wager the Seer would not find this funny.'

Bücka giggled, said, 'You look so pretty.'

She thought how whimsical the moment was. Shook her head at Jerune's quartz breasts. Realised it was all a shield against the dire nature of their task. They were both jesters in their own right, neither wishing to let the gravity of what was to come weigh too heavily upon them. Bücka smiled.

'You're actually a fool,' she said.

'Maybe.' Jerune moved the shells away from his chest and strode past. She followed with her gaze. Stopping at a large block of stone and iron, he said, 'Everything's here. The clamp, the net, this.'

Jerune stood beside a flat block with a metal sheen. A spherical recession was carved in the centre. He placed one shell in the depression, the other on the flat surface. Jerune stooped out of sight, returning to her view with a pair of tongs held in his hand. He displayed them to her, rotated the clamps. Two semi-circles of iron. Moving them above the shell, bringing them down to grasp it, he smiled.

'This is the forge.' He appeared amused. 'This simple bloody block is the Larian Forge.'

Bücka stared. It was no larger than a boulder from which to mount a horse. It appeared the power of the orb that had destroyed Petra's fort was created from humble beginnings. She had heard rumours and legend of Etherus; the industrial complex from which Kalleron had harnessed the Fury—the ferocious power of the Wind. By all accounts the place was a feat of human ingenuity and toil. The forge of Fire was nothing so special. An iron net, some tongs, and a mould. Pragmatic.

She looked at the seed of fire. For a moment she paused, feared what may happen. Recalled the balls of flame rolling over the edge.

'If I drop it, it'll go into the pit?'

Jerune nodded. 'Possibly.'

'Why didn't they make a hole? Like at Petra's fort?'

Pointing to the lip of the bubbling cauldron, he said, 'Perhaps down here, they have no need?'

It was a reassuring thought though it did little to help calm her frayed nerves. With a nod of her head, she said, 'Ready?'

'For this? Never. But go on, do it.'

Adjusting her grip, Bücka moved the clamp into position. Closing the handles together, she enclosed the fiery ball within the two hemispheres of iron. This is it, she thought; Bücka, the famed warrior, grasping the weapon of Fire. She glanced at Jerune. His eyes were wide, mouth hanging open. That expression laid her task bare. No mistakes. Bücka thought of every fight, every skirmish. Rallied by bloodlust and pride, she had won them all. Where was her vigour now?

'You can do it,' Jerune said. 'No one's got a steadier hand than you.'

She didn't need vigour. He gave her what she wanted. Driven by the desire to make Jerune proud, she moved the seed from the net and held it above the awaiting shell. So close. The clamps hovering an inch above the mark.

'You ready?' she asked.

Jerune brought the tongs to bear, holding them close. He nodded. 'Careful.'

An unwelcome twitch tickled her shoulder. She thought it strange, the weight not heavy. Noticed her hands, the whitest knuckles. It was an amateur mistake; gripping the handles too tight. *Breathe Bücka*, she willed herself. Opening the iron arms, she let the seed see the case. Ever so careful. Slow. It dropped from the cradle and into the quartz shell. She looked to Jerune who stared at the fiery ball.

'Now, Jerune,' she said.

As though awoken from a trance, he shook his head and lowered the upper casing. It was remarkable—the lack of catastrophe. A climax of withering disappointment as the sphere flared and died to a gentle glow. The two crystal shells appeared to have fused together. For a moment she stared, Jerune caught in a similar silence.

'That's it?' she said, still staring. It seemed so innocuous. So pretty.

Jerune put away the tongs, moved his hand above the seed of Fire.

'Hot?' she asked, leaning the clamp against the block.

'Warm. Just warm.'

Bücka found his words hard to believe. She moved her hand to his. *Warm*. Gentle, almost. What could be so destructive yet so peaceful? She knew it came from Fire; had felt the inferno as she lay underneath Jerune. But still, it was peculiar.

She startled as the quartz sphere wobbled in its place. 'What the...?'

Jerune retracted his hand. Bücka yelped with fright as the orb jumped from the depression and rolled across the block. Jerune lunged but she was faster, grabbing the orb in both hands before it hit the floor. For a second, she thought she was dead. The weapon held firm in her grip, she expected something grim. Once she had held an empty shell, now she cradled the essence of The Great Destroyer. Yet, she could not dismiss the contradiction. It was glorious and calming. Jerune came to her side.

'You alright?' he asked.

Mesmerised by the swirling colours of fire within the quartz, Bücka grinned. She held it for him to see. 'We've done it, Jerune, we've got Fire.'

He smiled. His eyes reflecting the flames. Bücka's heart sank. Jerune's expression had switched in an instant. Those traits of his. The flash of concern across his face.

'What?' she asked.

He looked to the upper ledge, to the flights of stairs zig-zagging to freedom. His head flicked this way and that, clear he was scanning for something.

'Jerune?' she said, her voice insistent.

He grabbed her shoulder, pointed to a recess in the wall. 'They're coming, damn it. We need to hide.'

Bücka allowed herself to be guided to the wall, her grip on the sphere as tight as she could manage. She trusted his senses, though she heard nothing above her own movement. At the recess, a natural flaw in the rock halfway between staircases, Jerune became silent. His hand pushed against her chest, moving her flat against the rock. A finger to his lips, he pointed upwards.

Voices. Now she heard them. Perhaps two. Thought that was a good thing. Their footfall was clear, not obscured by the march of many boots. There couldn't be more than a few. She could fight them. Attracting Jerune's attention, she whispered, 'I can take them.'

As she began to offer the seed of Fire to the scout, she stopped. A clear utterance from above.

'Three bloody days and nothing.' It was a man's voice. Impatient and angry.

A woman replied, her voice hoarse. 'It doesn't matter, Kharast, the seeds are on their way.'

The man, Kharast, muttered something else. Bücka couldn't hear what. She looked to Jerune, his eyes squinting, his posture tense. She gestured to her ears, he replied with an impatient shake of his head.

The woman's voice said, 'And the spies?'

'If they're foolish enough to come here, they'll find nothing but death.'

'You believe that little shit Porst?'

Again, his voice trailed off into a mumble. Bücka hissed with a quiet breath. Knew what she'd do when she found the gambler. She frowned at Jerune. A finger raised to silence her. His glare was intense. It was worrying.

After a few moments the sound of footsteps heralded the end of the discussion. They were moving away. But was it one set or two? Impatient to confirm what she heard, she whispered, 'That little bastard.'

Jerune appeared stunned. Thoughts racing across his features, he whispered, '*Sarellia!*'

Chapter XXXIX

I t wasn't something Goddard had considered; how to steer a floating mountain? The answer was more prosaic than he had thought. An oversized metal wheel sat atop the helm. Though, it was no ordinary wheel. A giant cog, it was recessed into the deck, as though a huge iron sun was sinking into a horizon of Larissian timber. A fat axle travelled from the centre and was met by two comparatively smaller wheels, both complete above the wooden boards. Each wheel was operated by a helmsman, and these men were the largest he had seen among Elazra's people. They worked in harmony with one another, finely tuned to their Captain's commands. The effort required to control the wheel appeared beyond the realm of ordinary flesh. Goddard considered the helmsmen were aided by herbal chemistry, their physique somewhat unnatural, veins bulbous across their taut skin. It was what prompted his humour when Chara repeated her question.

'Can I try?'

The starboard wheelman turned to her. A frown appeared on his brow and he said to Goddard. 'Is she serious?'

Nodding, he replied, 'I imagine she is but she's not to try.'

'Why not?' she asked.

Elazra walked forth, knelt close to Chara. She pointed to the two men. 'Arallas and Nazzar have trained for years to control the helm. My grandfather learned early on, and to his cost, that these Battleships are not so easily tamed.'

'What happened?'

Elazra held out her arm and with her other hand, she made a chopping motion. 'Took it right off.'

Chara flinched. Goddard chuckled as she frowned. 'Is that true?' she asked. 'Are you trying to scare me?'

'Not at all. Look here.' The Rotynian rolled up her white sleeve and displayed a wicked scar on her forearm. 'As leader of the Rotynian Claim, I thought it right that I steer this ship. I fought for my chance to prove myself. Forced my authority.' She glanced at the helmsmen. 'They tried to stop me but I'd not listen. Well, this scar is what's left of the damage. It broke my arm in three places. And I'm the strongest woman among my people. Yet, this ship chewed me up and spat me out without thought.' Elazra tapped

Chara's arm with a long finger nail. 'I don't know if we can mend what it would do to your skin.'

Chara took a pace backwards. She brought her arms close to her torso and looked to Goddard. She said, 'Goddard's strong enough; he could do it.'

'But I have no wish to try,' he replied, smiling at Elazra. 'Come on, let's find Sarellia, leave the Captain be.'

Chara nodded, glanced at the helm, and came to his side. Goddard tipped his head to Elazra and moved to the stairs. He led Chara across the main deck, strolling across to the fore. It was a marvel how little the ship rolled in the water. When it left the Rotynian camp, he had been caught off guard by the movement. Staring at the cliffs, he had thought *they* had begun to move, so smooth was the motion.

Walking past the massive cannons he stopped. Monstrous. There were only six, three for each side, staggered and rigged across the entire deck, each as long as a trader ship was wide. On wheels and rails they would recoil, held in check by multiple ropes of flexible Larian kelp. Again, he thought of Chara. The percussion would be as nothing she had known. He placed a palm upon the metal. Rapped his knuckles against it. Not a single chime. Nothing was returned to his ears. He imagined Allmatta herself would be impressed. Invoking her image brought him to his senses. He noted Chara at his side, staring at the cannon.

'What does it do?' she asked.

Pointing to the barrel, he said, 'A shot is fired from the end. It's to sink ships. This part,' he said, directing her to the firing cord, 'lights the chemicals within.' He clapped his hands. She startled. 'BANG!'

Apparently confused, perhaps nervous, she said, 'Why did you do that?'

'When these are fired, Chara, it's going to be loud.'

She nodded. It was clear she didn't understand.

He motioned to Bruch'ail, harnessed upon his back. 'You don't like the hammer, when I use it?'

Frowning, she shook her head.

Patting the cannon, he said, 'These will be worse. The sound will split the air. You'll feel it in your chest as though you'd been trampled by horses. I'm worried it'll affect you.'

Chara tapped the cold metal with her finger. 'You'll protect me, Goddard, you always do.'

A sigh. How could he? 'Yes, I will.'

Keen to remove another gloom, he spied Sarellia. She stood on the port side of the foredeck. A dark cloak rippled in the constant breeze, her hair whipping in the wind. He came alongside, followed her gaze to the distant horizon.

'See much?' he asked.

'I wanted to see what Water had made. The things Elazra spoke of—the creatures.'

'And?'

Sarellia shook her head. 'I don't much care to see them now. I know it's all her.'

'Kor'A?'

'Is it Kor'A? Is it some madness?' Goddard noted she glanced down at Chara. 'I don't mean to sound rude, little one.'

She replied, 'You're not rude.'

Goddard placed a hand on the back of Chara's head. She nestled into his leg. He said, 'I think we've been fools trying to understand Kor'A. What she thinks, what she does; none of it can be imagined by our minds.'

'But what Chara said, what you know; she's everything,' Sarellia said. 'Always has been. We've worshipped her in all her forms but she's always been one single creature. Does she even know? Did she know then?'

Goddard imagined she did not. What he knew of the Elementals, what he now knew to be a solitary creature, was that each manifestation was different. Allmatta's vision had made it clear that Kor'A's mind was at war with itself. A battle beyond comprehension. He shuddered, tried to push away the thought of the consequence should that war rage across the world. It seemed so probable, after all, mortals suffered from mental malaise. But nobody had ever considered that a god could fall to the same fate. Words floated in his mind, an old reminder spoken from Petra: Beyond human reckoning she may be but Kor'A was no god.

To Sarellia, he said, 'In my limited dealings with Kor'A, she never appeared conflicted. Aloof perhaps, indifferent. On our journey to Petra, Chara crossed Water, spoke with her.'

'What?' Sarellia's question sounded as though an accusation. It had never occurred to him that he should tell the others. It made sense now.

He nodded. 'Chara's world is her own. I'm not a gossip eager to tell all she sees. However, from what she said of that chance encounter, it sounds as though each Element of Kor'A is oblivious of its true identity. Truly independent.'

'It scares me,' Sarellia said. 'The thought that a living god is troubled by such an illness.'

Goddard felt Chara tug at his tunic. He turned, stooped and lifted her up, seating her upon the wide deck-rail. Peering over the edge, he thought it wise to keep a grip on her hand. An unnecessary precaution, the railing as wide as a temple seat.

Chara asked Goddard, 'Is it like you?'

'Like me?'

'Mother's different faces. Is it like Doga'rad and Baza'rad, Argan and you?'

A child's curiosity. Innocent and misplaced. Given Allmatta's meddling with his own truth, he considered it a valid question.

'I think we're different in some ways.'

'What ways?'

How to explain? What was the difference? Had he not been victim of his own mental fog? Days ago, he had known nothing of Doga'rad but from what legend told. Now he recalled fragments of that life. A broken mosaic slowly coming together. Baza'rad's time was clear in his mind, though a more ancient history was slowly manifesting. Those dull pieces more coherent by the day. Foreign to him, they seemed as though placed by another hand. Allmatta.

To Chara, he said, 'My fate has been guided by another. What I didn't know was held from me. I've been manipulated by Allmatta. Your mother, the one we know as Kor'A, was not made that way. What Allmatta created was one. Whatever happened, she became four. Who knows, she could be more.'

Chara frowned. 'Is she like a broken rock? Something in pieces that was once whole?'

A wise analogy, he thought. With a smile, he said, 'Very much so.'

'And you are a tree? One thick trunk connected to many branches?'

Sarellia laughed.

Goddard understood Chara's reasoning. Recognised Sarellia's humour. 'Yes, sometimes I do feel like a thick trunk with lots of branches.'

Chara smiled, then squinted. She glanced at Sarellia. 'Did I say something funny?'

'Oh, no,' she replied, 'you were quite accurate.'

A moment of silence, peppered by calls and whistles from across the deck, cast them into a surreal calm. Perhaps the ocean, Goddard thought. *Petra's medicine*—what Shadow had called it. No matter the worry, the ocean under a blue sky was a panacea. Sarellia removed the pleasant distraction.

'How long?'

'Elazra said a couple of days, maybe three, depends on the route we take.'

Chara asked, 'What will happen?'

A smile for the child. 'Don't you worry about that. When the time comes, I'll keep you safe. As always.'

Chara grinned, turned to stare at the ocean. Goddard's eyes met Sarellia's. She offered a faltering smile. A flag of regret. He replied with a gentle nod.

With sudden excitement, Chara pointed to the water. 'What's that?'

In the rippling blue, breaching in groups, a pod of whales ran parallel to their course. Of flesh, they were not the creations of Kor'A's split mind.

'They're whales, Chara. Natural.'

He noticed her expression, the side of her face bright in the sun. 'They're incredible,' she said.

Watching the majestic beasts soar and swim, Goddard's mood softened once more. Petra's medicine. He would need much more in the days to come. They all would.

It was a question he had expected. Elazra, well-travelled and wise of culture pointed to Bruch'ail. Allmatta's hammer stood haft up, as ever, within reach. Around a square table of Drohendrian Darkwood, they had been welcomed to the Captain's stateroom. The dark block of wood appeared incongruous with the lighter Larissian timber. Goddard imagined it to be a modern addition to the old relic. Sunset was an hour away and Chara sat beside him on a short bench. Sarellia to his right, sat opposite Elazra. A fourth seat, more elaborate and decorative than the plain benches they sat upon, lay empty. A peculiar thing, the head of the table absent.

Goddard said, 'I'll tell you about the hammer if you tell me of the empty chair.'

Elazra glanced at the empty seat. 'A Rotynian tradition. I've mentioned before how our ways differ. You saw our dry camp. We don't idolise Kings or Queens. We use terms that you mudfeet understand but leadership is not a birth right. If I had children, they'd have no claim to my position. The empty seat reminds us of that.'

Sarellia asked, 'You never sit in it? When you're alone?'

The Captain offered a wry smile. 'Again, a mudfoot's perception. To sit in that chair is to welcome death. No true Rotynian ever wishes to sit upon the empty chair. There have been times a drunken Captain has mistakenly sat an arse on the wrong seat.' Elazra shook her head.

'Punishment?' Goddard asked.

She frowned, nodded. 'Overboard.'

'Overboard?' Sarellia repeated. 'For how long?'

'If the Claim throws you overboard, it means you've been expelled. Forever.'

'Isn't that a bit harsh?' Sarellia asked.

'We don't think so, it keeps us level-headed.'

Chara asked, 'Have your people ever had Kings or Queens?'

'Not once. We had our ancestors, those who preferred the land. But once free of them, we made our own way. So, no, the true Rotynians have never known Kings or Queens.' Elazra flicked her finger in Bruch'ail's direction. 'Your turn.'

Goddard felt Sarellia's stare upon him. Anticipation. He hadn't told her of its origin. Hadn't known it a few days ago. To his side, Chara beamed up at him. What did she know? What had Allmatta shown to her? They knew his truth, Elazra did not. He found that division of trust to be dishonest. She had given them the Battleship. The Claim had shown him their loyalty.

'There are things I won't tell you Elazra. Better you don't know. Similarly, I don't wish to know all your secrets and rites. What I share with you, though, is the truth. The hammer has been in the Bruhadian royal line since Bruhale was founded. It existed before our nation did. It wasn't forged by our smiths. Nor retrieved in conquest. It has a power and a purpose that has rested for millennia. And I fear it's time draws near.'

Elazra maintained her stare. A piercing gaze. 'Go on,' she said as a matter of fact.

He chuckled. 'That's not enough?'

'A rather anaemic tale,' Elazra said. She waved a fan of fingers to the opulent cabin. 'You sail aboard a legend. One we made seaworthy. No others will ever have this privilege. Not, at least, mudfeet. This very ship sailed against Kalleron. It cast its firepower against the Iron Cloud, destroyed it. In doing so, she was struck by no less than two Furies.' Elazra leaned across the table. Her voice was animated with suspense. 'Imagine the explosions upon the deck as the twisted remnants of the Wind was released upon the crew. Larissian timber shattered by Elemental rage. Yet, she sailed on, dragged herself across the ocean. This ship gave Kalleron the bloody nose that brought the King to the shores of Hallan. That King was slain by you.' Elazra sat back in her chair. She sighed, looked to the ornate ceiling. 'We are bound by the world's fate, all of us. That you sit here is no coincidence. The immortals have planned all of it. Right down to the hammer you wield.'

Silence. Not even a creak of wood. Could it be true? Goddard forced his memory to the fore. A century past, the time of which Elazra spoke. His exile from Bruhada. Petra and the *Melody of the Sea*. A chance encounter that had led to the downfall of Kalle, King of Kalleron. The initial toppling of the order. Was it fate that had brought him here? Or was fate what mortal minds constructed to fathom reason from nonsense? He stared at Bruch'ail. Along for the journey. Coming closer to Allmatta's terrible goal. Fate. Coincidence. Which was it?

Tiring of the obfuscation, he said, 'It was created by an Elemental, to... stop an Elemental. It is the dawn of a new world.'

Elazra leaned forward, elbows on the Darkwood, she laced her fingers together. She appeared contemplative. 'I wasn't expecting that,' she said.

'Well, now you know.'

Separating her digits, she pointed at him. 'And you are chosen to wield it?'

He nodded.

'I suppose that will do,' she said. 'For now.'

Surprised by her acceptance, Goddard raised his brow at Sarellia who shrugged. Elazra rose, paced to a cabinet. She opened it, retrieved a bottle and returned with four crystal glasses. She placed it down, pushed a glass to each. Looking at Chara, she said, 'I don't imagine you drink but it would be rude not to offer.'

Chara's head turned to Goddard. 'Can I?'

'Drink?'

She nodded.

He was confused. She knew she couldn't. His brow creased and he noticed Chara smirk. 'You little...'

'Don't offend the child,' Elazra interrupted. 'Rotynian rules.'

Chara giggled.

'Oh, I see how it is,' Goddard said. 'You've found allies and it's time to ambush the old man?'

Sarellia laughed. 'I'm sure you can cope.'

He looked at Chara, her eyes glittering with mischief. And something else. Her stare was eternal, her smile as warm as a summer's sun. Another had once looked at him the same way. Just as tiny, certainly as cheeky. Bri'alla. But now he didn't lament her passing. Didn't confuse her with Chara. The girl by his side had assured her place in his heart. She was no surrogate. Chara was unique. Literally. And she had earned his love.

Goddard chuckled, wrapped an arm around the girl. Brought her close. Elazra was right. Fate. Doga'rad's journey had begun with Bri'alla. Now his could end with Chara. The world could turn full circle. Chara's words of destruction had not been shown to him by Allmatta's vision. All she had revealed was his past, not what was planned. From that he took solace. Allmatta's prophecy to Chara was not yet certain. The timespan of the immortals was unfathomable to flesh. Perhaps there was still time; Kor'A's fate not yet sealed. If he was the harbinger of the end of the world, he was certain he had a grasp on its destiny. There was another way to fix Kor'A. Another means to avoid the end. Chara wriggled in his grip, burrowing further in. There had to be another way.

Chapter XL

It wasn't the time for fear. Not yet. Jerune understood the danger of emotion. Had to control his reaction, focus on the present. In the flicker of fire and shadow, he scanned the lower ledge. It was traversable. The old machinery and abandoned lumps of metal provided ample cover. A forest of dead metal within which to become a ghost. Alone, Jerune wouldn't have hesitated. But he wasn't alone. And he wouldn't leave Bücka. A good student, in their time together, she had become more adept at stealth; more than her natural grace, she had evolved better awareness of silence. Though, Jerune doubted she'd be able to navigate the ledge. The stubby forest of shadow was better suited to his skills. A route through it already mapped in his mind, escape but fifty yards away. A staircase to freedom, or perhaps steps to another possible threat. Either way, Bücka's presence whittled his options down to the bone. He would have cursed the burden of a companion a few months ago. Now, after Sarellia and Bücka's grating had worn away his façade, he realised he valued the company. These very different women in his life. His heart sank, recalling confused fragments of what had been said above. Jerune pushed them away.

'Something's wrong,' he whispered.

'Have they gone?' Bücka replied.

He hadn't heard further noise. Though only one pair of footsteps had retreated. He imagined a figure not far from his head, scanning the ledge. He turned to Bücka, shook his head. One finger pointing above.

'I could rush him?' she said.

He pressed a digit to his lips, shook his head. She needed to be quiet. Bücka nodded, frowned an acceptance of his unspoken command. A scrape of stone sounded above the bubbling of the lake. Another. Movement. It was hard to concentrate with his thoughts floating back to Sarellia. Jerune tilted his head, angled his perception to the direction of the noise. Steady steps, moving along the ledge. Moving away.

Bücka's hand landed with weight on his chest. Shifting focus, he saw she had retrieved a small rock. Stone in hand, she pointed to the ledge further along. Her intent was clear; to throw it and create a distraction. He reached for her hand, closed his fingers around it. Another shake of his head. She had come far but there was much to learn. Thrown objects made noise, they rippled through the air. They flashed in the light; even a black stone across shadow was noticeable in the periphery. It was the realm of bards' tales; the distracting stone. He knew, he'd tried it. A long time ago. It was more likely to reveal their position. Besides, sudden noise created unease and it was a fool who investigated distractions without support. Jerune hadn't lived this long in the shadows by assuming all guards were imbeciles.

Though, one thing of which he was certain, the guard was moving away. Jerune whispered, 'That way, quietly, along the wall.'

Bücka nodded, placed the rock on the ground. She stowed the bright orb inside her fur. He thought she might leave it tucked inside—a risky gamble that it wouldn't fall free. But her hand remained within. The irony, now they had two good hands between them. She began to slink away, keeping tight to the uneven rockface. Jerune followed, his own sounds lost beneath Bücka's near quiet. A glance back, he couldn't see the guard. A worry to hasten his pulse; the ledge curved toward the pit. The farther away they travelled from the guard, the more visible they would become.

The escape was clear, they had almost reached the final flight of stairs closest to the cavern wall. Yards away from the goal, he tapped Bücka's shoulder. She stopped. Noise was returning. Voices echoing, one loud and agitated, the other more subservient. Had they been discovered? The arc of rock made their position vulnerable. They would have shelter in the shadow of the flight of steps, a jutting block of stone. They had to be quick.

Urging her on, he said to Bücka, 'Fast and quiet.'

A reckless pace, staying low, they moved to the steps. A check to the top, nobody was descending. Jerune followed Bücka behind the safety of the rock and sighed. A unique space, hidden from the ledge and concealed from most of the pit. It was a cage of secrecy. A cage for its lack of escape. Invisible as they were, Jerune knew if anybody came around that final block of stone, they had nowhere to run. Luck was their ally now, for better or worse. He thought of the arrow in his back. His broken wrist. All bad luck. What would today bring?

Checking the surrounds, Jerune noted the wealth of shadow. The stone stairs created a well of darkness, the ground marked by a contrast of light and dark. Within it, they were safe. But shielded from the voices, he couldn't discern the words. He wouldn't be able to hear what was known of their plan. Bücka leaned forward as though his own thoughts had prompted her to listen. Her auburn hair moved from shadow and into the light. It became ablaze with colour, painted bright by the fire from the pit. His hand was fast. The contact abrupt. He grasped Bücka and dragged her back to the darkness. In the dim light her eyes flared. A look of shock. A flash of anger for him.

'The light,' he said, pointing to her head. 'We're hidden here but the moment you peek out, you become a beacon.'

She agitated.

'It's an easy mistake to make,' he said, trying to appease her. 'I had to grab you. I'm sorry'

A frown. A huff. She asked, 'Was I that obvious?'

He nodded. An apology for the warrior. 'You were.'

Bücka's posture softened. A week ago, she would have fumed. Probably hit him. But she had matured; *they* had matured. She glanced to the canyon wall where shadow met light. With a finger, she poked toward the air, edging it closer to the light. Jerune thought to stop her. Allowed her the chance to see. The tip of her finger became a bright spot, she glanced to the wall. Jerune saw the shadow magnified by the distance. A protruding darkness to give away their position. Bücka retracted her finger. Stared at it.

She sighed, appeared to accept her mistake. 'I didn't think... Sorry.'

'Like I said, common move to peek. It's only natural.'

'But we can't hear them.'

That was true. And he wanted to know what was being said. Yet there was nothing he could do. He shrugged, shook his head.

Bücka paced deeper into the shadow. 'Now what?'

'What did you hear?' he asked. He knew he had heard more but he wanted another input. Perhaps he had misheard. Hopeful to be wrong. He wanted to be mistaken.

Bücka said, 'Enough to know I'll kill Porst if I see him again. That was us they were talking about.'

He nodded. Likely it was. But she hadn't heard the rest. 'The ships?'

She frowned. 'What ships?'

'Just dislocated words. Mentioned the hidden fleet would be ready. Why say hidden when it isn't?'

'I don't follow?'

'Sarellia's spies located the fleet in the north of Laria. Plain to see. Not hidden.'

She shrugged. 'So, there's another fleet.'

It was difficult to believe she couldn't put the pieces together. He tapped her on the shoulder with his palm. A solid thud. He squinted at her and said, 'And where are Sarellia and Goddard? Where are they going?'

Bücka's eyes widened. 'Oh. To attack the fleet.'

'Which isn't hidden.'

She paused, then with urgency said, 'It's a trap.' She looked to the ledge above. 'Just like us... They know? They know our plans? How the fuck do they know?'

Jerune concentrated. So many thoughts. Pushed away his fears for Sarellia—they wouldn't help him here. The cavern hadn't flooded with guards. They couldn't know they were inside. But clearly, they knew enough. He nodded, said to Bücka, 'Sarellia's spies. The information could've been a decoy. Porst, must be courting Larian favour.'

'Or sold us out for coin?'

Not the first time that treachery had sullied well-laid plans. Jerune looked to the pit. Noticed the blackened soot upon the nearby walls. If Fire returned, they'd be incinerated. If the guards explored the ledge, they'd be found. One option remained. A scouts' speciality.

'We need to wait,' he said.

'For how long?'

'Until I can't hear a thing.'

Bücka nodded. Without complaint or further chatter, she moved to the wall and sighed, slumping down to the floor. He knew she understood what he required. Silence to hear silence. Hopeful the voices would quieten and disappear in the distance, Jerune knelt down and closed his eyes to focus.

He opened his eyes. The pit whispered in the amber light and Bücka's breathing was a rhythmic sound. There was nothing else. He hadn't waited long. His movement caught Bücka's attention and accustomed to the dark, he saw her smile. She appeared happy he was back. Her eyes lingering with an expectant gaze. He nodded and stood. She followed his lead.

'Gone?' she asked, swapping her hands to hold the orb.

'I think so. It's been quiet for a while.'

'This thing's really weird.'

She nodded to her fur; the seed of Fire shielded within.

'Weird, how?' As he spoke, he realised the redundant question. It was strange in every possible way. Her reply was unexpected.

'It's warm. Comfortable.'

Jerune paused. 'It's a bloody weapon.'

'Is it?'

He reached out, touched her temple. 'Did you bang your head?'

She swatted away his hand. 'We saw them roll back. This was left. It's an orphan.'

'Orphan?' He wanted to shake her. It wasn't a child. It wasn't a living thing. Yet, he understood the comparison. 'Because it was left behind?'

She nodded. 'If this was deadly, we'd be gone by now.'

'Could still happen.'

'I almost want to put it down, see what it does.'

Curiosity. What Jerune considered a failing of humanity when not accompanied by caution. The pit at Petra's fort came rushing to his thoughts. Would Bücka's orphan roll with carefree abandon back to the pit? Or would it drive through the very rock, casting them all into a fiery end? It was ironic, they required the latter to destroy the forge. He needed it to be the weapon, not the comfortable orb that had taken Bücka's misplaced affection.

'I wouldn't put it down, not yet,' he said. He looked to the stairs. Still no noise. 'Come on, let's see.'

Turning to ascend the steps, he didn't wait for Bücka to agree. No more chat of warm orphans and maternal instincts. The seed had to become what it was feared to be. The thought was comedic. Jerune stifled the grunt of laughter. Behind him, Bücka clearly noticed.

'What?'

He stopped halfway. 'The seed. If we use it, imagine—what if it just trundles away.'

'Will it?'

'I actually have no idea.' He paused, a grim reckoning coming to the fore.

'Jerune?'

His heart sank. Bücka clearly noticing his sudden shift in mood. She repeated his name, her voice riddled with anxiety.

'Jerune, I know that look. What is it?'

If the seed didn't trundle away, it would perform as was expected. A vast pit would appear as it vapourised the ground. Rock turning to ash. As Petra had described it. Jerune looked to the cavern walls, his eyes drawn to the ceiling. He had to release the orb in the main tunnel. Bring it down and bury the place under rubble and rock. But the tunnel roof was too low to allow a great lob of the weapon. Even if Bücka had the strength for it, it wouldn't arc high enough to allow them time to flee. They couldn't release the seed without being within its sphere of influence. They would go down with it. All the way to Fire.

He said, 'If it doesn't trundle away, it'll go through the ground, right?'

Bücka nodded. 'That's the idea.'

Another thought. It came crashing down upon him as an avalanche. They had made so many mistakes. 'We've got one seed.'

'Right here.' She patted her fur.

In all the excitement to find the pit of Fire, to see the actual forge, he had overlooked their mission. So keen to acquire the weapon, he realised his folly.

'We didn't come here for just one,' he said.

'Oh...' Bücka's expression faltered. 'Shit. We came to destroy the lot. But that woman's voice. She said they'd taken the rest away.'

'We're too late. We've no idea where they've gone.'

'Can't you track?'

He hated when people asked that. Of course he could. But not ghosts. He needed a lead—they had none. Shaking his head, cursing their luck, Jerune said, 'I need a start, Bücka. I can't track thin air. Especially not in this frozen shit-pile.'

'What do we do?'

'Half of what we were meant to.' He pointed to her fur, the seed held within. 'We use that.'

'Two fools, half a job. That's us, eh?'

He offered her a smile. A darkly comedic failure.

Bücka stared. From a face of despondent expectation came her own smile. It was beautiful; if not misplaced. A warm hearth in a cold house. Her voice a breeze, she said, 'We've come a long way, haven't we?'

He looked to the pit, gestured to the orb beneath her fur. 'We have.'

She shook her head. Pointed to herself, then him. 'No. *We've* come a long way.'

Jerune allowed a sigh of laughter. 'Yes, we bloody have.'

Bücka said, 'I had no real friends before I found you lot. And I've not known you long but...'

He reached out, placing his good hand on her shoulder. 'Bücka, I never thought I'd like your company. But you know, I'm still working on it.'

Bücka's grin widened. 'You're such a shit!'

She was lovely. A fierce woman with a heart of gold. The wonder of a child in the mind of a killer. An enigma, a person the like of which he had never encountered. In time, after enough travels, he imagined he'd even call her a legend. But he couldn't tell her that. Not now. That would be admitting the end was near.

'So?' she said. 'How do we bring this place down?'

Jerune understood her words. More, what was hidden beneath. There was no safe way to release the seed. If it worked as intended, if the destruction matched Petra's fort, the entire cavern was coming down, possibly the hillside above. There was no way out. Not, at least, for him. Not something to tell Bücka.

'We'll figure something out,' he said, an image of Sarellia sailing away in his mind.

In the cavern all was still. The constant background noise of the pit the only sound. Jerune inched up the remaining stairs. The floor was deserted. He waved for Bücka to follow. Stepping onto the cavern floor, he glanced back at the pit. Wondered where Fire would be, what role she played in all of this madness and deception. Regardless, he knew what he had to do. His legs wobbled but he held the tremor from his voice.

'Come on,' he said, 'Let's cause mayhem.'

242

Chapter XLI

Time. What was it? Another sunrise over Anka. Petra staring at the fiery orb. Her eyes unhurt, her body immune to its distant rage. A century ago, as a new immortal, she had gazed upon her first naked sun. Diamond eyes never flinching, she had realised then that she would never regard time the same way. Sunrise was no longer a new day. It was forever. Back to the moment, she looked down upon the white city bathing in an amber glow but her eyes sought the coast. Always looking to where she could never be; once more sailing free upon the ocean. That was the pain that never truly faded.

Although she had lost count of the days, she still understood the revolution of the seasons. In past times she had ventured high into the mountains. Sat motionless for untold time and watched the vast frozen rivers scour across the rocks. She had wandered through lush valleys in spring, listening to the breath of the forest. It had delivered strange discomfort; immortality had given her the gift to see what the living could not, to feel what was not theirs to know. The unintentional gift from Kor'A. The curse. Petra could watch everything come to pass. Everything. And everyone.

Turning from the view, she paced toward Goddard's humble shack. A King's den. A snigger came forth to relieve the gloom. A wry smile. Petra imagined a grumbling old man heaving those rocks and beams into position.

'I bet you huffed like an old goat,' she said to nobody.

Goddard. Time. How long had he been away? Days at least, possibly weeks? The season hadn't shifted. No new threats had stumbled upon Anka. Petra assumed he would be safe. Nothing had killed him in over a hundred years. Not the Butcher, not even Kalle. It was difficult to concede that she would outlive her oldest friend. But she knew his end would come with peace. Nothing would vanquish Goddard. He who had been Argan, born from the shadow of Baza'rad, the world's greatest King.

Reaching for the rusted handle of the old door, Petra stopped. A feeling upon the earth. Footsteps. The rhythm of the touch was erratic. Two legs, of that there was no doubt. But ragged. Scraping and irregular. A lame soul. Injured? She turned, pacing slowly toward Goddard's staircase. A giant's causeway to his ramshackle lair. At the top she paused, unafraid and curious, peeking around the edge. At the base, struggling with the first block was a robed and hooded figure. Likely a man, his shallow breaths straining from labouring lungs.

Who would come, she thought? A beggar? Thief? Petra dismissed the idea. The robe was tattered by intent, not poverty. A lustrous blue-grey, a dense fabric, worn by wealth. Weapons were absent, a dagger at best hidden beneath the cloak. No jingle of coin, no need for currency, or perhaps already lost to the same fate that had spoiled his garb? Whittling down the possibilities, Petra watched the man fall; slumping as he conquered the first tier of Goddard's work. She listened to the earth. Silence. No further steps, no ambush behind. Not that such a thing was a concern. To be wary; it was a mortal habit, though it was one of many she still maintained. Better to recall something of flesh than relinquish her humanity to stone.

Petra descended the stairs. Elegant and super-human steps bringing her to the fallen man. Kneeling, she peeled back the hood. An old man. Wrinkles as deep and wise as any she had seen. Sparse white stubble spread evenly across face and scalp. Eyes tight shut. Opening his robe, she saw the wounds. Blots of dark stained against the inner tunic, a grey vest of woven fabric. More expense. Sullied by the damage and the blood. Dagger or arrows? Upon his belt there was a large leather pouch. A perfect rectangle, suitable for a bureaucrat to carry his papers. Her fingers moved to the clasp that kept the contents secure.

'Petra, no,' she said to herself.

She held her curiosity to account. Scolded herself. They were his secrets.

'Whatever they are, they're not yours to know.' Looking to his wounds, she said, 'At least, not yet.'

Petra waited. On Goddard's bed the old man lay motionless. His wounds—from daggers and blade—cleansed and dressed; herbs applied from an old King's stash. If the stranger was going to live, she had given him the best chance. Beyond the glass panes the world turned to dark and again back to light. That was all Petra noticed. That and the constant, steady breath of the old man. As though the forest, he inhaled and exhaled. The way of the living. Not as she.

A mouse scurried across the floor. It stopped midway between her feet and the bed. It's heartbeat fast. Close to the earth, tickling the surface, it was as loud as that of the man. Two drums beating very different tunes. One was passing. One was passing by. She watched as the small mammal twitched away, disappearing under the pile of timber and fur that was the bed.

'Didn't catch your name,' she said to the rodent.

A wheeze was returned. Petra rose from her seat, paced to the man. His eyes had flickered open. His head rolling to the side. A smile graced his face.

'I died... or I've found you,' he said on rasps of breath. 'Which is it?'

'Who do you think you've found?'

A redundant question to ask. His lack of surprise and air of peace. No man looked upon her countenance with such serenity.

'The Queen, of course,' he answered.

Petra shook her head. 'Not my title.'

He grumbled an agreement. 'They gave it you.'

'A long time ago.'

Petra understood malice. She had experienced enough in her living days. In stone she had known ignorance. Neither of those traits were to be found in his eyes. They were kind, benevolent.

'Who are you? Why have you come to me?' She pointed to his wounds. 'Who tried to stop you?'

'Many questions. Too many answers.'

His words were carried on weak breaths. As he appeared ready to speak again, Petra placed a finger to his lips. She offered the man a smile.

'I have time to wait,' she said. 'Rest some more and...'

'No.'

'No? You're barely able to speak.'

His frown creased. Old eyes squinted at her. 'You don't have time.'

'I have all the time in the world. If you know of me, you must know that.'

The tranquillity of his countenance faded. A troubled expression clouded his features, and he shook his head with a weary manner.

'My name.'

Petra nodded.

A smile returned to his face. Though, she thought it appeared confessional. A grin bereft of joy.

'Taberas.'

She frowned. 'Uncommon name. Pleased to meet...'

He interrupted. 'Of Arkalla. Son of Allin. Son of Io'ther.'

A name. Lost in the mire of years. *Io'ther*. Petra knew of one such man. Better days. Walking the hot streets of Arkalla, hand-in-hand with Felicitra. She recalled one man who carried that name.

'The Seer?'

Taberas nodded. 'My grandfather.'

A pace backwards. It could not be. The Seer of Arkallon. Last man standing after its fall. He who had faced the Queen of Kalleron and walked away. Petra knew of the tale from Kallisa. A revelation of Fire. His flight was the origin of the new world. The Seer of Arkallon had found the Great Destroyer; at least, that was the story. Corrupted by it, he sacked Laria. Her homeland. A frozen world set aflame. Another step backwards. Taberas' eyes tracked her.

As though reading her thoughts, he said, 'Everything is lies.'

'Lies?'

Petra wanted to say more. Confusion wrapping itself around her consciousness. The Seer was mortal. Long dead. Taberas' father, he too would have passed. It left a single possibility. Her words carried as though a breath, vibrations from solemn stone, Petra said, 'You're the Seer of Fire?'

But Taberas shook his head. 'There is no Seer. Not of Fire.'

'More lies?'

'Truth. Truth, Petra.'

She stared. This man. This frail, old man. Was he the same as that of the stories? Petra knew the impossible. She recognised it now. Unarmed, no orbs of flame to provoke her anger. No army nearby to assail her new home. Courting death, he had come to her. Why?

'The truth. What then?' she asked.

A shaking arm raised, he pointed to his belt hung upon a beam. 'The journal.'

Petra nodded, retrieved it from the pouch, held it to him.

Taberas said, 'Not for me. Truth. For you.'

Awkward. Had scolded herself earlier for such a thought. Others' pasts were not hers to know. As it had been on the *Melody*, so too it was in stone. But Taberas insisted.

'Please, open it. Save me my breath.'

Unwilling but instructed by his plea, she opened the leather book. Surprised by the text, she glanced at the back of her hands. Upon the white skin, ancient lines of similar design were scrawled in lost decoration. Invisible to most; faint to her. A painful reminder of who she used to be. The family line.

'Sanhe?' she said.

'My fathers preferred it. Arkallon and Laria held many ties. You ought to know.'

Petra nodded. The script inferred a shared Larian ancestry. 'A mother?'

'Io'ther's,' he replied. 'Half-Larian.'

'The writing's beautiful.'

'It's why they used it.' Taberas drew a laboured breath. Petra looked up from the pages. His face was pained. Somehow, she knew it was not the wounds. Something worse. Taberas said, 'The beauty hides the ugly truth.'

Frowning, Petra began to read. The first page was an account of Arkalla's fall. A city of noble sculpture and spirit razed to the ground. Dust and destruction everywhere. The account was grim, the description vivid. The apocalypse of the Terrible Queen of Kalleron—Kor'A. Though she was absent from the pages, it was a reminder of Felicitra's death. Gone home to face the end with her family. Too feeble to flee, her father was bed-ridden. The pages told of the grim reality in which Felicitra would have perished. A description of horrific carnage. Petra wanted the book to be a lie. But the ink was old. Faded and vague. The parchment discoloured and cracked as though dried autumn leaves. The account of the city was real. Despair brought back to her in stabbing visions. Petra closed the book. Blinked. A single diamond falling to the ground.

'I can't read this,' she said.

'Felicitra?'

Shocked, Petra asked, 'You know of her?'

'No. I've studied you. Your friends. I know who you've lost, Petra. That journal is a century of history. After the first pages, I'd wager you'd not recognise it.'

'History?'

'It's not what you think it to be. Everything after Arkalla is a lie. *Everything*. This world is false. Laria schemes under devious manipulation while on the continent another trouble brews.'

Petra frowned. 'Another?'

Taberas nodded, the smallest tremble of his head. 'There is more to fear than what comes from the cold. Kalleron is awakening, Petra. Whispers from the Black Smoke.'

Petra shook her head. Disbelief of his words. Kalleron's ambition had been thwarted a century past with the death of Kalle. 'That's not possible,' she said. 'We freed their Queen; took away their weapon. I watched the immortal King die. I saw his army crumble under Argan's hammer.'

A weak smile found its way upon the old man's lips. 'Not everything that falls stays down.' A look spread across his face. Petra understood the wrinkles and hesitation. She had seen fear in the eyes of many men. With a drawn-out breath, Taberas uttered three terrible words. Words to cause her to shake.

'The Fury, Petra,' he said. '*Etherus is rising.*'

Chapter XLII

O ne hand on the seed, the other on the hilt of the Bruhadian blade, Bücka followed Jerune. Across the cavern he strode, steps so soft as to be made of shadows. Her own footfall, a gentle scrape of rock, was jarring in contrast. She wondered how many years it had taken him to become so quiet. An impossible stealth. Unnatural. Jerune moved to the cavern wall, skirted the edge. It was a strange place, at once both wonderful and terrible. Bücka had seen Fire. She and Jerune had created a seed of her flame. And all around, there were guards. She would have her battle; Jerune couldn't fight his way out of a hessian sack but she could. Bücka would defend him. Once they started the mischief, her world would come into play. Swords would swing in glorious arcs, blood would flow in torrents. Her foes would lament their mistakes. She and Jerune would run free, bring the forge down—escape to another tomorrow.

No. Just one last impossible dream. The smile disappearing from her face, feeling the muscles relax and become still, Bücka stopped. Jerune paced on another few steps. At the tunnel, he turned. She assumed he had noticed her lack of noise. Expected one of his stupid quips. But in the amber light his features were clear. Distress. For her.

'Bücka? What's wrong?'

Wasn't it all so obvious? With a feeble smile, she said, 'You have to ask?'

Silence. He didn't need to speak. She saw it in his face. A shared understanding of their fate. All humour gone. The bravery he had shown supplanted by a mask of grim doubt. He swallowed. Sighed.

Jerune said, 'Give me the seed.'

'No.'

'No?'

She wouldn't. Bücka knew enough of Jerune to understand the request. A curtain of confusion was lifting. Behind it, a new scene was unfolding. His eyes were dead. The muscles on his brow relaxed. Resignation. Dreams and desires, hopes and futures, slipping away on the coldest breeze.

'Please, Bücka,' he said, 'just give me the seed?'

'So you can fucking martyr yourself?'

An awkward grin appeared on his face. He nodded. 'You'll tell Sarellia I was brave, really brave, eh?' He held out his good hand. 'The seed Bücka, come on.'

'NO!'

He frowned, glaring at her. Raised that bloody finger to quieten her.

She said, 'We'll figure it out.'

Jerune shook his head. 'It's already figured out.'

'No.'

'You can get out, Bücka.' He held up his bandaged wrist and hand. 'I'm no help. I'll not get far if we need to run. You can get free, find Goddard. Fight by his side. That's what you want, isn't it? Your dreams of glory—you can still live them, Bücka.'

She could. Bücka recalled the citadel. The pride in her heart watching Goddard swing that monstrous hammer. To be by his side. A dream. Yet, staring at a man she had once considered no more than a puppy, Bücka knew she didn't need dreams. She had better. She had a friend. Another soul with whom to share her life. How much longer could she keep him? Not long. Her vision blurred. She sniffed.

'I'm not leaving you.'

He pleaded. 'Bücka, please!'

'I'm not.'

Pointing to her fur, shaking a finger at the bundle within, he said, 'It'll destroy us both. Needlessly. You can live.' He took a step toward her. She was surprised when she paced backwards. She tightened her grip on the seed. So warm.

'Bücka, don't,' he said.

She pulled out the orb. Held it firm.

'Bücka...'

She glanced at the rock above her head. 'It'll work here, won't it?'

A moment of surreal pragmatism. Jerune scanned the cavern. Nodded at the ceiling of the tunnel.

He said, 'No.'

Bücka frowned. Realised he was lying. 'Did you think I'd walk away? Let you die alone?'

Jerune stared. No smart words for the moment. She saw the look in his eyes. If she could love a man, she would have loved him. Her thoughts drifted. The stories Thelia had told. Legends. Of Petra and Shadow. Two violent peas in a pod. Lovers without sex. Family without blood. A bond her grandmother had said she had never seen before, or again. Bücka thought that perhaps, this was how it began. She smiled.

'What?' Jerune asked.

'You were right. It is like Petra and Shadow.'

A deep sigh from his lungs. A nod. 'I'm honoured.'

Bücka's throat tightened. A flurry of tears came forth. She blinked them away. More came when Jerune's face crumpled in sympathy. Through sniffs, Bücka said, 'I think I understand now.'

'Yeah.'

'But we're not going to grow old like they did.' She held the seed high. Watched Jerune's eyes track the orb. In that moment, she felt it between them. Everything ebbing away. Fear, doubt, conflict.

'Ready?' she asked.

Jerune smiled. 'You're a selfish cow. You still owe me a beer.'

She laughed. Snot bubbled from her nose.

Jerune said, 'And that's why I love you.'

Bücka nodded.

And dropped the seed.

A solid thud. A noise that would be greeted with relief had it been a priceless heirloom. Bücka looked at the sphere. Immediately it began to roll away, trundling toward the pit. Jerune, out of character, guffawed with loud laughter.

'I bloody knew it,' he said.

Bücka knelt and scooped the seed back into her hand. She looked at Jerune, his eyes bright, his smile wide.

'Can't even get this right,' she said.

'Well, nobody's perfect.'

Bücka nodded, said to Jerune, 'To beer!'

He closed his eyes and she hurled the seed at the wall. In a flash of flame, it exploded, a crashing of crystal and rock. Bücka braced for the heat, winced as a wall of warmth flowed toward her. As Jerune had, she shut her eyes. It was a second, perhaps more. But it was too long. She opened her eyes.

'I don't believe it,' she said. 'I don't fucking believe it.'

A perfect sphere of flame was rolling at walking pace toward the pit. In the light of the cavern, she saw the scorch marks on the floor. There would be no scooping it up now.

'You're kidding,' Jerune said.

She turned. Smiled. Together they crumpled in fits of laughter. It didn't matter where they were. They had failed. Their only weapon strolling home to mother. Their laughter rang as a chorus throughout the cavern. A distant crash of metal echoed down the tunnel. The door. Bücka drew both swords. Still grinning, she moved to Jerune, stood between he and what would come. Against the light she could see the guards pouring into the tunnel. Lots of guards.

'We're still going to die,' Jerune said without fear.

'With honour,' she replied. 'Stay close to me.'

'Move to the stairwell, they'll need to come one at a time.'

A good plan. She nodded. They had to travel across the cavern but the guards were further. She had time.

'Go,' she said. 'I've got your back.'

Jerune moved halfway and stopped. Bücka frowned, ran to his side.

'What?' she asked.

He pointed to the seed. A peculiar sight. It had wedged in between two flakes of natural rock. Close to the upper ledge. It was shimmering, growing brighter. Flames lashed out. Inches at first. Then a few feet. To her eyes, it appeared angry.

She said, 'Is it going to... what's it doing?'

Jerune's reply was a shrug. Together, forgetting their flight, they stared. The guards had closed. A huge rabble of clattering armour and swords. It didn't seem to matter. She and Jerune were transfixed. The little orphan was throwing a tantrum. Voices came from the guards. She recognised them—the man, Kharast. But Bücka didn't catch his words. Her attention absorbed by another problem. Mother had returned.

'By the gods!' Jerune said.

Rising, her wings already spread wide, the Great Destroyer was fear incarnate. The cavern was bathed in her fiery glory. Everything black or grey turned to amber and white. Instinct broke Bücka's trance and she pushed hard against Jerune.

'Run!' she cried.

He reacted and without looking to the Elemental, they raced to the stairwell. Yards away, Jerune stopped, catching Bücka in his arms. Confused, she babbled.

'What are you doing, let me go... this isn't...'

He spun her around, the momentum catching her off balance. She heard Jerune wince as he pushed hard against her, throwing her to the side of the stairwell. *What was he doing?* She fell to the ground, appeared to sink into it. A fissure. Unseen by her eyes, no doubts picked out by Jerune's heightened senses. As she rallied her thoughts, falling further into the hole, wondering how deep it was, Jerune bundled down on top. With a thud and a scrape, she stopped falling. A flash of blinding light and ferocious heat swept across her vision. A dagger of light pierced the dark, accompanied by a clamour of screams. She felt the air being drawn from her lungs and Jerune wrapping his body around hers. Gasping, she struggled to breathe. Seconds stretched into forever. Time lost all sense. Choking on suffocating nothingness, Bücka had but one thought: not Jerune, not him, don't take my Jerune.

Chapter XLIII

C hara giggled.

'Hold still,' Goddard said.

Standing behind him, Sarellia asked, 'How does she move around?'

A glance over his shoulder, he quipped, 'You could help.'

Another giggle as he pulled the belt tighter. He sighed. 'Will you stop that?'

Sarellia knelt down beside him. 'Poor Chara. You look like a pea in a very tight pod.'

Goddard frowned at her. Looked at the padded armour he had made for Chara. The battle loomed. The cannons would soon fire. He had wanted Chara to be safe. All he could find was the blanket. A double weave padded with feathers. He had folded it in two and wrapped Chara inside. But Sarellia was correct; the child appeared as a black pea enveloped in a bright blue pod. He sat back, resting his seat on the timber floor.

'You do look silly,' he admitted.

Chara, still giggling, beamed at Sarellia.

'Not silly,' Sarellia said, releasing the buckle of the belt and setting the girl free. 'Perhaps a little encumbered.'

'Do I need to wear it?' Chara asked.

Goddard shook his head. 'No. Doesn't work as I had planned. If you were a little taller, I'd have asked Elazra for armour. But you're a shade too small for a buccaneer.'

'As fortune has it,' Elazra said, 'I may have something that fits.'

Goddard turned. Elazra was framed in the cabin doorway.

'Been watching long?' he asked.

'Long enough to see a grown man fumbling like a fool.' She paced in, handing a bundle of fabrics and leather to Goddard. He examined the assemblage, a mixture of armour: chest plate, padding, leggings and jerkin. It was small. A child's fit.

Elazra, evident she had caught his confusion, said, 'Not all who serve are seven feet tall.'

'Even so', Goddard replied, holding up the soft-leather leggings, 'you have child-warriors?'

Elazra frowned. 'You've never seen a small person?'

He had. But not serving as a fighter. Not wishing to agitate his host, he nodded and turned to Chara.

'For me?' she asked.

'For you,' Elazra said. 'Your demented guardian can decide what else to swaddle you in. Goddard?'

'Yes?'

'A word, please?'

Goddard nodded to Sarellia, passed the bundle to her. He moved to the door, followed Elazra a few paces before she stopped.

'Problem?' he asked.

'No, just to say, we'll be in sight soon. Within the hour.'

Much had transpired since devising the original plan. And though it still stood, to Goddard, it was a cowardly attack. A necessary attack. They couldn't allow the fleet to sail. They had to stop the weapons of Fire reaching the Northern shores. He had witnessed the aftermath of just one dropped seed. The cost of more coming offset the price of his guilt. An unfair weapon had to be neutered by a gutless ambush.

He said, 'Use the cannons from afar, scatter the ships. Then plough forward and open the hatches?'

'My people have trained with the Windspitters. We've manufactured enough for two salvos each weapon. Anything that's left, or has fight remaining, we can board.'

'A more honourable fight.'

Elazra smiled. But her frown betrayed the expression.

'Honourable?' she asked.

'Hand to hand.'

Her stare was as ice. Piercing, cold. There was no warmth in that look. It was unusual; it unsettled him. 'What?'

'As far as I know, the false immortals—those like Kalle—are all dead. Only men remain. And you. There are no others that can hold a flame to your strength, Goddard. This Battleship is to other fleets, as you are to armies of men. There are no fair fights when you enter the fray. I'm not certain what honour that is.'

Her remark would have agitated a lesser man but Goddard understood her point. He said, 'I have faced power in my time, Elazra. Te'anor at Bruhale, Kalle and his Furies at Stranghame. I never assumed my victory. But it is not my honour I speak of; it is for those who stand against me. It is right that others are given the chance to strike me down,' he paused, considered his newfound knowledge, 'at least, to stand against me with anger and purpose in their souls. Besides, one man cannot stop an army. As rivers they flow around what impedes them. Even this ship. If we make mistakes, only one vessel needs to slip past. One ship carrying that damn weapon. I never consider my might; I consider the outcome and the safety of my companions. My friends. The price of my strength is to watch others fall.'

Elazra appeared to contemplate his words. True words. Perhaps at sea, combat was different. Cannons were cannons. One hit was enough to sink a ship, no matter its size. On the field, Goddard understood his position. Hadn't known it against Te'anor. Or Kalle. But over the years he had understood more. Those recent revelations laying bare the truth of his impunity.

The Captain nodded. 'Fair points. Three bells will signal the barrage.' She paused. 'What will happen if she breaks?'

Confused for a moment, he asked, 'Chara?'

Elazra nodded. 'What would her mother do?'

An irony. It was why he had sought to protect her. Imagining the wrath of a mother who had lost her child. But now that was no longer his concern. Chara was his daughter. His to nurture and watch grow. If, indeed, she could.

'I'll not let anything happen to her.'

'But... what if?'

In his mind's eye, an image of the hammer. Smashing the world apart. 'They will pay, Elazra. They'll all pay.'

Seated on the edge of the bed, Chara swung her legs to and fro. Sarellia sat cross-legged by her side, fussing with the last few pieces of armour. His head tucked down to avoid the ceiling, Goddard watched the pair with affection.

'Do I look less silly now?' Chara asked.

'Very sensible,' Sarellia replied.

'Goddard?'

He smiled. The little girl in armour. It was difficult not to see it as a game. And though the truth of their reality was close, the sight of her wrapped in armour tickled his ribs.

'We ought to find a stick for you. A wooden sword,' he said.

Chara squinted.

'He's teasing,' Sarellia said.

About to reply, A chime rang below decks. A hollow and low sound. Less of a bell, it was the noise of hammering upon an iron door. Another followed. Sarellia glanced at him, her eyes worried, brow furrowed. In the room they waited in silence. As the echo died away, the final chime was notable for its absence.

'Wait here,' he said, and left the room.

Goddard found Elazra at the prow of the ship. Ahead, under a cold blue sky, the land rose from the sea. The far northern peninsula of Laria. A grey mass looming. Nestled on the long finger of land, on its west coast, distant but visible was a harbour town of sorts. And upon the water, a myriad of ships bobbed in the bay.

He came to her side. Staring out across the grey murk, Elazra said, 'That's not right.'

'The fleet?'

'We have superior optics in the nest. Not one of those ships is seaworthy.'

'What? What do you mean?'

She turned, pointed to the crow's nest a perilous height above. 'Our Watcher came down the rigging. He's a skilled lad. Good for nothing but spotting. If he tells me the ships aren't sea-worthy, I trust his judgement.'

'You've looked?'

She smiled. That strange, sarcastic reaction. 'I don't have to.'

Goddard strained to see. Optics would have helped. From such distance detail was lost. He didn't want to question Elazra. But he did.

'In what way are they not sea-worthy?'

'Rigging, sails, mostly. But the direction of the hulls. Random, as though waiting to be salvaged. There's no order. It's less of a fleet than a timber scrapyard.'

'But you said you'd seen this fleet?'

'Hadn't ventured this close before, no need. But I can dispel your doubts.'

Elazra put her fingers to her mouth and let out a shrill whistle. A raucous sound of gearing and clunking emanated from below decks and the sails were hoisted higher. The ship moved faster, the land becoming clearer. So too, the ill-equipped fleet became more apparent.

'The whole place looks wrong,' Goddard said.

'Yes. You ought to get Sarellia. It was her spies that reported it, was it not?'

Goddard nodded, fetched Sarellia and Chara. Keeping the child close, he brought them to the prow. Sarellia stood beside Elazra.

'Goddard says something is wrong?'

Pointing to the harbour, Elazra said, 'What did your spies report?'

'This. They spoke of this fleet.' She turned to Goddard. 'Why are we not firing?'

'Look closely,' Elazra said, 'do you see ships ready for war?'

Sarellia leaned forward, brought her hand to her brow. The light was harsh, Goddard watched as she strained to see that which Elazra had mentioned.

'They're a little... tatty,' Sarellia said.

Goddard paced forward. 'The spies, Sarellia. They spoke of a fleet amassing. This can't be it.'

Sarellia turned to face him. Her confusion apparent, she shrugged. 'This is it. It has to be.'

Elazra shook her head. 'I'll not fire on these ships. Nor that port. An ambush is one thing. Murder is another.'

'I don't understand.'

'Your spies were wrong,' Elazra said.

Goddard noticed the Captain's brow. A slight furrow. Her eyes narrowing. Looking to the shambolic fleet, he found no comfort in its lack of threat. Such illusions of war were always intentional. Had Sarellia's spies been duped? Worse, had Sarellia?

'The spies,' he asked, 'you trust them. With your life?'

Sarellia appeared hurt. 'Of course. What are you saying?'

Elazra said, 'If your sincerity is so, then your spies were deceived. This is no fleet.'

'Then, what? What is it?'

A chill ran down Goddard's spine. The cold realisation of what was to come. Pulling Chara to his thigh, he said, 'A trap, Sarellia. For us.'

Haste in her voice, Elazra said, 'We need to return to...'

'SHIP AHOY!' The call from the crow's nest rand loud. 'Port side!'

Goddard looked to the east. As a slow crowd, the crew moved to the side of the deck. In silence they watched. Waiting. Elazra was right, her Watcher had superlative vision. A gasp came from the crew. A rustle of disbelief. Then he saw. Dots on the horizon. Five specks. Coloured grey by distance. They shouldn't have been visible. Impossible. An ancient feeling rising within. Memories of Bruhada. Before the fall. Before the coming of the Queen. Elazra spoke his desolation.

'*Battleships.*'

A murmur erupted upon the deck. Elazra waved a hand and all fell quiet.

She looked at Goddard, shook her head. He understood.

'You need to flee,' he said.

A moment of calm. A pause of uncertainty. Elazra's face, tempered with hesitation, became serene.

She shouted, 'Prepare the pinnace!'

'The landing boat?' Goddard said. 'Elazra?'

'Take the girls, I'll give a half-dozen crew. Get to land.'

Goddard reached to her, grasped her arm. 'Elazra!'

With surprising force, she swatted his hand away. 'King you once were but don't dare presume to lay your hand on the Captain.' Again, she roared. 'Lower the pinnace!'

He was being removed. Goddard could do nothing to stop it. His eyes pleading, he wanted to know why.

Elazra smiled. Now it was a grin of joy. 'We came to scuttle a fleet. A cowardly ambush—your own words. Now, I get to fight against the odds. A Rotynian's purpose. I'll not endanger mudfeet in this battle.' She pointed to the pinnace swinging near the hull. 'Let me fight this battle on my terms. You can fight yours on land.'

'We're leaving?' Sarellia asked.

'You're dismissed,' Elazra replied.

Goddard peered down, saw Chara stepping from the security of his thigh. To the Captain, she asked, 'Will you win? Will we see you again?'

Elazra looked at Chara. Her eyes lingered on the child. Goddard wondered what thoughts were animating her frenzied features. He thought he knew. Understood all too well the call of war. Once in the blood, forever stained on the soul.

The Captain knelt down, took Chara's hands in hers. 'Stay safe, little miracle. Look after him,' she said, flicking her eyes at Goddard.

Chara nodded. 'I will.'

Elazra stood and said, 'You mentioned you had friends in Laria, go find them, sail home another way.'

Goddard stared. He recognised the fire in her eyes. Had seen it in so many loyal commanders and warriors. The last look of honour. He knew he'd never see her again and he understood she knew it too.

He nodded, bowed. 'Give them hell.'

'Like the Northern Storms,' she replied.

A glance over her shoulder and he saw the ships closing. Still distant, too far by all reckoning to fire. Not long though. Another legend was about to be written. He hoped it carried Elazra's tale well. Shaking himself from misplaced envy, he gathered Chara and gestured for Sarellia to board the pinnace.

Onboard, he stared up as Elazra ascended to the sky. The water jostled the small boat as the oarsmen ferried them to the port. He wanted to watch Elazra sail to glory but he had his own concerns. They weren't alone on the peninsula. A group of soldiers in unknown insignia approaching. Weapons drawn, dozens of men were coming for them. A rush to disembark, chaotic splashing of froth and seaweed, he handled Chara and Sarellia to the shingle shore.

Reaching for Bruch'ail, he said to Sarellia, 'Keep back. Chara, stay with Sarellia.' A frown, looking to the crew Elazra had gifted. 'Sail back to your Captain. My gift to her is your safe return. Fight with your own.'

Hesitation, then as the hammer was lifted, they fell back, boarding the landing boat. Goddard turned to the approaching men, a smile upon his face. Allmatta's cruel purpose in his hands.

'Goddard!' Chara called.

Without turning, striding forward, he replied, 'Close your eyes, Chara. Keep them shut, you mustn't watch.'

Chapter XLIV

'It started with Edramus,' Taberas said. 'His ships sailed against Kalleron. You and your crew gave him that insight. The Queen had left. Abandoned her King, taking his weapon away. King Edramus sought to draw first blood for Laria. Foolish. Kalleron was always more than its Queen. It had Etherus and the engineers, the chemists.'

'I knew King Edramus,' Petra said. 'I know this much.'

Taberas sighed. 'You don't know what he became.'

Petra frowned. 'Became? He was a good man. A noble leader.'

'A noble leader felled by the reality of war. Kalleron brought the power of Etherus to bear on his fleet. Kalle sent Laria home with a bloody nose. Five great Battleships sent limping into retreat—two destroyed by all accounts.'

'I know this too.'

Petra recalled the days. The same year as her own death and resurrection by Kor'A's hand. The same Elemental who had killed her lover, destroyed her world. A cruel fate. Those days were confused, muddled as she transformed from flesh to stone, but through General Aracyse's military tales, she had learned of Kallerons naval victory. A stalemate of sorts had followed. It had left the neutral Northern Lands in Kalle's cold and callous sights.

Taberas said, 'Edramus changed. He became insular. Having witnessed the true power of the Elementals, he craved it for himself. For how else would Laria defend its borders? If Kalle brought the weapons of Etherus to bear once again—his kingdom would fall.'

'That is where Io'ther wanders into this sorry tale.' The old man sniggered. A weary and bitter chuckle. 'The worst timing. You know he survived the Queen's assault on Arkalla?'

Petra nodded. 'She told him of Fire. Where to find her.'

'Yes.' A frown. 'Of course, Kallisa told you? Kallerons Overseer, agent of the Cult.'

Petra nodding, said, 'She exchanged few words with the Queen but through those bizarre conversations she learned the fate of the Seer.'

Taberas wheezed. Petra, now standing by his side, reached to him.

'I'm fine,' he said, pushing her hand away. 'Yes, Io'ther sought Fire. It's in the journal. Though, the Sanhe becomes difficult. His emotions appeared to cloud his ability to write. Chaotic, disjointed. At first, I think he wanted to die but his religion forbid he take his own life. Confused, he travelled to find the Queen's more terrible sister.'

'We know he did,' Petra said. 'Laria fell because of it.'

Taberas smiled. 'I told you; it's all lies. Io'ther crossed the sea, made no secret of his journey. Most thought him mad but Edramus' spies brought news to their King. In the beginning they paid scant attention. The ramblings of a lost soul. But word reached the King of a change. Io'ther's search became more focused. Edramus sent men. Found what Io'ther had discovered.'

'Fire?'

'Yes, but that is where the story ends as far as the world was to know. Laria's days were numbered. Without an Elemental weapon such as the Fury from Etherus, they had no defence. Their greatest pride, the Battleships, had proven no match for the wrath of the wind. But now, Edramus saw a new possibility. Io'ther was imprisoned, though hailing from Arkalla, he had friends beyond the iron bars. The journal was smuggled to him, he completed much of it before sending it to reach his son, Allin, my father.'

Petra glanced at the bound book lying on the bed. How much mystery did it hold? How many new truths lay scrawled in its pages? How much was false? She frowned, found it difficult to disbelieve what was being said. Taberas had honesty in his voice. But still, why had he come?

'Taberas,' she said, 'if the Seer was behind bars, who sacked Laria?'

His reply came with a growl of discontent. 'Edramus, of course.'

'Edramus? No. Impossible—he was the King. Defender of Laria.'

Taberas' hand waved in the air, dismissing her words. 'Pah! He defended the old Laria, one he knew had had its best days. The Battleships had been tamed. The beacons abandoned for fear of more Fury. Laria had to be reborn. Edramus found a way. A new nation, born under the lie of Fire. It was he who scarred the Sarellian Plains; a sacrificial lamb for the slaughter. In truth, few died, it was a miracle overlooked by most. Edramus was conniving, but genocide was not his design.

'He scorched his own earth, proof to the outside world that a mighty power had come to Laria. Fire, brought by the Seer, had conquered Kallerons greatest foe. And under Fire, no nation would be so mad as to consider attack. It was Edramus that devised the Seed of Fire. Edramus that carved a new Laria. Edramus became the Seer of Fire. A myth to control a nation. A myth to defend it.'

Taberas fell silent save for his breath. He appeared to be preparing for more. Petra sought answers from her own memories but she had none. Bound by Kor'A's curse to never sail again, she had forever remained in the Northern Lands. In truth, the world she and Aracyse had created was apart from all others. At peace when Kalleron was at war with itself. Calm as Laria burned. Except, if Taberas' words were true, it had not burned at all.

'The past century,' she said, 'what was Laria doing?'

'Edramus knew he required the Seed of Fire. But his mistress was an unwilling accomplice. Just as Etherus, the orphans of the Elementals are not given with grace. They are stolen. It took decades for Edramus and his line to harvest enough.'

'Enough?' Petra paused. Absorbed what had been said. She stared at the old man; his eyes returning the gesture. Truth. She knew it. His face, lined with such scars of age. Honest creases on a troubled visage. Yet, if what was said was truth, the world was once more veiled in lies.

She asked, 'The Seer does not serve Fire?'

Taberas' head lolled from side to side. His eyes shutting slowly, accompanying a mournful sigh. 'You want to ask of the Covenant?'

Petra nodded. Expectant of his revelation. Fearing the answer.

'Why I've come to you. Why they tried to stop me. There's no such thing. At least, not from the Elementals. It's the last piece of the Larian plan. They've had spies in An'Korathall, Kalleron, even southerly Shaddenhine. Waiting. Watching. What is happening in Kalleron is a spur to Laria's haste. Old losses weigh heavily on the psyche. They know about Etherus and its resurrection. They know it is only time before Kalleron restores her glory. It is why Laria now moves. It has always acted on wise impulse, reacting to the world around. Decades ago, when you left An'Korathall, it drew up immediate plans to invade—to pre-empt Kalleron's ambitions. But your throne was taken by another. Laria abandoned such suicide. No man is foolish enough to wield the children of the Elementals against their own mothers.'

Petra tried to absorb it all. She said, 'But now Kor'A has vanished.'

'As soon as that presence lifted, the spies flooded back with word of it. An old plan thrown into play. Misinformation, Laria's greatest weapon working its charm. Sow the seeds of a false plot. They're expecting something to come from these shores, hopeful Kalleron pays it no attention. Laria needs to know your strength. I've travelled far to warn you. You mustn't fall for their tricks. They expect an attack; their spies have poisoned the well of truth. They've created a web of deceit so complex nothing can escape it. Don't lose yourself in that web, don't stray across that ocean. Those waters are unsafe. Guarded by old ghosts.'

'Guarded?' Petra was surprised by her own voice. A distant memory. Fear. Though not for her.

Taberas smiled. 'Edramus recalled the Battleships. Hid them. Repaired them. Fortified them. Told the world they had sailed away. They've been in Laria all this time. Weaponised with Fire.'

Goddard! Her thoughts raced. A sickening impotence gripping her. She was trapped in these lands. Her immortality nothing but a chain around her neck. Her friends were in grave danger and there was nothing she could do. Agitated, angered, she saw fear spread across the old man's face. Dust sprinkling his brow.

'Please!' he said.

Petra stopped. Realised her fury had travelled into the earth.

'I'm sorry. Oh gods!'

'What?'

The Covenant. Her commune with earth. It would... It dawned on her. Taberas' story. The false pact of the Elementals. A lie created to bind her hands. Kor'A's power was hers to use. A question returned.

'Why did she leave?' she said aloud.

Taberas frowned, clear he didn't understand.

'Kor'A. Why did she leave? Sarellia spoke of the Covenant. We had assumed it was Chara but the…'

Petra turned and paced away from the old man. Kor'A had left. But she had also abandoned a child. It had never been the Covenant. It all came back to a mother's disgrace. A mother's grief.

'Petra? What is it?'

She returned to Taberas. Considered the truth was a righteous reward for his own. 'Kor'A created a mortal child. Abandoned her after decades.' Petra hesitated, her thoughts cascading in torrents. Confusion addled her mind. Too many distractions. 'She's on the seas, with Goddard. They've gone to Laria… in a Battleship. To wipe out the northern fleet.'

Taberas stared. It was evident his brain was processing what had been said. His eyelids fluttered, eyes darting side to side. 'A child? Incredible… But a Battleship you say?'

'Rotynian salvage.'

He smiled. 'Fly buggers. Maybe there's a slim chance… But Petra, your friends… Whatever they have been told will be false. You must warn them.'

'I can't. I am bound. They have crossed a barrier I cannot.'

He sighed. Stared at the ceiling of beams and fur.

A cloud had descended. Petra tried hard to focus. Forced herself to think but the dilemma facing her friends loomed as a tower. Cast in its shadow, a strange light came to her. Bright. A Question.

'Taberas, why come to me? Why care about these lands?'

He frowned. Squinted his eyes as if to question hers.

She repeated, 'Why me?'

Speaking as though bemused by her query, he replied, 'My line has been destroyed by the Elementals, forsaken by its God, and betrayed by Kings. There is nobody in this world left to defend what is good and noble. Nobody but you.'

Petra stared at him. Lost his face to a vision of another man. A King. A legend. Her friend. She smiled, shook her head. Reaching to Taberas, she took his wrinkled hand in hers.

'There are others, Taberas. Let me tell you of a King called Baza'rad.'

Chapter XLV

C hara. Eyes tight shut. Held firm in Sarellia's grasp. Shingle under her knees, water tickling her toes. A mighty roar coloured the dark. A crunch of gravel; a great weight bearing across the shore. Lightning flashing, thunder crashing. The storm, the storm. Goddard becoming Allmatta's wrath. With every tremendous percussion of the hammer, she felt Sarellia flinching; felt her heartbeat. Racing, surging. Frightened, just as she.

'Close your eyes, it's better not to look.' Chara said.

She could not tell if Sarellia heeded her words but the grip tightened. Her head tucking down, encompassing Chara in the embrace. Huddled, fearful not of the enemy but of the man, Chara thought another soul was present. In her pitch-black world, a sliver of light appeared. Thought it was her imagination. Neither black nor white. Flickering colours. A dance of what humans called Gods, a visitation of power. Accompanying Goddard's battle, Allmatta's aura began to sing. Eerie. A song of loneliness. For her? For Goddard? She wondered, could he hear? She doubted it, another flurry of thunder and a furious roar. His storm was moving away. Taking the clouds of his foe from the sea. To the land. The wind sweeping the leaves away.

The woeful, confused cries of the many whittled down to a few. Bruch'ail punishing the air more than flesh. Farther away, still moving, Goddard's raging quelled. The storm almost over. Distant, passing. And the earth shook.

Chara screamed.

Goddard turned at the sound. Fearful one had slipped past. All around him lay the dead and dying. A marsh of blood and broken bones. Nothing stirred. Looked to his hands. Sweat and licks of red covering his skin. Bruch'ail lay at rest, head buried in rock. His final swing to crush another. Under the hammer, the bedrock had cracked. A deep scar dozens of yards long ran until the grassy dunes reclaimed their place. He had struck the earth with force. One last look around. The port appeared empty. Perhaps cleared for this very assault; more could come. Goddard sighed, huffed a nervous breath. He stormed back across the rocks, plunging into the loose shingle.

'You're safe,' he called. 'Chara, you're safe.'

Her head popped up. Sarellia's too. Worried faces greeted his call. Glancing back at his carnage, he waved a hand to them.

'Don't look, don't look.' He pointed to the water lapping the shore. 'There, look there.'

They did. But he had seen Sarellia's eyes. Fear. Worse? Horror. He felt shame. Why? He had done what was required. Saved them both. There was no other way. Yet the lingering guilt remained.

Looking to the water's edge, clear she was keen to avoid his destruction, Sarellia asked, 'They're gone?'

'Yes.' He came close, sunk to his knees beside them. 'For now, at least.'

'All of them?'

He met Sarellia's eyes, a surreptitious glance. Nodded. 'It had to be.'

She offered a hasty bob of her head. 'What now?'

Chara spoke. 'Can we help Elazra?'

Elazra. The fog of war had taken his thoughts away from the Captain. He stood, looked to the north. There, on the water, a single massive ship moving east. Out of view, hidden by the peninsula, she would meet her fate. He shook his head.

'Sorry, Chara, there's nothing we can do.'

'Mother could.'

He shook his head. Kor'A had no claim on the water. Realised his mistake. She was the water. He had lived too long to change his memories. It was a stubborn thing, age. The life that had been hidden from him was hard to adopt without challenge. But even so, Kor'A would not interfere. Not as Earth, not as Water. She was beyond humanity. Aloof with godly reason.

'She can't help. She won't allow herself to be brought into our affairs again.' He glanced at Bruch'ail. Considered Allmatta's words. 'I don't want her involved in this. Elazra made a brave choice. She will be honoured by it.'

'But she'll die,' Chara said. 'You protect your friends.'

Jarring. Did she know what she had said?

Sarellia intervened. 'Chara, we can't interfere. We don't know what your mother would do.' Her gaze fell on Goddard, her hand pointing to the hammer. Head shaking, she said, 'We need to find another way. Kor'A can't be trusted.'

Chara's shoulders slumped. Goddard watched as she frowned, her face crumpling in a familiar expression. A huff. A subdued tantrum.

'It's not fair.'

'I know,' he said.

'Why do people have to die?'

Goddard thought his answer was hypocrisy. 'Because we must.'

He looked to the horizon, tracked the Rotynian Battleship as it merged with the grey of the land. His eyes fixed on that spit of rock, he felt a tug on his sleeve. He looked down, expecting Chara, but was surprised to see it was Sarellia.

A smile for her. A frown.

She said, 'Where now?'

He looked to the fleet in the water. Closer, he could see the damage. Considered it a miracle so many were afloat, the sea filled with rotting hulls and ancient wood. A dummy fleet; the trap had worked well. A thought came to him; he offered it to Sarellia.

'How close did your spies come?'

'I assumed close enough.'

'Your web of intrigue is torn, Sarellia. Somebody has a better grasp on conspiracy.'

'The Seer?'

It was probable. He huffed. 'Whoever it is, we need to check the port.'

'Is there anyone else here?' Chara asked.

She was looking to the water, obeying his previous command. 'Keep your eyes on the boats,' he said. Moving to retrieve Bruch'ail, he returned to Chara. Reaching, grasping her hand, he said, 'Let's find out if we're alone. We'll pace the shoreline, move into the town farther up.'

The port was abandoned. The houses were unkempt: squat stone buildings with thatched roofs. Clumps of the dry material lay scattered in the streets. Glass panes were shattered or lost from the sea-facing front. The infamous Larian chill was less noticeable, no surprise given the location, the temperate winds from the north kissing the coast. A warmer ocean bathing the shore. This was as hospitable as things would be. To Goddard, it was strange that the place was abandoned, and from appearances, had been for years. He had navigated the field of corpses, bringing Chara and Sarellia to the centre of the town. A square surrounded by stone structures. In the middle, a large, dry fountain. On a pedestal, an effigy of a naked female. Goddard didn't know the likeness. Perhaps Water. Or any other lost goddess. Around her, there were stylised sculptures of fish. He imagined their pouting mouths once spewed forth water, wondered what colours and laughter the town would have held. Throughout the square, evidence of the armed men was abundant. Rags and rotten food lay scattered. A place to mingle away from the shore. Secluded enough to hide. Floating on the fresh breeze was the stench of decay. An unwelcome scent.

Sarellia said, 'You think they were here for long?'

'Judging by the mess, a few weeks.'

'It doesn't make sense.'

Goddard thought it did. 'Sarellia, we were fooled.'

She sighed. 'Yes. By my own people. But why? They don't know of you, of Chara. I never gave them that knowledge.'

'I've seen this before,' he said. 'A calculated prod. A stick in the hornets' nest.'

'To test our reply?'

264

He nodded. 'To show our strength.' He thought of the Battleships. 'They must have eyes on the sea. Communications across the land. We underestimated Laria.'

Sarellia sighed. 'What else do I not know? What other lies have I enabled?'

'It's not your fault.'

'I came to you, to Petra. I brought their lies. This is my doing.'

Goddard understood her malaise. Crestfallen, Sarellia shouldered a guilt that was not hers to bear. Circumstance and a cunning, invisible enemy had manipulated her with precision. She wouldn't be the last Cultist to leave the door open.

He was about to speak, attempt to soothe her with words of wise experience. Instead, Chara wriggled free of his grip and walked to the fountain. Brushing away a scrap of food, she sat facing them.

'Why do humans fight?' she asked.

'For power. Glory.' He listened to his own words. How foolish they were. 'For peace.'

'Peace?' Chara shook her head. 'That doesn't make sense.'

Goddard spread his arms wide. 'Is this peaceful?'

She nodded.

Without pride, he said, 'And what happened to make it so?'

Chara squinted. She drew a false breath. Unnecessary, but it mimicked what he assumed she felt. A gloomy realisation. She said, 'You killed people.'

'I kill many people. Because otherwise,' he pointed, first at Sarellia, then at Chara, 'you'd both be dead.'

'I still don't understand,' she said.

Her voice was quiet. Alone. A single living sound in the square. Appropriate. She *was* alone. Unique. And no matter how much he wanted to shield her from the toil of human existence, he could not. Not here. Nor in the Northern Lands. Chara needed a new world within which to flourish. A grim thought. He held such power. Allmatta could deliver to Chara what he could not. A world free of life. A rebirth of stone. Looking to the empty, dead square, Goddard caught Sarellia's eyes. She frowned. Had she noticed his inner turmoil?

'What?' she asked.

He shook himself. 'Nothing. We need to find supplies. There should be plenty, we'll need to look around.'

Sarellia nodded. 'Transport.'

'Yes, of course. Horses. They came here from somewhere.'

'I'll check the north,' Sarellia pointed, her eyes communicating a silent offer.

'Yes,' he agreed. He could travel south, away from the death he had left in his wake. Keep Chara free of the sight. 'Thank you.'

She smiled, 'I'll scream if I find trouble.'

'I'll come rushing.'

Walking through deserted stone streets, Goddard watched as Chara picked and played among old decay. In its time, the port would have been warm, bustling with chatter and life. Ghosts remained, a sad reminder of what once was. He imagined drinking ale as he passed an old tavern. Rotted benches crumpled under the weight of time. Wood, soft and yielding, compressing under foot. Goddard paused. Stared at the moss-covered wall. Chara's cheerful chirping brought a smile to his face. Together, alone, he realised he was happy.

'I could brew my own ale,' he said.

'What?'

Chara stood a few paces away. In her hand, a piece of stone. A figurine.

'What's that you've got?'

'A miniature man.'

'A toy.'

'Toy?'

'Children play with them. Did you never see? In Anka?'

Chara nodded. 'I think. Can I keep it?'

'Of course,' he pointed to her leathers and armour. 'And now you've got somewhere to carry it.'

She beamed. Located a pouch and placed it inside. 'I can find more.'

Goddard laughed. 'Once we've found supplies and horses.'

'Of course.'

She came to his side and he moved away from the tavern. He could swear he tasted the hops on the breeze. Comforts. Simple things. Chara's glass fingers fell against his hand, grappling to hold on. Now she was leading him. Her head turned, looked up to him.

'Come on, let's find horses.'

He followed, smiling for longer than he had in decades. It was perfect. The noise of just the two of them. The wind in his beard, the peace of nothingness. Again, his thoughts drifted to Allmatta. Bruch'ail and its purpose. Would it be his end too? When fate called, would his soul survive the new birth of Kor'A... His anger rose from within. A deep resentment of his own thoughts. He made to disentangle his fingers from Chara's hand, hesitated before upsetting the child. Maintaining the connection, he scolded himself. This was not his world to end. He cursed Allmatta. Wondered if her influence was corrupting his subconscious mind. He wanted a life for Chara. But he would not offer it on the death of all else. That was a god's decision. Goddard was just a man, no matter what the legends said.

'There!' Chara said, pointing.

He followed her finger. On the edge of the town, grazing on the lush shoots, horses dotted the grassland. His relief was all too brief. Over the horizon, a line of dark approached. More horses. With riders. Hundreds of yards away, enough time to flee.

He knelt and grasped Chara by the shoulders. Pointing to the town, he said, 'Go find Sarellia. Hide.'

Chara shook her head, 'But...'

'Now!'

His face stern; he knew she would obey. She would not dare defy him. Chara huffed and ran off. He reached to his back, freed Bruch'ail from its mount. Choosing to confront the riders, two score or more, he strode south.

The same insignia as those from the shore. Not reinforcements; there had been no call to arms, no battlefield horn. He waited as the line drew closer. One man rode forward, raised his fist and the others stopped. Well-drilled. Not mercenaries or bandits. A battalion? The Seer? The lone rider came forth, bringing his mount to a halt a dozen yards away. Enough space for both to retreat. Or for the cavalry to attack.

'Who are you?' the rider called.

'A lone traveller.'

Without helm, clad in rigid leather and silver chain, the horseman raised an eyebrow. He peered beyond Goddard. After a pause, those eyes focused on his own. Suspicion—Goddard knew the look.

His gaze settling on Bruch'ail, the rider said, 'A strange weapon for a lone traveller. Have you seen my men?'

'Men?'

'A small posting. Guarding this town from strangers.' He leaned forward on his saddle. 'Such as you.'

Goddard recognised the tone. It was deliberate, formal. The horseman would not suffer the game for long. Goddard presumed it was simple curiosity that had enabled such a brief yet courteous discussion. He would be sure to hasten the conversation along.

'Ah, yes. Those men.'

The rider's hand moved to the pommel of his sword. 'Where are they?'

Goddard shook his head. Not a denial. An apology.

The rider's face became a blank. Eyes wide, staring. A creaseless brow and soft jaw muscles. His mouth beginning to hang open, he rallied himself.

'All of them?'

'All.'

From his horse he scanned the port. Darting looks and a calculating frown. 'A poor ambush,' he said, his eyes searching for the enemy Goddard had not brought. 'The others?'

'No ambush,' Goddard said. He placed Bruch'ail on the earth, leant on the haft. 'Myself, alone.'

'Impossible.' The rider smiled. 'You try to trick me? My men are still in the town. Lazy bastards. You snuck past.'

Goddard looked to his own frame. To the rider, he said, 'Me, sneak?'

Clear he was lost for a reply, the rider dismounted. Another came forward, hailing the man on the ground.

'Commander?'

The Commander raised his hand. 'No further, Marilus. Stay your ground.' He paced toward Goddard, hands moving away from his weapon belt. He said, 'My name is Edramal, Commander of the Fifth Infantry. My Lord is Fire, who is yours?'

'I have none.'

Closer he came. Goddard appreciated his bravery. Few men willingly approached such as he had.

'From where do you hail?'

'I hail from Bruhada. Though, I sailed here from the Northern Lands.'

'Why come?'

Better. The point would soon be clear. No more subterfuge and forced pleasantries. It would take more than forty horsemen to bring down Goddard. It would be fair to tell the Commander. Let him choose a fate.

'I came to stop a war. One I've been told is coming.'

No reply. Silence and the wind. The Commander squinted, stroked his chin. Goddard imagined what doubts riddled his mind.

Glancing back to his cavalry, Edramal said, 'You really killed my men? All of them?'

Goddard nodded. 'We did.'

'We? You said you were alone.'

He patted Bruch'ail. 'We.'

Edramal stared at the hammer. A century was a long time. So many decades had passed since Kalle. Legends faded in times of peace. What did the Commander know of those days? Anything? A sliver would be enough to piece together the puzzle.

'Your name?' Edramal asked.

What to say? Goddard himself was conflicted. Tell the truth—Doga'rad—and the man was likely to be none the wiser. Best to stick with legend. There were occasions it paid well to live on past glory.

Goddard spoke with volume. Loud so all could hear. 'I am Baza'rad of Bruhale. I am Argan of An'Korathall.' He paused. Thought of one last verse. 'I serve stone. Not Fire. And you will not bring war to my home.'

Silence followed. It was welcome. Edramal broke it with a whimper.

'*Baza'rad?*'

Behind him a whisper rustled through the ranks. Edramal's face brightened. A strange response. A smile creeping across his lips. He repeated Goddard's kingly name.

'You know of me, I assume?' Goddard asked.

Edramal nodded. 'But you're... that was over a century ago.'

Why not serve a fatal blow? Send them home.

He called out aloud. 'Not even time itself can claim my life. What chance have you?'

Silence returned. Edramal shook his head. His breath heavy on the breeze. Huffs of disbelief, spliced with anxious laughter, escaped his lungs.

'But the Covenant,' Edramal said, his trembling voice ringing with doubt.

Goddard thought of Petra, the destruction of her home. Of Elazra sailing to her death. Covenant? He grasped Bruch'ail, hoisting it from the ground. With a mighty punch, he planted it back down and roared, 'DAMN YOUR COVENANT!'

All at once the line of horses reared. A fracture appeared on the earth, an arc of organic lightning ripping the turf and rock. Those men who could, reigned in their mounts and fled. Edramal was thrown to the ground, the other, Marilus, thrown from his horse. Leaving Bruch'ail in a depression of rock, Goddard strode forward.

Leaning over the Commander, he said, 'Take this message to your Seer. I defend the Northern Lands. Your Fire has left. Earth has left. But I remain. And I am forever. Every enemy that crosses the ocean will perish. An'Korathall will remain in peace. My home will stay in peace.'

Fear etched on his face, Edramal crawled backwards. His head shaking, he said, 'He will bring Fire. You will not...'

Goddard roared, 'I have killed immortal Kings; I will not be stopped by Gods!' He paced back to Bruch'ail, plucked it up with one hand and pointing to Marilus, said, 'Give this message to the Seer!'

Storming forward, Goddard brought Allmatta's malice down upon Edramal's skull, his scream cut short in an instant, the echo outliving the man. Once more the earth fractured. Marilus turned and ran, leaping over great chasms as they tore the ground apart. Watching, fearful, Goddard stared as the fissures chased the horizon. *What had he done?* A low rumble now tormenting the plain, he let go of Bruch'ail, retreated, and glanced to the port. All around the earth heaved but the town remained intact. No damage. A miracle. He turned back to the horizon. Reached for the hammer.

One fraction of time. Separated from all. Nothing moving but the blood in his veins. Her voice. Powerful, oppressive, everywhere. She had come and she spoke his name.

'Argan?'

He fell backwards. A crushing weight upon him. Staring, disbelieving. It was Kor'A. Risen from her Earth. A perfect sculpture of marble. Gems spiralling and sparkling around her slim physique. A beautiful face, a terrifying visage; oversized blood ruby eyes staring down upon him from beneath her piercing crown of diamond. He looked back to the town, saw the two figures running. Coming closer. Kor'A glanced to the side. She smiled.

'My child,' she said.

Collapsing in darkness under the weight of her mountainous presence, Goddard had but one thought.

She's mine, not yours.

Chapter XLVI

Perhaps another slap would work? Jerune, wrapped in furs retrieved from the guard room, lay propped and unconscious against a charred trunk. Above, the sky was a blanket of stars. Bücka watched as her breath rose in clouds. It would be a cold night. Bitter. But cold, not hot. No more fire. No more flame. Just the heavens above and Jerune for comfort.

She had awoken, drawing pained breaths, darkness everywhere. Pushing against the weight of Jerune, crawling from the fissure, the cavern had fallen to silence. Hauling his limp body from the crack, she had carried him across the forge. There was nothing left but ash. No bodies, no furs. Blobs of misshapen metal armour lay as solid pools, orange in the dim light. Striding, the life in her arms held tight, she had emerged into a glorious chill. Though shock had come to her. The valley, blasted and turned to cinder. The ponds were gone, nothing but soot and the fresh falling snow. A beautiful destruction. White flakes landing soft on Fire's wrath. What had happened? Why such annihilation?

Jerune had shivered, his breath shallow. Bücka had returned to the guard room. The inside charred by the inferno. In heavy Drohendrian crates she had found the fresh furs, brought them back to the valley. Comfort for her friend. Nature's warmth and a companion's affection. But he had not awoken. Perhaps another slap? Shaking her head, Bücka used salvaged charcoal branches and furs, building a canopy above Jerune. Half a tent. She considered moving back to the tunnel. Stared at the darkness, the depths flickering with gentle amber. Their escape was impossible fortune and even Bücka knew not to tempt fate again. As the snow continued to fall, she used her blade to scrape the flakes from the clumsy shelter. The branches, deadened by fire, would likely snap under the weight. She would keep Jerune warm and dry; she would keep the shelter from collapsing. It would be a long night, a precious night.

Light. Beyond his lids. His face cold, body warm. The pain in his wrist a heavy throb, at least it meant he was still alive. A sliver of daylight to greet his opening eyes. She was there. Fanning him with a sword? Bücka standing with a lethargic posture; she was the waking dead.

'What are you doing?' he asked.

Her grin was immediate. Her body animated. She hopped on the spot.

'Jerune!' She dropped her sword and crashed down beside him. Her eyes sparkled, her face flush with colour. 'I didn't know if you'd wake.'

Wake? He recalled the cavern. Had there been guards? Had he run?

'I... What happened?' he asked.

Her eyes became wide as full moons. 'You don't remember?'

'No. My head's foggy. Why are we in the valley? Why's it all...?'

Bücka fussed, moved some furs to cover his neck. She patted her work and said, 'Fire came back. We smashed the orb but it rolled away.' She giggled, though her laugh appeared cold. 'She bloody came back, Jerune. We ran, you threw me into a crack in the ground, came down on top of me. You know, you're pretty solid for a lightweight.'

'Thanks?'

'All sinewy and bony. Like a bag of blacksmith's hammers fell on top of me. Anyway, I guess we both blacked out. I came to, dragged your sorry backside out...'

Bücka stopped, the enthusiasm slipping away from her features. A darker countenance troubling her face.

'What is it?' he asked.

Shaking her head, she replied, 'I thought I'd smell it, you know? The death. I thought maybe they'd gone—the guards—ran, like us. But...' Again, she stopped. Stared past him. He reached with his good hand, took hers. She continued. 'Just lumps of melted metal. And ash. I've seen fire burn people. I've seen those bodies. It's horrible. But there weren't any. They'd been...'

'Incinerated?'

'Yeah, that's it. What can melt metal and... do that to people? I mean, I know Fire did it but... but, that sort of power is impossible. It's inhuman.'

What few words she had spoken painted a grim escape. Fire had returned. Destroyed everything, killing the men supposed to be her ally. It didn't make sense. That she was even present was a contradiction to the Covenant. The catalyst that had brought them to blasted Laria.

'Why was Fire here, Bücka? This Covenant,' he freed his hand from hers, pointed to the valley, 'this destruction, it doesn't make any sense at all.'

She shook her head, looking to the valley.

He continued. 'I remember that man. His words.' His heart jumped, once again recalling the mention of the fleet. For all Bücka's companionship, he wanted to see Sarellia, know she was safe with Goddard. Yet, he didn't want to diminish Bücka's pride. She didn't deserve to be second best. First equal among friends and lovers.

'Kharast?' she asked.

Jerune couldn't confirm the name, his mind cluttered by a fog of disjointed pain. 'Maybe? But he mentioned Porst. Or the woman did. This was a trap, Bücka. Goddard faces a trap. The Covenant—I doubt its truth. This reeks of the conspiracy of men.'

'Bastards.'

He looked to the dark mouth of the tunnel. 'Nobody's left?'

'Not that I saw. It's a miracle we survived.'

'Then we head back to that town. What was it, Golda?'

'Gulda. And if I see him, I'll fucking kill him.'

'Porst?'

'Sold me out. I wonder how much he was promised?'

Jerune wasn't one for revenge though it seemed to him a standard path for a warrior. Honour and all that. He wouldn't stand in Bücka's way.

He said, 'From there, we can try for passage but if Laria has eyes seeking us?'

Bücka nodded. 'Horses. We'll get horses. A few days ride should take us North.'

'The northern fleet?'

'You said it was a trap? We go to our friends. Our travel has been swift until now. We may have time.'

It was noble. But Jerune wondered what they could do to help? Though, it was another port. Sailing from there would be quick. They could return to the Northern Lands. Perhaps they all could. Jerune leant on his good hand, made to stand. Bücka grasped at him, brought him back down. He frowned at her.

'I watched you all night,' she said. 'If we're going to ride hard, I need some rest. A few hours, here, that's all.' Her gaze moved to the canyon. Jerune watched as the snow fell in gentle waves. Apart from their voices there was no other sound. Peace among the destruction. It would be a nice thing to steal some serenity from it all.

He patted the fur beside him. 'I'll keep watch. I'll wake you in a few hours.'

Bücka nodded, curled into a ball beside him.

'No touching,' she said, muffled.

He understood her humour. Placed a hand upon her shoulder and said, 'Wouldn't dare.'

Gulda. From afar, Bücka thought it appeared different. Perhaps darker, less snow. Since the canyon the features had changed. She and Jerune had noted a strange ice sprinkled across the landscape. Fallen drops of frozen water, a sheen across much of the land. Jerune had suggested that Fire's warmth had perhaps melted the surrounds, a brief thaw, quick to freeze over. Now, looking to the distant town, she shivered; though, it was not the chill that rattled her so.

'Jerune, what do you see?'

He stood beside her. Close. His breath mingled with her own, a cloud of quiet awe.

'Is it what I think?' she asked.

'What do you think?' he replied, though judging by his tone, she knew she was correct.

'Burnt?'

'To a cinder. I can see the stone. It's survived. But the roofs, anything else—it's gone.'

Bücka watched as Jerune paced away. He stopped, brought his hands to shield his eyes. Gazing to the West.

'What else?' she asked.

'Some people. Horses. Travelling this way. Towards the town.'

She trudged across the snow, the strange, brittle surface crunching loud underfoot. Peering, straining, she saw dots, nothing more. 'Guards? Troops?' she asked.

'No. Don't think so. It's a caravan. Traders, perhaps.'

Bücka looked back at Gulda. 'We should check the town for survivors.'

Jerune turned. His frown was accompanied by a slanted smile. He shook his head. 'We can go. But don't expect to find anything.'

Staring at the dark blemishes that were the remains of houses, she sighed. 'Why did she do it?'

'Fire?'

'Yeah. I've never seen... never known of anything like it.'

'Well, I think she's gone. Let's see what's left.'

She and Jerune travelled the remaining distance in silence. Wondering if his speculation of Fire's disappearance was true, she kept an eye on the sky. Reaching Gulda without a fiery intervention, she was greeted with a familiar sight.

'The same as the cavern,' she said.

'Ash and nothing else,' Jerune replied. He moved to the closest house, a small distance from the main settlement. She watched as he reached with his good hand, felt the wall. 'Still warm.'

Bücka scanned the surrounds as she marched forward, moving to the bulk of what constituted the town's centre. The wind provided a gentle background cry as she and Jerune poked around what was left of Gulda. The ground was slick, a treacherous ice upon the flagstones. The snow had ceased and the town appeared as though covered in oil, a shine coming from the stone. Nothing stirred. Nothing lived.

'Gutted,' Jerune called out from a nearby building. 'The insides are ash too.'

'She must have been furious,' Bücka said. Startled by a sudden commotion, she turned. Saw Jerune cursing on the ground, holding his injured hand in the air.

'Bloody ice,' he said with a scowl. 'Saved my wrist, at least.'

Trying not to laugh, she offered redundant advice. 'Careful, it's slippery.'

From the ground, Jerune replied, 'Goodness, hadn't noticed.'

'You're alright?'

'Sore arse,' he replied, standing, looking to the frozen gravel as though it was malicious. 'Let's get off the stone, it's lethal.'

Bücka glanced at the buildings and nodded. It was clear nothing was left. Everything organic had become brittle charcoal or powdered ash. Pools of solid metal textured the streets as though quicksilver. The Great Destroyer; what they called Fire. Whatever she was, the Elemental was a power beyond compare. Bucka thought of Thelia, her stories of Kor'A and Petra. Somehow the power of stone seemed feeble in comparison. A scope of destruction beyond reckoning.

She joined Jerune on the outskirts. 'You think Porst was there?' she asked.

'Where else would he be?'

'I hope he saw it coming.'

Jerune stared at her but said nothing.

'What? You think he deserved to live?'

He shook his head. 'Damn, no. I was thinking about seeing it coming. I mean, we saw her. But to see her here,' he pointed to the town. 'All this cold and then... gone. What in the hell, Bücka? This is... it's...'

Jerune didn't finish. He turned his head. She followed his gaze, saw the caravan approaching. Traders. He had been right. Those canny eyes, his unnatural senses.

'Think we can get a horse?' she asked.

His attention on the traders, he replied, 'And travel north. We need to find our friends.'

Chapter XLVII

Mother. It was what she was. Yet, she was so much more. Chara watched as Goddard fell. Beside her, Sarellia winced. They had fled from the town, the thunder and quaking a terrible omen. Coming to find Goddard, instead, she had watched the world turn.

'Mother!' she called out.

Sarellia fell to her knees, her hands tight upon her temples. She appeared to be in pain. What was happening?

'Mother, stop!'

And she came. In a blink the white form vanished, only to erupt a single pace away. Sarellia screamed, suddenly becoming still and silent on the earth.

'STOP!' Chara yelled.

'I am,' Kor'A said. 'I cannot be undone.'

'You're hurting them.'

Her mother's ruby eyes stared at Sarellia, and Chara understood the pain had been removed. In that moment, mother appeared different, diminished.

'She looks familiar,' Kor'A said.

Looking at Sarellia, asleep on the ground, Chara thought of her story, her history. To her mother, she said, 'Kallisa was her... Bruhsa. Family.'

'Kallisa, *yes.* They all look alike, don't they?'

Chara frowned. Realised she didn't know if they did. Had experienced so few human interactions. But those she knew; she knew them as unique people. Beyond her mother, she sought Goddard. Wanted to go to his side. Needed to care for him.

As though reading her thoughts, Kor'A said, 'I know him.'

'He was Argan.'

What her mother did next caused Chara to step away. Her white face turned to the sky, her ruby eyes finding Noctyrne and Ambyr.

Kor'A, staring at the moons, said, 'She has sent him to me.'

Chara didn't know what to say. Should she say anything?

Kor'A, her attention focused on the sky, said, 'As I am your mother, Chara, so too I look upon my own.' She brought her gaze back to Chara, a smile, wide and honest, appearing upon her face. 'But I am not as she is. I will not abandon you as she abandoned me.' Kor'A pointed to Sarellia and said, 'What I have learned from this thing called life; to be alone is to suffer. This is not to be your... purpose. I have created for you; that you will not be alone, as I am.'

Such strange words, her mother's voice so different from before. It was cold but warm. Chara didn't understand. She glanced at Goddard, far away and motionless on the ground.

'Go to him,' her mother said. 'Wake him.'

Conflicted, uncertain, Chara shook her head. 'Mother?'

Her smile remained. She pointed to Goddard. 'Go.'

Hesitant, Chara moved away, her eyes fixed on her mother. Furtive glances to Goddard were her way-markers. Soon she came to his side. Knelt on the earth beside his huge frame. Chara reached out, her hands upon his torso. She tried a gentle shake, his huge bulk barely moving.

'Goddard.'

Nothing.

Again, she pushed against his chest. 'Goddard, please. Please wake up!'

From darkness, a light. A voice across time. Young and forever, full of life and love. Daughters of flesh and stone.

'Chara!'

He pushed himself onto his hands. His seat on cold Larian soil. She was there, beside him. He reached out, grabbed her, pulled her to him.

'*Goddard,*' she said, her voice a song to his ears.

'I'm here...I'm here.'

In an instant he recalled the cause of his fall. Kor'A. He looked to the port, saw her standing above the crumpled body of Sarellia. Holding Chara, he launched to his feet. One hand reaching for Bruch'ail. An inch from the haft, he stopped. Serene. Kor'A appeared serene. Not a broken monster. Not a god in pieces. His hand lowered to his side, he released Chara.

'Why is she here?' he asked.

'I don't know,' Chara said. 'But she won't harm you. I trust her.'

Trust? An Elemental? Could such a thing be true? Perhaps, Goddard noting with relief that her aura was gone. A power he had last felt a century ago. The presence of an immortal too much for human transience. The omnipotence of forever a wicked oppression upon the fleeting existence of life. Yet, now, as then, she had controlled that aura. As though a flame controlling its heat. The irony. Here she was, Kor'A. Earth—the Great Destroyer—unknown to herself.

Goddard looked down; Chara's hand grasping his. A thought, to leave Bruch'ail or bring it? Better by his side. He hoisted it to his back, secure in its cradle. Chara nodded and began to move to her mother. Leading him, he followed. Walking as the lost child, he was soon face-to-face with unwanted destiny.

'Argan,' she said.

'Once.'

She smiled. Nodding at Chara, she said, 'You have cared for her.'

'I have.' A thought. He added, 'Still do.'

Kor'A paused. Appeared to observe the northern horizon. 'Petra?' she asked.

'Not here. This is Laria.'

Her focus returned, she asked, 'Is she... well?'

Confused by her humanity, a trait for which she was not known, Goddard nodded. But he did not speak, instead, he knelt beside Sarellia, shook her gently. Her lids flickered open and her dark eyes stared up.

'Don't be afraid,' he said.

She shook her head, though her eyes betrayed the fear. With a hand, he pulled Sarellia to her feet. He thought she might say something but she said nothing. Simply stared at Kor'A. No surprise, he thought. What could you say to a god?

'The hammer,' Kor'A said.

A jolt back to reality. What did she mean? He frowned. Glanced at Chara, aware she was fidgeting.

'Hammer?' he asked. Best play the fool.

'It brought me. I felt it as a... a summons.' She peered at the harness. Looking to Bruch'ail. Her hand raised to reach for it. Goddard turned his body, refusing her the chance.

Kor'A smiled. But it was not a pleasantry. 'I have been a pawn to human deception. Manipulated by your kind. Yet you and your own removed me from that lie. Would you hide the truth from me now? Do you seek to deceive me again?'

Goddard asked, 'You wish to see the hammer?'

'I wish to see what is not of my world.'

It was a moment. A single thought. Strike her down—begin everything anew. He reached to the haft, broke it free of its mount. His eyes on Kor'A, Goddard brought it to bear. Butchers and Kings. He had felled them all. And gods? One single moment.

On open palms, his head bowed, he offered it to her.

'You would give this to me?' she asked.

Raising his eyes to stare at those depthless pools of red, he replied, 'I have no need of it. No wish to wield it. Take it from me.'

Time. What was it? Seconds were seasons as the silence between them carried across the plains. Small fingers tugging on his tunic. Chara's silent anxiety. Goddard watched as Earth's marble fingers reached to the haft of Bruch'ail. An inch away, her fingers remained as stone. Not a single sign of fear or doubt, yet her hand did not grasp the hammer. But words that chilled his spine came from her unmoving mouth.

Why mother?

Unmistakable. A tone he could never had expected from the immortal. Pain. One single moment and Goddard understood his fate was a brutal deception. He could not kill Kor'A. Would not kill her. He moved the hammer closer to her grasp but instantly, Earth removed her hands. She paced one step back.

Goddard said, 'Take it from me. I do not want this.'

'Nor do I,' she replied.

Her head turned upwards, he tracked her gaze to Noctyrne and Ambyr. Allmatta. For a moment her eyes lingered before bringing them back to his own.

'We all have mothers.' A smile graced her sublime features as she looked at Chara. 'But remember, mine is crueller than all.' To Goddard she said, 'She has touched you too, I see that now. It eluded me before. Perhaps she deceived us both?'

'You know?' Goddard asked. 'What I am? What she wants me to do?'

'I understand what that is,' she said, nodding to the hammer. 'One day perhaps you will try. I will not judge you. Though, be warned; whatever her plan, it has no place for life. I cannot tell you how many more times you may strike against me; when the last blow will fall—but be warned, human, it will cost you everything.' Kor'A turned to gaze at Chara. She repeated one word. Her voice wavering. It was sadness. '*Everything.*'

Goddard was transfixed by her eyes. A swirling vortex of red, a storm on a faraway world, he felt as though he could fall into them. Yet, for all their inhuman appearance, there was something other than what he had known before. A century ago, those eyes had been unfathomable. What was once a gaze of terrifying power had become a well of hope. Earth had found her empathy.

Goddard retracted his offer. Careful not to cause Kor'A concern, he gently placed Bruch'ail down upon the ground. He looked to the southern horizon. All the horses now gone; they were alone on this fractured coastal plain. Yet a puzzle remained. The Covenant. The Seer's army. What had happened to Elazra?

'You're not meant to be here,' he said to Kor'A.

She stared. 'I am... always.'

He shook his head. 'Fire sent word to Petra. The Covenant.'

Blinking and silent, she did not respond. And though her character had changed, in contrast to her creations, Petra and Chara, her countenance remained emotionally impoverished. Did she understand his words? Goddard thought he had erred by mention of her sister. Did Kor'A know she was one and the same?

Breaking her silence, she replied, 'Covenant?'

'A pact. To remain away. The Seer of Fire, Ruler of Laria, he was given weapons by Fire, he...'

'There can be no pact with life,' she said. 'You are mistaken. We are—you are not. There is no Covenant; can be no Covenant with mortals.'

Now Sarellia spoke. 'The forge. The seeds of Fire. *It's a trap.* Jerune's walking into a trap.'

Kor'A turned to her. Goddard thought she might speak. In the briefest moment he saw it; Kor'A as stone, frozen. *Absent.* Looking into her eyes he was amazed. Among all of the blood red, a solitary spark of amber flared—a flame—gone in a blink. Goddard jolted as Kor'A suddenly moved, lowering herself to kneel beside Chara.

'Daughter, this is for you.'

She handed Chara a flake of black stone.

Chara asked, 'What is it?'

'My gift to you. A way home so you need never be alone. When you want to go, this will show you the way.' Earth smiled, placed a fan of fingers to her breast and said to Chara, 'My world for you.'

Kor'A stood. To Goddard, she said, 'You will go with her. When it is time. They will need you.'

They? Goddard opened his mouth, about to speak when Kor'A vanished. Her body dissolved to dust, blowing away on the breeze. He looked down at the flake of rock on the child's palm. Wondered how it would guide Chara. Guide them both. To where?

A stupefied silence was broken by Sarellia. 'What the hell was that? What just happened? Did I not ask anything?'

Looking at Bruch'ail, patient upon the Earth, Goddard said, 'Well, we know there's no Covenant with the Elementals. We don't have to fear their wrath.'

'Jerune. And Bücka,' Sarellia said. Her voice was haunted. 'We have to help them.'

Goddard nodded. A cold truth, they were days away. But he couldn't deny Sarellia her hope. Besides, there was no way to sail home, not from here.

'The horses won't have bolted far,' he said. 'We'll find a mount for you both, ride south as fast as we can.'

He slung Bruch'ail over his shoulder. Chara looked at him, her face a frown of confusion.

'Why did mother let you keep it?'

A glance to the moons. A dark thought. Inevitability. But on what scale of time—human or immortal? Kor'A's warning had settled his fate; he would never use it against the Earth. Not at *that* cost. He would not lose Chara as he had Bri'alla.

He said, 'She knows I'll not use it against her.'

Chara's brow relaxed, her lips parting to display a wide grin. A touching moment though Goddard knew the truth; a prophecy told from the creator of gods. It would not be by his hand, but one day, in an unknown future, another hand would wield Bruch'ail. Another pawn to herald the end.

Chapter XLVIII

I t wasn't a Western Star. Of that, Bücka was certain. Hands on the reigns, she pushed away the sense of regret. What would Goddard think? A Bruhadian relic traded for a piebald pony named *Koltur*, a name she knew better translated as *good enough*. They had left Gulda the previous day, ridden at a canter until sunset. She dared not press Koltur's endurance. The stallion's name spoke volumes of his capabilities. Though, as with all hybrids, the temperament was unique. A noisy horse, his huffs and chatter had kept her amused. It had brought relief to a night around a pitiful fire. Jerune had complained of the scarcity of fuel. Though, it had suited Bücka; she enjoyed his proximity. When the flames died, she had nestled close beside the one man in whom she had found trust and friendship.

With the rising sun scraping the far eastern mountains, and Jerune's good arm hugging tight to her waist, Koltur was moving with speed. Not a gallop. She didn't think he had it in him. Figured short bursts of his middling pace would be better than a steady canter. Five trots forward, two trots back; that was how she imagined the journey would unfold. A comedy of circumstance to end an abysmal mission. It cheered her, to think in such ways, but her smile was erased as she looked to the northern horizon. Pulling Koltur to a stop, she turned him to the side. It would allow Jerune a proper look. On the cusp of grey land and blue sky, a cloud rose above a line of black. Distant but unmistakable, she didn't need the scout's senses.

'Oh shit,' she said.

Jerune sighed. A dark humour in his tone. 'Riders. A century at least. What next? A blizzard, a rain of fire?'

Glancing behind, Bücka saw there was poor cover. Laria's western coast was an undulating bedrock of snow and stone, a flat terrain of solid earth with few hills to break the monotony. Occasional ragged peaks climbed toward the sea, falling sharply at the water's edge; the Larian port one of few places with a deep harbour. But they had travelled farther north, leaving behind those imposing stacks and cliffs.

Bringing her focus to the approaching mass, Bücka said, 'They're riding hard.'

'As fast as cavalry can.'

A thought occurred to her, a puzzle. 'Why are they travelling south?'

Jerune, possibly foggy with pain, replied, 'What do you mean?'

'The fleet is north. That's where they should be.'

'But the Forge, Bücka, we heard—it's a trap.'

'I know, I remember. But you don't charge your cavalry at nothing. You ride steady unless moving into battle.' She pointed back to the south. 'There's nothing behind.'

'Then... they're retreating? Is that what you mean?'

'I don't know.'

Bücka was confused. Though now wasn't the time to hesitate. They were coming ever closer and she had few options available.

'Hold on,' she said to Jerune, kicking her heels into Koltur.

As though considering the command, the stallion began to plod west. Bücka kicked again, careful not to alarm the beast. Koltur moved from trot to canter and with the rumble of the cavalry rising in the air, he finally broke into a *koltur* gallop.

In her ear, Jerune said, 'They're ignoring us.'

A quick glance to confirm. Not a single rider deviated from that strange, southern charge. No matter, she thought, security was distance and it was a fool who stopped to listen to the thunder of war. Pushing Koltur westward, she didn't stop until the quake of hooves had passed. Bringing the mount to a gentle trot, allowing her to stare at the disappearing mass, she shook her head.

'They *are* retreating,' she said.

'How can you tell?'

'The banners are down. You notice, no flags?'

Bücka imagined that Jerune, for all his skills and knowledge, wasn't an expert on martial matters. His answer confirmed her thought. A single shrug.

'I suppose you don't really need skills to track an army?' she asked.

Jerune shook his head. 'More feet, more tracks. More horses, more hooves, more mess. Though, I've never had to track more than a dozen bandits.'

Bücka nodded, watching the clouds of dust and dirt being emancipated from ice and dry snow. The riders continuing south. She said, 'A full retreat.'

'But what are they running from?'

She looked at him, craning her neck hard to stare at his face. It was hope that spoke. She said, 'Perhaps they met a man with a massive hammer?'

Jerune raised his eyebrows, appeared to consider her words. 'One way to find out.'

Bücka grinned, dug in her heels and turned Koltur to the north.

On her face, Bücka noted the bitter Larian sting had faded. Just cold, not freezing. It was warmer. Not so much that the snow had disappeared. She wondered how far they had travelled on Koltur. The day had passed as a dull memory, staying on the coastal trail, the Larissian Sea to the west. Hard to gauge distance when everything looked the same: a grey sea, the black and white land, and a sky that raced with flurries of clouds. But the climate had altered. A sure sign of progress north. Temperate winds ahead, a less hostile world.

Staring across that ocean, squinting at the golden setting sun, Bücka considered the contrast. Beyond her view lay Kalleron, the continent, not the fallen Kingdom. A vast swathe, by all accounts the largest of the three known lands. A hot place. She had been, several times. Good contracts, most of them. She had once asked Thelia from where on Kalleron she had hailed. The streets, she had replied. No home, no nation; a child of nothing, brought to freedom by Petra. Forgetting the present, Bücka indulged the past. A history she knew from bedtime stories. The downfall of Kalle, Kalleron abandoned by its Queen. The creation of the free lands of the North, guarded by three heroes: General Aracyse and his iron arm, Argan and that hammer, and Petra, the new Queen of Stone. Days of legend. Days of wonder. A melancholy settled upon her, an image of Goddard. Now she knew the legend, the world seemed smaller. An ageing man, though she wondered if his grey was incidental rather than a sign of decrepitude. If Goddard was failing, he must have started his life as a god.

'Fire's up,' Jerune said, appearing by her side.

'You found enough wood?'

'Along the shore. It'll have to do.' He sighed. Stared to the west. 'What's it like?'

'Kalleron? Warm. First thing you notice is the heat.'

'Hotter than home?'

Bücka turned to face him. Realised he didn't know how it felt to stand on sun-kissed shores. A scout who had spent all his days in the comfortable, temperate, northern world. She smiled, imagined his light skin would fare poorly.

'You'd fry,' she said, noticed his wrist. 'You took the bandages off?'

He raised his hand, wiggled some fingers, wincing as he did. 'Still hurts but I can use it. Helped with the fire.'

'Is that wise? What if you heal funny?'

Jerune paused, looked to his hand. 'Should be okay, no?'

Bücka grinned, made a claw with her fingers. Mocked him with love. 'You'll be like this... oh, my hand, oh Sarellia, please rub me better.'

'Fuck off,' he laughed.

'I'm glad it's better.'

'Yeah.' He looked to the north. 'Another day or two?'

'Two, maybe three with Koltur.'

'I swear, that horse farts more than you.'

Bücka let her mouth hang open, her eyes feigning shock. She jabbed his shoulder, making sure to hit his good side. 'After all the nice things I say to you!'

He frowned, 'What nice things?'

Bücka grinned. 'Yeah, truth.'

She returned her focus to the far horizon. The sun had slipped from view leaving a pastel of orange and dark blue across the skyline. The sound of the water lapping the shore and the crackle of the fire was hypnotic. They rode away from death to chase

possible despair. Yet here, for just this moment, she allowed her breath to soften, ı.
heartbeat to slow.

'Jerune?'

'Yeah?'

'I'm glad you're here.'

No quip. No gentle insult. She felt his hand rest upon her shoulder. A gentle squeeze.
It reminded her of an old mentor. That reassuring hand. Bücka smiled, her face relaxed.
No matter what was to come, she still had Jerune.

Chapter XLIX

As a human, Petra toiled. And though the effort was a façade, the labour was honest; it was physical, her hands upon rock and boulder. One final stone to top the cairn. Near death, the Seer had come to Petra. Her physician skills, nought compared to Argan's, should have sufficed. But that morning, after a restful night, his breath had ceased. Perhaps age. Perhaps duty. Petra stepped down from the resting place of whom she understood to be the last Seer of Arkallon. A figure whose relevance died a century ago when the Queen had brought Kalle's anger. She surveyed her work. Nodded an appreciation. It was a modest tomb compared to those in Anka but atop the cliff, overlooking the white city, it was a fitting bed to sleep unto eternity.

The journal he had brought lay within his granite sarcophagus. She had taken from it what she could. It would not travel with her essence, could not survive commune with the Earth. Journeying from Farenhyne the old-fashioned way had been a necessity brought by the lie of the Covenant. Now that deceit was laid bare, the free Earth was hers once more. And the pages had opened her eyes to a terrible new world. The old Larian ways, those memories from her youth, were gone. A hidden Kingdom of immense deception had arisen. A match for the lies of Kalle and his immortal ruse. Disguised under the oppression of the Seer of Fire, Laria flourished as no other. Once a naval power, she had built an army, vast and powerful. Her navy, once known for those floating fortresses, always present on the ocean, was kept from view. Laria had become the assassin in pauper's robes. Waiting for opportunity. Watching the weapons of Etherus in Kalleron. Waiting for the Northern Lands to relinquish its Elemental treasure. A patient, scheming eye on far flung shores.

More was learned of Etherus. And though there were few pages to record what machinations were being created, what was told rang a bell in her mind. The clockwork mechanics—the wonders of a mad engineer called Anders. It shouldn't have surprised her, after all, she had sat and discussed war with a man whose metal arm was proof of Kalleron's genius and guile. With Kalle defeated, she had thought—they all had—that the threat was gone. No Elemental Queen to crush her foe; no brutal King to subjugate its people. But they had forgotten Etherus, thought it rendered impotent by the Cult and its martyrdom. No. Etherus had survived. The Seer's own words ringing in her mind. Etherus was rising. What nightmares would it bring?

Petra turned to observe An'Korathall. How would it fare in this coming dawn? She needed to know. In a blink she was there, surrounded by shrieks and cries of shock. Standing at the top of the main avenue, she surveyed the streets. Behind her, the citadel; in front, the living city. In the noon sun, hands reached to cover blinded eyes, a piercing light cast from her marble form. The ripple of hushed whispers replaced the fear. Once their Queen, she did not savour the role. Though, of course, they were never her people—they were her ward. And with Laria's intent laid bare and Etherus' threat renewed, they needed her once again. One by one, those whose years allowed recollection began to kneel. Watching, others copied. The young, those she had abandoned, they would know of her through legend. What history had been told; what truths had been embellished?

'You know me?' she said to the crowd.

Words returned. All the same. 'Our Queen.'

Never comfortable with the title but keen to lift their spirits, Petra replied, 'I am your protector. And I have returned.'

'There is fear,' a voice called, a woman.

'Stand,' Petra said.

Slowly, her movements punctuated by hesitation, a figure robed in blue arose. Fine wrinkles upon her face, age worn well, she bowed her head.

'All of you, stand. Nobody need bow before me,' Petra said. As the crowd began to rise, she continued, 'There is no need for fear. An'Korathall will return to its rightful role. A sanctuary for all. When you see foreign faces, tell them of my return. When you hear whispers of violence, be sure to invoke my name.

'I do not return with peace in my heart; I come to you with purpose. A new war is coming. Old enemies are sharpening their steel. But I promise you, in this city you will be safe. Let no man or woman spill blood upon my Earth. I will be the mountain that crashes down upon those who dare challenge my law. And for those that doubt my strength, for those that doubt my intent, I give you this.'

Petra imagined the wall. Saw it in her mind's eye. A great white marble block. Gasps erupted from the crowd as the earth shook. Chatter and pointing animated the confused assembly. On the cusp of Anka, where essence met rock, a slice of Earth erupted from beneath. With care, Petra brought it forth. She smiled, tried to hide her reaction from the crowd. But it was not power that pleased her so. It was those many souls in random behaviour startled by the ground rising: a man hopping away with one boot on his foot, a woman cursing as baskets of fruit were toppled over, a mutt barking at the bare flank. All around the white city she raised the wall with care. Where she was familiar with common routes of travel, Petra opened the barrier creating massive arches, twelve in all. No doors to hinge, no barricades to control. If she wanted them closed, she would do so by will. When the rumbling ceased, the city was ringed by a wall five-feet thick and fifty-feet high. In truth, it could have been the width of a child's hand and still be stronger than any human fortress. But appearances were important to quell the ambitions of mortal men. This wall was more than its essence; it was a sign. An immortal shield for Anka's mortal souls.

285

To the chattering and pointing crowd, Petra said, 'People of Anka. Know this truth.' As the voices quelled, she spread her arms wide. 'The Elemental Earth has no care for human life. But I do, and I promise to serve you.' Suppressing the bitterness she knew her next words would bring, Petra called to the crowd, 'Tell the world that I have returned. Tell the world that An'Korathall has its Queen once again.'

Petra blinked. It was all that was needed to commune with the essence of Earth. To become one with what she desired not to be. Yet, as flesh yielded to pleasure, Petra could not refuse the power of Kor'A's curse. The tragedy of immortality only becoming a gift when it aided her friends. Opening her eyes, she stared out across the plateau at Farenhyne. A breathless sigh vibrated on the wind. The pit remained but the fire was gone. A vast scar marring the idyllic view. Lazy clouds rolled across an azure sky, the ocean beneath twinkling as a field of diamonds. Farenhyne sat nestled in the bay, smoke from chimneys bowing to the breeze. It was surreal; how the world of mortals trundled by, so unaware of the foreign hands that played dice with their fate, ignorant of what hell malicious minds might bring. Tranquillity before the storm. As it had always been. As it would always be.

Staring out across the ocean, turbulent waters she knew as the Sea of Silence, Petra scanned for signs of war. Though her diamond eyes carried her vision to distant places, as with all the Elementals, there were limits. The curve of the world, the haze in the air; these things were natural barriers to immortal sight. Within her sensory range there was nothing to cause alarm. Certainly, Taberas had told of the Battleships; if those great hulks came, she would see. To the east, she peered to the Rotynian Claim; the waters where no sailor of sound mind would enter. Distant sea-stacks and vertiginous peaks hid from view that which she sought. If Goddard had returned on that ship, Petra would not be able to see. Not from here. A thought. A blink.

East of Farenhyne, a place unknown to most, Petra rose from the earth. Keen to preserve the Rotynian way, from afar she observed the camp spread out below, her eyes searching for that one majestic colossus. Had she blood in her veins and a heart in her chest, it would have raced. There, moored against the high stacks, the Battleship sat proud in the water. Petra focused, scanning the decks and hull. Her stone heart leapt; damage apparent upon the leviathan. A gaping scar down one side, a scorch of blackened wood, her sails peppered with dark ringed holes; a clear sign of a brush with Fire. The Covenant exposed as a lie, nonetheless, the mark of the Elementals was clear. No time to delay, not for Goddard; decorum and etiquette would need to wait.

A raucous noise greeted her arrival, Petra striding down the vertical face of the cliff. The ranks of men and women stared at her. Awe, not fear, held their attention. Weapons hanging listless by their sides, their intent was clear. A welcome party of curiosity. The noise abated to a whisper as a woman strode forward. With minimal deference to human modesty, Petra grabbed a hessian rag and swung it around her marble form. And though this was not Anka, all would know the Queen of Stone. Yet the woman approaching Petra did not kneel. An uncommon courtesy that she found refreshing.

'You would be Petra?' the woman said. 'My name is Elazra.'

Petra scanned the crowd. Couldn't find what she sought. No towering King to greet her.

'Argan,' she said. 'You would know him as Goddard. Did he come?'

'Aye.' Elazra came forward, turned to the crowd. 'Back to your business, nothing to see here!'

Petra smiled at the command. Assumed the woman was the leader; as much as the Rotynians deemed to know such a thing. Amazed at the influence of her words, Petra watched the faces turn and disappear. All compliant without so much as a grumble. Elazra approached, nodded a more formal greeting.

'I'm honoured,' she said. A pause before adding, 'But your friends aren't here.'

There was no panic in her voice. No sign of distress. Petra asked, 'Then where?'

'Set ashore on Laria. We were ambushed.' Elazra gestured to the Battleship. A wry smile crept upon her face. 'And here I thought I had the only one.'

Petra nodded. 'I had an encounter with a man. The Seer of Arkallon. He told me there were more.'

'Arkallon? That place is long gone. The only Seer I know of is Fire.'

'Part of a greater lie. A new order approaches. A stronger Laria. Clearly, you know of the hidden fleet. But tell me, one sailor to one who used to sail, how did you survive?'

Elazra hesitated. Her eyes sought an answer, her face displayed doubt. She shook her head, inhaled a deep breath.

'I've seen a lot, you know. You say you've sailed; I know your past. Folks think the ocean is flat and featureless. It's not. But when I thought our end had come,' she pointed to the scar on the hull, 'when they launched those infernal weapons, the ocean split apart. I've seen what Water can do but never that. As though the earth was splitting apart.'

Although Elazra's doubt was clear, Petra recognised what she described. The same had happened a century ago when Kor'A had left Kalleron to come to these shores. The true Covenant; the oath that was the bond of Water and Earth. She nodded to the woman, urged her to continue. She wanted to hear her story.

'Those damn ships bearing down, one went right over. We were in retreat, tried to gain some distance, gather our senses to return fire. I was staring back, saw it go down. In the water they're majestic but as the bow leaned farther into the void... the sound, splintering and cracking like thunder, the hull collapsing under its own weight,' Elazra paused again. Petra imagined the echoes of what terror she was recalling. It was a sailor's fear; the end of the world, where ocean poured over the edge of the abyss. Petra wondered if Elazra knew what unfathomable truth lay behind the superstition.

'It went right down?' Petra asked.

As though startled from her thoughts, Elazra looked up. 'Not so deep there, seemed as though seconds passed when we heard it hit the seabed. But that void, that chasm saved us. Water saved us that day. I don't know why.'

Petra said, 'It was Kor'A. The passage of Earth across her sister's domain. She has travelled from one land to another, perhaps gone to Laria, perhaps returning here. It is how the Elementals interact. Fortune smiled upon you that day. Chance, not fate.'

Elazra frowned. Raised an eyebrow. 'I suppose you'd know.'

'Goddard, he was safe on land?'

'Aye, the lady and the child too. That he is safe, I have no doubt. A man such as he. But you know that, don't you?'

Elazra's face held a curious expression. Was she seeking more information? Or was she sharing a truth few mortals could ever dream to know? That a Rotynian leader understood history was no surprise to Petra. Their seafaring longevity relied on understanding the intrigue of the land. Legends from where Goddard and Argan had come—a King of Kings—would be hard to ignore.

Petra said, 'I know Goddard faces few dangers.'

'Fewer, I'd imagine, brave enough to face him.'

'Many have tried, Elazra, all have failed.' Maintaining her calm, keen to suppress her own interest, Petra asked, 'The woman and child. You saw them?'

Elazra grinned. 'Not to fear, the girl of black glass is our secret. We keep our own.'

Petra was thankful. It had been a wise decision to bring Chara. Only Laria, it seemed, held more secrets than the Rotynians.

'Thank you, Elazra. I'll trouble you no more.'

The Rotynian's reply was lost as Petra dissolved into the Essence. There she remained, not yet ready to return to Anka. One riddle to solve. An ocean split apart. She sought the shadow that loomed in the dark. Where was she? Where was Kor'A now?

Chapter L

G oddard pushed a fragile stick into the anaemic flames. Considered it a miracle they had enough to burn at all. Had he known how barren the place was he would have picked up every piece of dead bracken they had passed. Sarellia and Chara had ridden on one horse, he had run with the other. They would swap over tomorrow. Peculiar horses, a Larian breed, he thought. A smaller frame, blessed with a thick dark coat to ward away the cold. Gods knew what they ate in this forsaken land, though the scarcity of food did much to explain their size. The abandoned port was one day past and they had noted few places of interest on their journey south. A deserted homestead, a disused wharf; nothing to suggest habitation, never mind a mobilising army. They had followed the tracks of the fleeing cavalry. Not a tactical decision. Necessity keeping them close to the coast, a warmer breeze than what appeared to blow inland. Here, the bedrock poked through in dark patches, lichen, moss and hardy grasses flourishing where they could. Hardly enough for a mouse, let alone the horses, which appeared content to nibble around the rocky outcrops.

'You think they'll come back?' Sarellia asked.

He stared south. His eyes unable to penetrate the gloom of night. The moons, things he'd never again regard with innocent beauty, shone down between bursts of racing cloud. Chara lay curled up beside him, her face ablaze in the mirror of the flame.

'If they do, it'll not be favourable for us.'

She frowned. 'But they fear you.'

He pointed at Bruch'ail, always close. 'I can swing at them. But as flies, they'll swarm. You'll not be safe. Chara won't be safe. One man, no matter how strong, cannot defy an army.'

Sarellia nodded. He saw the acceptance in her eyes. Kor'A's warning about Allmatta's trickery. Bruch'ail was neutered by necessity. To use it again, to smash the earth—how much more until the end? It was a devious weapon. A cruel gift.

'You really think it'll destroy the world?' she asked.

Goddard's stick snapped as he pushed it deeper into the flame. 'I know it will.'

Sarellia sighed. A long, drawn-out breath.

Goddard chuckled. 'Rather selfish.'

'How so?'

'To believe we, or I, should wield a weapon so powerful I can chase away nations. Such a weapon, such power; Sarellia, it can't be given to men or women. We face our days as mortals.'

Sarellia cleared her throat, raised eyebrows and a questioning stare; it was a reflection of the words spoken by Elazra. He was no mere mortal.

Nodding, he said, 'I know, I know. But I was born mortal. I know death will come to me. It's not as simple as being like Kor'A. I'm not. Nowhere close.'

Her gaze fell upon Bruch'ail. 'What will you do with it?'

He wasn't sure. Shrugged his answer. He had tried to part ways with it. It had returned. Imagined, as though a devoted dog, should he walk away from it, it would follow. A curse to bear. Better he, than another.

Goddard said, 'I'll keep it. As it keeps me.'

'When we find...' Sarellia began but stopped. She drew a breath, started again. 'When we find Jerune and Bücka, what do we do?'

Her doubt was palpable. A brave cover for a fearful thought. Goddard said, 'He'll be fine. They'll both be fine. The man can practically hide behind a sapling. And Bücka's fiercer than you know.'

Sarellia rallied. 'Oh, hell, I know. She's a right brawler.' She laughed, though her anxiety was clear.

'Hey.'

She looked into his eyes.

He said, 'We'll find them. We'll get away from here. Go home.'

A nod to accept his words, though he saw the doubt remained. Sarellia frowned. 'I'll need to dismantle the Cult. It's clear we've been infiltrated. Our ignorance bloated on a banquet of lies.'

'Isn't that the risk of politics and subterfuge?' he asked.

'You prefer straight battle?'

Goddard stiffened. Realised it wasn't an insult. A genuine query. One to which he had a simple answer. 'A battle is a single word of truth. It may not win a war but in that moment, there is clarity, Sarellia. I don't desire to end others' lives but when all is said and done, those who walk away, understand the truth.'

He thought she might argue his point. She didn't. Sarellia huffed, blowing a flop of frizzy hair away from her face. Nodding to Chara, glass wrapped in fur, she said, 'The rock she gave Chara, what do you think it does?'

'The flake?'

Sarellia nodded.

'Chara will know.'

She questioned him with silence.

He hoped Chara would understand what she'd been given. Couldn't face the prospect of more riddles. A daunting task to decipher the gifts of Elemental creation. Goddard said, 'We'll find out in time, I'm sure.' Sarellia nodded, tried to stifle a yawn. Goddard smiled. 'You sleep. Tomorrow's another step closer to our friends.'

A stray? Goddard strained his eyes, squinting in the harsh glare. Yesterday's weather, far from glorious but at least hospitable, had been replaced by a colder front. The journey south a probable factor. Beyond the heavy clouds a bright sun cast an obfuscating light. Against the flat horizon, the sky was a razer of white. From that narrow line a rider emerged. A single horse. A quick glance to Sarellia on her mount. She too was straining to see. Friend or foe, soon they would be revealed. As he moved his hand to Bruch'ail, Chara jumped in her seat.

'It's them!'

'You're sure,' Goddard asked. 'It's bright. Could be anyone.'

She looked down to him, reached out her arms. He moved to her, grabbed around her waist and lowered her from the saddle.

'It's them,' she replied. 'Bücka's riding. I think Jerune's behind.'

Sarellia dismounted. She stood still, quiet. In the cold air there should have been plumes of breath. Goddard noted that not one wisp was exhaled. Expectations high, he imagined her nerves were equally elevated. Then it came, the slightest sound accompanied by fragile breaths.

'Please, please, please,' she said.

Goddard knelt. One last check. A whisper in Chara's ear. 'You're sure?'

Turning to face him, she frowned, pointing to her eyes. 'Not like yours. Better. I see.'

A smile returned for her explanation. He stood again, strode forward. Closer they came, not a gallop, not quite a charge. And he saw. Bücka's grin, widening as she approached. From behind, a head peered out. Both alive and well. A miracle.

'You should wipe your face,' Sarellia said.

'Huh?' He reached up, felt the moisture on his cheek. A precipitation of joy, not something he was comfortable to show so readily. He wiped away the tear and said, 'The glare. It stings. Your eyes too, it seems.'

She smiled, a crease of tears sent down her cheeks. Sarellia reached to her face, wiped it dry with hurried hands. Clearing her throat, sniffing, she said, 'Don't want him to get cocky.'

'Wise, he's enough of a smart arse. Don't want him gloating over your emotions.'

'GODDARD!' Bücka cried aloud.

She pulled the horse to a halt, dismounting in one deft movement. Jerune appeared to fumble and clutch at her as she went. He flailed, slipped to the side.

'Bücka!' he called.

She turned, caught him as a bundle. Placing Jerune down on his two feet, he straightened.

'Ta,' he said to Bücka. Turning to Sarellia, he smiled. To the three of them, he frowned and said, 'Shouldn't you be on a ship?'

Sarellia bolted. Slamming into Jerune, Goddard thought he might tumble over. Bücka shook her head. Glancing at the pair, she came forward. Her eyes were bright with tears but she kept them at bay. Though, falling in line with Jerune's words, she too appeared confused.

'You're safe,' she said. 'Of course, you're safe. It's you.' She reached to Chara, placed a hand upon her head. 'Kept him out of trouble?'

Chara looked to Goddard. He thought she might think Bücka's question a serious concern. But she smiled and said, 'I try.'

'She does,' he said. 'And you, Bücka, how did you fare?'

Bücka shook her head. 'Long story. We...' She paused. Opened her fur to reveal her belt, one Larian rapier and an empty scabbard. 'I had to trade it for a bloody hybrid.'

'If it brought you back, it was a worthy trade. Things can be replaced, Bücka. Lives cannot.'

She frowned. Looked to the shore, clear she was seeking something. 'But the ship?'

Goddard shook his head, looked beyond her shoulder to the south. 'Alone?'

'Yes. Though, we saw a century of cavalry fleeing south. Real fast.' She grinned. 'It was you, wasn't it?'

He nodded.

The smile slipping from her face, Bücka said, 'Nothing makes sense,' she said. 'We found the Forge. I think.' She paused, her eyes widening. 'Fire was there. Goddard, we saw her. We saw Fire.'

What to say? How to respond? Tell her the truth of Kor'A's broken mind, or wait until all was settled and safe? Even so, he thought, to see Fire, to survive her presence; it was remarkable. He shook his head, more pragmatic answers first.

'You're unharmed?'

Bücka nodded. 'Jerune broke his wrist but it's healing. Lost some hair, better that than flesh.'

So much had happened. That was clear. And their own stories had to be shared. They were family now, they deserved to know. Looking over at Sarellia and Jerune, he cleared his throat. His grumbling summons worked, the couple parting the embrace. Jerune, patting down his fur, returned a smug grin.

Sarellia said, 'There's so much we need to discuss.'

'I'd rather not do that here,' Goddard said. 'We should get away from this place. The northern port was a ruse. There's nothing sea-worthy there.'

'Laria port will be risky,' Bücka said. She hesitated, glancing over her shoulder. 'Though, come think, I doubt folks know we're here.'

A surprise to hear. Had Jerune's stealth been so successful? Had they escaped the forge without sight? He nodded to the scout. 'I'm impressed.'

Jerune appeared confused. 'Why?'

'Your stealth. You remained unseen?'

Bücka spoke. 'Oh, no, *everybody* saw us.' She was quick to defend Jerune. 'Not his fault. I mean, he did this ridiculous climb—that's how he broke his wrist, saving me. No, inside we were surrounded but then... she came. Fire, Goddard; Fire burned everything. Everyone. Jerune pushed us into a fissure and, well... we got out. Just us.'

Goddard peeked at Chara. Did she understand? Fire, her mother, destroyer of all. Did she know what Bücka was saying.

The child spoke. A mimic of a sigh to start. 'Oh, you were lucky.'

Bücka nodded. 'Lucky I had this one.' She thumbed back to Jerune.

It was unsettling. Trying to wrap his head around Chara's thoughts. Where were her emotions in all of this confusion? He wanted to ask but knew it would be awkward. A discussion for another time. Looking to Bücka, considering the story of their flight, Goddard stroked his beard contemplating the next step.

'You think we can make safe passage from Laria?' he asked.

Sarellia spoke. 'Not the main port, surely. But there's a smaller port just north. More discreet. I know of it through the spies.' She paused then huffed. 'Probably compromised.'

'But smaller?' Goddard asked.

She nodded. 'Shallow harbour, no good for large ships. Small traders mostly.'

If it wasn't suitable for ships with deep keels, Goddard supposed it unlikely to have a naval presence. There would be fewer soldiers, if any. Easy pickings for he and Bruch'ail, compromised or not.

'How far?' he asked.

Sarellia turned to Jerune but the scout shrugged.

Bücka blew into the air. A long puff of white haze. Pointing at Goddard next to the diminutive Larian mount, she said, 'You're on foot, so at your pace, two, three days. I mean, Koltur's not so fast but he'll manage.'

Koltur? Goddard had to ask; the translation not lost. It brought a mischievous grin to his face. Waving his hand at Bücka's mount, he said, 'He's called *Good Enough?*'

She replied with a sheepish nod.

'I know I said it was a worthy trade if it brought you here but... I recant. By the gods, Bücka, you traded a Bruhadian relic for a...'

Bücka thrust her finger awkwardly close to his nose. She said, 'Here now, I'll not have you besmirch the name of our heroic horse.'

'Yeah,' Jerune called out with defiance. Bravery behind the warrior's guard.

A stern silence followed. Broken by a beautiful sound. Bücka giggled. Goddard shook his head. Outrageous. He tried to convince himself to remain serious. Continue his charade. Couldn't do it. Sarellia and Jerune had begun to grin. Bücka was crumpling in fits. A soundscape of cold emptiness was replaced with a hearth of joy. A glance at Chara. Although she didn't join in, her amusement was obvious, those eyes wide and alert, glowing with the faintest aura. Goddard scooped her up, hoisting her high on his shoulder. She squealed with delight. It was perfect, a single golden moment between the hours of darkness. A reflection on time. What was a good life but fragments of this?

Better days.

Chapter LI

'That's new. Someone had the stonemasons in?' Jerune said.

An'Korathall. As Goddard remembered it, although the wall was a novel feature. He knew nothing could be built upon that sacred ground. Nothing but that which was the will of the Earth. A quandary: was it the hand of Kor'A, or Petra's gentler touch?

'It's impressive,' Bücka said as they drew closer.

'Where's the door?' Jerune asked.

Moving under the huge arch, Goddard noticed the difference beyond. Anka at peace. Gone were the worried faces. Replaced by the hustle and bustle of a trading town. Not a sword in sight, no arms to bear. Back to how it had been under her reign—Petra, the reluctant Queen of Stone.

Faces greeted them and though few knew him by name, he understood the hope behind those awestruck eyes. Perhaps his old lie had failed. That vacant tomb no longer needed. Besides, he thought, it had a more deserving soul sleeping within. He glanced at Bücka pulling the cloak around her belt. She flicked her eyes his way.

'Just one sword and I feel awkward,' she said.

'I think Petra's returned,' Goddard said.

'Then she must know the Covenant is false?' Sarellia said.

'Who told her, I wonder?' he replied.

Kor'A? It had to be. No other knew, unless she had confronted Larian spies. That would explain the wall. What had happened in Anka? Curious to know, he quickened his pace. Striding ahead, Chara squealed out.

'Wait for me!'

Although he marched to the marble tower, he wasn't certain she would be there. Stepping into the outer courtyard, another sight fell upon his eyes. The Citadel, altered. But not by stone. By human hand. Wooden troughs and lattice frames held a rainbow of petals. A fragrant scent carried on the passing breeze. A marvellous manufactured garden smothering the harsh marble.

'Flowers?' Sarellia said.

Jerune paced forward, his head tracking across the colourful scene. 'Such beauty.'

As though Jerune's praise called her name, Petra appeared from the tower. She stepped forth, a royal blue robe gathered around her shoulders, her body wrapped in the fabric. Petra smiled, gestured to the new flora.

'I wanted life to return,' she said.

'I like it,' Goddard said. 'The wall?'

'A precaution and a warning.' She nodded at the companions. 'I am cheered you've all returned. I'm sure you must know the truth by now?'

'As do you, it seems?' he replied.

Petra's face slipped into a brief memory of loss. An expression Goddard recognised all too well; although, she was quick to recover her composure. She said, 'A brave man came to me. Told me of the new Laria. You know the Covenant is a lie?'

Goddard nodded. 'We do. The fleet, the Forge. All of it.'

Bücka spoke, her words refuting his own. 'The Forge is real. But it's a death-trap.'

'Yes,' Petra agreed. 'The Elementals don't give their Essence willingly.' She looked to her own palms. 'With a few exceptions.'

Goddard, moving to Petra, reached for her hands. She placed hers in his. Amusing. Looking down at them, he said, 'Always so small. Little porcelain fingers.' He looked into her eyes. Wondered if she could read his gratitude?

'Little fingers to snap necks,' Petra replied.

'Not mine,' Goddard winked.

'Never yours.'

Petra released his hands, wrapped her arms around his body. They failed to encircle his torso. A petite god. But her grip was as a vice. She knew it. Goddard chuckled; her embrace unnaturally strong.

With effort he said, 'Always need to remind me?'

She withdrew. A diamond tear for his trouble. 'It is good to see you again, my old friend.'

He nodded. A single tear for her.

'No diamonds?' she whispered, her affection clear. 'Wipe that away before the others see.'

A quick hand to his face, Goddard asked, 'The man who came. Who?'

Petra shook her head. 'The last Seer of Arkallon. He brought the truth to my eyes.'

He gestured to the companions, Chara shifting under Sarellia's patient hands. All stood a polite distance away. A moment alone for he and Petra. Goddard said, 'I think we've witnessed that truth, all of us. And I have one from my own past, something I need to tell you. These past days have been... difficult to take in.'

Petra squinted.

Goddard pointed to the citadel. 'Inside?'

She nodded. He turned to the others, waved them on. Chara came running to his side.

'Hello Chara,' Petra said.

Chara looked to Goddard. Her eyes were probing. He knew she wanted to speak.

'Inside,' he said, pressing his hand to move her onward. 'Inside, all of us.'

Goddard looked out across Anka and the forest and plains beyond. High in the citadel, it was clear Petra had made changes, invoked a human touch. His memory cloudy, she said it had been that way a century ago but Kor'A had cleared it all away. Possibly to create a sterile home for Chara. Once again, the orbital rooms of the citadel were furnished, smooth blocks and sculpted solid chairs risen from the stone. With cushions and fabrics, it would be palatial. Though he knew better of Petra. This was functional. At least, he noted, she had brought the portal edge higher, no longer a suicidal ledge from which to observe the world.

The evening drawing near, they had discussed their combined journeys. Petra told her story of Taberas, her meeting with Elazra—a tale of survival that had cheered Goddard. Bücka and Jerune had relayed the cataclysm of the Forge. In turn, Goddard had explained everything he could. Nothing had been left out. Not even Bruch'ail or his supposed destiny. After all they had come through, he felt it only fair to include Bücka and Jerune in his revelation. Though, he had left that until the end, thought it a reasonable way to crown a tale of broken gods and psychotic mothers of creation. He was surprised how well the warrior and scout appeared to absorb his news. Though, after their encounter with Fire, Goddard thought his story seemed almost mundane. Now, with his back to the room, he was waiting for Petra's response. He had offered to tell her in private, such was the weight of his story. But as always, she had been firm; if he was to share a truth, she wanted it to be shared equally. Goddard wondered if that had been a mistake, Petra's reply coming after a long and weighted silence.

'I remember taking you aboard the *Melody*. Thought you had a past back then. The way you carried yourself. Quiet. You were so damn quiet. I knew then you could defeat anybody. Everyone did. Your humility, your civility; we all knew you were... *different*. We discussed it, just a little, Shadow and I. He persuaded me you were Royal Guard. Likely shamed to wander far from fallen Bruhale. It seemed plausible so I swore to never delve further. No point disturbing old ghosts. You know, not my place to intrude.'

Goddard, staring at the city painted amber in the descending sun, said, 'Rules of the *Melody*.'

'Her rules indeed.' Petra sighed. 'Way back, when I first learned of your truth; that you were Baza'rad, I realised, had I known, I'd likely not have taken you aboard.'

Surprised, Goddard turned. All faces were on his. Jerune and Sarellia, slumped on a curved slab; Chara beside Bücka, upright and attentive on a flat block; and Petra, standing across the space.

'You wouldn't have let me board?'

Petra smiled. 'I know we sailed a few dubious routes but harbouring refugee Kings would've brought undue attention. There were limits to smuggling.'

'No regrets then?'

She pointed to Bruch'ail resting on the ground. 'Now you lay new revelations upon me. You carry the destroyer of worlds. You're a thousand years old and your fate was to become friends with a petite Larian woman who became the Queen of Stone. I think... no, I feel as though we had little choice in this. And no, you silly old man, I have no regrets.'

'Good,' Goddard said, strolling to Bücka and Chara, a gentle push to move the warrior along. He sat down, Chara nestling in. 'Because nothing's changed. As you've not-so-politely noted, I'm still older than you. None the wiser, mind. And, for balance, you're still stronger than me.'

'Is she?' Bücka said, turning to him, her face etched with surprise.

He pointed to Petra. 'She's made of...' Goddard stopped. Thoughts of Petra flashing in his mind; the life and death of the bravest woman he knew. Her days of flesh, her nightmare of stone. All of it immaterial. It was not that which made Petra the legend that she was. Looking at his old friend, he said, 'She's made of tougher stuff than me. Than all of us.'

Sarellia raised a goblet, a necessity insisted upon by Jerune before their grand communication. Goddard hadn't refused.

She said, 'To Petra.'

Goddard raised his, Bücka and Jerune joined in.

Petra waved a hand. A clear gesture of indifference. 'Toast me again, and I'll kick your arses out of Anka.'

Sarellia looked to Goddard. He shook his head, said, 'Ever humble.' He raised his goblet. 'Then, to friends.'

'Now that, I can toast,' Petra smiled. 'If I could, of course.'

'What happens now,' Bücka asked. 'Will Laria still attack? And what of Kalleron, of Etherus; what you said of the Seer, could it be true?'

Goddard looked to Petra, awaiting her response to the warrior's questions. As much as he had lived lifetimes over what she had known, Petra's unfathomable bind to the Elementals carried as much weight as his unholy role in Allmatta's grand plan. Her eyes reached to his and he felt her sadness. The time of peace was over. The world was turning.

Petra said, 'Laria? I doubt their forces would rush to meet us. This whole deception was a test of strength.' She gestured to Goddard. 'I think they understand what will await them when they come to our shores. Elazra said they lost a Battleship—that's not a loss they'll suffer lightly; I imagine they'll be sorely reminded of history and how Kalleron gave them a bloody nose. But they have their weapons of Fire... yes, I think they will make good on their plans. Not immediately though. Their Covenant is shattered wide open. They've witnessed Goddard's strength and if they send more spies, they'll soon know I defend this city. Even the Rotynians are a force to be reckoned with.'

Sarellia, clasping her hands, asked, 'And Kalleron? How can it have...' She looked to Goddard. 'You destroyed the myth of the King. Kor'A was freed. I don't understand how...'

Goddard said, 'Kalleron gave the world General Aracyse. The figurehead of a military super power.' He paused, recalled the man with the metal arm; the soul behind the armour. 'We were lucky his heart was true. But more than Aracyse, Kalleron produced the world's finest engineers and craftsmen, the brains and brawn that built Etherus.'

Sarellia said, 'When Kalle fell, the lines of communication went dark. Few truths came to the Cult—they assumed it was in turmoil. I was always told that by the Bruhsa.'

'Indeed, it surely fell to chaos,' Goddard said, 'at least, what little news came from the continent confirmed. But resourceful nations don't die—they transform. And after a century? I think Laria's intent may be matched by Kalleron's intelligence.' Without thinking, Goddard turned his focus to Jerune and said, 'We may need reliable eyes on those shores.'

Jerune looked up. A finger turned to his chest, he said, 'Bücka says I'll burn.'

'Didn't you survive Fire?' Goddard asked with a raised eyebrow.

Bücka grinned and said, 'Another adventure, eh?' She turned to Sarellia and added, 'If you'll let him go?'

Before Sarellia could reply, Jerune said, 'Don't I have a say?'

In unison, Sarellia and Bücka replied, 'No.'

As the two women giggled at the scout's expense, Goddard said to Petra, 'And speaking of Fire, in all history, I've never known her to appear before men or women. What does it mean? What is Kor'A's game?'

Petra shook her head and replied, 'I don't know. I know Kor'A more than any other person except perhaps Chara. But I think she's oblivious to her true existence—I was never aware of it. What's she's become, what you say you were shown. It's not what it seems to us. I don't see madness in her actions.'

'How is that possible?' Goddard asked. 'How can she be Fire, let alone Water and Wind? How can she be all and not know?'

Petra paced to the open void that gazed out over Anka. She turned her back to the view and said, 'What I have felt in my years; the echoes of her steps inside my mind—I've never felt sadness or longing. She's not like us, Goddard. I know she wants to understand us but her empathy isn't found in the soul. It's not the same as the bond that keeps family together. All I can think to describe it is a driven curiosity. As though she strives to figure out what we are, what our purpose is.'

Chara, attentive and quiet, raised her hand.

'Speak little one,' Goddard prompted. 'We are family here.'

Chara lowered her hand, nodded and said, 'Mother said she didn't understand you. She said you were not meant to be. Yet you were. You are.'

Goddard looked upon Chara with fondness, his heart swelling at her maturity and intelligence. She was growing. Though, perhaps only in her horizons. He asked her, 'What else did she say?'

'She often said, *I am*, and that life was not. Because you can...' Chara stopped and her gaze fell to the floor.

'Go on,' Goddard said. 'It's all right.'

Chara, her eyes still facing down, said, 'Mother is forever. You are not. She doesn't understand that.'

Petra's voice brought Goddard's attention from the child. With a solemn tone, his old friend said, 'But through us, she tried to. She's always tried. Kallisa once told me of the sculptures of flowers...roses... that she created in her garden in Kalleron. A garden of stone petals and leaves. Even when she was destroying nations, she was struggling to create a simple flower.'

Bücka asked, 'But what does all this mean. Flowers and stone, death and life? What does any of this have to do with Fire and what we saw, Jerune and me?'

Petra said, 'Perhaps I understand a little.' She raised a hand toward Goddard. 'Perhaps you too?'

What did she mean? Goddard frowned, asked as much.

Petra replied, 'How long have we been alone? I left Anka thirty years ago. In those years I've felt the weight of isolation.' All of a sudden, she smiled, her laugh music to Goddard's ears. Through her giggles, Petra said, 'I built a ship inside a tower. Is that normal?'

Goddard twitched, a realisation of her meaning coming to his own mind. He said, 'You created something to dispel the loneliness. You wanted to belong to what you had known.'

Petra nodded. 'You feel it, don't you. The bind to memory, the memory of family.'

He thought of the lost past; of Bri'alla and the ghost of Bruhale. Goddard nodded.

'I think Kor'A, alone in the world, saw us.' Petra frowned, her tone animating with splendid curiosity. 'Did she see the first humans and wonder what we were? Saw us perish and reborn? Did she want to be as us, did she want family?'

Goddard stared at his friend. If anyone could know the contortions of consciousness inside Kor'A's mind, it would be her. Though, even this was a leap too far for his old brain.

He said, 'All we know; all we appear to know, is that she is unaware of her true identity. Allmatta gave me that insight. But there's more to Kor'A. I suppose you're right, Petra.'

'You've found your way to agree with me?' she asked. 'You think she's not mad?'

He turned his head and looked down upon Chara, her bright, black eyes staring at him. He said, 'Madness doesn't make this.'

'Then what?' Sarellia asked.

Goddard smiled. He wanted to say *love* but that was a human power. He was certain it was something of which Kor'A knew nothing. Instead, he offered Chara something else. His hand on her shoulder, he said, 'Your mother made you to be special—to be unique. Like nothing she knows.'

Chara frowned. 'What do you mean?'

As though reading his thoughts, Petra said, 'You live like them, Chara. And that means you're free.'

Chara beamed, her face animating with impossible empathy.

Goddard rubbed her head. It never mattered she had no hair to ruffle. He imagined it for her. He said to her, 'You're one of us, Chara.'

A silence settled upon them and for a brief moment Goddard forgot the worries of war and what was to come. But all too soon, Jerune cleared his throat and spoke.

'I don't want to break this moment but what Bücka said, there's more. What about the seeds? What happened at the Forge was a miracle for us but the same can't be said for your fort, Petra. Those weapons are real, terrifying. Laria has them hidden away. We lost them. And we have no idea where they are, where they will come from.'

Petra shook her head. 'You never lost them. The game was over before you set foot upon Laria, the deception was perfect—none of us knew. But yes, those seeds; we'll need to track them down. We know from Elazra and the Seer that they're the arsenal of the remaining Battleships. There may be more elsewhere. Wherever that is, they can't be allowed to keep them. We will find them.'

'But for now,' Goddard said, 'we rest and recuperate. That hand Jerune, we need that sorted before any more adventure.'

A twitching finger, pointing in the air, the scout said, 'Oh, I wasn't volunteering. And to be clear, Laria wasn't an adventure.'

'Oh shoosh!' Sarellia said, slapping his thigh. 'Be brave.'

'Shoosh!' Chara mimicked.

'That's you told,' Bücka said.

Jerune huffed. Goddard wasn't certain the gesture was made completely in jest. He couldn't blame the scout; he'd survived the coming of Fire, saved Bücka's life and had nothing to show for it. Though, in time, Goddard knew it would make the man. He had been willing to die for his friends. To allow Bücka to live. The stuff of reluctant heroes.

'Whatever we do,' Goddard said, 'we'll do it together, and by choice.'

Jerune nodded to him. A thanks, he assumed.

Petra moved to a seat. She said, 'Less talk of gloom then. I think we're done. How about something lighter?'

Bücka, sitting straight, put her hand in the air. Goddard thought it unusual, then realised her focus was solely on Petra; those brown eyes gazing at his magnificent friend. He called to her, 'It's not the schoolyard, Bücka. Speak freely.'

The warrior grinned. 'I've got a story. You'll all love it. You want to hear it?'

Looking to Chara, Goddard asked, 'Is it safe for little ears?'

Her stare lingering on Petra, Bücka said, 'Oh, absolutely. It's a tale about a dog. A very special mutt called Bücka.'

On the highest floor, Goddard stood alone with Chara. Together they looked out across Anka settled in the peace of the night. The *night*. And Chara was awake. No pretence she hadn't noticed the setting sun long lost behind the horizon. He had no urge to enquire. Just let it be. Let her be.

'Are we staying here,' she asked.

'In Anka? For now, yes.' He thought of everything that had been discussed. The past month of turmoil. It felt as though years. 'Things need to be done, Chara. These lands are under a dark shadow.'

'You mean Laria and Kalleron?'

Looking south to unseen Kalleron, he imagined what menace would be lurking on the continent. Taberas' journal had revealed many dark secrets to Petra. Etherus was rising; a new threat from the masters of the Fury. And though Laria had Fire, Goddard knew of Kalleron's might and prowess. What had it become this past century? What machinations of war had the engineers created? His heart sank thinking of the future. The world had become a game of three powers, two of which harnessed incredible weapons of destruction. The Northern Lands had but two. He, and Petra. Not enough to stop the suffering of thousands.

'There are those across that water that seek to destroy us, Chara. Men and their miserable ways.'

'Once you fix it all, will we stay with our friends?'

It was so simple to Chara. Or was it? He had stopped trying to guess the motive behind her words. Long since dismissed the notion that Kor'A's hand manipulated the puppet. Chara was unique and free. As Petra had said. Unbound to the Elemental gods. A perfect shard fallen from the rock. A shard. *The flake.*

'You've kept the stone Kor'A gave you?' he asked.

Chara nodded and rummaged in her Rotynian pocket. She held it out, the strange black mineral flat on her palm.

Goddard reached to it. Retracted his hand. The strangest thought: *Bruch'alma.* He didn't want to touch it. The Rock of Kings was first. The cursed hammer second. There would be no third interaction with their damn gifts.

'Do you know what it does?' he asked.

'I'm not sure.'

'Kor'A said it would take you home.'

Chara shook her head. 'It will show me the way home.'

He stared at the innocuous flake. A rectangle tapering at one end, a black icicle, though it had no sharp point. Its texture and colour the same as Chara's skin, it was difficult to discern. An illusion of being.

Chara's words repeating in his head, he asked, 'Aren't you curious?'

She frowned. 'Of what?'

'Your home. Where it is.'

Chara looked at the flake, curled her fingers around it. She put it away, closed the buckle on her pocket. She patted the fabric and shook her head.

'Not curious?' he asked. 'Not at all?'

Smiling, she reached for his hand. Her fingers grasped his; little pincers on his huge digits. She tugged and walked forward, leading him toward the portal. Staring out, both of them looking to unseen futures, she sighed. Goddard thought it such a relaxed and contented sound.

On a breeze of breath, her tiny fingers squeezing his, Chara said. 'I don't need to be shown where home is, it's standing right beside me.'

About Author

James D. McEwan once struck a friend on the head with a six-foot sword. That he was 16 years-old and the sword was made of foam doesn't diminish the warrior's achievement. Now substantially older, he has become a fantasy world-builder, creating relatable heroes and troubled villains to populate his epic Kalleron saga, of which Hammer & Glass is but one small chapter. You can delve further into his mind and learn more about Kalleron at jamesdmcewan.com.

Coming soon: Kalleron Book I

The Terrible Queen of Kalleron is the destroyer of worlds. Beholden to Kalle, a devious and—some say—immortal King, the Queen is a weapon of such cataclysmic power the mere whisper of her name invokes terror. Decades of omnipotence have brought Kalleron's enemies to their knees; from glorious and green Tormelor, to golden Bruhada, throne of the legendary King Baza'rad. But something stirs in the shadows of Kalle's empire; a rumour echoes in all the dark places. Some speak of an Elemental cult come to free their Queen, and one woman seeks their truth. Petra, whose rage is fire and will is stone, will uncover a world beyond Kings and Queens. With her loyal crew by her side, she will learn the frightening truth behind the lie that is the majesty of Kalleron.

Visit jamesdmcewan.com to read more about the Kalleron series.

Printed in Great Britain
by Amazon

11644251R00181